MURDER IN DUBLIN

By Christina Koning

MURDER IN DUBLIN

CHRISTINA KONING

Allison & Busby Limited
11 Wardour Mews
London W1F 8AN
allisonandbusby.com

First published in Great Britain by Allison & Busby in 2023.
This paperback edition published by Allison & Busby in 2024.

10 9 8 7 6 5 4 3 2 1

ISBN 978-0-7490-2998-2

Typeset in 11/16 pt Sabon LT Pro by Allison and Busby Ltd.

By choosing this product, you help take care of the world's forests.
Learn more: www.fsc.org

FSC
www.fsc.org
MIX
Paper | Supporting
responsible forestry
FSC® C171272

Printed and bound by
CPI Group (UK) Ltd, Croydon, CR0 4YY

For Eamonn

Chapter One

It was getting on for ten o'clock at night when the Liverpool ferry docked at North Wall Quay after what had been as smooth a crossing of the Irish Sea as one could have hoped to enjoy, thought Frederick Rowlands. It was of course high summer, he reminded himself as he lit a cigarette; he supposed it might be a very different story in the depths of winter when storms would make the crossing a far less pleasant experience. Standing by the ship's rail, he savoured the first few moments of arrival in a strange city as around him the business of disembarking passengers and unloading cargo began.

'I always think this is the best way to approach Dublin,' said his companion, who was standing next to him, close enough so that he could catch the scent of her hair, and the perfumed smoke of the Turkish cigarettes she favoured. 'With the lights of the buildings along the waterfront shining on the river, and the loafers on the quayside, and the feeling one has – here, more than in London, I feel – of having arrived in the heart of things . . . although I imagine,' she added, as if it had just occurred to her, 'it isn't the same for you.'

'Not exactly the same,' he replied, offering her his arm as the two of them started to move towards the gangplank, across which groups of foot passengers were already making their way. 'But I can picture it, from what you've said. The lights and the buildings. The loafers, too – one finds them in every port. Then there's the smell of the place – or rather, that of the warehouses along this stretch of the river. Coffee, and pepper, and beer – there must be a brewery nearby. And the sounds of the voices. Is that Irish they're talking, those fellows?' She said that it was. 'I knew it was a language I hadn't heard before although heaven knows I met enough Irishmen during the war . . .' But she was only half-listening.

'Now, where's O'Driscoll got to?' she murmured, looking out for the servant who was to meet them. 'He should be here. I wired before we left Liverpool.'

They had, by this time, reached the quayside where a crowd of those meeting the ferry jostled against those who were getting off; there seemed to be no particular organisation. 'Perhaps,' said Rowlands, feeling himself pushed this way and that, and doing his best to protect his companion from the same, 'we should find a quieter spot to wait until this crush clears?'

But just then there came the clatter of hurrying footsteps along the cobblestones. 'Milady! Oh, milady! I was afeared I'd come too late and missed you.'

'You certainly might have been earlier,' said his mistress. 'But no matter. Where have you left the car?'

'Over the way, milady. Was it a good journey, now?'

'Not bad.'

'And the sea as calm as a millpond,' said the man, sounding as satisfied as if he'd arranged this himself. 'Would there be any luggage, milady?'

'Yes. There are my two bags and one of Mr Rowlands'. See to it, will you? And then let's waste no more time. We've had a long journey.'

'To be sure,' was the reply. 'Patsy's after collecting the luggage now. Hi there, Patsy! Over here with the bags, now! Car's this way, milady. Just a few steps,' added O'Driscoll in an encouraging tone. Within a few minutes, the travellers were seated in the back of the Bentley, with O'Driscoll taking his seat next to the silent Patsy, whose functions evidently included that of chauffeur. 'Merrion Square, is it, milady?' enquired the former. Being assured that it was, he conveyed this fact to the latter. Then they were moving, at a steady but not excessive speed, along the river – 'The Liffey,' murmured the woman beside him to Rowlands – and across O'Connell Bridge. Trinity College soon appeared on their left, so Rowlands' companion told him, after which it was more or less a straight line to their destination where they arrived in little more than ten minutes.

'Here we are,' she said as they drew up in front of a house about halfway along the far side of the square. As he got out of the car, Rowlands had a sense of a freshness in the air that came from the presence of trees, and of a fountain playing softly somewhere. There was something else – the quiet that hung about the wealthier parts of cities where the raucous sounds of the poorer streets seldom, if ever, penetrated.

Rowlands followed the mistress of the house up a short flight of steps, to a door that already stood open. A sensation of warmth and light met him as he entered the spacious hall. A smell of fresh flowers and polished wood, with a faint, underlying scent of something else – fine cigars, he thought, wondering if he was shortly to meet the man whose indulgence they were. Invisible hands, like those in one of the fairy tales his girls had once loved, divested him of his coat. 'Baths first, I think, don't you?' said his hostess, preceding him up the stairs. 'And then we'll see what Mrs Keane has left for us. You needn't dress,' she added. 'Half an hour, shall we say? John will show you to your room.'

Left to his own devices in the room to which he had been conducted by the servant, Rowlands took a few moments to familiarise himself with its layout, something which had, of necessity, become habitual in the more than twenty years since he had been blinded by an exploding shell at Passchendaele. Having first ascertained the position of bed and fireplace (in which a fire had been lit against the evening chill), and finding that his suitcase had already been brought up, he undressed, and having put on his dressing gown, took his sponge bag and found his way across the corridor to the bathroom that served this end of the house. Here, a bath had already been drawn; he got into it gratefully, finding the water as hot as he could have wished.

It had been almost twelve hours since he had met, at Euston station, the woman at whose behest he was here. As he let the tensions of the day slip away, in the warmth of the pleasantly scented water, he reflected on what had led up to that meeting, and why it was that she had sought him out after so long.

Two days ago, if you'd mentioned her name to him, it would have conjured memories already almost a decade old: memories of a dangerous sweetness that threatened his carefully maintained peace of mind. He'd had news of her over the years, of course. A woman who occupied the place she did in society, and who, moreover, had been briefly notorious, couldn't expect to disappear entirely from public awareness although her marriage six years before, to an Irish peer, had seemed to guarantee her removal from the epicentre of London society. There'd been nothing in these occasional snippets of information, concerning her appearance at a Dublin ball, or a race meeting, perhaps, that might have pointed to her sudden reappearance in Rowlands' life.

He'd stayed at work later than usual on that particular evening because, with Edith and the girls away in Cornwall at the start of the summer holidays, and Edith's mother seen off that morning on the train to visit friends in Scotland, there was no special reason to hurry home. Miss Collins had already left, taking the letters for posting with her, and Rowlands was making notes in his careful script – guiding his hand by means of a ruler so as to avoid going off the page – to remind him what needed to be addressed with his secretary the next day. Absorbed in this task, he wasn't aware that anyone had come into his office until the intruder spoke: 'I hope I'm not disturbing you? I asked at the house and they said you hadn't yet left.'

For a moment, Rowlands found himself unable to utter a word. Was it really her – or was this merely a soft-voiced hallucination, come out of the past to torment him? 'Lady Celia,' he managed at last. 'I . . .'

'You don't seem awfully glad to see me, Mr Rowlands.'

'I'm just surprised, that's all. It must be seven years . . .'

'Eight,' she said. 'Almost to the day. It was at that party in Richmond where the girl was attacked. Awful business. I drove you home after the police had finished with us, didn't I?'

'You did,' said Rowlands, for whom every detail of that night was etched in memory. 'And I *am* glad to see you,' he added. The obvious question, which was what it was that had brought her there, hung in the air between them. But if she sensed this, Celia Swift evidently wasn't in any hurry to answer it. 'So this is where you work?' she said. 'Rather nice to be right in the middle of Regent's Park.' For this indeed was where the St Dunstan's HQ was located. 'It took me quite a while to track you down. I had to ask at the other place – Gerald's old office, you know.'

'Yes.' The mention of his late CO, Gerald Willoughby, briefly transported Rowlands back to his former place of work where he'd been for seven years until disaster intervened, a disaster in which Lady Celia (Celia West, as she was then) had been intimately involved. 'I came there once, if you recall.' He did, all too vividly. Because it had been then that he'd come to realise the power she had over him. It was a power she was exercising at that moment as she moved about the room. It had to do with her voice, her scent – musky, exotic – with the languor of her movements, the rustle of her silk dress. One might have called it seductive, except that it seemed artless.

Pausing for a moment in her restless wandering, she fiddled with the objects upon his desk: a paperknife; a painted jar that one of his girls had made, containing pencils; a wave-smoothed stone, picked up on Brighton beach.

'I was hoping,' she said at last, 'that you'd have dinner with me.' She was staying at the Savoy: 'We can get a bite to eat in the Grill,' she said. 'Then we needn't dress.' It was all the same to Rowlands, although he rather wished he'd been wearing his best suit instead of the one he wore to the office; he reminded himself that while he was in Celia Swift's company, no one would be looking at him anyway.

In the taxi on the way from Regent's Park, their conversation had necessarily been confined to pleasantries. She enquired after the health of his wife and family; he reciprocated by hoping that she herself was well. 'Never better,' she replied with an airiness that made him think she wasn't being entirely frank. Then, changing the subject: 'I remember your daughters. Dear little things! I've a boy of my own now, you know.'

He hadn't known, and said that that was good to hear. 'Yes, he's quite a jolly little chap. Just turned five. Ned – that's my husband – is keen to start him off with his first pony, but I think he's too young.' A brief silence ensued.

'I haven't seen you since your marriage,' said Rowlands, deciding to follow up on this conversational opportunity. 'It must be very different, living in Ireland ... I mean after London.'

'Oh, it *is*. Although I've only just begun to realise *how* different.'

Before he could discover what, if anything, she meant by this cryptic remark, they arrived at the hotel. Greeted by the manager in that fashionable establishment's lofty entrance lobby, they were conducted by another factotum to the restaurant. From the subdued murmur of conversation that met them as they walked in, Rowlands judged that the place was far from full. It was still early, of course. A waiter led them to a table on the far side.

'I believe the steaks are good here,' said Lady Celia as they were seated. Rowlands said that, in that case, he'd have the steak. 'We'll have a bottle of Burgundy to go with it,' said his hostess to the waiter. 'And I'll have the fish.' She waited until the man had brought the wine, poured it, and left them to their own devices before she spoke again. 'Tell me . . . how's your sister?' Rowlands, who'd been wondering for the past hour what her reason was for inviting him here since he assumed it couldn't simply be for the pleasure of his company, was nonetheless taken aback.

'My sister?' he echoed, recalling the circumstances under which the two women had last met – circumstances no doubt highly uncomfortable to both. 'She was very well when I last saw her. She . . . she married again, you know. Seems very happy.'

'I'm glad,' said Lady Celia. She took a sip of wine and set down her glass. 'And the child? I forget his name . . .'

Rowlands had the feeling this wasn't true. 'William,' he said. 'Known as Billy. He's not such a child any more. He's seventeen.'

'I suppose he must be,' she said drily. 'You know there was money left to the boy . . . in my late husband's will?' She seemed reluctant to mention him by name.

'Yes,' said Rowlands. 'I believe I did hear something about that.' Was this why she'd sought him out? 'But I don't think she – my sister – cares about the money,' he added, wanting to disabuse her of the idea that he, or his sibling, might harbour such mercenary designs.

'Perhaps not. But I do,' replied Celia Swift impatiently. 'That is . . . I *don't* care about it. I don't want it. It's his. The boy's.'

'Lady Celia—'

'I've been to see my solicitors,' she said, cutting across him. 'It's one of the reasons I came to London. Ned, my husband, agrees with my decision. He says it's my money, to do with as I please. I've put it in trust for the boy . . . for William,' she said. 'He'll get it when he's of age.'

Somewhat stunned by this information, Rowlands did not at once reply. 'What about your own boy?' he wanted to say, but did not.

She must have read his thought, however, for she said: 'I don't need, or want, his money.' Rowlands knew it was her late husband, Leo West, of whom she spoke. He thought he understood the reason for this. After the shocking events that had ended her marriage to the wealthy entrepreneur, she would doubtless regard the money as tainted.

Their food arrived, and for the next few minutes they occupied themselves with the agreeable business of consuming it, or rather, Rowlands did. Lady Celia merely pushed her food around her plate. He remembered her figure as slim and girlish; he guessed she hadn't changed in that respect. She would have kept the same graceful form he had once, briefly, held in his arms, just as the same delicious scent – a heady mixture of expensive perfume and Turkish cigarettes – clung to her skin and hair. What was different was a new hardness in her voice. She pushed her plate away, and lit a cigarette. 'That wasn't the reason I wanted to see you,' she said. 'Or not the only reason.'

He hadn't finished eating, but he put down his knife and fork, and waited to hear what she had to say.

'That was the reason I gave *him* – Ned, I mean – for my coming to London. Setting up the trust, and some other business I had to see to. The sale of some property . . .' She broke off as if the subject bored her. 'No, it was something else I wanted to ask you about,' she was saying. 'The truth is, I need your help, Mr Rowlands . . . or may I call you Frederick? You helped me once before when no one else did.'

Rowlands waited. His companion seemed to be nerving herself for what she had to say. Even so, it was a shock when it came: 'I think someone's trying to kill my husband,' she said. 'In fact, I'm sure of it. You must help me prevent it.'

There had been letters, she said: vaguely threatening in tone at first, latterly of increasingly violent language.

'Have you kept them?'

'Only the most recent ones. Ned threw the first couple in the fire.'

'Can you give me an idea of what they said?'

'Well . . .' She lit another cigarette. 'Shall we have our coffee in the lounge? We can be more private there.' When they were settled in a corner of this vast apartment, whose atmosphere of hushed opulence was made more so by the luxurious thickness of the carpet, Lady Celia resumed her tale, which sounded all the more luridly fantastical by contrast with these civilised surroundings. 'To begin with, as I said, the letters contained vague threats. "We know how to deal with your kind." "Go home, English scum." That kind of muck. Then they got more specific. "You'll be sorry you ever set foot in Castletown and your English whore with you . . ." I don't think,' she added wryly, 'that they approve of me, either.'

'Who are they? Do you have any idea?'

'Ned thinks they're IRA malcontents, or they could just as well be Blueshirts. That's the Protestant lot,' she explained. 'They're all as mad as each other. The one thing on which they agree is that they hate the English. Unfortunately for Ned, he's only a quarter Irish, on his mother's side, and I haven't a drop of Celtic blood.'

'But . . .' Rowlands refused her offer of a Turkish cigarette, preferring his own. 'Why *now*?' he said when it was lit.

'Haven't you heard?' was the faintly mocking reply. 'There's going to be a war. And Ireland's keeping out of it if de Valera has his way. Ned says it's a golden opportunity for them to rid themselves of the enemy.'

'The enemy?'

'Us. The British.'

'And you believe these letters are part of a campaign to force you and your husband out?' said Rowlands.

'I do,' she said. 'It's not just letters, either. One might ignore those, although it's not very pleasant to know one's hated. But it was when they killed Ned's favourite dog that I really started to worry. Oh yes,' she said, seeing his horrified expression. 'Shot the poor beast in cold blood and left him for Ned to find. *He* says it was probably an accident – some farmer letting loose at what he thought was a stray – but I don't believe it. Especially not when another letter came the next day. "You'll be next, my lord," it said. If that isn't a death threat, I don't know what is.'

'Have you informed the police?' said Rowlands. 'Surely they—'

'The Gardai are as mixed up in politics as all the rest,' said Celia Swift crisply. 'Ned did talk to the local man, Sergeant Flanagan, who said he'd look into it, but I don't imagine he'll exert himself overmuch. To be blunt, Frederick, they want us gone. We're the oppressors, in their view. The sooner we, the English, get out of Ireland, the better, in their estimation.'

Rowlands was silent a moment, reflecting on what she had said. 'I still don't see how I can be of help,' he said, at last. 'I've never set foot in Ireland . . . and my knowledge of its politics is shaky, to say the least.'

'I've come to you because you stood up for me, all those years ago,' she said. 'You saved me from the gallows. Now I want you to save my husband from being murdered. Please, Frederick. You're my only hope.'

* * *

Having bathed and changed his shirt, Rowlands made his way back to the entrance hall where the obliging John was waiting to conduct him to the library. Here he found Lady Celia seated in front of a good fire. 'There's a chair directly opposite mine,' she said. 'And there are sandwiches and coffee . . . unless you'd prefer a whisky?'

'Coffee's fine.'

She poured them each a cup. 'Black or white?'

'Black, please.'

She placed the cup on a low table at his side, and handed him a plate of sandwiches. 'Mrs K's made enough to feed an army. I hope you're hungry.'

He was, as it happened. It seemed a long time since they'd lunched on the train to Liverpool. The sandwiches were ham, and very good. He had eaten two before his hunger abated. Celia Swift seemed content to watch him eat while she sipped her coffee and smoked a cigarette. 'I'm so glad you agreed to come,' she said. 'It makes me feel so much *safer* to have you here.' Although what good his being there would do was debatable, thought Rowlands. A blind man, with little knowledge of the country in which he had just arrived.

'I don't know what you expect me to achieve that the police can't,' he said. He pushed away his plate, and lit a cigarette. 'And . . .' He hesitated.

At once she picked him up. 'What?'

'Just that . . . I don't imagine your husband will take kindly to having a man he's never met interfere in his business,' he said. 'I mean, surely he must have his own ideas about all this?'

'Oh, Ned just dismisses it as some kind of nasty prank,' she replied. 'As for what he'll think of *you*,' she went on. 'He'll think what I've told him to think, which is that you're an old friend I happened to run into in London and that you've had considerable experience of this kind of thing.'

'You told him *that*?'

'Don't look so alarmed. It's true, isn't it?'

'Well . . .'

'Ned's much more likely to listen to you than he is to take notice of what a mere wife might say,' said Celia Swift. 'I want you to convince him to take these threats seriously, that's all.'

Rowlands doubted whether anything he could say would make the slightest difference, but he held his peace. He was here now, wasn't he? He might as well go along with what she'd proposed. 'Will we see Lord Castleford tonight?' he asked.

The answer was in the negative. 'He's at the estate. We'll see him tomorrow with all the rest of the crew. I'd better put you in the picture about Ned's family,' said Lady Celia.

Edward Swift was the younger son of an earl. His elder brother, John, had been killed at the Somme, and so the title had passed to Edward, on the death of his father. The latter had been married twice – the boys' mother having died when Edward was an infant – and there was another son, Jolyon, by the second marriage, to Eveline, the much younger daughter of a local landowner. 'I wonder what you'll make of our dear Eveline?' said her daughter-in-law, with a faintly satirical edge to her voice. The Dowager Lady Castleford had been given a home by her stepson, to which, naturally enough, her own son was frequently invited. 'Jolyon lives with us most of the time,' said Lady Celia. 'At least . . . it *feels* as if he does, he's about the place so often, with that wife of his.' The couple had a young son, Reginald. 'He's two years younger than our boy, and so he's not much company for him. Besides which . . .' She left whatever comment she'd been about to make unsaid.

In addition to these people, she went on, there was 'Cousin Aloysius, a retired canon. I'm not sure what relation he is to Ned exactly, but he's a dear old boy. The best of the lot, in my opinion. You'll also meet Robert Butler – he runs the estate – and his wife, Elspeth. She's rather a starchy sort, but she means well. And there's Sebastian Gogarty, who's been cataloguing the Castleford library for the past few weeks. Now,' she said as if the subject held no more interest for her, 'I want to hear all about your girls,' which was no hardship to Rowlands, whose three daughters were the delight of his life.

And so he told her about Margaret, midway through her studies in mathematics at Cambridge; and about Anne, who was currently torn between following her sister to St Gertrude's College, or pursuing a career in fine art; and finally about Joan, the youngest, whose preoccupations at present were those of any healthy schoolgirl: hockey, the games mistress, and getting enough to eat. 'You never saw such an appetite!' said her father fondly. 'I think she'll end up being the tallest of the three.'

Chapter Two

They set off for Castleford after a leisurely breakfast; the journey would take no more than an hour if they went at a comfortable pace, said Lady Celia. They'd take the road that passed through Dundrum. 'It's quite a pretty little place although Enniskerry beats it by a mile – or so *we* think,' she said, meaning herself and her spouse, Rowlands supposed. 'Of course, we can't compete with Powerscourt. That's frightfully grand, you know. We prefer our place even if it *is* a bit of a barracks. All the houses of that era are. But we like it. It's a working farm too, you know.' Rowlands said he was glad to hear it. 'Oh yes,' went on this surprising convert to the joys of the rural life. 'We produce all our own butter and eggs. And we've one of the best flocks of Blackface sheep in the county. Prizes at all the local fairs.'

As she chattered on, it struck Rowlands that her enthusiasm cloaked a deeper anxiety. It was as if she were trying to convince him, and herself, that she had made the right choice in abandoning the whirl of London life for the seclusion of the Irish countryside. Although, as the powerful car rolled smoothly along through the verdant scenery of County Wicklow, 'it really is greener here. I thought it was a myth before I came.' He wondered what choice she had had. A series of unfulfilling affairs with dubious playboys (he'd met one or two of them); living off the interest from the money her (detested) husband had left her; the vague notoriety of belonging to the fast set: an ageing beauty, with no one to care whether she lived or died. Except that one man *had* cared – too much for his own good. At the thought of his late employer and friend Gerald Willoughby driven half-mad by a hopeless passion for the beautiful Celia West, Rowlands shook his head to dispel the memory. As for his own sad case . . .

'What did your wife say when you told her you were coming to Ireland?' said Lady Celia as if she'd guessed the way his thoughts were tending.

'I told her I'd got some business to see to, and that I'd join her and the girls in Cornwall next week,' he replied, not quite answering the question.

'Well, I'm grateful to her for sparing you,' she said. 'If you could just convince my husband to take this matter seriously, I'd feel that our "business" had been concluded successfully.'

'But . . . Lady Celia . . . I still don't understand. Why should Lord Castleford pay attention to anything *I* might say? He doesn't know me from Adam.'

'He knows you saved my life once,' she said in a low voice, although the glass screen separating those sitting in the back of the car from the driver's compartment was closed. 'That'll be good enough for him. And the fact that you're a detective . . .'

'I'm not a detective.'

'. . . who's worked with the police on numerous occasions,' she went on, ignoring his protest. 'Ah, here's the lodge, and Nancy coming out to open the gate for us.'

Rowlands surmised that this must be the lodge-keeper's child, for as the Bentley slowed down to a crawl, and began to move through the open gates, Celia Swift wound down the near-side window, and spoke to the child. 'Here's sixpence for you, Nancy.' To which the little girl gave some reply unintelligible to Rowlands, but which seemed to satisfy his companion, for she laughed. 'Droll little thing! She always looks at me as if I were going to bite her. Maybe I will, one day. Her cheeks are so *very* round and red.' Settling back into her seat, she went on: 'The approach to Castleford is really very pretty. Would you like me to describe it?'

'Please,' he said.

'All right. In the distance you can see the

Wicklow Mountains – they're famous, you know. On a day like this, you can see for miles across the valley. Of course,' she added, 'the same can't be said when it's raining . . . which it does rather a lot, in Ireland. There's a river at the bottom of the valley – hence Castle*ford*. That part of the demesne is quite wooded . . . and the park itself has some fine oak trees. An avenue of lime trees leads to the house, which is set on rising ground. It was built by Ned's great-grandfather, and is in the Palladian style, if you know what that is?'

Rowlands said that he did.

'That's more than I knew before I came here.' She laughed. 'But then I'm ignorant about lots of things. My father believed that educating girls was a waste of money. The house is rather a good example of its kind,' she went on, like a dutiful child reciting a lesson. 'It's built of Wicklow granite, faced in ashlar. Rather grey and austere until one gets used to it. There are two symmetrical wings on either side of a central pedimented section. It's called a "breakfront",' she added. 'Each wing has three sash windows on each floor – there are two floors – except in the breakfront, which has three floors, with three windows on the second and third floor, and two arched windows on the ground floor. There are steps leading up to the front door, and pillars on either side of it, going up to the roof of the pediment, which is triangular, like a Greek temple, or so Ned says. There! I've told you all I can about the outside. You'll have to wait to hear about the rest.'

Rowlands said he looked forward to that.

The car drew up on a gravel sweep in front of the house, to a chorus of barking dogs. 'The reception committee,' said Celia Swift as they got out. 'Down, Juno! Down, Jess! Down, Jason! They're quite well-behaved as a rule,' she added apologetically to Rowlands, who found himself the centre of attention from the beasts, one of which, he guessed – from its size and shaggy coat – to be an Irish wolfhound. Lady Celia confirmed this supposition. 'That's Jason. The brother of Jasper – the one that was shot. He still misses him, poor beast . . . Ah, here's Ned,' she cried as the master of the house appeared at the top of the steps. 'Darling, I want you to meet Frederick Rowlands, one of my oldest friends.'

More than a little startled at this description of himself, Rowlands held out his hand. 'How do you do, my lord?'

'Ned Swift. No need for the handle,' was the reply as they shook hands. From this brief contact, Rowlands got an impression of a strongly built man, of around his own age and height. His hand, though well-shaped, had the slightly roughened texture of a hand used to outdoor work. 'Good to meet you. My wife's spoken about you quite a bit.'

This was even more startling. 'Has she?'

'Indeed she has.' There wasn't a trace of an

Irish accent, which was hardly surprising, thought Rowlands, given that, from all Lady Celia had told him, the family was of English origin. 'Come in, why don't you?' Lady Celia linked her arm companionably through Rowlands' as they mounted the steps, and crossed a broad stone terrace before passing through the open door into a lofty entrance hall. Rowlands' impression was of warmth and light – no doubt an effect of the sunshine that streamed in through the door, and the two tall arched windows, of which his hostess had spoken.

'We're very proud of the floor in this room,' she said. 'It's Irish oak.' Which would explain the absence of the usual chill to be found in houses of the grander sort, whose halls were floored with marble, thought Rowlands. 'It was installed in 1824 when the family were expecting a visit from George IV. He was staying at Powerscourt – that's our grand neighbour, you know. But he didn't turn up.'

'Too busy enjoying himself with his mistress, the dirty dog,' put in Swift.

'The decorations are . . . . what do you call it, Ned? Greek Revival? That's it. There are fluted Ionic columns on either side of the door that leads to the main staircase and—'

'I'm sure your guest doesn't want to hear all this stuff, Celia,' interrupted her spouse.

'Sorry! I was only trying to give him a picture.'

'Actually,' said Rowlands. 'I was enjoying it very

much. Lady Celia might not have mentioned the fact that I'm blind. So I'm grateful for any description of my surroundings even if it might strike others as odd to hear them described.'

'In which case, I'll say nothing more,' said Swift, opening a door. 'Carry on with your tour, Celia.'

But his wife said she felt too self-conscious to continue. 'Although the morning room is one of the best rooms in the house,' she said. 'It used to be the music room, and so the mouldings on the ceiling are all of harps and flutes and violins. It gets the morning sun, so we often sit here before lunch if we've nothing better to do. Do take a seat, Frederick. There's a sofa straight ahead of you, in the sunny spot by the window.' She must have touched a bell, because a moment later the door opened.

'Yes'm?'

'We'll have our coffee in here, Mary.'

'So you were in the war?' said Swift, throwing himself into a seat adjacent to Rowlands'.

'Yes. Royal Field Artillery.'

'I was in the Irish Guards. You were at the Somme, I suppose?'

'That, and Ypres,' replied Rowlands. 'It's where I got my Blighty one.'

'Bad show,' said Swift.

'It was – for a lot of people,' agreed his guest. 'I made it home.'

'If you're going to talk about the war, I'm leaving

you to it,' protested Lady Celia. 'Since I'm not allowed to describe the room, I don't see why you men should swap war stories.'

'You're quite right, my dear,' said her husband. 'We'll leave it until after dinner. Do you ride, Rowlands?'

The sudden change of topic was disconcerting. 'I *have* ridden,' admitted Rowlands after a moment. 'When I was a boy, on my great-uncle's farm in Norfolk. But not since.'

'I thought, as you were in the war . . .'

'I was a gunner,' said Rowlands. 'The only horses I and the other men in my battery had to deal with were the poor broken-down beasts that drew the limbers.' It was generally the officers who rode, he recalled, but did not say.

'To be sure,' said Swift as if he'd suddenly remembered this, too. 'But if, as you say, you used to ride as a lad, you'll find it comes back to you – wouldn't you say, Celia?'

'Oh, don't drag me into it!' she said. 'As you'll have gathered, Frederick, my husband doesn't consider a day well spent unless he's ridden ten, or preferably twenty, miles. Put it on the table, would you, Mary?' she added to the parlourmaid, who had just returned with the tray. She busied herself with pouring out as her husband pursued his theme.

'The fact is, one never forgets how to ride. It's instinctive. Put you on a quiet animal, with a companion to ride alongside you, and you'll be fine,' he said to Rowlands, who was beginning to realise that, for Swift, the subject was indeed a passion.

'Your coffee cup's on the low table in front of you,' said Lady Celia. 'And there are some of Mrs Malone's ginger biscuits.'

'If you'd care to, we can walk over to the stables before lunch, and I'll show you the horse I've got in mind for you,' Swift went on, picking up his own cup, and stirring sugar into the coffee.

'I'd like that,' replied Rowlands, thinking it best to go along with his host's obsession. He could always find some excuse later.

At that moment, the door opened, and somebody stuck his head in. 'Aha!' said a voice. 'I thought I smelt coffee! Hello, Celia. So you're back, are you?'

'As you can see,' she replied. It seemed to Rowlands that there was a distinct coolness in her tone.

'And who are *you*?' said the newcomer, evidently addressing Rowlands.

The latter was about to supply his name when Swift intervened: 'Sorry. Ought to have introduced you. This is my brother, Jolyon Swift.'

'Half-brother, if we're being precise,' said the other, pouring himself a cup of coffee.

'Half-brother, then. Jo, this is Frederick Rowlands, a friend of Celia's.'

'Oh, so *you're* the man, are you? Celia's been very secretive about you! All we knew was that she'd picked you up on her London jaunt. Positively mysterious, we all thought, didn't we, Neddie?'

'Leave me out of it, will you, Jo?' said Swift, with an edge of impatience. 'And cut the fooling. You're making our guest feel uncomfortable.'

'Not at all,' said Rowlands. 'And there's no mystery about it. Lady Celia and I had a mutual friend, at one time. He was my commanding officer during the war. After his death, we – Lady Celia and I – kept in touch, that's all. When she was last in London she was kind enough to look me up.'

'Oh,' said Jolyon Swift flatly as if he'd suddenly lost interest in the topic. 'This coffee's cold. Can't stand cold coffee. Ring for some more, would you, old girl?' It struck Rowlands that any man who could bring himself to address the exquisite Celia Swift as 'old girl' was either being very stupid or deliberately provocative. He suspected the latter.

Her Ladyship evidently thought so, too, for she said languidly, 'Don't be a bore, Jolyon. The bell's there. Ring it yourself.'

'I assumed,' he replied, 'that you'd prefer to give the order yourself since you've asked us – Henry and me – not to "give extra work to the servants", as you put it. But heigh-ho, it shall be as you wish.'

He must have pressed the bell, for after a brief interval, the door opened again. 'Yes'm?'

'Bring Mr Swift some coffee, will you, Mary?' said Lady Celia. 'Will Henry want some, do you think?' she added to her brother-in-law.

'No idea,' was the reply. 'Haven't seen her all morning.' From which Rowlands gathered that the person referred to was female. This proved to be the case a moment later when a young woman, accompanied by a small child, entered.

'*There* you are!' she exclaimed ill-temperedly. 'I've been looking for you all over.'

'Well, you've found me, my angel,' said Jolyon Swift. 'We were just debating whether or not you'd like some coffee, and here you are, to clarify the matter.'

'Oh, don't be such an ass! Of course I want some.'

'Bring some coffee for Mr and Mrs Swift,' said Lady Celia to the maid, who disappeared on this errand.

'And you've brought Reggie with you – what joy!' cried the irrepressible Jolyon. 'Henry, I must introduce you. This is Mr Rowlands, Celia's Man of Mystery. And this, Rowlands, is my adored wife, Henrietta, and the son and heir of my heart, Reginald Castleford Swift.'

'Delighted,' said Rowlands, wondering why the honeyed words should have left such a sour aftertaste. At the mention of his name, the child, whom Rowlands guessed to be about two or three years old, set up a whining noise, of which the only distinguishable words were 'Mama' and 'bickie'.

'Don't pester,' said his mother wearily. 'You know Nurse said not before lunch. He wants a biscuit,' she added superfluously. When the chant of 'bickie, bickie' grew more insistent, Mrs Swift relented: 'All right. Just one.' With which the child, seizing his booty, ran triumphantly from the room, to general relief, Rowlands suspected.

'You spoil him, Henry,' said her husband, taking a biscuit from the plate and biting into it. 'If he goes on like this, he'll turn into a greedy, selfish little beast.'

'Like his father,' was the tart retort. From which Rowlands deduced that the Jolyon Swifts were the sort of couple who enjoyed sparring in public.

Ned Swift evidently decided he'd had enough, for he got to his feet. 'I'm off to the stables,' he said. 'Coming, Rowlands? I can show you the mare I've got in mind for you.' Rowlands readily agreed, although privately he was dubious about the idea of getting on a horse again after so long. Even if he managed the first part successfully, he wouldn't be able to see where he was going, so what would be the point? But it would be good to get out in the fresh air, on such a glorious day, and besides, against his expectations, he was starting to warm to Swift. 'Are you coming too?' said the latter to his wife, who replied that they should go on ahead, as she had things to see to. The dogs had been waiting patiently in their baskets for just such an eventuality; they now rose as one and followed the two men out.

'Ever been to Ireland before?' said Swift as they crossed the hall, and passed through a door to one side of the staircase (a double sweep, Rowlands was later to discover). Rowlands said that he had not.

'Hmm. You'll find it quite a change from London. The people are good-hearted. But it can take a while for an outsider to be accepted.' It was more or less what Lady Celia had said. Rowlands, who had no expectation of staying long enough to be 'accepted', gave a non-committal grunt. A corridor led to the back of the house, past kitchen and scullery – from which agreeable smells of luncheon being prepared were issuing – to a boot room. 'What's your footwear like?' was the earl's next question. 'Good enough' – on seeing Rowlands' well-polished and well-mended brogues – 'but I'll find you some gumboots. It's pretty dry underfoot today, but you know what stable-yards are . . . You don't use a stick, I notice.'

'My wife is always telling me I should.'

'Well, take this one,' was the reply. A stout hawthorn walking stick was pressed into Rowlands' hand. 'You won't need it for the stables, but we might walk up afterwards to take a look at the home farm.'

They passed the open door of the kitchen, and Swift put his head in. 'Morning, Mrs M,' he said, interrupting a dressing-down the cook was giving to one of her staff on the unsatisfactory polish this unfortunate had given to the knives.

'Morning, my lord. And a fine one it is to be sure.'

'This is Mr Rowlands. He's from England. He'll be staying with us for a few days.'

'And doesn't he look as if he needed some good Irish food and country air, the poor cratur,' said the woman after a glance at the newcomer. Rowlands smiled at this, but didn't think it required a reply. It had been a busy few months at work, and he'd been looking forward to his two weeks' holiday in Cornwall; evidently, he looked as if he was in need of it. After a further exchange of pleasantries, the two men exited through the back door onto a cobbled yard.

'Celia tells me you're a detective,' said Swift, whose conversational style seemed to be that of getting straight to the point.

Rowlands met this with equal directness. 'Yes, of a kind. I don't work in any official capacity, of course. But I have assisted the police, from time to time.'

'Hmph. You know, you're wasting your time if you think there's anything here for you to detect,' said the Irish lord as, accompanied by the dogs, they strolled across the yard. 'My wife's got some notion into her head that someone's out to get me. But it's all rot.'

'Those letters were real enough,' said Rowlands.

'Ah, she told you about those, then?' Swift didn't sound too pleased.

'Yes. And then there was what happened to the dog.'

'That was an accident. Jasper was an excitable creature. He must have got out, and one of the local farmers thought he was worrying sheep. Whoever it was mightn't have known it was my dog.'

'But the note . . .'

Swift made a scoffing sound. 'The Irish are a

dramatic people,' he said. 'I should know – I'm part-Irish myself. That note, like the letters before it, was just somebody making a drama out of a perfectly ordinary, if regrettable, occurrence. In my view, the best thing to do with such things is to ignore them.'

They passed through a gateway. That they were now in the stable-yard proper was evident to Rowlands, from the smells of newly raked straw and fresh horse-droppings; of leather tack and warm horseflesh, familiar from his boyhood days. The sounds, subdued but unmistakeable, were those that human beings adopt when conversing with horses: the low crooning of a stable hand to the beast whose coat he was engaged in brushing; the soft clicking of a tongue by which a rider signalled to his mount that it was time to 'walk on'. Swift led the way to the far side of the yard where the stables were, greeting this employee and that one en route: 'Morning, Davy, morning, Mike. How's the brown mare's foot coming along?'

'Grand, me lord. Sure, she'll be lepping fences again in no time.'

'Well, make sure you keep that poultice on until the thing's healed.' They reached the first of a row of loose boxes. 'This is Lady Molly, the horse I had in mind for you,' said Swift. 'She's as gentle as a lamb, aren't you, old girl?' He leant in to pat the mare's nose, murmuring sweet nothings as he did so. 'Give me your hand,' he said to Rowlands; when the other did so, he found something in his palm: a sugar lump. 'Always carry a few in my pocket for the beasts.' Rowlands offered this tribute to Lady Molly and she took it delicately between her lips and crunched it with her strong teeth. He stroked her face, feeling the soft puff of her breath on his cheek. He could tell from the quiet way she submitted to his caress that this was an even-tempered creature. 'I think you'll do very well together,' said Swift.

They moved along the row, coming to a halt in front of a stall three places along from the one occupied by the mare. 'Now *this*,' said Swift, 'is another kettle of fish altogether. Name's Lucifer. And doesn't he live up to it, the devil! Proud as can be, aren't you, my lad?' He reached a hand in to pat the stallion's neck, and there came a snorting and stamping of hooves as the high-mettled beast responded to this presumptuous contact. 'Six-year-old. Thoroughbred. Came first in his class at the County Wicklow trials. Good jumper, too. Careful!' he added as Rowlands reached out a hand to the horse. 'He's got a bit of a temper.' This Rowlands had just discovered for himself, for as his hand touched Lucifer's nose, the beast gave an indignant snort, and jerked his head away. 'Behave,' ordered his master. 'Don't you know a friend when you see one?'

'Fine animal,' said Rowlands, stepping back a pace to allow Swift to take charge.

Just then, one of the grooms came hurrying up.

'Ah, me lord,' he said. 'I was just after giving himself

a nice warm mash. Quiet him down a bit. Were you after taking him out, now?'

'Not until first thing tomorrow, I think,' was the reply. 'He's had one good ride already today. Rowlands, this is Mr Pheelan, my head groom. Pheelan, Mr Rowlands will be taking Lady Molly out this afternoon. You might get her ready. He'll need a lead rein.'

'Very good, my lord.'

'I'll lend you some clothes,' Swift went on as he and Rowlands resumed their stroll. 'We're more or less the same size. And I've a spare pair of boots I think might fit you.' Resigned to the inevitable, Rowlands nodded. It'd be good to get up on a horse again although he doubted whether he'd be able to go very far. But he was fast learning that, with these people, one was hardly worth noticing if one didn't ride.

'How many horses do you have here?' he asked as, after a few more words with the head groom on matters of a technical nature relating to the type of reins, bits and saddles best suited to an inexperienced rider, they continued their walk.

'Six, at present. That is, the two you've just met and two more, one of which is Celia's horse, Delilah, and the other a gelding – Duke Humphrey. I'll be riding him when we go out later. My brother doesn't care for riding although he was brought up to it, the same as I was. The other two horses belong to a neighbour, who stables them here. In my father's day, we kept a dozen hunters, as well as what he liked to call "good, quiet, ladies' horses", and ponies for the children. I'm thinking of getting a little pony for my boy, you know. Celia isn't keen. But I think one has to start them young.'

Chapter Three

There was still an hour to go before lunch, said Swift. If Rowlands was interested, they could stroll up to the home farm. He wanted a word with his cowman, and it was a pleasant enough walk. The dogs would appreciate it, too. Rowlands said he'd be happy to come along, and the two set off across the fields. 'You'll need your stick now,' said Swift, pausing to light cigarettes for them both. It was a glorious day, Rowlands thought, savouring the feel of the sun on his face, and the sweet smell of hay and wildflowers arising from the meadows on either side of the path. After they had been walking for a few minutes, Swift said as if there had been no break in the conversation: 'Yes, I think Celia's got herself worked up about nothing. The fact is, Rowlands, my family have lived in this part of Ireland for two hundred years. We've seen famine and revolutions come and go. Of course, there's some resentment against us – the English, I mean – and why wouldn't there be? We've treated the Irish abominably over the years. Now they're getting some of their own back. Inevitably, some of the nationalist crew are getting a bit carried away.'

'That's one way of putting it,' said Rowlands drily. 'So you think it's all a lot of . . . what did you call it? Dramatics.'

'I do,' replied Swift. 'Listen,' he went on earnestly. 'I know these people. I don't mean the Irish in general, I mean the people who live on or around this demesne. I've known them all since I was a child, and they know me. I can't believe any of 'em would wish me ill. I grant you, there may be a few hotheads – young fellows who fancy themselves as "soldiers" for the Republican Army – but that's all just hot air. Why, I could name you a few names, if it would make any difference . . . except that it wouldn't. Taking these threats seriously is the best way of encouraging them, don't you see? If . . . call him Paddy, or Mike . . . thinks he's made an impression, he'll be much more likely to keep on with his foolish tricks. Ignoring them's the only way.'

Rowlands guessed that the unusual length of this speech was indicative of how seriously the speaker meant what he said. And so he held his peace as, having scrambled over a stile, they found themselves on the rough track that led to the farm. Swift was obviously the type who would only become more entrenched

43

in his position, the more one tried to persuade him he was wrong. Rowlands began to see why Lady Celia, despairing of convincing her husband of the seriousness of the threats against his life, had called in reinforcements.

They reached the cowshed where Swift sought out his cowman, O'Brien, for an exchange of views on the question of milking machines against which, it became apparent, the worthy O'Brien had set his face. Rowlands, with nothing to contribute to this, lingered in the door of the large and airy building – empty now of its bovine occupants – which smelt pleasantly of clean straw and, faintly, of disinfectant. Evidently, the home farm was run on strictly hygienic lines. 'Our cows are Kerries,' said Swift on rejoining his guest. 'The black ones, you know. Smaller than some of your English breeds, but they do well here.'

Rowlands said that he believed Irish cream and butter was the envy of the world. 'To be sure,' was the reply. 'Of course it's only a small herd, kept for our own uses. The sheep are what bring us in our real income. I've a few pigs, too – again for home consumption – and there are Celia's chickens, which keep us in eggs.' Still talking of these bucolic matters, he set off back down the track, with Rowlands throwing in an occasional polite enquiry to keep the conversation going. Like many another man who had been through the war, Ned Swift seemed to have been only too glad to retreat to the comfortable monotony of domestic life. 'Why, here's Celia, come to meet us,' he said as they neared the house, the dogs running ahead to greet their mistress.

'So,' she said to Rowlands. 'Have you fallen in love with Lady Molly yet?' He admitted that he had, at which she let out a crow of laughter. 'I knew it! Ned was determined to get you up on a horse. But you needn't worry. Molly's the sweetest-tempered creature.' Rowlands said he believed it.

'The plan is to go out after lunch,' said Swift. 'You'll be joining us, won't you, Celia?'

'I suppose I must, since you've bullied our guest into doing so,' was the reply. 'I've put you in the yellow room, by the by,' she added to Rowlands. 'Lunch is at one. Sherry in the library at a quarter to.' She touched a bell, and a moment later, the servant appeared. 'Show Mr Rowlands to his room, Biddy,' she said.

'Yes'm.'

Rowlands accordingly followed the girl up the broad sweep of staircase, and along a corridor to a door at the far end, which she opened. 'Mistress said you was to have this room as it's the sunniest,' she said shyly.

'I can tell.' He smiled. 'It's so nice and warm.'

This must have raised a doubt in her mind, for she said hesitantly, 'Will I draw the blinds down?' He told her to leave them, saying he liked the sun. 'There's hot water in the jug, for your wash,' she went on. 'A new cake of soap on the washstand.' Lady Celia – or more likely, the housekeeper – had evidently been precise in her instructions for his comfort.

There wasn't time to do much more than wash his hands and comb his hair before joining the others, and so Rowlands made only a cursory survey of his room. Bed – a four-poster, he discovered – the aforementioned washstand, dressing-table, chest of drawers, writing desk, armchair. Someone – another pair of those 'invisible hands', no doubt – had unpacked his suitcase and hung his evening clothes in the wardrobe.

With his ablutions completed, he was about to go down when the sound of voices from below the bedroom windows – the sashes of which were raised, to air the room – drew his attention. 'I just need a few more days,' said a voice Rowlands recognised as that of Jolyon Swift. 'You'll get it, never fear . . .'

'I'm sure I shall, sir,' was the cool reply, a voice Rowlands didn't recognise. 'You've never let me down so far . . .'

'And I shan't now,' said Swift irritably. 'Let's go in, shall we? I think I hear the gong.'

There came a knock at the door. Rowlands moved hurriedly away from the window. 'Come in.' He was expecting it to be the maid who had conducted him here, but it was a man – a boy, rather – who spoke. 'Master said as I was to bring you these.' It was the promised riding clothes, Rowlands guessed, as the youth proceeded to lay these out upon the bed. 'Master said he'll have the boots ready for you to try on directly,' added the lad – whether groom or trainee valet, Rowlands could not have said.

'Thank you.'

'Will you be wanting me to help you dress?'

'I'll manage,' said Rowlands. 'And now, perhaps, you can point me towards the library?'

But, as it happened, Rowlands would have found his way without assistance, being guided, as he often was, by the sound of voices. These emanated from a room to the left of the staircase and across from the room where he'd had coffee that morning. As he entered, the murmur of conversation abruptly ceased, then resumed, as those present registered the arrival of a stranger in their midst. 'Ah, Frederick, there you are,' said Lady Celia, coming to meet him. 'I hope the room's to your liking?' He said that it was. 'Good. Come and have a sherry, and meet the rest of the tribe.' She steered him towards the centre of the room where a library table held cut-glass decanters and trays of sherry glasses. Here, the other inhabitants of Castleford were assembled. The talk was of horses.

'Now, if I were twenty years younger, I'd buy that two-year-old from you, Neddie my boy,' said an elderly gentleman. 'Train him up. He'll be a beautiful thing in a year or so. Plenty of bone. And the legs on him! Built for a runner.'

'Frederick, this is Canon Wetherby. Cousin Aloysius, I want you to meet Frederick Rowlands, a friend from London.'

'A pleasure,' said the old gentleman, shaking

Rowlands' hand. 'Neddie tells me you ride.'

'Not for many years,' said Rowlands, accepting a glass of sherry from his hostess.

'Oh, one never loses the knack,' replied the clergyman. 'Even an old crock like myself, crippled with the rheumatics, can still get up on a horse.'

'Go along with you!' said Ned Swift. 'You know it'd take more than a twinge of rheumatism in bad weather to make you hang up your hunting boots, Cousin Aloysius. The Enniskerry Hunt couldn't do without you, and that's a fact.'

'If you're really planning on giving up hunting, Canon Wetherby,' said a woman standing nearby, 'you might want to sell me that bay mare of yours. I think she'd be just right for my weight.'

'My Sally's not for sale,' said the old gentleman with a chuckle. 'But if she *were*, you'd have first refusal, Mrs Butler.'

'Rowlands, let me introduce you,' said Swift. 'This is Mrs Butler. Her husband's my land agent. Helps me keep the place ticking over . . . Oh, there you are, Butler! Didn't see you come in. This is Mr Rowlands.'

'How d'ye do?' said the land agent as he and Rowlands shook hands. 'Over from London, are ye? Can't say I fancy it there myself. Got used to the quiet life, haven't we, my dear?' Rowlands recognised the voice of the man who'd been talking to Jolyon Swift in the garden half an hour before. Evidently a man of some weight and presence at Castleford, to judge from his firm handshake, and confident tones.

Of Mrs Butler, whose hand he did not shake, Rowlands gained only the most superficial impression. Her rather drawling tone gave her utterances a condescending sound. 'So *you're* Celia's friend?' she said coldly when Rowlands was introduced, then addressed not another word to him.

Since the only others in the room were the Jolyon Swifts – too busy muttering to one another on the far side of the room to have time for anyone else – Rowlands found he could let his thoughts drift, paying only the most cursory attention to the conversation that flowed around him. It seemed an easy, untroubled world in which he now found himself, with its talk of horses and dogs, and its leisurely pace. Yet not many miles from here, across the English Channel, something dark and violent was brewing. There was the potential for violence here, too, if Celia Swift's fears had any foundation. He shook his head as if to dispel such thoughts. Swift was probably right. There was nothing to them.

The door to the library opened and someone came hurrying in. 'Sorry I'm late . . . G-got a bit caught up. Forgot the time.'

'You'd better make it quick,' said Swift as the young man, still muttering apologies, joined them. 'We're lunching in five minutes. Rowlands, this is my secretary, Sebastian Gogarty – fresh out of Trinity College. He's cataloguing the library.'

'H-how do you do?' said Gogarty, shaking Rowlands' hand. His own was cold and slightly clammy.

'That sounds like an interesting job,' said Rowlands, who felt sorry for the young fellow, who now stood nervously gulping his sherry, ignored by everyone else.

'Oh!' Gogarty sounded startled to be thus singled out. 'Yes, it is quite. Lord Castleford owns a number of r-rare first editions. Byron's *Poems*. G-Gibbon's *Decline and Fall*. S-several in very good condition.'

'Probably because no one has ever opened them,' put in Celia Swift, who was standing beside Rowlands, a fact of which he could not be unaware, given that there was no other woman in the world with just that delicious smell: expensive scent, and Turkish cigarettes. 'The only volumes anyone at Castleford actually *reads* are the *Stud Book* and bound copies of *Horse and Hound*.'

'Oh, Lady Celia . . . S-surely not?' cried Gogarty. 'I . . . I . . . m-mean . . .' He broke off, in apparent confusion, and Rowlands guessed that he wasn't the only one to find himself beguiled by Castleford's lovely chatelaine. The secretary was saved from further embarrassment by the announcement that luncheon was served. There was a general movement towards the dining room, across the hall. As he took his seat on Lady Celia's right, at the far end of the table where she presided, Rowlands wondered just how many rooms this 'barracks' had. It was probably as well that there *were* so many, given the numbers of people the place had to accommodate.

Just then, the door opened and a querulous voice said, 'Oh dear! Am I late?'

Beside him, Rowlands heard the mistress of the house emit a small sigh. 'I thought you were having a tray in your room as usual, Eveline? Lay another place for Lady Castleford, would you, Monckton?' she added to the butler.

'Very good, my lady.'

Rowlands, who had risen to his feet at the entrance of the dowager, now found himself the centre of attention once more. 'And who are *you*? I don't believe we've met.'

'Mr Rowlands is over from England, Eveline.'

'Really? Which part?'

When Rowlands said he lived in London, Lady Castleford replied, 'You must bring me up to date with all the news. We see so little really *good* society here.'

Fortunately, he was saved from having to confess how little he had to do with 'really good' society by the arrival of the soup. The talk reverted to its familiar topics – horses, dogs, and the news that the current MFH was to retire at the end of the next hunting season. There was speculation about who would replace him: 'Dunphy's your man,' opined Canon Wetherby. 'Those dogs of his are the best in the county.'

'Yes, but he hasn't the experience of, say, Martin Foley,' said Swift. 'Why, that bitch of his with the white patch has killed more foxes than the rest of the pack put together.'

The argument raged on, with some for Dunphy and some for Foley. Rowlands naturally took no part in this, occupying himself with eating his mutton chop while around him the contesting voices rose and fell. 'I loathe hunting, don't you?' said a voice in his ear. It was Henrietta Swift. Rowlands said that he had no opinion about it, as he had never hunted. 'You don't know how lucky you are,' she replied. 'It's the *only* thing people care about here, apart from racing, of course. My dear husband's the worst of the lot in that respect. I hate to *think* how much of our money he's lost over the years. Sometimes I think we're the only thing keeping Ireland's bookies from penury.'

'What terrible stories have you been telling Mr Rowlands about me, my love?' said Jolyon Swift from across the table.

'Only the truth,' said his wife.

'So I like a little flutter at the races now and then,' he said silkily. 'Where's the harm in it?'

'You know perfectly well—' she began, then broke off as if she'd said more than she'd meant to.

An awkward silence was broken by Lady Castleford, who, busily plying her lapdog with scraps, had caught only the end of the conversation. 'I like a day's racing, myself. I always get Pheelan to place my bets for me. He knows a good horse, does Pheelan.'

'So he should,' said Ned Swift mildly. 'Although I don't know that I want you distracting him from his work, Eveline. He's supposed to be looking after my stables, not giving you racing tips.' It was said in a jovial tone, but there was a steeliness underlying the words that made Rowlands think that he wouldn't like to be the man – or woman – who crossed Ned Swift.

'Yes . . . well . . .' Lady Castleford sounded flustered. '*Leave* it, Mitzie! You'll make yourself sick.' This was to the dog, which had taken advantage of his mistress's discomfiture to stage a raid on her plate.

'One does ask oneself,' said a voice from along the table – it was Robert Butler – 'whether racing, or hunting, or any of it, can carry on much longer, with things the way they are?'

'What the dickens do you mean?' said Canon Wetherby.

'I mean the fact that we'll be at war soon – or at least, England will. I'm rather afraid,' said Butler, in his suave, self-satisfied voice, 'that'll bring an end to the kind of life we've all enjoyed up till now.'

'Nonsense.' This was Wetherby again. 'Ireland'll stay neutral if de Valera has his way.'

'Then it's to be hoped that our German friends are as keen on the thrill of the chase as we are in Ireland.'

'You can't think that the Germans are likely to invade?' said Ned Swift sharply.

'What's to keep them out?' was the cool reply.

'B-but s-surely . . .' Sebastian Gogarty's stammer got worse, the more excited he became. 'Ireland's of no s-strategic importance to the G-Germans?'

'As a base from which to invade England, what

could be more convenient?' said Butler. 'Besides which, it'd stop the English using Irish ports.'

'Y-yes, but . . .'

'Coffee, I think,' said Lady Celia, bringing this political discussion to a close. 'We'll have it in the drawing room, Monckton. We should set out as soon as possible if we're to take advantage of the weather,' she added to Rowlands, slipping her arm through his as they made their way out. 'The forecast said it might break tonight. And I want you to see Castleford at its best.'

Having dressed himself in the jodhpurs and hacking jacket Swift had lent him and pulled on the boots (they were slightly too small, but he wouldn't be walking far in them), Rowlands descended the stairs to the hall where the others were waiting. 'Ah, there you are!' cried his host. 'I've asked Pheelan to bring the horses round to the front of the house. Thought you might like to walk Lady Molly up and down for a bit before we set off.' Rowlands said he was happy to do this, and having handed him a pair of leather gloves and a tweed cap the latter said he thought might fit him, Swift led the way out of the front door. Outside, on the gravel sweep, the three horses stood, attended by their respective grooms. 'Well, Pheelan?' said Swift. 'Is everything ready?'

'Yes, my lord. I put the lead-rein on Lady Molly, as you instructed.'

'Hmph,' was the reply. 'We'll see if it's needed. You

can help Mr Rowlands up, Pheelan. It's his first time on horseback since he was a lad.'

'Very well, my lord. This way, sir,' said the head groom to Rowlands, placing a hand on the latter's shoulder to guide him towards the horse.

Unable to suppress a feeling of trepidation as he approached the animal, even though he was satisfied that her nature was of the quietest, Rowlands spoke softly to her: 'Remember me? I'm the one you're going to be looking after.' He stroked her nose, murmuring words of reassurance that were as much for himself as for the horse.

'Ready, sir?' Pheelan guided him so that he was standing on the left side of the horse. 'Just take a hold of her mane there, and put your other hand on the saddle while I give ye a leg up,' said the groom, suiting the action to the words.

Grasping Rowlands' shin and ankle, he pushed him upwards so that the former was able to swing his right leg over the horse and settle himself in the saddle. Having satisfied himself that Rowlands' feet were firmly in the stirrups, Pheelan checked that the girth was tight enough. All the while that he was performing these necessary tasks, Rowlands sat completely still, accustoming himself to the feel of the thing: to the warm, solid presence of the animal on which he sat; to the perfect fit of the leather saddle, and the feel of the reins in his hands; to the extraordinary sensation of being at one with the horse – or at least, of being accepted by her as her rider.

He was conscious, also, from the terse remarks of his two companions – 'The girth a little tighter, I think', from Swift to the groom assisting him, and 'I don't know if I really *like* this saddle', from Lady Celia, to nobody in particular – that they, too, had mounted their beasts, and now stood waiting for him. A sudden feeling of anxiety overtook him at the prospect of having to move. Couldn't he just sit here, drinking in the warmth of the sun, and the pleasant smells of leather tack and horseflesh while the others rode on ahead? But then Pheelan said, 'Will I walk a bit with you, sir? I've Lady Molly on the lead-rein. She's as good as gold, aren't you, darling? She'll follow me like a lamb.'

Rowlands assented and, at this, the groom made a clicking sound with his tongue, signifying 'walk on'. At once the horse began to move sedately across the gravel. The surge of emotion Rowlands felt mingled elation and alarm. What if he fell off? But, he reassured himself, they were going along so slowly that – even if he did – he was unlikely to hurt himself very much. And he was secure enough in the saddle. 'We'll go down the drive,' said Swift, who rode beside him on the gelding, Duke Humphrey. 'Then cross the road to the big meadow. It's fairly level for the first hundred yards or so.'

They continued at the same stately pace, with Rowlands holding the reins loosely in his hands as he recalled how to guide the horse, using the pressure of his knees. Suddenly, he'd had enough of being led like a child. 'I think I might manage it myself from here,' he said to Pheelan. 'If somebody would guide me as to direction, and so on.'

'I'll take over, Pheelan,' said Lady Celia, bringing her horse level with Rowlands'. 'Delilah and Molly are old friends. They're quite used to walking along together.' The leading rein was taken off, and Rowlands took the reins into his own hands. A few minutes' practice was all it took.

As they crossed the road that bounded the estate, and entered the meadow on the other side, he said, 'You won't want to spend the whole afternoon at a walking pace, Lady Celia. If you don't mind carrying on talking so that I can follow your voice, I think I might be ready for a canter.'

'Good idea. There's a nice flat stretch of meadow ahead, with no obstacles until you reach the fence at the far side – about two hundred yards away. Here.' She handed him the riding crop she had been carrying. 'Just give her a touch with this if she doesn't respond to your kick . . .'

But this proved unnecessary for, at a signal from her rider, the obliging mare broke into a canter and set off across the field, with Lady Celia's horse in hot pursuit. Then it was just a matter for Rowlands of keeping himself as firmly in the saddle as he could, and trying to avoid the tendency to bounce, to which inexperienced horsemen are prone. 'All right,' called his companion, as in a very few moments they drew near to the edge of the field. 'Pull on the reins a bit to slow her down.

That's it.' The two of them came to a halt, just as Swift cantered up.

'I'll take over now, Celia, if you want a gallop. You might open the gate for us first.' She went to do so, and Swift said to Rowlands, 'You're doing fine. I watched you over that last bit, and you kept your seat like a champion.'

'I don't flatter myself that I cut a very elegant figure,' said Rowlands. 'But Lady Molly was kind enough not to throw me off.'

'Oh, she wouldn't do that,' said her master, sounding a little affronted at the suggestion. 'She's too much of a lady, aren't you, old girl?' At this unconscious echo of Jolyon Swift's mode of addressing his sister-in-law, Rowlands smiled, at which Swift, misunderstanding the smile, went on: 'You might think it absurd, but horses are much like people in their behaviour. You get those like Lady Molly, who knows exactly what her rider wants, and does it, without fuss. Then there are the other kind – like the stallion I showed you earlier. Wonderful beast, but with a filthy temper at times. One simply can't generalise where horses are concerned – any more than one can with human beings.'

Rowlands said that he understood this, and the two men set off again, passing through the gate into the next field, and quickening their pace to a canter. Once again, Rowlands found himself able to place absolute trust in his mount while the ride lasted, and to exult in the sensations of well-being it promoted. The feel of the warm breeze in his face was delightful, and the smell of new-mown hay and wildflowers arising from the meadows. Memories of his boyhood in Norfolk when he and Harry roamed about the fields (his brother, two years his senior, was the one who'd taught Fred to ride, in the first instance) filled his mind. He felt a tremendous sense of gratitude to the Swifts for providing him with an experience he'd never thought to have again, and was glad he had overcome his foolish fears.

Chapter Four

'I must say, Frederick, you look very comfortable on that horse,' said Lady Celia as the two men caught up with her. 'I think you've been pulling the wool over our eyes about your lack of riding experience – don't you, Ned?'

'Indeed I do. You'll be jumping fences next,' said Swift; but at this, Rowlands smilingly demurred.

'Even with a horse as even-tempered as Molly here, I don't think I'd attempt anything so ambitious. But it's been a wonderful afternoon.'

'Glad you've enjoyed yourself,' said Swift as they walked on. 'Celia was keen to show you around the demesne a bit.'

'Is this all your land?

'Some of it,' was the reply. 'The boundary lies on the far side of the river. Beyond that, it's the Langtons' place. You'll meet them at dinner tonight. There's a path through the woods ahead of us – it's a good, broad one, and Molly knows it well. I want to take you up to the ridge. There's a splendid view from there. I'm sure my wife will enjoy describing it for you.' There followed a pleasant walk through shady woodland, then a more strenuous canter across open country before they reached the prospect Swift had mentioned. At the summit of the hill, they dismounted and lit cigarettes.

'When it's clear like this, you can see as far as Dublin Bay,' Lady Celia said. 'Just between those two far mountains. They look almost purple at this time of day. I've often thought that if one were a painter, this would be the best time to capture this view – with that golden, late-afternoon light over everything. There's a lake at the bottom of the valley, fed by the river that runs through Castleford.'

'It's a decent trout stream,' put in Swift. 'If you care for fishing, I can fix you up with a rod.' Rowlands said he'd like that very much. At least with fishing, he thought, one only had to sit there.

For a while, he and his companions stood without speaking, enjoying the warmth of the sunshine and the immense quiet. That quiet was broken only by the harsh cawing of a carrion crow, circling above whatever tasty morsel of dead flesh it had sighted.

'Time we were heading back,' said Lady Celia after another few minutes had elapsed. 'I'd like to introduce you to Georgie.' This, Rowlands guessed, was the five-year-old son, of whom both parents had spoken with such pride.

'Which reminds me,' said Swift as they turned their horses' heads for home, 'I want to stop off at Doolan's cottage . . . That's my gamekeeper,' he added to Rowlands. 'His spaniel bitch has just had puppies. I thought we could pick one out for George to rear as his own.'

'Don't you think he's got enough to do, looking after his rabbits?' said Lady Celia.

'To hell with rabbits. A boy needs a dog,' was the trenchant reply, at which George's mother, perhaps realising that this was another argument she couldn't win, spurred her horse to a gallop, leaving the two men behind. 'We'll skirt the wood,' said Swift, making no comment upon this sudden desertion. 'Doolan's cottage is on the far side of it. He'll be having his tea about now.'

Rowlands nodded, but made no other reply, his attention fixed on the other's voice, without really paying attention to what was being said, except as a guide to where he was to follow. So it came as a shock as they neared the keeper's cottage, when Swift suddenly reined in his horse with a sharp exclamation: 'What the devil?' Then, in a sterner tone than Rowlands had heard him use hitherto: 'Come out of there at once, Christie Doherty. It's no use your trying to hide.' From which Rowlands gathered that the individual Swift was addressing must have taken cover behind a wall or hedge when he saw the master coming. 'What are you doing here?' the latter continued. 'You know I told you to keep clear of my property.'

'Sure, can't a man visit his relations?' was the truculent reply. 'And didn't the mammy say to me this morning, "Time you went to see your uncle Pat, Chrissy. Mebbe he'll have some work for you, now that His Lordship's after letting you go."'

'You can cut all that nonsense,' said Swift. 'I don't want you working here, or anywhere else on my land. I thought I'd made that clear.'

'Mebbe you did and mebbe you didn't, *my lord*,' replied Doherty, with a sarcastic emphasis on the honorific. 'The fact is, I've a living to get, like any man.'

'Yes, by stealing and poaching,' snapped Swift. 'I won't have it, do you hear? Now take yourself off, or—'

'Or *what*, my lord?' There was an unpleasant note in Doherty's voice. He must have been rolling a cigarette throughout the exchange, for he now lit it, releasing a whiff of rough tobacco. 'It's a free country. And if things go on the way they're going, mebbe it'll be yourself who'll be the first to leave.'

'Are you threatening me, Doherty?'

The man laughed. 'Now why would you be thinking such a thing, my lord? All right, all right! I know when I'm not wanted,' he added hastily as Swift's horse, perhaps sensing the animosity between the two men, took a frisky pace or two towards the speaker.

Before things could get uglier, the keeper, Doolan, came out of his cottage. 'Afternoon, my lord. I made sure it was you. Come to look at Bessie's pups, have ye?'

'I have. And I've been telling your nephew that he's not welcome here. I'm surprised you didn't tell him yourself, Doolan.'

'Indeed I did, my lord,' replied the gamekeeper. 'But it's a terrible stubborn lad, is our Chrissy.'

'Well, you can tell him from me,' said Swift as if Doherty was not there, 'that if I see him around these parts again, I'll know what to do . . .'

'Set the dogs on me, would you, my lord?' was Doherty's parting shot as he sloped off. 'I wouldn't run the risk, meself. Shame what happened to that old dog o' yours, wasn't it? Wouldn't want there to be any more *unfortunate* accidents . . .'

To which piece of impudence, Swift made no reply. Having dismounted, he helped Rowlands to do the same. 'Let's see these pups of yours,' he said to the keeper, who – still apologising for the way his nephew had behaved – led the way into the cottage. This consisted of a single room, comprising bedchamber, kitchen, sitting room and kennel in one. There was a pungent smell of dogs, tobacco and some kind of lineament that was boiling away on the stove. In a basket in front of this, the spaniel bitch and her puppies were ensconced. Swift spent the next few minutes examining these in turn, remarking on their colour and the condition of their coats. But in the end, he came to no conclusion. 'The black one's the liveliest,' he said. 'Bit my finger, little devil. However, I think it best if I bring Master George along to choose for himself.'

'Right you are, my lord.'

'I'm sorry you had to witness that unpleasant little episode with Doherty,' said Swift as, having refused the offer of tea, he and Rowlands rode away. 'Doolan's a good man – and a very competent keeper. He's worked for me for years. Of course, like most of the men of his age, he fought on the rebel side. But I don't hold it against him. That nephew of his is a different matter. Had to sack him when I caught him smoking in the stables. There'd been incidents before that, too. Petty pilfering. I can stand a bit of poaching – what's a fish or two, or the occasional rabbit? – but stealing money from the other stable-lads I will not have.'

Rowlands said he quite saw that. 'You don't think Doherty might have had something to do with those letters?' he said cautiously, knowing his host's stubbornness where the subject was concerned. 'It's a possibility, surely? A disgruntled employee . . .'

'Christie Doherty doesn't have the wit to have written those letters,' was the reply. 'He's all piss and wind. No, of the two, his uncle's the more formidable character. He was a quartermaster in the IRA during the Troubles. I should think he's killed a few men in his time. Fortunately, he and I get on pretty well. Come on, if you're game, we'll take the last field at a canter.'

Tea was being served in the library when they got back to the house. Lady Celia presided, with the rest of the company – the Jolyon Swifts, the Butlers, Lady Castleford, Canon Wetherby and young Gogarty – disposed about the large and comfortably appointed room. 'Ah, there you are!' said the mistress of the house as they entered. 'Come and sit by me, Frederick. There's someone I want you to meet.' This turned out to be the child, little George. 'Say "how do you do" to Mr Rowlands, Georgie,' prompted his mother. The former dutifully complied, and Rowlands responded in kind, holding out his hand for the boy to shake. This proved more awkward than anticipated, as the child was holding his pet rabbit.

'Really, Nurse,' said Swift impatiently to that member of the household, who had been standing silently by. 'I've told you about letting him bring that animal into the house.'

'He *would* have it so, my lord,' was the unruffled reply. 'Said he wanted to show the gentleman what tricks his old bunny can do.'

'Well, make this the last time,' said Swift. 'George, I think I've found a nice dog for you.' Then, when his son made no response: 'Celia, this tea's stewed.'

'If you will turn up half an hour late . . .'

'In my opinion,' said Jolyon Swift, with a laugh to

show it was a joke, 'the best place for a rabbit is in the pot.' At this, Rowlands felt the child shift uneasily beside him on the sofa.

'Does your rabbit have a name?' he said quickly.

'He's called Peter,' was the timid reply.

'Of course,' said Rowlands, reaching to stroke the rabbit's soft fur. 'It was clever of him to get out of Mr McGregor's garden, wasn't it?' This reference to a story beloved of Rowlands' girls when they were young seemed to calm the child, for he stopped his fidgeting.

'He *is* clever,' he murmured, so quietly that only Rowlands heard. 'He can sit up on his hind legs an' . . . an' he knows how to play dead.' Which, thought Rowlands, was a useful accomplishment for a creature whose days, from the sound of it, might well be numbered.

'All right, Georgie, time for your bath,' said his mother after a few more minutes had passed. 'You can take him now, Nurse.'

'Yes, m'lady. Come along, Master George.'

'He's rather shy,' said Lady Celia apologetically as the nurse and her charge left the room. 'But he was *very* excited when I told him he was going to meet a famous detective . . .' Her words, falling into a momentary lull in the conversation, seemed to hang in the air for rather longer than Rowlands would have liked. Fortunately, not many minutes elapsed before it was time to go and dress, so he was spared any inquisition about his alleged profession. He wondered, as he ascended the stairs to his room, whether Celia Swift's remark had been merely a tease – or whether it had been meant as a warning to one of those present. Surely she couldn't think that a member of the household was responsible for the poison pen letters, and the killing of the dog?

After what he himself had witnessed that afternoon, Rowlands was inclined to think that it must have been someone with a grudge against Swift who had carried out that heinous act. Christie Doherty was the obvious candidate.

Having luxuriated in the pleasures of a hot bath, which he hoped would mitigate the after-effects of his ride, he put on his evening clothes – already laid out for him on the bed – and made a poor fist of tying his bow tie, a task for which he usually required Edith's help. At the thought of his wife, Rowlands felt a pang, although it had only been forty-eight hours since they'd spoken on the telephone. When he'd informed her that, rather than joining her and the family in Cornwall straight away, he'd be spending the first few days of his annual holiday in Ireland, she'd made surprisingly little objection, even when he'd admitted that he'd be staying with Lady Celia. 'She wants my help on a matter concerning her husband,' he'd hastened to explain. 'She believes his life has been threatened.' Given that this wasn't the first time that Rowlands had been caught up in a life-and-death affair involving Her Ladyship, Edith had taken the news very well.

'Just don't get yourself into any scrapes, Fred,' she'd said. Quite what she meant by that, she left for him to work out, which was unusually reticent for Edith.

Now he stood at the top of the stairs, still fiddling with his confounded bow tie. Was it crooked or straight? He couldn't really tell. There came the sound of a light footstep. A waft of scent. 'Anything I can do?' said a voice. Hers, of course. Having sized up the problem, she went to work at once, fingers deftly untying and retying until the offending article was as it should be.

'Thank you,' he said, feeling the momentary frisson of pleasure of being close to her.

'Can't have a man let down by his tie,' she said, giving him an approving pat on the shoulder as she completed her task. 'Let's go down, shall we?' She linked her arm through his, and he caught another whiff of her perfume.

'Chanel Number 5,' he murmured, without thinking.

'It's my favourite,' she said. 'How clever of you to identify it. But I expect you're rather good at such things.'

'Sometimes,' he admitted, conscious of the feel of her bare arm resting lightly on his, and of the liquid folds of her satin gown brushing against him as they descended the stairs. They crossed the wide hall to the drawing room. This struck Rowlands as a grander, more formal room than either the morning room, with its cosy muddle of sofas and low tables or the library, with its wing chairs and walls of leather-bound books. A state room, almost – its acreage of slippery parquet floor, covered at intervals with rugs, and dotted here and there with flimsy articles of furniture, seemed designed to trip the unwary, and made him glad of his hostess's arm.

'Cocktails first, I think,' said Lady Celia. 'Unless you'd prefer a whisky?'

He said that he would, and she led him towards the side table where the drinks had been laid out. Here, a number of the other members of the party had already congregated. He heard Jolyon Swift's petulant whine rising above the general murmur: 'But *Mummy* . . .' and Lady Castleford's reply – 'Not *now*, Joly . . .'

From another part of the room came the canon's jocular tones, describing a salmon he'd caught, and the rod he'd used to catch it, for the benefit of young Gogarty. And here was Swift himself, in conversation with his land agent: '. . . no question but that we'll have to retrench. What with the war coming . . . Ah, Rowlands, there you are! Not feeling too saddle-sore after your ride, I hope?' Rowlands said that he was fine, but expected he'd know all about it tomorrow.

'So you've been given a tour of the demesne?' enquired Butler, in his smoothly insinuating tones. 'Ah, it's a lovely spot, a lovely spot. Some of the best land in the county – wouldn't you say, my lord?'

'Well, naturally, I'm biased, but . . .' The sound of a motor car pulling up outside distracted Swift from what he'd been about to say. 'That'll be the Langtons,' he said. 'Do excuse me, won't you, Rowlands? I need to have a word with old Langton before we go into dinner. See about those figures, will you, Butler? I want them on my desk first thing tomorrow.'

Then he was gone, leaving Rowlands and the land agent in awkward tête-à-tête. 'I suppose His Lordship'll have taken you up to the ridge?' said Butler after a moment's silence. 'There's a grand view from there although, to be sure, it might be lost on one such as yourself.' Rowlands said that they had indeed ridden up to the lookout point, and that Lady Celia had described the view to him. 'Did she so?' replied the other. 'That's grand. I wonder did Her Ladyship mention the fact that one can see beyond the Castleford demesne, to where it abuts onto the next estate? My late father was the steward there.'

'I don't believe she did,' replied Rowlands.

'Ah! No reason why she should, no reason at all,' the other man went on. 'I grew up there, you know. Happy days. Avalon was the name of the house. Burnt down, in the last Troubles.'

'It was falling to pieces, even before the rebels burnt it,' said a voice. It was Mrs Butler. 'Death duties,' she added, for Rowlands' information. 'Most of the big houses in Ireland have gone to rack and ruin, on account of that. Sheer greed on the part of the government, if you want my opinion,' she added bitterly. 'People have had to sell up – those that still have anything to sell.'

Rowlands said that it must have been a difficult time – and really, what more was there to say? Many people had lost homes and livelihoods in the bleak years since the financial crash. He supposed this was just another example of the same. He was relieved when, before the subject could be explored further, dinner was announced. Accompanied by Butler and his wife, he began to make his way towards the dining room. 'So tell me,' Mrs Butler went on, slipping her arm through his so that he was forced to match his step to hers. 'Are you really a detective? Or was that just some story of Lady Celia's?'

'Well,' he began, not liking the implication that his hostess had been telling stories, 'I *have* worked with the police, on a number of occasions, but—'

'Frederick's being modest as usual,' said Celia Swift, overhearing this. 'He's solved quite a number of celebrated cases. But of course he's far too discreet to talk about them.'

'Fancy!' said Elspeth Butler, sounding as if she wasn't sure whether or not to believe this.

'Lady Celia is too kind,' said Rowlands. 'But I can't claim to have done anything more than being in the right place at the right time.' This seemed to have settled the matter for the time being although Rowlands was glad, as they took their seats at table, that he hadn't been placed next to Mrs Butler. There was something about her cold inquisitiveness that chilled his blood.

But his right-hand neighbour, Lady Castleford, proved to be no less tiresome in this respect: 'Well,' she said as the soup was served. 'You *are* a man of mystery, to be sure! A man who knew Celia during her London days, as it were . . . We know so *little* of her past . . . other than the fact that she was *very* famous at one time . . .' Malicious old cat, thought Rowlands, hoping that none of this was reaching the end of the table where his hostess sat – nor the opposite end where her husband presided. 'Quite the *queen* of the smart set, was she not?' She spooned up her Mulligatawny with noisy gusto. 'Life must seem *very* quiet to her now. So you see, Mr . . . er . . . You've an advantage over the rest of us at Castleford. You knew my daughter-in-law when she was the name on everybody's lips . . . the . . . what's the word? The *cynosure* of all eyes.'

That had certainly been the case, thought Rowlands, recalling that day in Court 1 at the Old Bailey when Celia West (as she was then) had been summoned to give evidence at a notorious murder trial. This had been the affair that had brought them together, and in which he had played a not insignificant part. He guessed that this was what the dowager was referring to now. Doubtless, Lady Celia's incautious remark about his being a detective had roused suspicions in the old girl's mind as to the nature of their past connection. 'I think you must be confusing me with someone else,' he said. 'I've never had anything to do with the smart set. My association with Lady Celia is purely coincidental. She was a childhood friend of Gerald Willoughby, my commanding officer during the last war. After he died, she was kind enough to keep in touch.' It was the account of their relationship he'd given to Swift's half-brother; while it left out a good deal, it covered the essential – and least interesting – points.

Lady Castleford evidently felt that she'd been short-changed as far as the conversation was concerned, for she said, with what seemed to Rowlands an odious coyness, 'And there was I thinking you were one of Celia's admirers! I'm sure there must have been many . . .'

It was Canon Wetherby, on Rowlands' left, who came to the rescue. 'So what do you think about all this talk of war? Will your government manage to keep Britain out of it?'

'I think it's increasingly unlikely,' replied Rowlands. 'Now that Hitler's violated the Munich Agreement, and with Stalin getting in on the act, I don't see how we *can* stay out of it.'

'I thought dear Mr Chamberlain had settled all that a year ago?' interjected Lady Castleford. 'What I say is, we should live and let live. Let Mr Hitler run things his own way.'

'Appeasement isn't the answer,' said another voice. It was Sebastian Gogarty. 'One can't *n-negotiate* with tyrants.' Rowlands realised that the young man was making an effort to contain his anger. 'We've n-no alternative but to fight back – or risk being crushed by the N-nazi war machine.'

'Really, I think you men are *obsessed* with war!' said Eveline Swift peevishly. 'My late husband was just the same. Never happy unless he was talking about his soldiering days in South Africa . . . No, take it away,' she said to the servant who was serving the next course. 'It's my meat-free week. Don't you find,' she added to Rowlands, 'that quail is a rather *unsatisfying* dish? Never enough flesh on the bones, to my mind.'

'Tell Cook that Lady Castleford would like an omelette, Stevens,' said Celia Swift to the man. 'Eveline, we'll carry on eating, if it's all the same to you? Mrs M gets so offended if her dishes aren't enjoyed at their best.'

'Oh, don't mind little *me*!' was the reply from the dowager. 'Although heaven knows why anyone should *need* a heavy meal at this time of day. So bad for the digestion. But then I've always had a sensitive system. Why, dear Doctor O'Leary says it's a miracle I'm still alive.' She continued in this vein until her own meal was brought, and the first course replaced by cuts of roast beef for all the other guests. The talk was of the continuing spell of good weather and the imminent start of the shooting season.

Intermingled with this came snatches of what sounded to Rowlands like an amiable – and perhaps long-standing – dispute: 'I'm telling you, Swift old man, you'll never get a better price for that land . . . not with the war coming.'

'I beg to differ,' was the reply. 'And, in any case, I'm happy to sit it out. That land's been part of the demesne for generations. My father held it in trust for me as his father did for him, and *his* father before that. I intend to pass it on in its entirety when George comes of age.'

'How pleasant that would be – if 'twere only possible,' said Langton, of whom Rowlands had so far been able to form only a superficial opinion. He sounded a bluff, genial sort of fellow. A typical gentleman farmer – Rowlands supposed there must be many of his kind in this part of the world. 'I'm afraid you're living in Cloud Cuckoo Land if you think that the war won't change all that. Why, the value of land – to say nothing of other kinds of property – will fall through the floor.'

'Well, thanks for your opinion,' replied Swift. 'But you're wasting your breath if you think you'll get me to change my mind about selling that land. As long as I've breath in my body, I mean to keep the demesne intact. Darling, it's time . . .' This last remark was addressed to his wife, at her end of the dining table, whose job it now was to collect the ladies so that the men could enjoy their port and cigars.

'All right,' she said, getting up. 'But don't be too long, will you?'

Once the ladies had left, the talk turned once more to the war, and the likelihood or otherwise of Ireland's being out of it. Of those assembled, two – Butler and Langton – took the view that de Valera had it right, 'It isn't our fight,' said the landowner. 'We should stay clear of it.' Two others – Jolyon Swift and Canon Wetherby – were neutral (the latter, as a man of the church, said he deplored fighting even if the cause were a just one) and two – Swift and young Gogarty – were of the opinion that it was Ireland's duty to enter the fray. Swift had seen service in the last war, as had Langton, who was of an age with him. (Butler had been exempt on the grounds of his being the only son of a widowed mother.)

Sebastian Gogarty, whose age Rowlands guessed to be around twenty-one or -two, was the most passionate in favour of going to war: 'W-we *have* to fight,' he said, his fierce tone belying the impression Rowlands had received on first meeting him of a bookish, mild-mannered young man. 'If we don't, it'll look a-as if w-we're afraid. Or . . . or as if we s-support Hitler's gang.'

'There are some in this country who'd consider that a better option than supporting the British,' said Langton, who seemed to Rowlands to be enjoying the argument. 'It's not so many years since they were blowing up British soldiers on our country roads, and shooting informers.'

'B-but that's all in the past,' protested Gogarty, who must have been about two when the events to which Langton was referring had taken place.

'The past is never really over in Ireland,' said Canon Wetherby. 'Why, men are still fighting battles from three hundred years ago. For which,' he added drily, 'the church must take some responsibility.'

''F you want my opinion, I think it's a frightful

bore,' interjected Jolyon Swift, who sounded as if he'd had rather more to drink than was wise. 'Dragged into a war none of us want. I *object* to it, persh . . . personally.' He let out a loud hiccup.

'If you gentlemen have done,' said his half-brother quickly, 'I suggest we join the ladies.'

Chapter Five

As Rowlands, in company with the other men, crossed the hall towards the drawing room where the ladies awaited them, he felt a touch on his shoulder. 'Rowlands, I don't believe I've introduced a neighbour of mine, Oliver Langton. Langton, this is Frederick Rowlands. Got so caught up in all that nonsense about the war that it slipped my mind.'

'So you're the man from England,' said Langton as they shook hands. 'Should have got *your* opinion about what Chamberlain's up to, instead of pontificating about the subject ourselves. A man who's been on the spot is bound to know more than we provincials do.'

'I'm not so sure about that,' replied Rowlands. 'It seems to me—'

'I *shay*, Ned,' said Jolyon Swift, cutting across this exchange. 'Lemme have a word, will you?' He sounded agitated. 'Somethin' need t' discuss.'

'Can't it wait?' Swift did not attempt to conceal his irritation at this interruption.

'No, it can't. Rather important, *ack-shully*, ol' man. Been wanting to talk to you all evening, 'smatter o' fact.'

'All right,' said Swift curtly. 'You'd better come along to my office. But I can't think what can be so urgent that it can't wait until morning.'

Swift and his half-brother accordingly absented themselves, the latter babbling nervously that it wouldn't take a minute, but that he was rather keen to tackle the matter tonight. 'I can guess what *that's* about,' muttered Langton in Rowlands' ear. 'Young Swift's a terror for the horses. He's been losing heavily at the tables, too. If he goes on the way he is it won't be long before he ends up in Queer Street.'

Further discussion of this unsavoury topic was curtailed as they entered the drawing room, by Langton's being hailed by his wife to come and make up a four at bridge: 'There you are at last, m'dear! Can't *think* what you men find to talk about that's so fascinating. And here's Lady Castleford and myself just *dyin'* for a game.'

'Rowlands, let me introduce my wife,' said Langton. 'A fiend for bridge as you can tell. Venetia, this is Celia's friend, from London.'

'Delighted,' said Rowlands, adding that he was a bit of a fiend for bridge himself.

'A man after me own heart,' said Mrs Langton. 'I'd suggest you join our table, except that it would mean disappointin' the poor canon, who's no doubt been longin' for his game for the past half-hour.'

Rowlands said that he wouldn't dream of depriving Canon Wetherby of his game, and withdrew to a suitable distance, from which he could follow the play. 'Coffee, Frederick?' said Lady Celia, joining him at that moment.

'Thank you.' He took the cup from her.

'You know there's no reason why you shouldn't make up another foursome with Mr and Mrs Butler and Henrietta,' she said as trumps were called and the game began. 'Although of course . . .' She hesitated as if she'd remembered something.

'As it happens, I do have my Braille cards with me,' he said, guessing what it was she had remembered. 'One never knows when one might be offered a game. I could fetch them now – that is, if the other players wouldn't consider it an unfair advantage?'

'What's that?' said Robert Butler, overhearing this. When it was explained to him that Braille cards differed from the usual kind only in having their denominations indicated by a series of small raised dots in the top right-hand and lower left-hand corners, he grunted that he didn't mind if it didn't interfere with play, and that after the day *he'd* had, he'd been looking forward to a rubber or two. Mrs Butler concurred, adding rather acidly that she supposed it must be like playing with marked cards. Henrietta said she was dying of boredom and didn't mind what kind of cards they played with as long as she got her game. And so Rowlands went off to fetch the cards, saying he wouldn't be a minute.

'If you see my husband,' said Lady Celia, 'do tell him to hurry up. His guests are waiting.' Rowlands smiled, but he had no intention of doing any such thing. Whatever Swift and his half-brother had to say to one another was no concern of his – nor did he relish interrupting their colloquy with his hostess's message. As it turned out, he didn't have to.

It took him no more than a couple of minutes to return to his room and retrieve the pack of cards from his suitcase. As he was descending the stairs to rejoin the rest of the company, there came the sound of angry voices from behind the door of the room he guessed must be Swift's study. 'Not standin' any more of this!' shouted Jolyon Swift. 'Bein' *leckshured* like a schoolboy . . .' A moment later, the door burst open and he rushed out, followed by Swift himself.

'That's right!' shouted the latter angrily. 'Run away, like you always do, you little coward! By God, if you come near me again tonight, I swear I'll kill you.'

'Get away from me!' The younger man came running upstairs, pushing past Rowlands in his haste to get away from his adversary, who, however, made no attempt to follow. Before Rowlands could reach the hall, Swift, too, must have decided to take himself off, because there came the sound of rapid footsteps crossing the hall, and the front door opening and slamming shut.

The dumbfounded silence that greeted Rowlands as he entered the drawing room once more told him that everyone – with the possible exception of Lady Castleford, who was busily engaged in totting up her bridge score – had heard Swift's angry words. 'Oh dear!' said Lady Celia softly as he joined her. 'I do wish my dear husband could learn to control his temper. You'll have to take my word for it, Frederick, but his bark really *is* worse than his bite.' There was nothing to say to this, and so Rowlands merely smiled, and took his seat at the second of the two bridge tables. Conversation – largely consisting of bids and counter-bids – flowed once more. For Rowlands, who usually enjoyed a game of bridge, the bitter exchange between Swift and his half-brother had soured the mood, so that it was as much as he could do to concentrate on the business of taking tricks and winning rubbers. That his partner in this endeavour was Henrietta Swift made him all the more uncomfortable, although she herself made no allusion to the row.

Neither of them was 'on form' as far as their bridge-playing went, and Rowlands, for one, wasn't sorry to concede victory to the Butlers, who had played a skilled and ruthless game. 'Bridge is such a bore,' yawned Henrietta Swift, throwing down her cards. 'I'm off to bed.' And she was gone, without further ceremony. Mrs Butler remarked that it hadn't seemed a bore to *her*, but since she was just then collecting up her winnings (amounting to several shillings), this didn't seem to require a reply. So Rowlands excused himself from the table, and went out through the open French windows onto the terrace to smoke a cigarette before turning in.

Too late, he realised that he was not alone.

'. . . the man's a p-perfect brute,' said a voice he recognised as that of young Gogarty. 'You deserve better. You must k-know how I f-feel about you, Celia.'

'Now you're being impertinent,' said the woman at whom this passionate outburst was directed.

'I . . . I'm sorry, I m-meant "Lady Celia",' stammered the boy.

'It's not my title I mind your forgetting, Mr Gogarty,' was the cool reply. 'But your manners. I think you'd better go.'

'B-but . . .'

'Good night, Mr Gogarty.' At which the young man must have fled, because Rowlands heard hurried footsteps descending the steps to the lawn below. He, too, was about to beat a hasty retreat when Celia Swift said, 'Hello, Frederick. Come to enjoy a breath of air? After this evening's events, you must be regretting having let yourself be persuaded to come to Castleford. As you see, we're a set of lunatics.'

'I wouldn't say that. Cigarette?'

'Please.'

He lit it for her, then lit his own. For a short while, the two of them stood in silence, leaning on the balustrade that ran the length of the terrace. Somewhere in the darkness an owl hooted softly. 'What you witnessed just then . . .' she began hesitantly, but he didn't let her finish.

'There wasn't anything to witness. A young man let the wine go to his head, that's all.'

'Thank you.' She rested her hand on his for a moment. 'I don't suppose,' she went on, 'you heard Ned come in?' Rowlands said that he hadn't, and she sighed. 'He's probably gone off for one of his long tramps. He does that when something's upset him. What he said . . .'

'People say things they don't mean when they're angry.'

'You're right. I just wish he and Jolyon didn't fall out so often. That man's a waster – even if he is Ned's half-brother.' They finished their cigarettes, and then went back inside – Lady Celia to say good night to her guests, who were on the point of leaving (Mrs Langton very pleased with her winnings at bridge), Rowlands to add his good-nights to hers before making his way up to bed. Before he did so, he decided to fetch himself a glass of water. It wasn't worth bothering one of the servants for so small a request, he thought. He found his way easily enough to the kitchen, now deserted of all its staff, for it was well past midnight. He found a glass on the draining board and filled it.

As he stood drinking, he heard a footstep in the passage outside, and the sound of the back door opening. He was about to make his presence known when it became apparent that whoever it was – one of the maids, he supposed – was talking to someone who was standing just outside. An exchange of urgent whispers followed, of which Rowlands could make out only a few words. What was obvious from these was the increasing agitation of the young woman. 'Ye're out o' your mind,' she said. 'Haven't I told you and told you it'll come to no good?' The other must have replied, but in such a low voice that it was impossible to make out what was said. 'Oh! I've no patience with ye!' cried the girl. A moment later, there came the sound of the door being closed and footsteps hurrying away along the passage.

A lovers' quarrel, evidently, thought Rowlands, making his own way back towards the stairs. He put the incident out of his mind. It had been a tiring evening.

He had expected to fall asleep straight away, but in fact sleep took a while to come as, tossing and turning in the unfamiliar bed, he considered the events of the past few hours. Even before Swift's outburst against his half-brother – for what misdemeanour one could only guess – there had been a definite atmosphere. He couldn't say from whom or what it emanated, but it had become increasingly oppressive. Hatred, jealousy and suspicion were its elements; violence and death might be its outcome. His was not the only restless night, it seemed: as he lay there, drifting in and out of consciousness, he was dimly aware of footsteps in the passage outside, of the low murmur of voices from another room, and once, of a window being raised – perhaps to admit more air, for the night was stiflingly hot. All these added to the prevailing feeling of disquiet, so that it was only in the small hours of the morning that he fell asleep at last.

He woke around seven, to the sound of horses' hooves – Swift going for an early ride, he supposed, grateful that he wasn't obliged to join him. On rising from his bed, he discovered that he seemed to have aged twenty years overnight; only an immersion in as hot a bath as he could stand alleviated the stiffness in his limbs. Having shaved and dressed, he went down to breakfast, finding his way to the breakfast room (an annexe off the dining room) by the simple expedient of following the agreeable smells of bacon, kippers, toast and coffee coming from that direction. Canon Wetherby and young Gogarty were ahead of him, he found, the latter bolting his breakfast and offering no more than a muttered 'Good morning' before taking himself off, presumably to his labours in the library.

'Always in a tearing hurry, the young,' observed Canon Wetherby placidly as he worked his way steadily through his porridge, toast and marmalade. Rowlands, helping himself to bacon and eggs, agreed that this was so. Privately, he thought that Gogarty's flight was probably due to embarrassment on seeing the man who had witnessed his foolish behaviour the night before. 'The older I get, the more I come to the conclusion that one should take life slowly,' went on the affable clergyman. With which unexceptional piece of philosophy it was impossible to disagree, but the elderly gentlemen seemed inclined to pursue the topic. 'All this rushing about,' he said. 'It does no good, no good at all. I said as much to young Swift last night, but he wouldn't listen.'

Only half-listening to this gentle complaint, Rowlands murmured his agreement. The door opened and someone – Butler, as it turned out – put his head in. 'Have either of you gentlemen seen Lord Castleford? I've some papers for him to sign.'

'I believe I heard him going for his ride about three-quarters of an hour ago,' volunteered Rowlands.

'Ah, yes, to be sure,' was the reply. 'In which case, he won't be back for a while.' At that moment, the clock in the hall struck eight. 'Goodness, is that the time already?' exclaimed Butler. 'I had a late start this morning. To tell the truth, I wasn't feeling too well last night . . . something must have upset my system. Hardly slept a wink. My wife was quite worried. She was all for calling the doctor, but I dissuaded her.'

'You're fortunate to have such a devoted spouse,' said Canon Wetherby.

'Indeed I am, indeed I am,' was the reply. 'Well,' the land agent concluded, 'mustn't stand here chatting. Lots of things to see to.' Then he, too, took himself off.

'Busy fellow,' said Canon Wetherby, pouring himself some more coffee. 'Of course, it's a lot of work, keeping an estate like this one running.'

Rowlands said that he imagined it was. He was just starting to wonder what had happened to the other members of the Swift family when Lady Celia came in.

'Morning, Cousin Aloysius,' she said, kissing him. 'Morning, Frederick. Hope you've got all you need? Breakfast tends to be catch-as-catch-can in this house.' She helped herself to coffee. 'Has anyone seen my husband about?'

A little surprised that she wasn't aware of this already, Rowlands repeated what he'd told Robert Butler about having heard Swift go off for his morning ride.

'Oh yes,' she said carelessly. 'He always goes for a brisk canter after a late night. It must have been going on for two o' clock when he came in.'

'Now, isn't that strange?' said the canon. 'Because I was just saying to Rowlands here—'

But whatever he'd been going to say was cut short by the sudden appearance of Monckton. 'Apologies for the intrusion, Your Ladyship . . .' His imperturbable manner seemed to have temporarily deserted him. 'Pheelan's just sent a boy up to the house to tell me that His Lordship's horse has come home without him.'

Events, after this alarming revelation, moved both quickly and slowly – the way they often seemed to in a crisis. For while Lady Celia displayed admirable presence of mind in commanding that all the available men should be conscripted into the search for her missing husband, it seemed to Rowlands an age before the search got going. It began, of necessity, at the stable-yard to which the runaway horse had returned. Here, it was only after a great deal of running hither and thither, and a great shouting of orders by the head groom to his underlings, that the search party moved off, with Lady Celia leading the way on her own horse.

Knowing he'd be of little use to the searchers, and might only hinder their efforts, Rowlands remained behind, resolving to find out as much as he could about the circumstances that had led to the accident before its outcome were known. With this aim in mind, he heard once more the account by the excited stable-lad who'd first spotted the riderless horse – none other than the notorious Lucifer. 'Chargin' across the big meadow, he was, as if the divil himself were after him,' said the boy, whose name was Mickey. 'I thinks to meself, I thinks, "What's His Lordship's horse doin' out alone, and His Lordship nowhere to be seen?" So I sets meself to catch him' – the horse, not His Lordship, he left it to his listeners to surmise. 'Took me the best part o' ten minutes, he's that artful, the cratur . . .'

'I should think Lord Castleford's a very experienced horseman, isn't he?' said Rowlands to the head groom.

'Indeed he is, sir. One o' the best in the county, in my opinion.'

'Isn't it rather surprising that he should have let himself be thrown?'

'Not a bit of it, sir. His left-hand stirrup leather broke. If he was getting up any kind of speed, he'd have found it hard to hold the horse. They're sensitive beasts, especially one like this Lucifer. Soon as he realised His Lordship had lost control – which he would've done, ye see – that horse'd have been off like the wind. No way of stopping him, see? I've seen many a man break his neck after being thrown off a galloping horse,' he added sombrely.

'If you don't mind,' said Rowlands, to whom an idea had just occurred, 'I'd like to take a look . . .'

'At the horse, d'you mean, sir? He's shut up in his

stable, the divil, with a nice warm blanket over him. Sweating like fury, he was, by the time the lad here caught him. Snorting and stamping as if he wanted to trample the life out o' somebody. Gentle as a lamb he is, now,' he added. 'You wouldn't think to look at him that he'd likely killed a man.'

'We don't know that Lord Castleford is dead,' said Rowlands severely, thinking that Pheelan seemed to be relishing this grim prospect a bit too much. 'And I was talking about the stirrup leather. I'd like to examine it, if I may.'

'Certainly, sir. Not that there's much to see. Snapped right through, it is. No wonder His Lordship couldn't hold the cratur.' He ordered the lad, Mickey, to go and fetch the thing; a moment later, Rowlands held it in his hand. It was a strip of leather, about an inch wide and four-and-a-half feet long, with holes punched at intervals of an inch and half an inch, and a buckle to fasten it so that it could be adjusted to suit the length of the rider's leg. The leather passed through a slot at the top of the stirrup iron and doubled back on itself, but in this instance, the stirrup iron was missing. 'Must've dropped off somewhere along the way,' said Pheelan, seeing that Rowlands was examining the place where the leather had broken. 'We'll find it not too far from where we find His Lordship, I reckon.'

But Rowlands wasn't paying attention, preoccupied as he was with what he had just discovered. 'This leather didn't snap of its own accord,' he said. 'It was cut – or rather, scored across with a sharp knife – so that it would snap under pressure. Feel for yourself.'

'Jaysus,' muttered the head groom when he had done as Rowlands suggested. 'I believe you're right, sir. Here's the mark where the leather was slit. Cunningly done, too, so that it doesn't show on the outside. Who could have done such a thing?'

'I don't know,' said Rowlands. 'But I'm taking charge of this piece of evidence. Whoever did this intended no good to come of it, that's for sure.' An examination of the stirrup leather on the right-hand side found that it, too, had been tampered with.

'Not enough to cut it through, but enough for it to break if any strain was put upon it,' said Pheelan. 'Which it would be once His Lordship got up any speed. Devilish, I call it,' he added, in a tone expressive of disbelief that anyone should be capable of such a heinous act of sabotage. 'Why, the man's neck'd be broken for him in that very minute.'

'Let's wait until we know what's happened before we jump to any conclusions, shall we?' said Rowlands. As he spoke, his sharp ears picked up the sounds of the search party returning.

First came Lady Celia, who dismounted from her horse in one swift movement, shouting for the groom to take charge. 'We've found him,' she said as Rowlands hurried towards her.

'How is he?' He was almost afraid to ask the question.

'Alive, thank God,' was her curt reply. 'But unconscious. No limbs broken, as far as I could tell . . . Ah, here they are now.' This was the rescue party, Rowlands surmised – consisting of three of the stable hands and the gardener's boy – who now entered the yard, carrying the unconscious man between them. 'Call a doctor, will you?' said Lady Celia, and Rowlands at once went to carry out this instruction. This, at least, he could do for her.

Entering the house through the back door, he found Mrs Malone, the cook, hovering anxiously in the kitchen doorway. 'Have they found His Lordship?' she asked, but he waved her aside, not stopping until he reached the big entrance hall. Here, he found several of the servants gathered: Mary, the parlourmaid, who was weeping softly; the manservant John; Bridget, the chambermaid; and Philomena, the nursemaid. On seeing Rowlands, these at once set up a clamour:

'Is His Lordship killed?'

'Is it his neck that's broken?'

'Ah, it's a terrible thing to come upon the house.'

'Will one of you fetch Mr Butler?' said Rowlands, cutting across this jeremiad. 'He's to telephone for the doctor at once.'

'I can do that,' said a quiet voice. It was the housekeeper, Mrs Doyle, who had emerged from her room at the commotion. She went to do so, and Rowlands found himself once more besieged by questions, which he brushed aside. For the rescue party were even now carrying Lord Castleford into the house, by the same route that Rowlands himself had followed.

'Carry him upstairs to his room,' said Lady Celia. 'Be careful now! I don't want him jolted about. Has the doctor been telephoned?'

'Yes, my lady,' said Mrs Doyle, returning from this errand. 'He'll be here directly.'

'All right. Well, don't just stand there, the rest of you. Mary, tell Mrs Malone I want a cold compress for His Lordship's head. John' – to the manservant – 'fetch some brandy. The rest of you, get back to your work. Where's George?' she asked, seeing the nursemaid standing there.

'He's after having his breakfast, my lady.'

'Well, keep him in the nursery for now. I don't want him frightened, do you hear?' Her voice was calm, but Rowlands could detect an underlying note of fear that the man she loved might still be taken from her. 'Where's Cousin Aloysius?' she said suddenly.

'Here I am, my dear,' was the reply as the elderly gentleman emerged from the morning room.

'Come upstairs with me to Ned's room, will you? You, too, Frederick. I want you both to be there when he wakes up.' She began to ascend the stairs, with the two men following suit.

'My lady,' said a voice from below as they reached the top. It was the land agent, summoned from his office. 'I came as soon as I heard. Is he . . . is His Lordship badly hurt?'

'I don't know,' was the bleak reply. 'We're waiting for

Doctor O'Leary now. Send him up as soon as he arrives, will you? And keep everyone else away. I don't want my husband disturbed any more than necessary.'

'Very well, my lady. May I ask . . .' But she had already forgotten him, it seemed – preoccupied only with reaching her husband's side.

In the master bedroom, Ned Swift had been laid upon the four-poster bed in which, Rowlands guessed, he had been born. Whether he would die here, in the course of the next few hours, remained to be seen. Having dismissed all the servants but Biddy, who was delegated to act as auxiliary nurse, Lady Celia sat down on a stool that had been placed for that purpose beside the bed. 'You *have* got yourself into a pretty pickle, Ned my boy,' she said. 'Frightening us all half to death! Maybe *now* you'll believe me when I tell you that you should have sold that horse long ago . . .'

Her voice tailed off as if she suddenly realised the futility of what she was saying. 'Well, don't just stand there,' she said to the two men who had accompanied her. 'Sit down, won't you?' Then, as Rowlands went to do so: 'What have you got there, Frederick?' Because all the while, Rowlands had been holding the broken stirrup leather. He held it out to her.

'I assume that's the feller that's responsible for Ned's accident?' said Canon Wetherby.

'Except that it wasn't an accident,' replied Rowlands. 'The leather was cut.' At this, there came a gasp from Biddy, the maidservant, who burst into tears and rushed out of the room. Her mistress hardly seemed to notice this extraordinary behaviour, her attention focused entirely on what Rowlands had said.

'Let me see,' she demanded, taking the leather from him. She examined it for a moment in silence. 'I think you're right. It's been cut across one half of the strap, to weaken it. One wouldn't have noticed it at first.'

'Yes,' said Rowlands. 'That's what I thought, too.'

'Oh, Ned!' cried his wife, sounding as close to breaking down as she'd been throughout the whole episode. '*Now* do you see how wrong you were? They were trying to kill you all along.'

'What are you saying, my dear?' said Canon Wetherby. 'Do you mean to tell me that there have been attempts on Ned's life before this?' She must have answered him with a look, for he burst out, 'But this is terrible! Surely it can't be so, Rowlands? Why, Ned is liked and respected by everyone who knows him.'

'I'm afraid it *is* true,' replied Rowlands. 'Lady Celia has been concerned about Lord Castleford's safety for some time.'

'Good heavens! I had no idea,' said the old gentleman, sounding distressed. 'You should have come to me, my dear.'

'I doubt whether you could have persuaded Ned to take the matter seriously – any more than I could,' said Celia Swift. 'You know how stubborn he can be. Oh, Ned, Ned, why didn't you listen?' she cried softly. 'Now it may be too late . . .'

The door opened. 'What's this?' said a jovial voice Rowlands guessed must belong to the doctor. 'Too late? Come, come, Your Ladyship, this isn't the kind of talk I like to hear. Now, let's take a look at the patient, shall we? Hmm. Still breathing, at any rate. You gentlemen' – addressing the canon and Rowlands – 'can make yourselves scarce while I conduct a more thorough examination. But one thing's certain: His Lordship isn't dead yet – nor will he be if I have anything to do with it.'

Chapter Six

A hush lay over Castleford – as if for a death, Rowlands found himself thinking, then dismissed the thought at once. Hadn't the doctor said Swift would pull through? But such robust affirmations aside, an atmosphere of gloom and dread prevailed. No cheerful chatter of servants came from the kitchen quarters, and in the rest of the house, a profound silence reigned. With nothing else to do but await further developments, the two men accordingly descended the stairs and seated themselves in the morning room where the canon occupied himself by looking over the papers and tut-tutting – whether about the state of the world, or troubles nearer at hand, Rowlands was unable to determine.

On quitting the room where the unconscious man lay, he himself had first returned to his own room in order to put away the broken stirrup leather until such time as it needed to be produced. It struck him as he did so, slipping the thing out of sight at the back of a drawer, that it would be best to say nothing of this piece of evidence to the other members of the household. Although at present it seemed likely that the sabotage had been carried out by a disaffected employee of Swift's – Christie Doherty being the obvious suspect – past experience had taught Rowlands that where murder was concerned, one could rule nothing and nobody out.

Suddenly, the quiet was broken by the sound of rapid footsteps crossing the hall. A moment later, Henrietta Swift rushed into the room. 'Have either of you seen Jolyon?' she demanded without preamble. 'Only his bed hasn't been slept in . . . I think he's left me.' With which she burst into noisy tears.

'Calm yourself, my dear young lady,' said Canon Wetherby. 'It's surely not as bad as you say? Why, when I saw young Jolyon late last night, he assured me that he would only be away for a few days . . . "until things cool down" was how he put it.'

'You mean you saw him leave and didn't stop him?' shrieked the girl. 'How *could* you have been so stupid?'

'I . . . I suppose I thought you must have known about it,' replied the poor old gentleman. 'I don't think I could have persuaded him to remain against his will, in any case.'

'What time was this exactly?' intervened Rowlands.

'Oh, didn't I say?' said the other. 'It must have been around half past one or a quarter to two this morning.

I . . . I couldn't sleep, and so I was reading . . . St Thomas Aquinas, you know. Very comforting when one's mind is a little uneasy . . . Anyway, it was then that I heard a footstep in the passage outside my door. When I put my head out, I saw that it was Jolyon, creeping past on tiptoe. "Don't give me away, will you, Cousin Aloysius?" he said. "It's getting a bit hot for me around here, so I'm clearing out for a bit."'

'Did he say where he was going?' was Rowlands' next question. A suspicion had been forming in his mind while the clergyman had been talking. Why exactly had Jolyon Swift decided to 'clear out' at precisely that moment? Could it be that he had anything to do with his half-brother's near-fatal accident? His absenting himself at the crucial time seemed too much of a coincidence to be overlooked.

'I'm afraid I didn't ask,' replied Canon Wetherby.

'Oh, *I* know where he'll have gone,' interjected Mrs Swift, in a scornful tone. 'He'll be off with his Dublin cronies – taking the car, too, and leaving me all alone. It's so typical of his selfishness!' It didn't seem the moment to remind her that she wasn't quite alone, since she had a child to care for. 'Well, that's that, I suppose,' she concluded glumly. 'Jolyon's gone, and I'm stuck here until such time as he deigns to come and collect me. It really *is* the limit! Why is it so hard to get a cup of coffee in this place?' she added, jerking the bell-pull angrily. 'And where *is* everybody? The house is like a morgue.'

Before the others could put her in the picture, a maidservant appeared and was duly scolded for her tardiness in doing so. 'I'm afraid there's some bad news about Lord Castleford,' said Rowlands, amazed that the young woman could have remained in ignorance of the events of that morning. 'He's had an accident while out riding. The doctor's with him now.' But if he'd expected further tears or any expression of concern from Mrs Swift, he was disappointed.

'It was bound to happen, one of these days,' was all she said. 'Let's face it, Ned's not as young as he used to be – and he *will* insist on riding that great brute of a stallion . . . Ah, here's the coffee at last!'

But it wasn't the maid with the coffee who stood in the doorway, but the chauffeur, Patrick Connolly, who had driven Rowlands and Lady Celia from Dublin the previous day. He was breathing heavily as if he had been running, and seemed to be having difficulty getting his words out. 'Oh, Jesus, Mary,' was all he could say.

'What is it, man?' said Canon Wetherby. 'Take your time, now.'

'I need to speak to the master,' Connolly managed at last.

'The master can't speak to you now,' was the reply. 'You can talk to me.'

'I . . . Oh, Jesus, Mary . . . It's a terrible thing,' stammered the other. 'I wouldn't have seen it for the world. I opened the door of the garage and . . . he was lyin' there . . . Oh, miss' – evidently noticing Henrietta for the first time – 'I don't know how to tell you. He's dead. Mr Jolyon. His brains blown out, in the car there.'

At this dreadful news, Henrietta Swift gave a cry, and fell to the floor in a dead faint. Just then, the door opened to admit the maid with the coffee. 'Oh!' she exclaimed, on seeing the prostrate woman.

'Fetch some water for Mrs Swift,' said Canon Wetherby to the girl. 'And ask Mrs Doyle to come at once.' To Rowlands, he said, 'Lend a hand to get her onto the sofa, will you? The poor lass is out cold. You might have broken the news more tactfully,' he added to Connolly. 'You've given the lady a nasty shock.'

'I'm sure I didn't mean any harm, Father,' was the reply. 'Oh Jesus, Mary, say she isn't dead . . .'

'No thanks to you if she isn't,' was the severe reply. 'Ah, here's Mrs Doyle now. Have you the smelling salts handy, Mrs Doyle? The young lady's had a bad fright.'

Leaving the housekeeper in charge of the unfortunate Mrs Swift, Rowlands and the canon marched the reluctant Connolly back to where he had found the body. On the way, he reiterated his account of how he had made his appalling discovery: 'I'd just left my cottage, to begin work . . . Not that the master generally asks for me until later . . . but I always give the Bentley a good rub-down first thing, in case His Lordship wants me to drive him anywhere after lunch . . . So then I opened the door of the garage, like I always do, and that's when I saw him . . . Dead as a doornail, the poor feller.' When they reached the door of the garage, Connolly flatly refused to go in. 'I can't do it, Father,' he said to Canon Wetherby. 'Seein' him lyin' there in his blood fair turned me up. Sure, it's a horrible sight . . .'

'That, at least, won't affect me,' said Rowlands as he and the canon went inside, leaving Connolly at the door, with instructions not to let anyone else in. He didn't add that there were other aspects to a violent death of which he was all too aware: the smell, for one, although in this instance the metallic tang of blood was masked, to some extent, by that of petrol and motor oil. In silence, the two men walked towards where Swift's car, a Talbot convertible, was standing – next to the Bentley, which, presumably, Connolly had been about to clean when he made his grisly discovery. It was immediately apparent that the canvas roof of the vehicle must be down, and that – as the chauffeur had said – the occupant of the driving seat was past help.

'Poor fellow,' said the canon after no more than a glance. 'He's quite dead, I'm afraid. And here's the gun that did the mischief, on the seat beside him. It must have fallen from his hand.'

'I shouldn't touch it,' said Rowlands quickly. 'It's evidence.'

'To be sure,' replied the other mildly. 'Although it seems pretty clear to me what must have happened. Young feller gets himself into a jam, and decides he can't go through with things . . . Terrible, terrible,' he said, in a broken voice.

'So you think it might be suicide?' asked Rowlands.

'Well, what in the name of goodness could it be otherwise? You're not suggesting *murder*?' Canon Wetherby lowered his voice as if the word were too dreadful to pronounce.

'It's not for me to speculate,' replied Rowlands. 'The police will have to decide from the evidence – of which the gun is an important piece. Do you recognise the weapon, incidentally?'

'I couldn't say, without handling the thing,' said Wetherby. 'But it looks like a standard Webley Mark VI service revolver. Sort of thing they handed out by the tens of thousands to serving officers in the last show.' Rowlands, who possessed a similar model, which he'd neglected to surrender when invalided out of the army in 1917, merely grunted. It seemed an odd choice of weapon for someone like Jolyon Swift, who'd presumably been too young to be in the last 'show' unless of course he'd stolen it from someone else . . .

While he stood considering the implications of this, Canon Wetherby was engaged in private reflections of his own, murmuring what sounded like a brief prayer under his breath before he turned away from the car and its lifeless occupant. 'Poor young feller! I can't help feeling I failed him,' he said sadly as – leaving Connolly on guard outside the garage – the two men walked back towards the house. 'If I'd only been able to *talk* to him, it might have prevented this dreadful thing.' Rowlands, who had his own suspicions about what had happened the previous night, made no reply. He knew that nothing he could say would stop the old gentleman from blaming himself, in part, for the tragedy.

In the hall, they met Robert Butler. 'Mrs Doyle has just told me the news,' he said. 'Is it true that Mr Jolyon . . . ?'

'I'm afraid so. There's nothing we can do for him. It's now a matter for the police,' said Rowlands. 'They must be called at once. I'll take the responsibility,' he added, sensing that the land agent was reluctant to take such action.

'You'd better do it, Butler,' said Canon Wetherby. 'I'll inform Her Ladyship.'

'Very well, sir,' said Butler. 'What a shocking business it is, to be sure,' he added piously. 'Following so soon after His Lordship's accident, too.' He duly hurried away to perform this task, leaving the others alone in the hall.

'I suppose there's nothing to do but wait until the police get here,' said Wetherby. 'Dear, dear! What a terrible day it's been, with Ned's accident, and now this awful thing. I can't say I'm looking forward to telling Celia.'

'Telling me what?' said Lady Celia from the landing above, then, when neither spoke: 'I was coming to say that Ned has woken up. He's very shaken, of course, and Doctor O'Leary says he must have complete rest for a day or two. But he's going to be all right.' She had by now descended the stairs and stood facing them.

'That's good news,' said Rowlands, wondering how to tell her that news of another kind had befallen the household.

She must have seen something in his expression, and that of his companion, for she said sharply, 'What is it? What's happened?'

'Celia, my dear,' began Canon Wetherby. 'You must prepare yourself . . .'

'I'm afraid it's your brother-in-law,' said Rowlands, who thought there was no point in beating about the bush where news of this kind was concerned. 'He's been found shot dead. I'm very sorry.'

Celia Swift was silent a moment. 'Was it an accident?' she said at last.

'Impossible to say. But it rather seems not,' replied Rowlands gently.

'I was afraid something like this might happen,' she said, then: 'You're to say *nothing* of this to Ned, do you hear? I won't have him upset when he's in the state he's in. When did it happen?' she went on.

'It's not certain yet,' replied Rowlands. 'Canon Wetherby saw Mr Swift leaving the house at around two o'clock this morning. So he was still alive then. The police will establish precise times . . .'

As if on cue, Robert Butler now appeared, to say that the Gardai were on their way. 'You should have consulted me first, Cousin Aloysius,' said Lady Celia angrily. 'Now we'll have the police crawling all over the house. It'll be impossible to keep Ned from knowing what's happened.'

'It was my decision to call the police,' said Rowlands. 'In a case like this, one can't afford the slightest delay. I'm sure Lord Castleford would agree.'

'I expect you're right,' she conceded. Another thought appeared to strike her. 'Are you sure there's nothing that can be done for Jolyon? Perhaps a doctor . . . Call Doctor O'Leary, will you, Mr Butler? Tell him it's urgent. Biddy can stay with my husband.'

'Yes, my lady.' The land agent hurried away to carry out this instruction.

'What exactly happened, do you think?' said Lady Celia. 'Was it suicide?'

'That was my thought,' said Canon Wetherby. 'The poor lad's mind must have been disturbed. He was in a very excitable state last night.' Rowlands was silent. In his view, there was no doubt that this was murder.

'And where's Henrietta?' demanded her sister-in-law suddenly. 'Has she been told?' It was explained to Her Ladyship that Mrs Swift had indeed been told the news about her husband's untimely death, and that she was being looked after by the housekeeper. 'Poor Henry!' cried Lady Celia. 'It isn't her fault, any of this. If only I could have prevented it in time . . .'

But just then there came another voice. It was the doctor, O'Leary, coming downstairs. 'I gather there's been another accident,' he said, in his richly jovial tones. 'You Swifts are an unlucky crowd, I'll say that for ye.'

Canon Wetherby at once stepped forward to offer to conduct the doctor to where the body lay, but before the two men could set off on their grim errand, Lady Celia intervened. 'I'm coming with you.'

'I don't think that's a very good idea,' said Rowlands. He didn't need to add that the sight of the dead man might evoke painful memories.

'Nevertheless,' she said. 'I want to come. Jolyon was my brother-in-law, you know. I owe it to Ned . . . Speaking of whom, how is he, Doctor?'

'Asleep,' was the reply. 'I've left that girl of yours in charge of him.'

'Then there's no reason why I shouldn't leave him for a few minutes. Biddy's a competent nurse.'

Since she refused to be dissuaded from accompanying Wetherby and the doctor, Rowlands decided that he, too, would return to the scene of the crime. There wasn't much he or any of them could do until the police arrived, but he could at least offer his support, in case of need. Lady Celia, however, turned out to be made of sterner stuff than her sister-in-law since she neither screamed nor fainted when confronted with Jolyon Swift's corpse. 'Poor Jo,' was all she said. 'So it's come to this, has it?'

At Rowlands' suggestion, all the members of the party, with the exception of the doctor, kept their distance from the car in which sat the pathetic remains.

Since the floor of the former stables was made of flagstones, it was unlikely, Rowlands thought, that any footprints could have been left which might have indicated the presence of an intruder, but it was as well to be on the safe side where a crime scene was concerned. But if he'd hoped by this simple strategy to protect Celia Swift from the worst of it, he failed. Because as Doctor O'Leary began his examination, muttering under his breath as he did so, 'Hmm. Not much doubt about the cause of death . . . One shot through the temporal fossa on the right side . . .', she stepped forward.

'That looks like Ned's gun,' she said. 'I wonder how it got here?'

'Lady Celia . . .'

'It's all right, I'm not going to touch it,' she said, in response to Rowlands' protest. 'I'm just puzzled as to how Jolyon got hold of it. Ned always kept it locked up in his desk, on account of the children.'

The arrival of Sergeant Flanagan on his bicycle meant that the whole sequence of events had to be gone over once more, for the benefit of the said officer. After an initial inspection of the body, he took the precaution of locking the garage behind him before beginning his enquiries – starting with the doctor and Connolly, and proceeding methodically through the rest of the witnesses, of whom Rowlands was one. At Lady Celia's suggestion, the household had assembled in the morning room for this purpose. 'So,' said Flanagan, flipping back through his notes. 'The first that anybody knew of this gentleman's death was at nine o'clock this morning when your man Patsy Connolly discovered the body.'

'That's right, Sergeant,' said Celia Swift.

'And yet,' went on the policeman, 'the doctor puts the time of death between two and four o'clock this morning – that's five to seven hours earlier,' he added, in case any of them had failed to grasp the point he was making. 'It's a little surprising that his absence wasn't noticed earlier.'

'It was the middle of the night, man,' said Canon Wetherby. 'Most people were asleep.'

'But not you, sir.'

'No. As I've explained, I was the last to see young Mr Swift alive.'

'Not the last, sir,' was the laconic reply. He allowed the implications of this to hang in the air before proceeding. 'Mrs Swift, now. I'll need to ask her when she first noticed her husband's absence.'

'Mrs Swift is resting,' said Lady Celia sharply. 'She's had a bad shock. You'll have to wait before you ask her any questions.'

'Certainly,' said the Gardai officer smoothly. Rowlands noticed that he avoided using Celia Swift's title when addressing her. Perhaps he was one of those who resented the presence of the 'Englishwoman' at

Castleford. 'And you yourself,' Sergeant Flanagan went on. 'Where were you when you heard the news?'

'I was looking after my husband,' she replied. 'As I told you, he can't speak to you at present, because he's incapacitated. Now I think it's time I returned to him. If you have anything more you want to ask, Canon Wetherby or Mr Rowlands here will help you.'

'I've no further questions at present,' said the Gardai officer. 'But I'll need to use the telephone.'

'Very well.' She pressed the bell, and a moment later the butler appeared. 'Conduct Sergeant Flanagan to the telephone room, will you, Monckton?'

'Yes, m'lady. Come this way,' he added to the policeman, making no attempt to hide his disapproval of the intruder. Then Lady Celia herself went out, leaving Rowlands and the canon at something of a loose end after the frenetic activity of the morning.

The latter sighed. 'They do resent it, the servants – having police in the house,' he said. 'One can see why, of course, but it does make things rather difficult.'

'Yes, I gathered there's not much love lost between the local constabulary – or indeed between the local people overall – and the Big House,' said Rowlands. 'A historic dislike, one imagines.'

'Oh, the people round here are all right in the main,' said the old gentleman. 'They get on with their lives, just as we – the English – get on with ours. But when something like this happens, it stirs up a lot of ill feeling. People start remembering the days when such

horrors were commonplace. Fingers were pointed –
sometimes at the wrong culprits. Reprisals followed.
It all got very ugly.'

The door opened and Sergeant Flanagan put his head
in. 'Just to let you gentlemen know that I'd prefer it if
you remained within call for the time being. Dublin's
sending a car – it should be here within the hour. We'll
see what our Inspector Byrne makes of all this.'

Inspector Thomas Byrne of the Dublin police turned out
to be a quietly spoken individual in his late thirties – an
altogether more formidable character than the sergeant,
Rowlands thought. *This* man seemed more at ease with
the 'quality' than his subordinate. Rowlands guessed that
his approachable manner would make him a dangerous
adversary when it came to ferreting out evidence –
something he was able to put to the test when it was his
turn to be questioned. He had been preceded, as before,
by the doctor, Canon Wetherby and Patrick Connolly.
The latter came out of the study where the inspector
had set up his centre of operations, muttering under his
breath about 'too-clever-by-half city boys who think they
can catch a man out by twisting what he says', to which
Rowlands paid no attention, being familiar with the way
that authority took some people.

'Come in, Mr . . . Rowlands, is it?' said the inspector
courteously, then, after sizing up the situation: 'Help
the gentleman to a chair, Rooney . . . the one in front
of my desk.'

'Thank you,' said Rowlands, who needed no more than this direction to find his way unaided. 'I can manage.'

'War veteran, are you, sir?' said the other. 'I had an uncle fought at Gallipoli with the Royal Dublin Fusiliers.'

'A brave body of men,' said Rowlands.

'Indeed,' was the reply. 'We haven't always kept out of our neighbours' quarrels. I understand that you're a detective, Mr Rowlands?' Byrne went on.

The question, coming straight after his remarks about Irish loyalties, was doubtless calculated to catch Rowlands off-guard. He smiled. 'I wonder who told you that, Inspector?'

'You don't deny it, then?'

'There's nothing to deny. It's true that I've worked with the police on a number of occasions – in a strictly unofficial capacity. But I'm here because Lady Celia, who's an old friend, asked me to come. She was worried about her husband's safety. He had refused to take her concerns seriously. I agreed to talk to him, that's all.'

The inspector considered this for a moment while his sergeant's pencil scratched busily away. 'And what exactly was the substance of Her Ladyship's concerns?'

'She was afraid that there might be an attempt on her husband's life.' Briefly, Rowlands explained about the letters, about the shooting of the dog and about the supposed accident that had befallen Swift that morning.

'You're saying that the fall His Lordship took from his horse was caused deliberately?' said the inspector when he had heard Rowlands out. 'Have you any evidence for this?'

'I have, as a matter of fact.' Rowlands told him about the cut stirrup leather. 'I can fetch it if you'd like.'

'I would. Sergeant, you're to go with Mr Rowlands to collect the item. First, however, I'd like to ask you about your movements last night, sir – or rather, this morning. The crucial times are between the hours of two a.m. and six.'

'That's easy. I was in bed, asleep.'

'What time did you retire, out of interest?'

'It was about a quarter to midnight. I said good night to Lady Celia and her guests, Mr and Mrs Langton. Then I went upstairs, and went straight to bed.'

'Thank you, that's very clear. Can you help me as to the movements of the rest of the party? I gather there were several others present that night, apart from those you've just mentioned?'

'Yes, that's right. We were playing bridge.'

'An interesting game,' said the inspector pleasantly. 'I believe it's supposed to train the memory. So who was playing that evening? Could you list them, for the benefit of Sergeant Rooney?'

Rowlands was certain that the sergeant would have compiled this list already, but he did as he was asked, knowing that such routine questions are the bedrock of an investigation. 'Let's see,' he said. 'There were two tables. Canon Wetherby and Mr and Mrs Langton were at one of them, with Lady Castleford. I myself was at the other table, with Mr and Mrs Butler, and Mrs Swift.'

'Ah, to be sure. The deceased's wife. And was she still in the room when you said your good-nights?'

'She'd already gone up to bed, I think.'

'Accompanying her husband, no doubt?' said Byrne, his tone so non-committal that this could easily have been mistaken for an unimportant query. Rowlands perceived the trap, and decided not to fall into it. 'No, that's not right,' he said. 'Mr Swift had already gone up.'

'Any idea what time this was? I'm trying to build up a picture.'

Rowlands knew exactly when it was, but he saw no reason to make things easier for the inspector than he needed to. 'It was some time earlier,' he replied. 'I don't think Mr Swift wanted to play cards.'

Byrne gave a short, dry laugh. 'Do you know,' he said, 'that's almost exactly what the other gentleman said – the priest, I suppose you'd call him.' From which Rowlands deduced that Canon Wetherby had been no less reluctant than he had to mention the quarrel that had resulted in Jolyon Swift's furious exit, nor the words his half-brother had used to precipitate it.

Chapter Seven

On his way upstairs to fetch the broken stirrup leather, with the police sergeant on his heels, Rowlands met Lady Celia coming along the corridor that led from her husband's room. 'I gather that Sergeant Flanagan has summoned reinforcements,' she said drily.

'Yes.' As they passed one another, Rowlands touched her hand. 'It's all right,' he said softly, hoping that she would understand by this that he had not betrayed the confidence she and Swift had placed in him. But then the sergeant, puffing slightly at a too-rapid ascent of the stairs, caught up with him, and conversation was at an end. Quite how long the truth about what had happened the previous evening could be kept from the police was another matter. There had been too many witnesses to the quarrel for it not to leak out eventually.

As Rowlands came downstairs again, having handed

over his piece of evidence to the Gardai officer, he met Sebastian Gogarty coming out of the library where it appeared he had been sequestered since breakfast time – missing the day's excitements, evidently. 'What's g-going on?' he said, accosting Rowlands in the hall. 'There've b-been people tramping up and down all m-morning.'

Rowlands hesitated, uncertain how much he ought to tell the young man. From past experience, he knew that the police generally preferred to keep the element of surprise on their side. Young Gogarty didn't seem the type who'd have the know-how – let alone the murderous intention – to have fixed Swift's horse, but appearances could be deceptive. And there had certainly been animosity in the remarks Rowlands had overheard the previous night. Whether the young man had it in him to translate his dislike of his employer into action, Rowlands was unable to decide. As for motive – well, the lad's infatuation with his employer's wife offered one that was all too plausible.

Before he could reply to Gogarty's question, however, the sergeant, who had followed Rowlands downstairs, intervened: 'And who might you be, sir?' Gogarty identified himself. 'Thank you, sir,' said the officer, making a note. 'The inspector'll be wanting a word, just as soon as he's finished with the lady.' Rowlands guessed that this was Celia Swift. 'If you'll step in here, sir,' the policeman went on, opening the door of the morning room. 'He'll be with you directly. You, too, sir,' he added to Rowlands.

'But the inspector and I have already spoken.'

'He wants another word with you, sir, if it's all the same to you,' said the Gardai officer. 'There are one or two things he'd like to clear up, he said.' Rowlands didn't doubt it. And so he, too, joined the rest of the company, which included Butler and his wife, and Canon Wetherby.

'Well,' said the land agent portentously. 'This is a pretty how-d'ye-do, and no mistake! Who'd have thought we'd see so much death and disaster in one day? First His Lordship struck down, and now—'

'What's that?' cried Gogarty, cutting across him. 'Are you saying Lord Castleford's d-dead? But that c-can't be. He was p-perfectly all right when I left him.'

'You've got this all wrong,' said the canon, in a soothing tone. 'It isn't Ned who's killed, but his brother, poor feller. Why don't you sit down, Mr Gogarty? You've gone as white as a sheet, man. And that's a nasty black eye you've got there. Don't tell me you've been fighting?'

'I . . . I w-walked into a door,' was the not very convincing reply.

But Rowlands had been struck by something Gogarty had said. 'What did you mean when you said of Lord Castleford just now that "he was perfectly all right"?' he demanded sharply. 'Was there some reason he *shouldn't* have been?'

'I t-told you, he was fine!' cried the young man. 'I . . .

I barely t-touched him. H-he might have stumbled a bit, but that w-was because I'd t-taken him by surprise.'

'I think,' said Rowlands, 'that you'd better tell us what happened from the beginning.'

'It w-was after I'd left the terrace,' muttered Gogarty. 'You w-were there, weren't you? I . . . I'd had a b-bit to drink, so I th-thought I'd walk it off.'

'Where did you go?'

'Nowhere special. I w-walked in the garden for a little while, and then I w-went up the lane towards the farm. I th-thought I'd walk across the fields. Get some f-fresh air.' He hesitated. 'Only I d-didn't get that far, because it was then that I m-met him. Lord Castleford. He was c-coming along the lane. He asked me w-what I was doing, out so late, and I . . . I told him it was n-none of his b-business. I think I w-was still a bit lit,' he added apologetically. 'I w-went to pass him, but he blocked my path. He t-told me not to be such an ass. I'm afraid I s-saw red. So I t-took a s-swing at him. I don't think I h-hit him very hard.' Gogarty sounded so crestfallen that it was almost comical.

'What happened then?' said Rowlands.

'H-he staggered a bit, b-but he d-didn't fall,' said the young man in a small voice. 'Then he knocked me down. S-said it'd teach me n-not to go about assaulting m-my elders and betters. After that he walked off. He was p-perfectly all right then.'

'No one doubts it, Mr Gogarty,' said Canon Wetherby. 'My cousin was injured by a fall from his

119

horse, early this morning. There can be no connection between that terrible accident and whatever passed between the two of you late last night.' Which was true enough, thought Rowlands – unless Gogarty's wounded pride had led him to take more drastic measures against the employer he had come to detest.

Further speculation on the matter was curtailed by the appearance of Lady Celia, to say that a cold luncheon had been set out in the dining room for those who wanted it. She herself would be returning to her husband's bedside directly. 'Oh, and Mr Butler, the inspector wants a word with you,' she added as she went out.

'I can't imagine what *I* can tell him that will be of the slightest use,' said the land agent, in reply. 'I was laid up all last night, wasn't I, my dear?'

'Oh, yes. I've never seen you so poorly,' agreed his wife, to whom this last remark had been addressed. 'I blame that second helping of sherry trifle. Far too rich for a stomach as sensitive as yours, Robert.' The couple went out together, although if Mrs Butler imagined that the inspector would welcome her sitting in on her spouse's interview, she'd another thing coming, thought Rowlands. He and the remaining members of the party made their way towards the dining room although Rowlands, for one, didn't have much of an appetite.

Fortunately, the sandwich lunch on offer didn't make too many demands on the three distracted individuals who now seated themselves at the table, nor on the fourth member of the party, Mrs Butler, who joined them after a few minutes had elapsed. 'Well, really!' was her opening remark as she swept in. 'If *that's* the type of person they're employing as police officers these days, it doesn't bode well for the future of the country, in my opinion. Very *low* sort of person, I thought. Calls himself an inspector – ha! I fancy the only thing an oaf like that is fit for is inspecting the pigs on his father's pig farm . . . Very rude to me, he was. Told me he'd be "obliged if I'd mind me own business"' – she assumed a thick Dublin accent – 'and leave *him* to mind his. The cheek of the man! Robert was quite incensed on my behalf.' She pushed away her soup plate and reached for the plate of sandwiches. 'Hmph! Tongue, ham, egg and tomato, bloater paste,' she remarked disgustedly. 'Can't say I think much of the standard of catering. It seems to me that Cook is taking advantage of the fact that the house is at sixes and sevens to slack off from her duties. I must have a word with Mrs Doyle. This sort of thing won't do.'

They were joined at that moment by Robert Butler, to whom his wife repeated her remarks about oafs and pig farms, and who added a few derogatory comments of his own regarding Inspector Byrne: 'Time was they'd appoint a college man to a post of responsibility like that,' he said, piling his plate high with sandwiches until reminded by Mrs Butler that his stomach was still in a sensitive state. 'Now they get any old hobble-de-hoy in to do the job. Can you believe that this fellow had no idea what a land agent does? Seemed to think I spend all my time grubbing about on the home farm, whereas in fact . . .'

'In fact you run the estate,' his wife finished for him.

'Thank you, Elspeth my dear. I said as much to the good inspector,' said Butler, taking a bite of his sandwich. 'Didn't make a blind bit of difference, though. He still wanted to know when I'd last visited the farm, and the stable-yard – as if I have anything to do with the horses! Told him I hadn't visited either place for over a week. Confined to the office, most days,' he added, perhaps for Rowlands' benefit. 'Job's largely paperwork, y'know.' Rowlands murmured his appreciation of this fact, whilst wondering how soon he could escape. He found the Butlers rather hard work.

As if in answer to his thought, the door of the dining room opened and the parlourmaid, Mary, came in. 'Beggin' your pardon, sir,' she said, addressing Rowlands. 'But m'lady says would you come at once. You too, Father,' she added to Canon Wetherby.

'Perhaps there's been some improvement in Ned's condition?' said the elderly gentleman. Rowlands, who knew that a man with a head injury could take a turn for the worse just as easily, said nothing. But as they reached Swift's room, it became apparent that the canon's optimism had been justified. For here was Swift himself, up and dressed, and resisting all attempts on the part of his wife and doctor to persuade him of the rashness of this. 'Nonsense, Celia,' he was saying. 'I feel as right as rain. Took a bit of tumble, that's all. No bones broken. Hi, Rowlands, old man! Tell this woman of mine that she's making a fuss about nothing, will you?'

'I think you're being ridiculous, Ned,' retorted his wife with spirit. 'An hour ago, you were out cold. You can't possibly be well enough to get up yet.'

'Lady Celia's right, my lord,' said Doctor O'Leary, following his recalcitrant patient out of the room and onto the landing. 'You need time to recover. As your medical advisor, I strongly suggest that you should spend the rest of the day in bed.'

'Bosh!' said His Lordship rudely. 'I'm fine. And I'm as hungry as a hunter. What I need is some breakfast – or is it time for luncheon?' But he was never to receive a reply to his query, because at that moment there came a piercing scream from one of the rooms along the left-hand corridor – a scream that seemed to go on and on. 'What the devil?' exclaimed Swift, then, as the screaming drew nearer: 'Why, Eveline, what on earth's the matter?'

But she was unequal to speech. 'Jolyon,' she managed to gasp out at last, between inarticulate cries. 'My boy . . . My Joly . . .'

'Who was it who told her?' demanded Lady Celia furiously. 'I suppose it was you, Biddy?', addressing the frightened chambermaid, who now appeared.

'Please, m'lady . . . I never meant any harm,' wept the girl. 'I was after bringing Madam her lunch, and she asks me why was I cryin' and I says . . . it was along of Mr Jolyon, lyin' there stiff and dead . . .' Another torrent of tears drowned out the rest of her words.

Above the wailing of the dowager, and the sobbing of the maid, another voice – Swift's – now made itself heard. 'Is it true? Jolyon's dead? But how? I don't understand . . . and why wasn't I told at once?'

'I was going to tell you—' began his wife, but he cut across her: 'Then why didn't you?'

'Ned, my dear boy . . .' said Canon Wetherby, but was also rebuffed.

'Where is he? I want to see him. Now.' Swift's tone brooked no demur. He began to descend the stairs at a run, with the rest of the party, including his stepmother, whose wails had now dwindled to a subdued snivelling, trailing in his wake. As he reached the bottom of the stairs, two things happened. The door of the study opened, and Inspector Byrne, followed by his sergeant, came out. 'Who the hell are you?' demanded the peer.

'Good afternoon – Lord Castleford, is it?' replied Byrne, unperturbed by this trenchant mode of address. 'The name's Byrne. Dublin police. Glad to see Your Lordship up and about.'

'What's it to you? And what are you doing in my house?'

'I'm doing my duty, sir. Investigating a crime,' said the other coolly. 'To wit: the suspicious death of Mr Jolyon Swift. Your half-brother, I believe.'

'What do you mean, a suspicious death?' cried Swift.

'He means it was murder.' The voice, devoid of emotion, came from the top of the stairs. It reduced them all to silence. 'Deny it all you like,' went on Henrietta Swift, beginning to descend the stairs to where they all stood, transfixed by this intervention. 'But I heard you. We *all* heard you. You said, "If you come near me again, I'll kill you." And so you did.' She drew near to Swift, and almost spat the word in his face. '*Murderer.*'

Another silence, which seemed to last a long time, followed Mrs Swift's words. Then everybody started speaking at once. 'I say . . . S-steady on,' muttered young Gogarty, who had emerged from the dining room at that moment.

'My dear child, consider what you're saying,' protested the canon.

'You're mad, Henrietta.' That was Lady Celia, her clear tones rising above the rest. Beneath this general hubbub, the low keening sound emitted by Lady Castleford added a note of melodrama to the scene. Because there was something decidedly theatrical about the whole thing, thought Rowlands – with the accused, Swift, now standing in the middle of the 'stage', which was the hall, and his accuser, Henrietta Swift, denouncing him from her elevated post on the stairs.

She herself seemed unrepentant, at the furore her intemperate words had created. 'It's true, though, isn't it?' she said. 'You can't deny it, Ned. You threatened Joly – you know you did – and now he's dead.'

'I think, ma'am,' said Inspector Byrne drily before

Swift could reply to this challenge, 'that it would be better to leave the police to draw their own conclusions from the evidence. And you'll have your chance to say what you want to say. First I need to talk to Lord Castleford here, about *his* recollection of what took place last night. I've taken the liberty of setting up my centre of operations in your study, my lord, so if you'll step this way.' He opened the door of the room from which he had just emerged.

'I don't suppose I have any choice in the matter,' said Swift pleasantly. 'Let's get this over, shall we?'

'Wait!' Following young Mrs Swift's dramatic intervention, they had all almost forgotten about Lady Castleford, who had seemed lost in grief, huddling in one of the armchairs to the side of the hall fireplace. Now she spoke up: 'I want to see him – I want to see my son.'

'Eveline,' said Celia Swift gently. 'I don't think that's a good idea.'

'Her Ladyship's right.' This was the Inspector. 'You'd only distress yourself, ma'am.'

'But . . .' she began; before she could make any further protest, Canon Wetherby took charge.

'Come, Eveline, I'll see you back to your room,' he said. 'You've had a bad shock. You need rest. Perhaps Mary'll bring you up a nice warm drink.'

'See to it, will you, Mary?' said Lady Celia to the parlourmaid, who had been hovering in the wings, with some of the other servants. 'The rest of you, go back to your duties,' she went on, still addressing the staff. 'Biddy, go and wash your face. Monckton, I don't want any visitors admitted to the house today – apart from the police, of course. And tell anyone who telephones that Lord Castleford and I are otherwise engaged.'

'Yes, m'lady.'

There came a discreet cough from the far side of the hall. 'I take it that you'd like me to return to my duties also?' said Robert Butler. 'Although it hasn't of course been possible for me to speak to His Lordship about any particular matters he might want me to deal with today.'

'I'm sure you've plenty to be getting on with, Mr Butler,' was the reply. 'You too, Mr Gogarty', for the young man was still in the vicinity. 'Unless you're wanted by the inspector, of course.'

'I . . . I . . .' The combination of recent events, and his unruly emotions where Lady Celia was concerned had rendered Gogarty even more inarticulate than usual, it seemed. He turned and fled, without another sound.

'As for you, Henrietta,' said her sister-in-law. 'I don't know what you think you were playing at, just then. You must know as well as I do that Ned had nothing to do with Jolyon's death. It's ridiculous to suggest otherwise.'

'I know what I heard,' replied the girl defiantly.

'Well, you'll have your chance to tell it to the police,' said Celia Swift. 'Until then, I suggest you keep your thoughts to yourself. There's such a thing as the law of libel, you know.' At which the younger woman gave a contemptuous snort, and stalked off. Lady Celia sighed. She put a hand on Rowlands' arm. 'Do you know,' she said, 'I feel as if I can't stand being in the house a minute longer, with all this madness going on. Any more of it, and I might go a bit mad myself. Let's take a turn around the garden, shall we, Frederick? The roses are looking rather lovely.'

It was good to be outside in the fresh air although the sun was already blisteringly hot on the terrace, onto which they exited through the French windows of the morning room. Fortunately, it was cooler in the yew walk, which ran between topiary towers. These, said Lady Celia, took a lot of upkeep. 'They're one of the features of Castleford's formal gardens,' she went on. 'Although they're looking a bit ragged just now. It's so hard to get good gardeners these days.' She must have heard how it had sounded, for she laughed, and added: 'That may not seem like a priority, with a war about to start, but I can assure you that McGurk, our head gardener, talks of little else.'

By unspoken consent, they didn't speak of the matter that was uppermost in both their minds, Rowlands guessed, until they'd entered the rose garden – instantly perceptible to him as such from the ravishing scent that arose from the ramblers and climbing roses covering its walls: Madame Hardy, William Lobb and the Queen of Denmark (with other varieties whose names Rowlands couldn't guess) intermingled their perfume in the still, warm air. A stone bench stood against the south wall; they sat down on this, and lit cigarettes. After a brief silence, Celia Swift spoke: 'He didn't do it.'

'I never thought he did,' replied Rowlands. He was glad that he was able to do so without a moment's hesitation.

'Well, that's something.' The warmth in her voice told him how much she appreciated the fact that his support was unqualified. 'I imagine the police think otherwise,' she added flatly.

Rowlands considered this. 'Not necessarily. Inspector Byrne seems like a shrewd kind of man. He'll look at the evidence before coming to any conclusion.'

'Yes, what *about* the evidence?' she said angrily. 'Henrietta accused Ned of murder.'

'That's her word against his. Your sister-in-law was obviously upset.'

'Deranged,' said Lady Celia. 'And yet we all heard him say what he said.'

'People say things they regret in the heat of the moment,' said Rowlands. 'I don't think for one moment that your husband translated his hot words into cold-blooded murder.'

She rested her hand briefly on his. 'Thank you for that. And it's true. Ned and Joly were always sparring with one another, but there was never any real animosity. It was the same with my brothers, I think. Johnny – he was the eldest, you know – used to rag Rollo about his lack of prowess at cricket and rugger – that sort of thing. And Rollo'd get his own back by making apple-pie beds, or hiding Johnny's riding boots. Silly boys' stuff. But they were devoted to one another, really.' Both her brothers had been killed in the war, Rowlands knew, as had his own elder brother, Harry.

He nodded. 'Brothers do fight. But when it comes down to it, blood is thicker than water. Do you have any idea what the quarrel last night was all about?'

'None. I think I've already said that it was very late when Ned came to bed. I was already asleep, so there wasn't the opportunity to ask him . . . even if he'd have told me,' she added under her breath. 'Then, this morning, he went out before I was properly awake. So I've as little idea as you have . . .'

Before she had finished speaking, Rowlands' sharp ears had detected the sound of brisk footsteps on the flagstone path. 'Perhaps,' he said, 'we could ask Lord Castleford himself?'

'Ask me what?' said Swift. 'I thought I'd find you here,' he added to his wife, without waiting for an answer. 'I couldn't wait to get out of the house, either. Place seems to have turned itself into a blessed police station, with Gardai wandering about, and my own study commandeered.'

'Yes, it's been an unpleasant few hours,' said Lady Celia evenly.

'So what was it you wanted to ask me?' said her husband, sitting down beside her. 'Did I kill my brother? No. Anything else?'

'Frederick was just asking if I knew what the quarrel with Joly was all about,' was the reply. 'Since you're the only person who knows—'

Give me a cigarette, will you, Celia?' said Swift, cutting across her. 'I've left mine in my other jacket.' She did so, and when he'd lit it and taken a deep drag, he said: 'I'll tell you what I told that inspector – Byrne, isn't it? The fact is, I don't remember a thing about last night. Not the quarrel, as you call it, nor any of what came afterwards – going out for my ride, and the stirrup leather breaking, and Lucifer throwing me . . . Nothing, in fact, up to the moment when I woke up, a couple of hours ago, with a bump on my head. The last thing I remember is going into dinner, and talking to old Langton about selling the Long Meadow. After that, it's all a blank.'

'You're still suffering from concussion,' said his wife. 'I told you to stay in bed.'

'Nonsense, I'm perfectly fine. Bit of a headache, that's all. You don't imagine I could have stayed in bed, knowing what had happened to Jo? Poor little blighter.' His voice was not quite steady.

'He – Byrne – got me to identify him, you know. I guess he thought the shock of seeing him like that would get me to confess.' Swift gave a short, unamused laugh. 'It was a shock all right, but if that's what the good inspector hoped, it didn't have the desired effect. I've still got no idea why he was sitting in the car with a bullet in his brain nor whether I'm the one responsible for putting it there. I might be, for all I know.'

'Of course you're not,' said Lady Celia fiercely. But the vehemence with which she spoke had an element of 'protesting too much', thought Rowlands uneasily. Certainly her husband appeared to think so.

'Loyal of you to say so, my dear. But Jo and I were hardly the best of friends, as was all too obvious to anyone who saw us together. And I *had* threatened to kill him, a few hours before he was found dead, if young Henry's account of what I said is accurate, which I suppose it must be since none of the rest of you contradicted her. So you see, I'm Suspect Number One.'

'That's absurd,' said his wife. 'Whatever differences you might have had with Jolyon, no one could doubt that you were fond of him in your own way. Besides which, you'd never have stooped to such a method. I can well believe that you might have strangled him in a fit of rage – he could be awfully exasperating – or hit him a bit too hard. But to shoot a defenceless man in cold blood . . . No. The man I married wouldn't be capable of such a low trick.'

Swift made a sound that was midway between a laugh and a cough. 'There's wifely devotion for you,' he said. 'And I'm grateful to you, my dear. Unfortunately, the police may take a different view of my character.'

'They might,' agreed Rowlands. 'People under pressure *do* act out of character sometimes. All the same, before they come to any conclusions, the police will have to take into account the attempt on your life.

I suppose you *could* have faked it yourself, to throw them off the scent, but it was taking a hell of a risk that you might have been killed in so doing.'

'What's this?' said Swift sharply. Rowlands explained about the stirrup leather having been tampered with. 'The police have the evidence at present, so I can't show it to you,' he concluded. 'But I think, in the light of what's happened to your half-brother, they'll be taking it very seriously.'

'Are you suggesting that someone was out to kill us both?' said Swift.

'It rather looks like it,' was the reply. 'Unless of course Mr Swift himself was responsible for the tampering and someone else – let's call him X – happened to stumble upon him as he was on the point of leaving Castleford in the small hours of this morning, and chose that moment to shoot him.'

Swift considered this a moment. 'That does seem unlikely. For a start, Jo wouldn't have gone anywhere near Lucifer. He was terrified of horses. No, that won't fly.'

'He might have bribed someone else to do the tampering,' suggested Lady Celia.

'But why?' Swift's bewilderment was that of a man grappling with a nightmare. 'If I could only remember what it was we fought about, it might supply an answer. Until I *do* remember, I'm completely in the dark about why Jo – or anyone else – should have wanted me dead.'

'There is one other possibility,' said Rowlands

cautiously. 'For obvious reasons, I've only the vaguest idea what you look like, Lord Castleford—'

'I've said you can drop all that,' interrupted the other impatiently. 'The name's Ned, or Swift, or whatever you please – just not that bloody handle. And what the blazes does my appearance have to do with it?'

'Of course,' said his wife excitedly. 'Don't you see, Ned? Whoever it was that shot Joly thought he was you . . . They're both tall,' she said to Rowlands. 'Ned's the more athletic in build. Jolyon was thinner and more round-shouldered. Both have sandy-coloured hair. Joly's was a darker red, but at a glance . . .'

'One of them might have been taken for the other,' said Rowlands, finishing her sentence for her. 'I wondered if that might have been the case.'

Swift groaned aloud. 'All this is making my head ache. Are you saying that whoever shot Jo was intending to shoot me?'

'As I said, it's a possibility,' replied Rowlands. 'It's likely that whoever sent those death threats and shot your dog was also the person who tampered with – or got somebody else to tamper with – the stirrup leather. Then when X saw Mr Swift about to drive off in his car last night he – thinking Mr Swift was you – seized the opportunity to make certain that his murderous plan would be fulfilled.'

'It makes sense,' said Celia Swift. 'It was dark, remember, and the garage is poorly lit . . . Oh, Ned, don't you see that you've got to accept it, now? Someone's out to kill you – and they very nearly succeeded.'

'All right, I take your point,' said her husband testily. 'The question is, how do we find the blighter before he has another go? It'll soon leak out – if it hasn't already – that X has failed in his attempts to rub me out . . . Poor old Jo,' he added, in a softer tone. 'Whatever our differences, he didn't deserve this.' He gave a bark of laughter. 'How he'd have hated it! Being mistaken for me.'

Chapter Eight

The body had been taken away in the mortuary van, and the police had gone, Inspector Byrne having completed, for the time being, his interrogation of the various members of Castleford's household, including its staff. Now, a sadly depleted group sat listlessly drinking tea and eating scones in the smaller of the two sitting rooms while outside the sun continued to shine with the same intensity as it had throughout the whole of that long day. From time to time, subdued remarks were let drop from the lips of one or other of the company – remarks about the weather: 'Too hot. One doesn't feel up to anything . . .' and speculations as to when it would break. By common consent, none of those present – who included the Swifts (minus the younger Mrs Swift), the Butlers, Canon Wetherby and Rowlands himself – alluded to the topic that was surely uppermost in all their minds: the murder.

Henrietta Swift's outburst earlier that day, and the questions each of those present had been forced to answer when interviewed by the inspector, had drained all desire to speculate about who might have been responsible for the atrocity, or indeed any wish to pursue an alternative explanation for Jolyon Swift's death. Canon Wetherby confined himself to an occasional sigh, and a murmured 'Dear, dear.'

Only Elspeth Butler, stirring her tea with what seemed to Rowlands an unnecessary vigour, seemed unaffected by the lowness of spirits that otherwise prevailed. It was she who broke the taboo on mentioning what had happened, and which had caused Lady Castleford and Mrs Swift to keep to their rooms. 'What I *don't* understand,' she said brightly, 'is why the police aren't out looking for the man – I assume it *is* a man – instead of wasting time putting us all through the third degree? I mean,' she went on, into the silence that greeted this sally, 'surely it stands to reason that it's somebody from outside? A hooligan, or one of these political troublemakers. The country's swarming with them.'

'But all that was years ago, surely?' objected Canon Wetherby mildly. 'I'm not aware of any trouble of that kind having taken place in the neighbourhood since . . . well, since that unfortunate affair with poor Captain Hammond – it must be twenty years back.'

'The IRA never owned up to that one,' said Swift

carelessly. 'There was talk it was a jealous husband who shot him, because Hammond was a bit of a ladies' man. But that's all in the past,' he added. 'I don't believe that the Republicans murdered Jo, nor that they're out to get me. I mean, what could they hope to achieve? They can't imagine that I'll be scared off by such tactics.'

'Oh, you're not scared of anything, we know that,' said his wife, in a fondly mocking tone. 'More tea, Frederick?'

'Thank you.' He held out his cup, and she took it from him, refilled it, and handed it back. Privately, he thought that Swift was being over-hasty in dismissing Mrs Butler's suggestion. If, as Lady Celia had explained, the nationalists saw the forthcoming war as an opportunity to push their case for independence, then a good start would be to force out those members of the landed gentry with English antecedents who had hitherto refused to be forced out. And yet, he reflected, sipping his tea, there seemed something altogether more *personal* about this crime – a feeling that individual resentment rather than political expediency had been the driving force.

'Well,' said Swift, breaking into this reverie, 'I think I'll take a walk up to the home farm. Want to see how that newborn calf's doing. Coming, Rowlands?' Rowlands said he'd be glad to. 'You'll get to see the Kerries when they're brought in for milking,' His Lordship went on. 'Jolly little beasts.'

'You might take Georgie with you,' said his wife. 'He could do with stretching his legs. Nurse has had both the boys on her hands all day – and you know what a handful Reggie can be.'

'Don't I just! Little blighter. Yes, I'll take George along. He's a good little walker, thank the Lord. Wouldn't have much use for a boy who wasn't.' Swift got to his feet, and was making towards the door with Rowlands after him when he added, as if the idea had just come to him: 'Thought I'd stop by the stables first and have a stern word or two with Lucifer.'

'You're not thinking of taking him out, are you?'

'I haven't decided yet.'

'Really, Ned . . . I don't think that's a very good idea – not so soon after your fall.'

'I'll have to get back up on him sooner or later, you know,' was the reply. 'Let him know who's in charge.'

'Yes, but surely . . .'

The door opened and the butler, Monckton, put his head in. 'Telephone, milady.'

Lady Celia sighed. 'I thought I said no calls?'

'It's Mrs Langton, milady. Shall I tell her you're not at home?'

'No. On second thoughts, I'd better speak to her. She won't have heard about all this business yet. Although I expect she'll hear soon enough, from the police . . .' She got up, following her husband and Rowlands out of the room. 'I'll take it in the telephone room. Oh, and Monckton, could you tell Nurse to get

George ready to go out with his father? He'd better wear his gumboots if they're going up to the farm.'

'Yes, milady.'

They separated in the hall – Lady Celia to put her friend in the picture regarding the events of the night before, and the two men to go to the boot room in order to collect caps, boots and sticks. Before they got there, however, there came the sound of footsteps behind them as someone came rushing out of the library. A voice said: 'M-my lord? M-may I h-have a word?'

'Certainly, Mr Gogarty. I say, that's a splendid black eye you've got there. How did you get it?'

'You know p-perfectly well, my lord,' replied the young man with dignity. 'A-and I've come to give notice that I'll be leaving a-as soon as p-possible.'

'I see.' Swift sounded more amused than affronted. 'May I ask why?'

'You k-know why.'

'I'm afraid I don't. It may have escaped your notice, but I took a fall from my horse earlier today. Knocked everything that took place after about nine o'clock last night clean out of my head.'

'I d-don't believe it.'

'I hope,' said Swift pleasantly, 'you're not calling me a liar, Mr Gogarty? Because then I really *would* have to call you out. Good shot, are you? No, I thought not . . . Why, man, you've gone quite green!'

'You . . . you . . .' With this stifled imprecation, Gogarty rushed off.

'What on earth's got into the feller? Highly strung, these Trinity types,' said Swift. 'Suppose I must have given him that black eye, if he says so.'

'You did,' said Rowlands. He related what the young man had said to him and the canon concerning the events of the previous evening.

'Hmm,' said the other. 'Well, I don't remember it – although I expect he deserved it. Impudent puppy! Always moping after my wife.'

'What does he look like, young Gogarty?' asked Rowlands suddenly. 'I mean, as to build and so on.' From the brief handshake they'd exchanged, it hadn't been possible to deduce much, except that the lad was tall, and obviously nervous (the hand had been clammy).

'Skinny sort of feller,' said Swift, confirming this impression. 'Yet to grow into his height, if you get my meaning. Type women want to mother, with those big puppy-dog eyes. Tell you the truth, I'd as soon he took himself off. It was Celia's idea to have him catalogue the library. Never saw the need for it myself. Why are you interested in him, anyway?' he added sharply. 'You don't think *he* could have shot poor Jo, do you? Feller doesn't have it in him.'

Rowlands wasn't so sure. It seemed to him that Gogarty would have been eminently capable of pulling a trigger . . . and of fixing the stirrup leather, too. Neither required much physical strength, so a slightly built youth might have managed both. Whether the impulsive young librarian would have had the ruthlessness to carry out either of these murderous acts was another matter. Then there was the question of motive. Was a crush on his employer's wife enough of a reason for a man to commit double murder? Rowlands rather thought not. Although it was true that men had killed for less – women, too, as he knew from past experience.

Accompanied by the dogs, the two men, with the child in tow, strolled across to the stable-yard where the wolfhound and his two red setter companions were ordered to sit by their master. 'Can't have dogs running around a stables,' he said. 'Might upset the horses – or get themselves kicked in the head. Sit, Juno!' – this to the more excitable of the setters. 'You'll have your walk in a minute.' Despite what his wife had said, Swift was determined to get back up on the stallion as soon as possible. 'Can't let him get it into his head that he can throw me off whenever he feels like it. Horses are funny beasts. Temperamental. Doesn't take much to turn a good animal bad, if you know what I mean.'

Rowlands supposed the same could be said of human beings.

'Ha, ha! Indeed. Which reminds me, I'd better take a look at that stirrup leather – the one you *didn't* hand to the police. I'm intrigued to see the method by which some ingenious blighter tried to do me in.'

The head groom, when applied to for this

piece of evidence, sent Mickey the stable-lad to fetch it, all the while deploring his master's stated intention of taking Lucifer out once more before the day was over. 'He's settled down in his stall now, me lord. He's been quiet as a lamb since this morning . . .'

'Probably planning his next piece of mischief,' said Swift. 'Ah, here we are!' – acknowledging the return of Mickey from his errand. 'You were the lad who first spotted Lucifer running around the field after he'd played his tricks with me, I'm told?' Mickey admitted that this was so. 'I'm grateful to you,' said Swift, clapping the boy on the shoulder. 'I might have lain there a good while longer if you hadn't been so sharp-eyed.' Then, as Mickey took himself off, muttering that it was nothing at all, any of the lads would've done the same, Swift said to Pheelan, 'I want ten shillings added to that boy's wages this week. We need more of his stamp at Castleford.'

'To be sure, me lord.'

'Bring Lucifer out, will you? I want to take a look at him.'

The groom acquiesced, and went off to see to it, leaving Swift and Rowlands together. The former's attention now shifted to the stirrup leather. Carefully, he ran it through his fingers, pausing at the place where – as Rowlands had discovered earlier – it had been scored through. 'Devilishly clever,' he said. 'If you hadn't spotted the sabotage, my fall would have been passed off as an accident . . .'

'As the saboteur intended.'

'Yes. You don't really think Jo could have been responsible, do you?' said Swift urgently. 'I know he and I had our differences, but I can't believe he'd want me dead . . . any more than *I* wanted him dead. He was my brother, damn it! That counts for something, doesn't it?'

Before Rowlands could reply, the sound of horses' hooves on the cobbled yard signalled Pheelan's return with Lucifer. 'Ah, here's the creature himself,' said Swift, going up to the animal. 'Well, sir,' he said, addressing him rather than the groom, Rowlands surmised. 'You think you've been very clever to get the better of me, don't you? But you've another thing coming, my lad – as you'll find out shortly. Get him saddled up, will you?' he said to Pheelan. 'I'll take him out in an hour. No, make that two. Mr Rowlands and Master George and I are going to walk up to the home farm first, and I'll need to change into my riding things.'

'Very good, me lord.'

'Like to come along, Rowlands?'

'Well . . .' Rowlands wasn't at all sure that he *did* like.

'Go on,' said Swift. 'It'll do us both good after a day spent hanging about indoors. You'd better put a saddle on Duke Humphrey,' he added to Pheelan. 'I know you'd got accustomed to Lady Molly,' he said to Rowlands, 'but we don't let the stallion go out with the mares, as it gets him excited – and we don't want that! Humphrey's a nice steady mount, you'll find.'

'All right,' said Rowlands resignedly.

The Kerry herd was filing into the miking shed when the three of them arrived. Swift was soon deep in conversation with the cowman, O'Brien, who was supervising this operation while his two assistants – his daughters, it emerged – got on with the milking. Distant memories of being allowed to 'lend a hand' milking the four or five beasts on his great-uncle's Norfolk farm now surfaced in Rowlands' memory, amid the sweet smells of straw and warm milk that filled the airy shed. This herd, he gathered, was a much larger concern – perhaps two dozen animals in all – but the methods employed by the two young women introduced as 'my Mary' and 'my Carmel' were the traditional ones. 'We tried one of the new milking machines not so long ago,' said Swift as they stood waiting for O'Brien to join them. 'But it didn't take. Cows didn't like it, and the girls said it was harder to keep the animals clean than when it was just a matter of washing 'em down with soap and water. So we went back to the old way. A machine would increase the yield, of course, but O'Brien won't hear of it.'

A pleasant half-hour ensued while Swift discussed the progress of the newborn calf with the cowman, and Rowlands amused himself by scratching the heads of this cow or that as the patient beasts awaited their turn in the milking stall. A lifetime had passed since those carefree day on Great-Uncle Horatio's farm – a lifetime in which the world Rowlands had known as a child had been utterly transformed by war, pandemic and economic collapse. And yet, standing there in the sweet-smelling cattle shed, with the gentle beasts around him, he felt himself transported back to that earlier time, and a country where the shire horse was king, and where warplanes and tanks were horrors yet to come.

This agreeable illusion was sustained by the presence of little George, who had attached himself to Rowlands, and whom he had evidently decided to consult on those questions of most importance to small boys. 'Have you got a knife?' was one such, to which Rowlands replied that indeed he had, producing the object for the child's inspection. This, a souvenir of his soldiering days, was a standard issue jackknife, made of Sheffield steel, with a double blade, tin opener and a marlin spike. The body of the knife was textured steel, with a belt loop at one end. An old friend. The boy examined it critically. 'It doesn't have a corkscrew, or a thing for taking stones out of horses' hooves,' he said.

'It doesn't. But it's a good knife,' said Rowlands, shutting up the blades again.

'I'm to have a knife, Daddy says,' the child went on

when Rowlands had returned the knife to his pocket. 'Just a penknife, he says, until I'm old enough to use a proper knife. You can cut quite a lot with a penknife,' he added.

Swift had now finished inspecting the calf, and whistled to the dogs that it was time to leave. 'I thought, as we've got George with us, we'd walk over to Pat Doolan's cottage to see about that puppy,' he said. 'You'd like that, wouldn't you, Georgie? A dog of your own.' George agreed that he would. 'It's a good tramp across the fields,' said his father. 'You'll have to keep up. No whining about being tired, mind.'

They set off. The sun was going down, and it was cooler now than it had been, but it was still a fair distance for a small child, thought Rowlands, glad to see that, despite his stern words, Swift was not above hoisting his son upon his shoulders after they'd been walking for a while. The smell of woodsmoke was the first indication that they were nearing the cottage; the second was the sound of barking dogs – a greeting returned with interest by Swift's wolfhound and red setters. 'Quiet, Juno! Quiet, Jess! You too, Jason . . . Hello! Who's there?' Because as they reached the place, there came the unmistakeable sounds of a door slamming, and someone running away. 'If I'm not mistaken, it's that no-good Christie Doherty,' said Swift angrily. 'Hi, you!' But if the young man heard him, he made no reply. 'If I find that Doolan's broken his word to me about letting that feller on the premises, there'll be hell to pay,' muttered the landowner, pushing open the gate and marching up to the door. He rapped once, and without waiting for an answer, went in. Rowlands followed with young George – the former's feelings of apprehension about this meeting increasing by the minute. Because it was at once apparent from the rumble of male voices, which rose above the yapping of the spaniel bitch and her offspring, that the gamekeeper had company – a fact that did not appear to please Ned Swift in the slightest. 'Clancy. O'Donovan. Brennan. I'm surprised to see you men here.'

'Evenin', me lord,' said one of these three, in a tone of heavy irony. 'Sure, it's a fine night for visitin' old friends.'

'That's as may be, O'Donovan,' replied Swift coldly. 'But I'll remind you that this is my property. If you want to meet your *friends*' – he laid a sarcastic emphasis on the last word – 'you can do it elsewhere, and as soon as possible, if you please. I've business with Doolan here, as he knows.'

'We was just going, me lord,' said another of the men. 'We know when we're not wanted, don't we, boys?'

'Ah, to be sure,' said the man who had not yet spoken. 'Wouldn't want to outstay our welcome . . .' Rowlands, who'd stepped aside to allow the men to pass, caught a whiff of rough tobacco, sweat and something else – hard spirits, he rather thought. 'Glad to see you lookin' so *well*, me lord,' went on this character – whether Clancy or Brennan,

Rowlands could only guess. 'Heard you took a bit of a fall from that horse o' yours . . . Bad luck, that.'

'An' then the *unfortunate* news about the brother,' put in O'Donovan, with what seemed a malicious satisfaction. 'Bad luck does seem to follow your family about.'

'Thanks, but I don't need your sympathy,' said Swift curtly.

The three men went out, one of them spitting pointedly on the hearthstone as he did so. Outside the door, the dogs once more set up their barking, which drowned out any further riposte the interlopers might have made. 'What do you think you're playing at, Doolan, inviting those IRA scoundrels into this house?' demanded Swift of his tenant. 'I tell you, I won't have it.'

'No, me lord,' said the craven Doolan. 'But ye see, it's like this . . . When Donnie O'Donovan decides to pay ye a call, it's not easy to say you're not at home. These are hard men, mc lord.'

'Don't give me that rubbish,' said Swift. 'And by the by, I think I saw that reprobate of a nephew of yours slinking away just now. I've already said I don't want him in this house – or anywhere within a mile of my land. Is that understood?'

'It is, me lord.'

'Good. Well, you've kept me and Mr Rowlands here waiting long enough with your shenanigans. As you see, I've brought Master George along to pick out his dog.' He turned to his son, who had been clinging to Rowlands' hand throughout the exchanges with the IRA men. 'Come, George. I think you'll like the pure black pup best. Plenty of spirit, that one.'

But after a moment's consideration of the tumbling mass of puppies, George said that he liked the 'little red one' best. 'Ah, that's the cream o' the crop,' said Doolan, fishing out the little creature from amongst his brothers and sisters. 'Nice, gentle little feller.'

Swift, to his credit, did not attempt to persuade his son to change his mind, but took the spaniel puppy from the keeper, and made for the door. 'Want to carry him yourself, Georgie?' he said when they were outside once more. George said that he would, although privately Rowlands resolved to lend a hand if the puppy became too much for the child to carry. He *was* only five – a fact his father rather tended to overlook, in the other man's opinion. Perhaps if he himself had had sons instead of daughters, he'd have been the same, he thought. Not that his girls hadn't learnt all they'd needed to learn as soon as they'd needed to learn it – and all without being pushed or harried. Poor George, he fancied, would have a harder time of it.

With the boy there, Rowlands didn't think he could say what was in his mind, which was that the presence of the cabal of IRA men put a different complexion on the matter of Jolyon Swift's murder. Surely Swift, intransigent as he was, could see that? Here were hard men, clearly antagonistic to the

English landowner and his family – men who wouldn't scruple to resort to violence in the pursuit of their ends. As he and the landowner talked idly of other things – a record barley crop; a plan to build new piggeries – he resolved to have it out with Swift as soon as the two of them were alone. The man might think he knew these people, with whom he'd grown up and who had worked his land for generations, but a war was about to begin that would throw even long-established relationships into disarray. For the hard men of the Republican movement, this was an opportunity like no other. Getting rid of the Swifts would be only the start of it.

They reached the house. Having delivered George and his new pet to the care of the boy's nursemaid, the two men went to change for the proposed riding excursion. Rowlands was feeling slightly less apprehensive about this, as he had just learnt that Pheelan was to accompany them. 'I'll need to concentrate on making sure that Lucifer behaves himself,' Swift explained. 'So I won't be able to keep such a close eye on Duke Humphrey. He's a well-behaved horse, as a rule. But one horse can affect the behaviour of another, you know. Pheelan'll make sure to keep him on the straight and narrow.' All of which was a relief to Rowlands as he went to put on his riding clothes. No more than five minutes later, he was descending the stairs.

From the hall below came voices – one of them was

Celia Swift's; the other belonged to Monckton, the butler. He sounded unusually agitated. 'What am I to *say* if they ask me, milady?'

'You don't need to say anything. You can leave all that to me.'

'But milady . . .'

At that moment, Swift himself must have appeared from the back of the house, for he said impatiently, 'There you are, Monckton! I can't find my new gloves anywhere. It was the same this morning. Had to wear my old, worn-out gloves when I went out first thing. Any idea what's happened to the new pair? I'm quite sure I left them on the table here. Most annoying.'

'My lord . . . the fact is . . .'

'Well, spit it out, man! Haven't got all day. Do you know where they are, or not?'

'Tell him, Monckton.'

'Yes, milady.' Then to Swift, who was tapping his whip impatiently on the edge of the hall table: 'If you'll wait a moment, my lord, I'll fetch the glove directly.'

'What's this all about, Celia?' demanded Swift, then, catching sight of Rowlands on the stairs: 'Ah, Rowlands, be with you in a moment . . . just as soon as I get to the bottom of this mystery, which everyone apart from myself seems to be in on.'

'If you'll let me get a word in edgeways, I'll explain,' said his wife, with some acerbity. 'As you know, Venetia rang about an hour and a half ago –

very upset about something. I could hardly make sense of it at first. Apparently, she lost one of her diamond ear-clips after last night's bridge party . . .'

'That woman's always losing valuables. I'm surprised any insurance company will touch her.'

'. . . and she sent Baines over in the Lagonda to look for it as soon as she noticed it was missing. She thought she might have dropped it getting into the car last night after Baines had brought it round . . . It got caught up in her scarf, or something. Anyway, Baines didn't find it . . . hardly surprising, as it was dark, but Venetia was convinced she'd dropped it just below the steps leading up to the terrace . . .'

'Celia, I hope this is going somewhere?'

'. . . although he didn't find the earring, but he *did* find something else on the steps. A glove. One of yours, it would seem. As it was late, he took it back to Slaney Park with him, thinking to return it next day. Venetia was ringing to say that he was about to do so, and would I mind if he had another look for the earring while he was about it. Only it was then – after I'd told her the news about Jolyon – that she realised that what he, Baines, had found might be important. Your glove, that is. . .'

'I fail to see why,' said Swift. 'A lost glove. It's hardly of much significance.'

'So she sent Baines round with it, about an hour ago. Monckton, you'd better fetch it.'

'Yes, milady. '

'Here it is, my lord,' said the butler, coming back at

this moment. 'I put its fellow aside, intending to search for the other one, and then, after what happened . . .' He fell silent as Swift took the glove from him and examined it.

'Yes, it looks like mine . . .' he began, then broke off. 'Why, man, it's stained – with blood, from the look of it.'

'Yes, my lord.'

'*Now* do you see?' said Lady Celia. 'Whoever was wearing that glove – and its fellow – was the one who shot Jolyon. Since the gloves are clearly marked with *your* initials, the implication is that *you* were the one responsible for his murder . . . At least, that's the impression someone wanted to convey.'

'But . . .' Swift was still struggling with the implications of this. 'How long have you known about this, Celia?'

'As I said, Venetia telephoned about four. Baines brought the glove round at half past.'

'And you didn't think fit to inform the police?'

'No. Do you suppose I wanted to incriminate my own husband?' she said, with a flash of temper.

'It'll look far worse when the police find out – which they assuredly will.'

The telephone rang. 'It's all right, Monckton, I'll get it,' said Lady Celia.

'If it's that fool Venetia, tell her that her meddling's caused enough trouble,' called Swift after her. 'Well, Rowlands old man,' he added in a humorous tone, 'I'm afraid we'll have to forgo our ride until another day.'

'Yes,' said Rowlands. 'I'm afraid you're right.' Because as he spoke, there came the sound of a vehicle, recognisable to them all as the police Wolseley, pulling into the drive. A moment later, came the slamming of car doors and the tramp of boots coming up the steps to the front door.

Lady Celia returned. 'Ned, that was Venetia. The police have just questioned Baines about his movements this afternoon. I'm afraid they know about the glove.'

'So it would appear,' replied her husband.

'I'm sorry—' she started to say, but he cut across her.

'You were only trying to protect me. I know that.'

'I seem to have made matters worse,' she said miserably.

The heavy thud of the door knocker resounded through the hall where their party stood as if transfixed.

'Answer it, Monckton,' said Swift.

'Yes, my lord.' With stately, unhurried steps, Monckton crossed the wide oak floor, and opened the door. 'Good evening, Inspector. May I be of assistance?'

'You know why I'm here,' said Byrne, stepping into the hall. Two of his men followed close behind. 'Evening, my lord. I've some business to discuss with you, as I believe you know.' He must have spotted what was in Swift's hand, for he added to his sergeant: 'Take charge of that glove, Rooney. Careful, mind! Although there'll be no fingerprints left to speak of after it's been handled by all and sundry. Now then, my lord – perhaps there's a quiet spot where we can talk?'

'Just here is fine,' was the reply. 'I've no secrets from my wife – or from Mr Rowlands.'

'Very well,' said the inspector grimly. 'Don't say I didn't try and make it easier for you.' He adopted a severe, official tone for what he said next: 'Edward George Swift, I'm arresting you on a charge of murdering Jolyon Reginald Swift, on the night of 19th August 1939. You do not have to say anything, but anything you do say may be taken down—'

'You can cut all that,' said Swift. 'As a magistrate, you know, I'm familiar with the form. Was it the glove that tipped the scales against me?'

'That, and a couple of other things I needn't go into at present,' said Byrne. 'If you'll come with me, my lord.'

'Of course, Inspector. May I at least change out of my riding clothes, and pack an overnight bag?'

'I'll pack your things while you're changing,' said his wife, who had drawn nearer to his side while this exchange was going on.

'Thank you, my dear. And get Brian Murphy on the telephone, will you? Tell him to come to the Gardai station in Enniskerry as soon as he can. I assume that's where you're taking me, Inspector?'

'For the present, my lord,' was the reply.

'Very well. I'll just . . .' Swift took a step towards the stairs, and at once a uniformed officer made as if to accompany him. 'You can call off your man, Byrne,' said the accused. 'I'm not about to throw myself from the bedroom window, or blow out my brains, even if I still had my revolver . . . Perhaps,' he went on, 'Mr Rowlands could accompany me to my dressing room? He's had a good deal of experience of dealing with felons unless I'm much mistaken.'

Byrne gave his assent to this plan, and the two men followed Lady Celia upstairs. While she busied herself putting clothes and other necessaries into a bag, Rowlands went with the beleaguered lord into the latter's dressing room where Swift changed into tweeds and flannels, and looked around for his cigarettes and lighter. 'Confound it!' he muttered. 'This is a bad blow for Celia. You'll look after her for me, won't you, old man? She rather depends on you.' Rowlands said that he would. 'Good man. I know I can trust you. And I'm sorry about our ride.' Swift gave a good imitation of a carefree laugh. 'When all this is over, we'll go out again, I promise you.'

'I look forward to it,' said Rowlands, with a smile, although his heart was heavy.

Chapter Nine

The trial for murder of a member of the aristocracy (albeit one belonging to the Irish peerage) might have been headline news at any other time; as it was, reports of the arraignment of Edward Swift, Lord Castleford, for the murder of his half-brother, Jolyon Swift, were relegated to a small paragraph on an inside page of *The Times* and other London papers. Even the Dublin papers gave the affair far less attention than might otherwise have been expected, the news on both sides of the Irish Sea being all of the coming war. Following Swift's arrest and subsequent incarceration in Mountjoy Prison, there seemed little that Rowlands could achieve by remaining at Castleford, and little comfort he could offer to either the peer or his wife, beyond expressing the vague hope that things would turn out all right in the end. He was not, in any case, convinced that this would be so, since the evidence against his friend was looking increasingly black.

Apart from the incriminating matter of the blood-stained glove, the police had found other indications that the acrimonious encounter between Swift and his half-brother, overheard by the other guests on the night of the murder, had not been the last time the two had met. The butt of a freshly smoked cigarette, of the brand Swift favoured, had been found in the garage where Jolyon Swift had died, dropped down beside the car. Fingerprints corresponding to those His Lordship had consented to have taken had also been found on the door of the vehicle itself, indicating that at some time during the preceding twelve hours since the Talbot had last been cleaned and the time of the murder, Swift had rested his hand upon it although, as he said with some sarcasm, he'd hardly have taken his gloves off to lean upon the car if he'd worn them when committing the murder. Not that he could remember doing either, he'd said: the whole evening after about nine o'clock remained a blank to him.

Bail was applied for, and refused. Had the times been different, the magistrate said, making clear his reluctance at having to stick to the letter of the law, he might have been able to waive the rules; as it was, with the current political situation being especially volatile, allowing a man accused of murder to roam the streets, as he put it, was out of the question. And so Swift remained in prison, visited once by Rowlands, on his way back to

London (for there was no good reason for him to stay, and a great many reasons for him to return, not least his anxiety about the safety of his family, now war with Germany was imminent). He found his friend cheerful but resigned. 'I didn't do it, you know,' he said as Rowlands rose to take his leave. 'But I'm damned if I know how I'm going to prove it. If we *don't* meet again,' he added, with that gallows humour Rowlands had come to recognise as characteristic, 'it's been a pleasure knowing you, old man. I wish we'd had that ride together, that's all. You were getting your confidence back, you know. Another few days would have done it.'

As they shook hands, Rowlands replied in the same jocular vein, adding that he was sure they *would* see one another again, and soon. Surely he'd be called as a witness? But it transpired that Inspector Byrne didn't think his evidence essential after all. And it was true, said Rowlands to Edith when he'd arrived home after his long and exhausting journey, that he couldn't contribute anything of particular significance. He hadn't been the first to discover the body, nor was he on the scene when Swift had had his fall. His discovery of the sabotaged stirrup leather aside, there was nothing he could add to the main body of evidence. He didn't even know if Byrne was taking the attempt on Swift's life seriously, or not. As far as the police were concerned, it certainly complicated the affair – otherwise a beautifully simple one of brothers falling out, a threat being made and followed up on.

Edith agreed that it was all very tricky. 'There's

nothing you can do about it, Fred. You've already given up as much time as you could spare.' Which was true enough. There had been no Cornish holiday for *him*, that year.

'I can't help thinking that there's something I've missed,' he said, lying awake that night, his mind too active for sleep. 'Something obvious. But every time I try to pin it down, it eludes me.'

'Let it go,' said his wife wearily. 'We've enough to deal with here, without taking on other people's problems.' Which was also true, he thought.

Chamberlain's ultimatum had been ignored. Britain and France had declared war on Germany. And on that fateful day, the SS *Athenia* had been sunk by a German U-boat off the coast of Ireland, with the loss of 112 lives – the first act of war against Allied powers, at the start of a war that would last for six years and cost untold millions of lives. But in England in September 1939, none of this could have been foreseen. People still struggled to come to terms with what the war would mean for themselves and their loved ones. Those who had sons of an age to be called up dreaded what was to follow. Those with daughters – like Frederick Rowlands – thanked their stars that they didn't have sons. Everybody began accustoming themselves to the exigencies of wartime: the prospect of food rationing, the imposition of the blackout, and the strangeness (as described to Rowlands by his wife) of seeing barrage balloons in the skies over London. An air of unreality lay over it all, intensified by the spell of beautiful autumn weather with which the month began.

It was hard to believe that anything bad could happen on such a day, thought Rowlands, feeling the warmth of the sun on the back of his neck as he strode across the lawns of Regent's Park towards his office in St John's Lodge. Yet underlying the holiday mood that the unseasonal weather engendered was a feeling of foreboding. The news on the wireless that morning was that Warsaw had fallen. They really were in for it at last, he thought.

As he opened the door of his office, he immediately became aware – as he had been six weeks before – that he had an unexpected visitor. Only this time it was the smell of pipe smoke rather than that of Chanel No. 5, that alerted him to the fact. 'Good morning, Chief Inspector,' he said, closing the door behind him. 'To what do I owe the pleasure?'

'Can't a man drop by to see a friend?' said the other blandly. 'Couple o' things to discuss, that's all. Your young lady here,' Alasdair Douglas went on, referring to Rowlands' secretary, 'kindly said she'd make me a cup of tea.'

'In which case, I'll have one too, Miss Collins,' said Rowlands. When she had disappeared on this errand (the kitchen being at the end of the corridor), Douglas said, 'I don't really want that tea, although it was good o' the lassie to offer. The fact is, I've a proposition for ye, Fred. Ye'll no' have heard me mention a man named Brian Murphy?'

'No,' said Rowlands. 'But the name's familiar.'

'He was my commanding officer during the last show. An Irishman by birth, but Scots on the mother's side – which was how he ended up leading a platoon in the Scots Guards. Anyhow, he's written to me. It's about this Castleford case.'

'Of course,' said Rowlands. 'He's Lord Castleford's solicitor, isn't he? I knew I'd heard the name. But I still don't see . . .'

'He wants you to go over there,' said Douglas bluntly. 'Apparently there's been a development. Things are looking bad for Castleford, or Swift, or whatever he's called. He's asked for you – Swift, I mean.'

'But . . .'

'I said I'd ask you, as a favour to the OC . . . I've asked you. Ah, here's the lassie with our tea.'

'I'm afraid that's the last of the sugar ration,' said Miss Collins, setting down the tray.

'Och, I'm giving up,' said Douglas quickly. 'Better for my waistline. So will you go?' he said to Rowlands.

The latter frowned. 'Am I being called as a witness for the defence?'

'No idea. All I know is Captain Murphy thinks you might be useful to his case.'

'I'll talk to Edith,' said Rowlands with a sigh.

As it turned out, she already knew all about it. 'I've had a letter,' she said as Rowlands let himself into the house that evening. 'From your friend. Lady Castleford, is it? She signs herself Celia Swift, so I wasn't sure. She's

163

written to me, but of course it's intended for you.'

'Let me take my coat off, at least,' he said. When he had done so, he followed her into the sitting room. It hadn't been the easiest day. Apart from Douglas's surprise visit, there'd been a lot to get through in the way of paperwork. Miss Collins was leaving soon, to get married – her fiancé was in the navy, about to be sent abroad – and so there were letters of application for the post of secretary to consider as well as everything else. St Dunstan's was making arrangements to move most of its long-term residents out of London, away from the risk of bombs. Organising this, on top of all the usual demands of running a large organisation, would be another headache. The war was going to make a lot of extra work, that much was certain. Now there was this. Rowlands had hoped to have a few minutes to think out what he was going to say before putting Douglas's proposition to his wife. But that was not to be. 'What does she say?'

'I'll read it.' He couldn't tell from her voice whether she was annoyed by or indifferent to what the letter contained. She cleared her throat. '"*Dear Edith (if I may; Frederick has talked of you so much that I feel our acquaintance has gone beyond mere formality)*—"' She gave a sniff.

'Edith,' interrupted her husband. 'Couldn't we do this later – perhaps after dinner? It's been a long day.'

'It won't take long.'

With a feeling of resignation, he sat down. 'Go on.'

'"*Dear Edith, I'm sure Frederick will have told you of our present difficulties . . .*" That's a way of putting it, I suppose. "*. . . difficulties which have been complicated by the current emergency. Ireland has of course remained neutral . . .*"' Another disapproving sniff. '"*. . . but I am well aware that things in London must be unsettled, to say the least. I hope you and your girls (whom I remember so fondly) are coping with the many restrictions and regulations . . .*" I suppose she means the blackout. "*. . . which wartime has imposed. We are not entirely free of these in Ireland, with food and other essentials in short supply, owing to the blockade. But I'm not telling you anything you don't already know . . .*" That's true. "*So I'll get to the point. My husband's solicitor, Mr Murphy, who is a family friend, and has handled most Castleford business on the legal side for the past twenty years or so, has learnt from Ned, my husband, of the invaluable help Fredrick gave us both during that terrible week in August when my brother-in-law died—*"'

'I didn't *do* anything,' Rowlands protested.

Edith paid no attention to this, but went on reading: '"*. . . and so he thinks (as I do) that it would help the defence case to hear what your husband has to say about the events of that week, given that he was present when most of them took place, not least the attempt on Ned's life, which might never have been recognised as such if not for Frederick's quick thinking . . .*" When did all this "Frederick" business start?' said Edith, with a hint of mischief in her voice. He opened his mouth to protest, but once more she ignored him. '"*So I implore you*,"' she read on, '"*as one woman to another, to persuade him to say yes. I realise that these are dangerous times to ask anyone to travel, and I can assure you that I would not have asked if it had not seemed like our last hope, Ned's and mine . . .*"'

'Edith,' he began again, but she hadn't quite finished.

'"*As you will doubtless recall, there was a time when your husband stood by me when I was in the gravest peril. It is thanks to him that I am alive to write to you now, in the hope that he will once more be willing to lend his service. Please remember me to your daughters. I am, yours ever, Celia Swift.*"'

Neither spoke for a moment. Then Rowlands said, 'I know it's a lot to ask, but—'

'If you think,' said Edith, cutting across him, 'that I'd stand in the way of your going, you must think me a poor kind of wife, that's all.'

Lady Celia had sent a car to collect him from the North Quay, with apologies for not meeting him in person.

'Her Ladyship's at the Mountjoy just now,' said the chauffeur, Connolly, hoisting Rowlands' bag into the boot of the Bentley. 'Says to me to tell you that she'll be after joining you for dinner, most like.' Rowlands, tired from his journey across England, with the trains packed with troops on their way to God knows where, poor blighters, and then the crossing – on this occasion unpleasantly rough – wasn't altogether disappointed at the prospect of a few hours to himself. It would give him a chance to bathe and rest before engaging once more with what he privately termed the 'Irish question'. But when they reached the house in Merrion Square, it was to find that Lady Celia had already returned and was anxious to see him.

'Milady says would you join her in the library,' said the Merrion Square butler, O'Driscoll as he ushered Rowlands into the hall, adding with a fervour at odds with his formal role: 'God be thanked that you're here, Mr Rowlands! Her Ladyship's been out of her mind with worry these past weeks. Ah, now, Patsy' – addressing the chauffeur – 'will you bring Mr Rowlands' bags in directly?'

Leaving O'Driscoll to see to the disposition of his luggage, Rowlands went at once to find his hostess, recalling the night he had first come here when she had awaited him in the same room. She rose at once as he entered and came to greet him. 'I'm so glad you're here,' she said, taking his hand. Hers was cold although the room was warm. 'Come over to the fire.' She shivered. 'The nights are drawing in. Soon it'll be winter.' Then, to the servant who came at the touch of a bell: 'Bring us some tea, would you, Molly? Unless you'd prefer a whisky, Frederick?' He said that tea would be fine. 'Let me look at you,' she said when the door had closed behind the maid. 'I can hardly believe you're here. It was good of you to come.'

He said that it was a pleasure.

'Oh, hardly that! To have come halfway across England and then have to cross a sea full of German U-boats, for the sake of a man you only met six weeks ago . . . I know it was asking a lot. But something's happened since you were last here, Frederick.' She lowered her voice although there was no one else in the room. 'The fact is, he's *remembered*.' Over tea with – at her insistence a dash of whisky to keep out the cold – Celia Swift put Rowlands in the picture as to how, and when, her husband's memory of the night of the murder had come back. It had been preceded by an extraordinary discovery – 'If anything can be called "extraordinary" after what's happened,' she said wryly. This was the news that the Long Meadow, a piece of land that lay on the border between the Castleford demesne and the one belonging to the Langtons, had been sold – but not, it transpired, to Langton. 'Ned was adamant that he wouldn't sell,' said Lady Celia. 'Even though Oliver Langton was offering a good price for a piece of land that wasn't of the best quality. Too boggy, for one thing – it lies along the river, you know. We use it for grazing, during the summer months, but in the winter, it's practically waterlogged. Oliver had plans to extend his fishing rights – at present, he has to beg permission to fish above the bridge. Anyway, it made no difference to Ned. He refused point-blank to break up the estate.'

'I remember some conversation about it,' said Rowlands.

'Of course. You were there that night,' she said. 'It's one of the reasons I wanted you here – because you'd had a chance to form a picture.' Suddenly, she seemed to become aware of his weary, travel-stained state. 'But I'm keeping you from your bath,' she said. 'Dinner's in an hour. No need to change. We're keeping wartime habits here although we're not officially at war.'

'You might as well tell me the rest,' he said, keeping his seat.

'All right. Well, a few days ago there was a letter. Addressed to Ned, of course, but I opened it. It was from a firm of Dublin solicitors – not one we've used ourselves – saying that they were representing a certain Mr Clarence Deasy in the matter of a sale of land to the said client from Lord Castleford. The letter said that, as there had been no further communication between His Lordship (the vendor) and his client (the purchaser) since the sale was effected on 14th August 1939—'

'What?' interjected Rowlands. 'But that was . . .'

'Five days before the conversation with Langton. Precisely. Anyway, our man – a Mr Higgins – begged to enquire on behalf of his client when it might be convenient for him (the vendor) to take possession. He wants to build houses, this Deasy character,' added Lady Celia in a tone of incredulity. 'Although whether he realises that he'll be building them in a swamp is another matter.'

'I don't understand,' said Rowlands. 'I thought Lord Castleford was opposed to the very idea of selling off parcels of land.'

'He was. Still is. He says he knows nothing about it.'

'So that means . . .'

'It means that the signature on the deed of sale was a forgery. Quite a good one, actually. But Ned certainly didn't sign anything of the kind. According to Mr Higgins, Lord Castleford came into the office in person to sign the document, and to collect a cheque for £10,000. He – Higgins – remembers him well, he says. A tall, well-spoken gentleman with red hair.'

'Jolyon Swift.'

'It sounds like him, doesn't it? Although it could also describe my husband – which I imagine he, Jo, was counting on . . .' She was silent a moment. 'I was dreading the prospect of breaking it to Ned – that his half-brother, whom he'd always treated so decently, had tried to defraud him. As it turned out, I didn't have to. As soon as I mentioned the cheque, he said "So that's what the row was about!" It all started to come back to him then – Jolyon confessing what he'd done, because he knew it'd come out eventually. He'd got into a tight spot, he said – his creditors were hounding him, and it was the only way he could think of to hold them off. Naturally, Ned lost his temper – we all heard that – telling Jo to get out of his sight, and rushing out himself. After he'd walked a bit, he cooled down, he said, so that when he found the little wretch in the garage later that night, on the point of running off, he tried to reason with him.'

'Ah,' said Rowlands. 'That would explain the fingerprints on the car, and the dropped cigarette that the police found.'

'Exactly. Oh, he admits he was there all right,' she said. 'And he and Jo certainly had high words. Ned told Jo he was going to get that land back if it was the last thing he did. Even if it meant dragging his own brother through the courts . . . or wringing his blasted neck.'

'He said that, did he?'

'Oh yes,' she said, with a tremulous little laugh. 'Ned never holds back when he's angry. And he was very angry with Jo. But he didn't kill him. Unfortunately, his memory of that last encounter has given the police the one thing they lacked. A motive.'

'Yes,' said Rowlands. 'I'm afraid they *would* see it like that.'

Chapter Ten

They found Swift's solicitor, Brian Murphy, in the library at the Four Courts. This, Lady Celia explained to Rowlands, was where their solicitor had to present himself in order to brief the barrister who would be taking on the case: in this instance, Sir Anthony Griffin, KC. 'Mr Murphy says he's the best man for murders,' whispered Lady Celia as they stood waiting for the solicitor to conclude his business at the desk, a large, horseshoe-shaped object in the centre of the great domed room, which hummed with the voices of those assembled there – barristers, solicitors and their clients as well as the clerks who served their needs and on whom, said Rowlands' companion, the whole edifice depended. At length Mr Murphy saw them and came over, full of apologies for having kept them waiting.

'Good to see ye, good to see ye.' He seized Rowlands'

outstretched hand and pumped it up and down. From this contact, Rowlands received the impression of a short but powerfully built man, with an iron grip – perhaps expressive of a tenacity of character to be desired in one of his profession. 'Mr Rowlands, is it not? Her Ladyship has spoken very highly of ye.'

With which encomium he led the way, still throwing remarks over his shoulder, to a desk in an annexe of the lofty chamber, whose walls, Rowlands discovered, were lined with large tomes, presumably of a legal nature. 'Sit ye down, sit ye down,' went on the solicitor – evidently a man somewhat given to repetition. That this conversational habit did not lessen his acuity was apparent from the first question he directed at the newcomer: 'Well, Mr Rowlands, and what can you tell me about this case that I don't already know?'

Rowlands smiled. 'I wish I knew. The police—'

'Ah, let's have no more of the police! They have their way of doing things and I have mine. I've no doubt,' said this disconcerting little man, 'that they asked you all the right questions in the right order. Wrote them down, too, in their notebooks – and then promptly forgot 'em. What I want to know,' said Brian Murphy, suddenly dropping his jovial manner, 'is what they *didn't* ask you about. Anything that struck you as untoward.'

'I'll do my best to remember,' said Rowlands. 'But I still don't see why you've asked me here. There were a number of witnesses to what happened that night in

August – several with a better view of events than I could hope to offer,' he added wryly.

'Perhaps so, in the literal sense,' was the reply. 'But no one else who was at Castleford between the middle of August when you arrived, and the end of the month when you left, had quite your view of things, as you put it. Nor had they your experience in such matters – your eye for the salient detail, if you'll excuse another visual metaphor—'

'I've told Mr Murphy what you did for me all those years ago,' interjected Lady Celia. 'And about the other murder cases you've solved.'

'That's putting it a bit high,' protested Rowlands. 'I happened to be on hand during the cases in question, that's all.'

'The Percival case – that was one of yours, wasn't it?' said Murphy, ignoring this. 'Fine bit of detective work, I call it . . . and then there were those London murders. Oh, we read the papers here, you know,' he added with a chuckle. 'Dublin's quite a civilised city – even if the same can't be said for some of its citizens. Why, it's not so long ago that they blew up this very building that we're sitting in. You wouldn't guess, to look at it now, but all this fine Palladian architecture was reduced to rubble.' He was silent a moment. 'To return to the subject of Castleford, and the night of the 19th August . . . I'd like to hear it from your point of view.' He gave an apologetic chuckle. 'Impossible to avoid using words to do with sight.'

'I use such phrases myself all the time,' said Rowlands.

'So where do you want me to begin, Mr Murphy?'

'I think at the beginning, don't you? Lady Celia has told me that she asked you to come to Ireland in the hope of persuading Lord Castleford that his life was in danger – am I right so far?'

'You are,' replied Rowlands.

'And what was your impression, on arriving at Castleford?' the other persisted. 'Did you find Lady Celia's apprehensions to be justified?'

'I did.' Rowlands marshalled his thoughts. 'My impression from the first was that there was a definite *atmosphere* at Castleford – a feeling that things weren't right. I suppose I was on the look-out – to use another visual phrase – for signs of trouble after Lady Celia had informed me of the death threats made to her husband, and of the killing of the dog.'

'Indeed,' said the lawyer. 'The first murder, one might say.'

'One might. And I certainly detected signs of unease. There was a feeling of resentment, directed principally towards Lord Castleford. A quarrelsome mood overall.'

'Can you be more specific?'

Rowlands hesitated. 'Well, there was the animosity between the late Mr Swift and Lord Castleford. A feeling, I might add, that seemed to me to be more on one side than on the other.'

'That's true,' put in Lady Celia. 'Ned was really quite fond of Jolyon, in his own way.'

'I had that impression, too,' said Rowlands. 'There

also seemed to me to be some negative feeling between Mr Swift and his wife.'

'Oh, Joly and Henry were always at each other's throats—' began Lady Celia, then broke off, presumably at a look from Murphy. 'I'm sorry,' she said. 'It's *your* impressions Mr Murphy wants, not mine. Do carry on, Frederick.'

'That was the feeling I had in the house itself,' he said. 'Not a good feeling. It even seemed to affect the staff . . .' He thought of the conversation he'd overheard between the land agent and Jolyon Swift, the morning of his arrival, of the whispered exchange he'd intercepted between one of the maids and her supposed paramour at the kitchen door, and of the terror, perhaps unrelated, perhaps not, that Biddy the chambermaid had displayed when it emerged that Ned Swift's accident had been no such thing. 'There were other matters, too,' said Rowlands. He described the encounter with Christie Doherty at Doolan's cottage, and the subsequent meeting with the three IRA men. 'It seemed to me that there might well be a connection between the threats sent to Lord Castleford earlier and the attempt on his life that followed. Doherty seemed the obvious candidate, both for the shooting of the dog, and for the sabotaging of the stirrup leather that led to Lord Castleford's accident.'

'Ned didn't tell me about meeting O'Donovan and his crew,' interjected Lady Celia, forgetting her earlier resolution to let him speak. 'Nor about the quarrel with

Doherty. Do you think, then, that it was the IRA who tried to murder him?'

'It's one possibility,' said Rowlands. 'And I'm sure the Gardai won't have neglected that particular line of investigation. But it still doesn't explain who killed Jolyon Swift.'

'Unless it was Ned they were after, and they mistook Jolyon for him,' she said excitedly. 'It's what you suggested yourself, Frederick—'

'What's this?' interrupted Murphy. 'A case of mistaken identity? That's one I hadn't thought of.'

'It's another possibility,' said Rowlands. 'But . . .' He fumbled for the words. How to say that, in spite of appearances to the contrary, he felt sure that the murderous impulses he had detected at Castleford were coming from *within* the house, not from outside? It was true that it was he who'd suggested the IRA men as suspects – but even as he'd said it, he didn't believe it. 'I think we ought not to jump to conclusions,' he said lamely.

'What choice do we have?' cried Lady Celia. 'Ned's trial starts in a week's time. We have to show that he couldn't have done it. That he wasn't even—'

'Ah, there's the man himself,' said Brian Murphy, cutting across his client's impassioned outburst. 'Hi there! Sir Anthony, now! Over here, sir!' In an undertone, he added, 'Tony Griffin's your man, to be sure. If anyone can get your feller off, it's Tony.'

A moment later, they were joined by the said Silk:

an affable presence, with a stately, almost theatrical manner – no doubt entirely suited to his calling, thought Rowlands. 'Afternoon, Murphy! These your clients? How d'ye do? Griffin's the name. I'll be in charge of your husband's defence, ma'am.' With which he swooped low over the hand Lady Celia had held out to him, and kissed it. 'And you're the witness from England, I suppose,' he went on, addressing Rowlands.

'He is, indeed,' said Murphy. 'Mr Rowlands, may I present Sir Anthony Griffin, KC.'

'Delighted,' said Rowlands, extending his hand. The hand that took it was smooth, well-shaped and warm, the handshake vigorous, and the voice, with its rolling cadences, was pitched from a height that indicated that its owner was well over six feet tall. Rowlands briefly entertained himself with the thought of the contrast that this would make with the diminutive Murphy.

'Pleasure's all mine,' said Griffin. 'Getting down to business, I see, Murphy.'

'Indeed we are. Mr Rowlands was just giving his impressions of Castleford.'

'To be sure. You're the man who spotted the cut stirrup leather, are you not? That's a very strong point in our client's favour, you know – the fact that he was himself the victim of a murder attempt. Yes,' said the KC, 'I think we can make quite a good thing of that. Well, mustn't stop, you know. I'm expected in Court Four at eleven. Nice, straightforward little poisoning case. But we'll meet again ere long, I don't doubt. I said

I'd look in on our client later.'

'We're off to the Mountjoy ourselves directly,' said Murphy. 'His Lordship's anxious to keep abreast o' the case.'

'Splendid, splendid. Well, keep your spirits up, won't you, dear lady?' he added to Lady Celia. 'Never could bear to see a good-looking woman with a sad face.' With that he swept off, as across the echoing vaults of the library his name was called by the court usher: 'Sir Anthony Griffin to Court Four, if you please.'

'There you are,' said Murphy happily. 'Didn't I tell you he was the man for the job? Now, if ye'll permit me to offer ye a wee bite of luncheon in my office beforehand, we'll make our way to the Mountjoy.'

They entered the gaol by a wicket gate to one side of the main entrance, whose fortress-like appearance, said Lady Celia, made her blood run cold. 'Each time I visit, I get the feeling that I might not be let out again,' she confessed, taking Rowlands' arm as they passed through another gate, which the guard accompanying them locked behind them. 'Of course, it's worse for poor Ned.'

'Now then, my lady, no need to despair,' said Murphy. 'We'll have His Lordship out o' here in two shakes, you see if we don't.'

They were to meet Lord Castleford in the visitors' room of E Wing, Murphy went on – adding for Rowlands' benefit, that each wing formed one of the spokes of a wheel, radiating from a central courtyard. 'Like Pentonville,' said Rowlands, realising that this apparently inconsequential information was the solicitor's way of giving him a physical idea of the place. Although frankly, he thought, but did not say, the layout of the gaol was of far less interest to him than the state of mind of the man he had come to see.

On a first impression, this was better than expected. Swift's greeting was almost effusive: 'Celia! Here you are at last! I thought you'd never come. Afternoon, Murphy. I suppose you've no good news for me? Rowlands, old man, welcome to the Joy, as we old lags call it. It was good of you to come.'

Rowlands murmured that it was a pleasure. Although it soon became apparent to him that the other man's cheerfulness was only a veneer. 'Has Celia put you in the picture?' the latter went on, still addressing Rowlands. 'The police have a cast-iron motive for Jolyon's death now, you know. It seems I shot him because I found out he'd sold off part of the Castleford estate to pay off his creditors. I lost my temper – as I'm sure you recall – and threatened him. Later, I made good on the threat, and killed him.'

'Ned, please . . .'

Swift ignored his wife's protest. 'It all hangs together, doesn't it? Just as it will end up by hanging *me*.'

'Except that it didn't happen like that,' said Rowlands quietly.

'Didn't it? Glad to hear you say so, old man.' There

180

was a hectic quality to Ned Swift's levity. 'Then perhaps you'll tell me how it *did* happen? Damned if I know,' he said.

'That's just what we're after doing, me lord,' put in Brian Murphy. 'Mr Rowlands was giving me his thoughts on the subject earlier.'

'Oh? And what *are* your thoughts?' demanded Swift, half-humorously. 'Don't tell me . . . let me guess . . . a gang of IRA men, intent on driving me away, shot first my dog and then – mistaking Jolyon for me on account of our red hair – shot my brother, and nobbled my horse in order to kill me. Rather a complicated way of going about things, but then the Irish are a subtle race.'

'I don't think that's what happened at all,' replied Rowlands. 'But if it *was* like that, then the attempt on your life was arranged before, not after, your half-brother's death. And I *do* think the shooting of your dog was probably carried out by one of the men we encountered at Doolan's cottage – Christie Doherty seems the obvious candidate. He had a grudge against you. As a former stable hand, he also had the know-how to have nobbled the horse, as you put it. But I don't think that he, or Donovan, or any of those men, killed Jolyon Swift.'

'Then who did?'

'I don't know. But I've a feeling it was someone closer to home.'

'Surely you don't mean a member of the family?' The humour had gone from Swift's voice.

Rowlands gave an embarrassed shrug. 'Not necessarily. It's just that—'

'You *can't* mean one of the servants?' Lady Celia sounded as horrified as if she herself had been accused. 'Why, they've all been with us for years. I'd trust most of them . . . well, with my life.'

'I'm not accusing anybody,' said Rowlands. 'It's only a feeling I had when I was at Castleford.'

'"An atmosphere of suspicion", I think you said,' put in Murphy. '"A feeling that something was wrong".'

'Yes. It's just a . . . call it what you like . . . An intuition. I hope I'm proved wrong, but . . .'

'It's all we've got to go on so far,' said Lady Celia. 'And I'd trust your intuition over most other people's, any day.'

They dropped Murphy off at the Four Courts where he was meeting another client. He'd see them next day, he said. The trial was to begin on the following Monday. 'Actually,' said Lady Celia, 'I think I'd rather walk from here, if you don't mind, Frederick?'

'Not at all,' he said. It would be a relief to get a breath of fresh air, and clear the prison stench out of his lungs.

'Good. I can show you a bit of the city,' she said. 'You can take the car home, Connolly,' she told the driver. 'I shan't be needing you until tomorrow morning.'

'Very well, milady.'

The Bentley drove off. Rowlands and his companion began walking along Inns Quay, and from thence along

Upper Ormond Quay, on the north side of the river. It was she – Lady Celia – who informed him of these topographical details as they strolled down the tree-lined embankment; otherwise she was silent, apparently preoccupied with her thoughts. But there was more than enough to occupy that part of Rowlands' mind that was not taken up with the details of the case, for Dublin was for him a new, and delightful, experience. From all around arose the sounds and smells of the city as it settled into its early evening routines: from the river came shouts of men unloading a barge; from the roadway, the clanking of trams and the throaty roar of motorbuses as they bore their human cargo homewards. Nor was there any shortage of the older form of transport: horse-drawn vehicles clattered past – one, loaded with scrap metal, might have run him down if Lady Celia's cry and the unmistakeable sound of horses' hooves had not alerted him. Then, too, there was the charm of hearing his own language spoken with the gentle lilt that transformed its prosaic cadences into something altogether more lyrical. A shopgirl, arm in arm with her friend, related the latest gossip: 'I says to him, Millie, I says, "I've had enough of your cheek" and what do you think he says to that, the rascal?' A girl and her boy lingered on the Ha'penny Bridge for a kiss: 'Leave off, now, Donal O'Kelly. Ye're messing me hair, so ye are.' A woman hurried past, with a small child: 'Come along now, *acushla*. Yer pa'll be wanting his tea'.

As they turned down Temple Bar, smells of sawdust

and spilt beer drifted from the open doors of public houses. Sounds of a fiddle being tuned up from within reminded the Englishman that this was a nation as renowned for its music as for its fondness for spirited debate. These pleasant impressions could not distract Rowlands very long from his underlying thoughts, however. That these were of a similarly melancholy tendency to those of his companion was obvious from her next remark: 'It's not looking very hopeful, is it?'

'I don't know,' he replied. 'All the evidence is circumstantial. There's no actual proof that he – your husband – did what he's accused of.'

'No,' she said. 'There's no proof, as you say.' They had by now reached the Stag's Head, a large establishment, halfway along Temple Bar. 'We'll go in here,' said Lady Celia. It struck Rowlands, as they did so, that there was no pleasanter place than a pub at opening time, with its smells of tobacco and freshly poured beer, and its quiet hum of male voices – 'Well, Seamus. How's life treating you?' 'Grand, Tommy, grand. And yourself?' – interspersed by the click of dominoes. He and his companion made for the snug, however. 'We can talk in here,' she said, closing the glass door behind them. 'There's less chance of being disturbed than at Merrion Square.' When their drinks were in front of them – a pint of Guinness for him, and a glass of sherry for her – she fell silent for a moment.

'There's something you should know,' she said at last. Rowlands took a sip of his drink, and waited.

'I don't think the quarrel that night was about the

sale of the land,' said Lady Celia. 'In fact I'm sure it wasn't . . .' She broke off. 'I'm not sure I've got the courage to tell you.'

'Oh come now! It can't be so very dreadful.'

'All right,' she said. 'I'll tell you. But I'm afraid it will make you think badly of me . . . that is, if you don't already.'

'Lady Celia, I . . .' He was going to say that nothing she could tell him would do that but fell silent. It would only make an awkwardness between them, reviving feelings he had done his best to bury. 'Go on,' he said.

She took another sip of her drink, and set it down. 'Do you remember the last time we met?' she said. 'I don't mean at that party, I mean afterwards. It must have been the summer of 1931.'

'At the air race. Of course,' he said. 'You introduced us – my wife and I – to the gentleman who won the race. Flight-Lieutenant Howard, I think it was.'

'Bryan Howard, that's right. What a memory you've got!' He forbore from saying that whcre she was concerned, he remembered everything. Places they'd met. People with whom she'd had a connection. 'We were, well, *involved* at the time,' said Celia Swift flatly. 'It didn't last. He was a bit young, I suppose. Or I grew tired of going to watch him win races – perhaps both.' She lit a cigarette. 'Oh, sorry. Would you like one?' He said he'd smoke his own, if it was all the same to her. 'Yes, well, it ended a few months after that meeting. That autumn, I met Jolyon Swift, at a house party. In

Buckinghamshire, I think it was . . . not that it matters.'

She took a deep drag on her cigarette, and exhaled a mouthful of the aromatic smoke. 'We hit it off, rather. Jolyon is – or was – very amusing company. Things went on from there. For a week or so, it was rather fun.' Her tone had the brittle insouciance he recalled from past exchanges about previous affairs. 'But it came to an end, as these things do. I don't think either of us minded much. The following spring, I met Ned, at a point-to-point. It was rather a whirlwind courtship.' She gave a brief, unhappy laugh. 'When Ned makes up his mind to do something, it's very hard to dissuade him from doing it. Not that I wanted to,' she added quickly. 'Do you think I could have another one of these?'

'Of course. Amontillado all right?' She said it was, and he went to get it, deciding to limit himself to the one drink. After what he'd just heard, he felt he needed to keep a clear head. 'Are you telling me,' he said when he returned with her drink, 'that Lord Castleford knew nothing of your relationship with Mr Swift?'

She thought for a moment. 'Until lately, I'd have said just that.' She took a sip of her sherry and gave a little shudder as if it had suddenly become bitter. '*I* certainly haven't told him. After we were married, the question of my past *relationships*, as you so tactfully put it, didn't arise. Ned knew I'd been married before, and that there'd been other men since – as there had been other women before me, for him. It's something we agreed never to discuss. The past is the past – or so I thought.'

Again, she was silent. 'It might strike you as strange,' she said at last, 'that I didn't make the connection between them at first. Oh, I knew Ned had a half-brother somewhere, and that they were estranged, but it never occurred to me that it could be Jolyon. I mean, Swift isn't an uncommon name, in Ireland. Anyway,' she went on, 'nothing happened for a couple of years until, out of the blue, Jolyon wrote to say that he was getting married. Ned was very pleased that his wayward sibling had bothered to get in touch, and there was a rapprochement of sorts. It wasn't very long after the wedding that Jolyon brought Henrietta back with him to Ireland. They found a flat in Dublin to begin with, but after their child was born, they began to spend more and more time at Castleford. Jolyon's excuse was that he wanted to see more of his mother – Eveline was already living with us by then. What he really wanted was money,' she added bleakly.

Rowlands took this in. 'He was blackmailing you.'

'Yes.' Her voice had sunk to a whisper. 'There were letters I'd written to him. Nothing much in them – beyond the usual silly things that one says at such times – but the very fact of their existence was damning.' She took another sip of her drink. 'He – Jolyon – said if I didn't pay up, his conscience would force him to confess to Ned about our affair. He was gambling pretty heavily by then – even Henry had started to notice – and they'd had to let out their flat in Dublin to economise. Jolyon said that if I didn't give him what he needed to pay off his creditors, he'd have no choice but to involve Ned. So I paid him. It wasn't a lot of money, at first.'

'It never is – at first.'

'Just lately, he'd started to demand more. Of course I had some money of my own . . . but I knew that would run out eventually. It was one of the reasons I went over to England,' she said. 'I had to oversee the sale of some property. . . and set up that trust fund for your nephew,' she added. 'I was determined that Jolyon wasn't going to get his hands on *all* of it.'

'It must have been terrible for you,' said Rowlands gently. He felt a surge of anger against the dead man. Blackmail was one of the worst of crimes, in his opinion, laying waste to all the lives it touched. Driving its victims to suicide . . . and murder. In the same moment, a dreadful thought occurred to him, which he tried at once to suppress.

It seemed that Lady Celia had anticipated the thought, for she said gravely, 'The fact that Jolyon was blackmailing me gives me a motive for murder just as plausible as Ned's, don't you think, Frederick? And I won't deny that I often wished him – Jolyon – dead. But I didn't kill him,' she said. 'Although I'm afraid Ned thinks I did. That quarrel he and Jolyon had that night wasn't about the sale of the land at all. I think Jolyon told him about our affair. I think they quarrelled about me.'

Rowlands, taking this in, thought that it all made sense. Swift's violent outburst against his half-brother that night, and the amnesia that had followed it. One might have put it down to the blow on the head he had received as a result of his fall from the horse. Or it might simply have been because what had been said was too painful for him to want to remember it.

Nothing more was said on the subject until after they had left the Stag's Head and, having turned down Anglesea Street, began to walk back in the direction of Trinity College. At that time of day it was quiet, its boisterous crowds of undergraduates dispersed to lodging houses and pubs. 'So you think your husband knows about this?' said Rowlands after they had been walking for a while in silence.

'I'm afraid so,' was the reply. 'His whole manner towards me has changed – didn't you notice?' Rowlands said that he had not. 'Well, it has. He's become more . . . distant. It accounts for his refusal to do anything to save himself. He believes I did it. He'll let himself go to the gallows rather than give me away, the poor fool. Oh, Frederick, what *am* I going to do?'

They were surrounded at that moment by a gaggle of students, emerging from a nearby pub. 'I say,' cried one, overhearing this last remark. 'Things getting a bit hot, are they?'

'You mind your manners,' said Rowlands sternly. 'Come on,' he said, steering his companion away from the laughing crowd. 'Let's get out of here.'

The encounter, trivial as it was, seemed to have brought her to her senses, for she said in a calmer tone, 'You see *now* why I had to get away from the house. I couldn't run the risk of one of the servants overhearing . . . well, any of this.' He said that he did see. A few more minutes brought them to Merrion Square, and the end of all but the most general conversation. Lady Celia, sounding suddenly exhausted by the afternoon's events, said that she'd rest for an hour before dinner. Rowlands, too, was glad of a brief respite, and the chance to think over what he'd just learnt.

Chapter Eleven

The trial of Edward George Swift, Lord Castleford, began on the following Monday, 2nd October, in Court 1 of the Four Courts. Rowlands and the defendant's wife were in the public gallery to hear a plea of not guilty entered. It was Rowlands who persuaded him to go through with the farce, as Swift called it. 'Really, it hardly seems worth the waste of time and energy that will be expended in order to achieve the result of my being hanged,' he said, with the ghastly levity he had adopted in recent days. 'Isn't it better to call it quits, plead guilty, and take one's medicine like a man?'

'Better for you, perhaps,' said Rowlands. 'But surely worse for your wife and son, to have you branded a murderer.'

'Ah yes. My son,' said Swift sadly. 'Poor little devil. He hasn't deserved this.'

'No more have you, and you know it,' said Rowlands stoutly. 'You owe it to George – to both of them – not to give in to faintheartedness, but to stand up and fight.'

The other man laughed. It had a hollow sound. 'It's what we do, isn't it, we old soldiers?' said Swift. He sounded infinitely weary. 'All right. I'll go through with this charade, for George's sake.' He didn't mention his wife. 'But I'm telling you, old man, it won't end well.'

As Rowlands took his seat next to Lady Celia, a buzz of voices from the courtroom below told him that the defendant had just been brought up from the cells – a commotion quelled, a few moments after by a loud injunction to silence by the clerk of the court, heralding the arrival of the judge, Mr Justice Walsh. 'Ned looks quite calm,' whispered his companion to Rowlands as the hubbub subsided. Rowlands nodded, but did not reply, as the opening statement for the prosecution was beginning, and he didn't want to miss a word. Once before, years ago, he had sat in the public gallery at the Old Bailey to hear the evidence given in a murder trial by the woman who now sat at his side. Perhaps she recalled the same occasion, for she shivered slightly, although the courtroom was if anything too warm, and laid a gloved hand on his as if seeking reassurance.

'. . . that on the night of 19th August 1939, he did wilfully murder Jolyon Reginald Swift . . .'

So the sonorous phrases rolled on. Prosecuting counsel was a Mr Patrick Riordan, of whom Lady

Celia had said, on first glimpsing him in the corridor leading to Court 1, 'He looks like a fox. Sharp-featured. Clever. I hope our man's a match for him.'

It was Sir Anthony she'd meant. *He* was now rising to his feet to raise some point of law, his orotund delivery lending even his most trivial remarks an importance they might otherwise not have had. 'My lord . . . I am sure Your Lordship will find . . .' He was establishing in the minds of the jury that he and the presiding judge were on equal, if not intimate, terms. This was a case concerning an English gentleman – wrongfully accused, as it happened – who was being tried by others of his kind, under the obligation, disagreeable as it might be, of having to refute the fallacious evidence put forward by the Irish upstart Riordan. Rowlands wondered if this was an altogether wise strategy at a time in history when England and Ireland were once more at odds. He supposed the man must know his business, however, and settled down to listen to the evidence as the first witness was called to the witness box.

This was Inspector Byrne. Having been sworn in, he was invited by the prosecuting counsel to summarise the events of the fatal night, and the day that followed: 'Inspector, you were the officer called to the house on the morning of 20th August by Garda Flanagan, who was first on the scene, were you not?' Byrne confirmed that this was so. 'Good. I'd like you to tell the jury what you found on arriving at Castleford that morning. You may consult your notes if that would help you.'

Byrne did so. 'Having been informed by a telephone call from Sergeant Flanagan that the body of a man had been discovered, shot dead, in the garage adjacent to the property, I and my men proceeded to Castleford demesne, arriving at 9.55 a.m. After calling briefly at the house in order to notify the defendant's wife of our intentions, we – Sergeant Rooney and I – went to the garage where we found the body of a man of about thirty-five years old, slumped in the driver's seat of a motorcar that I later ascertained was registered in his name: that is, Mr J. R. Swift. On a cursory examination of the body, it appeared to me that the deceased had been shot through the head. Leaving Sergeant Rooney on guard outside the garage, I then interviewed the chauffeur, Patrick Connolly, who had discovered the body at around half past eight that morning. Connolly said that he had entered the garage as usual—'

'That's all right, Inspector,' interrupted Riordan. 'You need not tell us what Mr Connolly said, as he will tell us himself, in due course. Confine yourself to your own account, if you please.'

'Yes, sir,' said Byrne, in the colourless voice he had employed throughout. 'After speaking to Connolly, I returned to the house and questioned several members of the household, including Doctor O'Leary, who examined the body, the elderly gentleman . . . I mean, Canon Wetherby, and Mr Frederick Rowlands – both of whom had viewed the body. I needn't go into detail about their evidence, either, need I?'

'No, indeed. A brief account will do very well,' replied Riordan to the policeman, who continued after a moment.

'Having asked to speak to His Lordship – that is, the defendant – I was told by Her Ladyship that he was unconscious, following a fall from his horse earlier that day. I later discovered, from a witness, that this mishap might have been caused deliberately. I asked the witness, Mr Rowlands, to produce evidence of this, and he did so. I then spoke to Her Ladyship, and to several other members of the household.'

'That would include the servants, would it not?'

'My sergeant questioned the servants,' replied Byrne. 'Everyone who had been present during the crucial hours was interrogated as to their movements.'

'And what of the defendant?' persisted Riordan. 'Were you able to question him, too, eventually?'

'I was, sir. Around two hours after my arrival, Lord Castleford – the defendant – had recovered sufficiently from his injuries to give me a statement.' He was silent a moment, so that it appeared to Rowlands, and to the rest of those listening, that he had come to the end of his evidence. But then he said, 'Will I tell the court of what was said when the defendant came out of his room, immediately after his recovery?'

'Since you heard what was said at first hand, Inspector, I think that is quite in order,' replied the counsel for the prosecution.

'Very well, sir.' Byrne cleared his throat before proceeding. 'Sergeant Rooney and I were discussing our findings that morning in the room – His Lordship's study – which had been allocated to our use, when we heard a commotion outside the door. Emerging into the hall, we found the defendant, apparently recovered, and several other members of the household, including the deceased's wife, Mrs Henrietta Swift, and his mother, Lady Eveline. Both ladies were distressed, having just heard the news of Mr Swift's demise – Mrs Swift going so far as to accuse Lord Castleford of his murder—'

'Can you tell us exactly what was said?' interrupted Riordan.

'I can, sir.' Byrne must have consulted his notes once more. 'Mrs Swift said: "I heard you. We *all* heard you. You said, 'If you come near me again, I'll kill you.' And so you did. Murderer."' A silence followed this rendition of the scene Rowlands himself had witnessed. Stripped of all drama by the inspector's flat, emotionless voice, it nevertheless created a stir in the courtroom.

'Silence,' said the clerk, in response to this.

'Go on, Inspector,' said Riordan once quiet had been restored, his dry tones conveying nothing of the satisfaction he must have been feeling at this coup de théâtre.

'I then asked to speak to Lord Castleford – the defendant,' Byrne went on. 'He accompanied me into the study to give his statement.'

'Thank you, Inspector,' said Riordan. 'I think you may stand down unless my learned friend has any questions for you?'

'I do have one question, as it happens,' said Sir Anthony, rising to his feet. 'If you'll permit me, my lord?' This to the judge, who told him to proceed. 'Thank you, my lord. Inspector Byrne,' he continued, his tone becoming markedly less unctuous as he addressed the Gardai officer. 'You have described your investigations into the sad death of Mr Swift with admirable thoroughness. I am sure you left no stone unturned when it came to collecting hard evidence of this terrible crime.' He laid a particular stress on the phrase 'hard evidence' as if to emphasise that nothing less would satisfy *him*. 'Is it not the case that, up until the scene you have just described, you had no particular suspect in mind for the murder of Mr Swift?'

Byrne took his time before answering. 'I had not then completed my investigations, that is true,' he said.

'And is it not the case,' said Sir Anthony, 'that it was not until Mrs Swift's hysterical intervention—'

'My lord,' said Riordan. 'I must protest. The inspector said nothing of hysteria.'

'I withdraw the word. It was not until Mrs Swift's *distressed* intervention that you, Inspector, began to consider my client as a potential suspect?'

'I was bound to consider him,' said Byrne coolly. 'Since he was one of those most intimately related to the deceased.'

'And yet, by your own admission,' said the counsel for the defence, 'Lord Castleford had been lying unconscious – close to death – for several hours before your arrival at Castleford. Surely he was the *last* person you should have suspected of carrying out this brutal crime?'

But if Sir Anthony had hoped to throw the inspector off his stride, he was disappointed. 'The medical evidence indicated that Mr Swift had died the previous night,' said Byrne. 'Therefore the defendant would have been quite capable of carrying out the murder at some time during the hours *before* he took the fall from his horse. I saw no reason to exclude him from my investigations,' he added, his tone as unemotional as it had been throughout.

It wasn't the tactical victory the defence counsel might have hoped for, thought Rowlands, but it *had* placed a doubt in the jury's collective mind. Had the good inspector's judgement been unconsciously affected by the ravings of a hysterical woman? He began to see the way Sir Anthony intended to conduct the case for the defence. Undermining the prosecution's case by implying that it wasn't based on hard evidence, but on prejudice and supposition, wasn't a strong defensive strategy, but in the absence of anything else, it would have to do.

The Gardai officer's evidence was followed by that of Doctor O'Leary, who had first examined the body, and by the police surgeon, Doctor Feeny, when he had carried out the post-mortem. Nothing of much interest arose from these grim testimonies, aside from the bare facts that the death had been by gunshot, and would have been instantaneous (a fact no doubt of consolation to the bereaved), and that the contents of the deceased's stomach had included a fair quantity of alcohol. Time of death was established as having taken place between two o'clock and four o'clock on the morning of 20th August. An attempt by the counsel for the defence, during his cross-questioning of the family doctor, to turn the minds of the jury towards the injuries Lord Castleford had incurred as a result of his riding accident that day was quashed by the judge. 'We are here to consider the cause of death of Mr Jolyon Swift – not whether the defendant was suffering from concussion,' he admonished Sir Anthony, who apologised for leading the jury down this path.

Apologies or not, thought Rowlands, he had once more succeeded in reminding the jury that the defendant himself had been the victim of a murder attempt. Whether that would count for much once the rest of the evidence had been heard, remained to be seen. A ballistics expert named Rutherford was the next to be called, and gave as his opinion that it was a .38 revolver – a Webley Mark VI – that had fired the fatal bullet, and that it was this gun that had been produced in court. The fact that this weapon belonged to the defendant caused a mild sensation in the public gallery as those seated around them digested the information already known to Rowlands and his companion. 'Ah, so 'twas himself's gun,' muttered a man sitting behind them to his friend. 'Stands to reason it was himself who pulled the trigger, does it not?'

Fortunately, before Lady Celia could summon up a suitably withering riposte to this casual slur on her husband's name, the judge announced that the court would rise. 'Come on,' said Rowlands. 'Let's get a breath of air.'

Since the court was not due to reconvene until two o'clock, there would have been time for the two of them to return to Merrion Square for a bite of lunch, but Lady Celia said she wasn't hungry. 'Let's walk, shall we?' she said. 'I feel as if I've been sitting in that beastly courtroom forever. Poor Ned looked as if he were facing a firing squad. He must be hating every moment – having his private life trampled over by these people.'

It would only get worse, Rowlands knew (and she must have known it, too), but he said nothing, only giving her his arm as they began to pace slowly along the quayside. 'I'm sure he thinks I did it,' she burst out after a moment or two. 'It's why he wanted to plead guilty. Thank God you dissuaded him from that,' she added with a shudder.

'I'm sure he thinks nothing of the kind—' Rowlands began to say, but she cut across him.

'I can't *ask* him, do you see? Because that would

mean confessing to the affair with Jolyon – and if there's a chance he *doesn't* know, then I don't want to have to tell him.' Her argument, though flawed, made a kind of sense, thought Rowlands. Like his wife, Swift might prefer to leave what had happened between her and his half-brother in the realm of possibility rather than actuality. Denial was often the best form of defence against unpalatable facts.

They crossed the river by the Grattan Bridge, and were soon once more in Temple Bar. Here, the pubs were just opening, admitting straggling queues of regulars to their beer-smelling interiors. 'I need a drink,' said Lady Celia suddenly. 'Terrible of me, I know, but I don't think I can get through the rest of the afternoon without some Dutch courage.' The establishment into which they turned was smaller and more crowded than the Stag's Head had been, and Rowlands was momentarily afraid that the presence of a woman – especially one who was obviously a lady – might excite comment from the clientele. Happily for his peace of mind, the talk from those propping up the bar was of a rugby match that had taken place the previous day while another group, ensconced at a corner table, debated the merits or otherwise of a racehorse called Beginner's Luck, and whether placing a bet on the same would be a sound investment, or no.

Even so, Rowlands was relieved when, having finished her sherry, his companion said that she'd like to get back. They were far enough from the Four

Courts for her not to have been recognised by anyone who'd been in the public gallery that day, but she was still conspicuous, if only because of her beauty, and the way she was dressed – silk dresses and furs not being typical wear for the denizens of Temple Bar public houses, he supposed. He downed his half of bitter, and was following her out onto the street when he heard a muttered comment from one of the men standing at the bar: 'Not often you see the likes o' *that* in Malone's Bar, is it, now?'

And the reply: 'Know who that is? Her man's the one who's up for killing his brother.' So the story *had* spread. He hoped she hadn't heard the remark, which would only confirm her worst fears.

The first of the afternoon's witnesses to be sworn in was Patsy Connolly, who seemed nervous and ill at ease, stumbling over the oath, and addressing the prosecuting counsel instead of the judge as 'my lord'. Yes, he had been the man who found the body – 'A terrible sight. Terrible,' he opined, and would have said more if Riordan had not told him to confine himself to the facts. It had been around half past eight that he had made his discovery. He had been going to clean His Lordship's car, as he always did, and . . .

'Just the pertinent facts, Mr Connolly, if you please,' said Riordan. There was a pause while the chauffeur made an effort to call these to mind. He had seen at once that the man – Mr Jolyon – was dead.

No, he had never seen a dead man before, but it was obvious. The blood . . . Poor Patsy shuddered at the memory. 'Thank you, Mr Connolly, that will be all,' said Riordan, then, at a signal from his opposite number: 'Stay there, if you please. My learned friend has some questions for you.'

Sir Anthony rose to his feet. 'Mr Connolly.' His tone was kindly. 'I wonder if you can help me? You say that it was your custom, every morning, to clean His Lordship's vehicle before it was called into use each day – am I right in that assumption?'

Connolly confirmed that this was so.

'Thank you. That is very clear. And was it also your habit to clean the, ah, *other* vehicles in the garage? For instance, Mr Swift's car.'

The chauffeur seemed nonplussed by the question.

'To put it, ah, more *succinctly* . . .' Sir Anthony was at his most mellifluous. 'Did you, or did you not, clean Mr Swift's car – the Talbot, that is – the morning before the, ah, tragedy?'

Connolly seemed to infer from this that he was being criticised for *not* doing so. It wasn't his job to see to the other cars, he said, sounding affronted. Sometimes he'd give them a rub-down if it was called for, but . . .

'Quite,' said the counsel for the defence, with some satisfaction. 'So what you're saying is that Mr Swift's vehicle would *not* have been cleaned in the days leading up to his, ah, unfortunate demise unless he'd specifically requested it. Is that correct?' The chauffeur, now thoroughly discomfited, said that it was. But his duties lay with His Lordship's car, not with any of the others.

'Sir Anthony, is this going anywhere?' said the judge wearily.

'My lord, I merely want to establish a fact,' was the reply. 'Mr Connolly has now done so. I have no further questions for the witness.' Which might have mystified anyone unfamiliar with the rest of the evidence, thought Rowlands, but was a deft ploy on the part of the defence. Because if Jolyon Swift's car hadn't been cleaned in the days before the murder, then any fingerprints found on the body of the car might have been placed there at any time, and therefore had no bearing on the crime. In this way, and by increments, Sir Anthony was undermining the case for the prosecution. Whether the cumulative wearing-away of evidence would affect the outcome of the trial remained to be seen. And the evidence of Ned Swift's fingerprints being found on Jolyon Swift's car was far from being the most damning in the case.

'I should now like to return to the night of the murder, my lord,' said Riordan, in his precise, even tones – a sharp contrast to Sir Anthony's more theatrical delivery. As he listened to these introductory remarks – setting the scene, he supposed one would call it – Rowlands tried to form a mental picture of the man, for his own amusement. A 'foxy' type, hadn't

Celia Swift said? He envisaged a narrow face, with deep-set, watchful eyes, and a sandy colouring. A wiry build. That, too, would offer a piquant contrast to the tall, full-fleshed figure of the defence counsel. Rowlands shook himself out of these enjoyable, but useless, speculations in time to hear the swearing-in of one John Cavanagh. It took him a moment to recognise the voice as one belonging to the Castleford manservant – Rowlands had never been quite sure what his function in the household was. Footman? Under-butler? At any rate, he, along with the other servants, Rowlands supposed, had been present on the night in question – taking charge of the guests' coats, serving drinks in the drawing room and, later, handing round the food at table.

'Mr Cavanagh, you have been in the employ of Lord Castleford for a number of years, I believe?'

'I have, sir. Four years, come Candlemas.'

'Thank you. And during that time, you have received a good report of your work, have you not?'

'Yes, sir.'

'Good. So that there could be no justification in saying that you had reason to dislike – or indeed, hold a grudge against – your master?'

'No indeed, sir. Master was always very fair in his dealings with all of us.'

'By "all of us" you mean yourself and the other servants?'

'I do, sir.'

'Thank you, Mr Cavanagh. I wanted to establish that – just to make it clear that you are an impartial observer.' Rowlands began to see where this was going. Riordan certainly was a sly fox, spiking the defence counsel's guns like that. 'And now, I want you to cast your mind back to the night of Saturday, 19th August. You were waiting at the dinner table that evening, I believe?'

'Yes, sir. I always help out when there are guests.'

'As there were that night, I understand?'

Cavanagh answered in the affirmative. 'Good,' said Riordan. 'And was there anything about the *early* part of the evening that stays in your mind as having been at all untoward, or unusual?'

'Well . . .' The man hesitated a moment before continuing. 'Not to say it was unusual, but Mr Jolyon was quite free with his wine. I noticed because it was my job to go round the table, filling up as needed . . .' Another pause. 'It seemed to me that Mr Jolyon's glass needed filling more often than the rest.'

'I see. And did this cause any unpleasantness?'

'I don't follow, sir.'

'Let me be clearer. Did Mr Swift's heavy drinking bring about a quarrel between him and Lord Castleford?'

'Not as such, sir. But the master must've said something to Mr Monckton about it, 'cause he told me to go easy when filling Mr Jolyon's glass.'

The counsel for the defence was already on his feet.

'Yes, yes, quite right, Sir Anthony,' said the judge. 'Mr Riordan, as you well know, that is hearsay, and can't be allowed. The jury will disregard what the witness alleges was said to Mr Monckton – he's the butler, I assume? You must confine yourself to what was said to *you*,' he added to Cavanagh, who mumbled something unintelligible.

'I apologise, my lord,' said Riordan. 'I merely wanted to establish for the benefit of the jury something of the mood of the occasion.' The counsel for the prosecution sounded highly pleased with what he had 'established' so far: the fact that the mood had been quarrelsome, with Swift (allegedly) forbidding his half-brother any more wine. Oh yes, he was a clever old fox, thought Rowlands.

'Can we please get on?' said Mr Justice Walsh irritably.

'My lord,' murmured Riordan, then turning once more to the witness: 'I now want to come to the *latter* part of the evening of 19th August – the few moments when the gentlemen who had been seated in the dining room began to move towards the drawing room, to join the ladies. You were present in the room when this was going on, were you not?'

'In the room, and out of it, sir,' was the reply. 'I opened the door for the gentlemen when they rose from table, and remained behind to start clearing away.'

'While you were thus engaged, did you hear Mr Swift say anything to Lord Castleford while both were still in the room?'

'I did, sir. He – Mr Jolyon – said "I must speak to you, Ned." That's the master's name in the family,' he added as if apologising for the liberty.

'And what did Lord Castleford say in reply?'

'He said, "Not now, Joly. You're half-cut. Can't it wait until tomorrow?" And Mr Jolyon said—'

'One moment, Mr Cavanagh. Did this exchange take place while you were in the dining room?'

'Well, in the room and out of it, like I said, sir,' replied the manservant. 'His Lordship had gone out of the room by this time, and Mr Jolyon was following him out into the hall. I got the impression he was trying to shake him off.'

'Lord Castleford, you mean?'

'Yes, sir. He – the master – said something to Mr Langton about having forgot to introduce him to the blind gentleman . . . Mr Rowlands, I mean.'

'And you were able to hear all this from within the dining room?'

'Well, sir, the door was open.'

'Quite so. You were therefore able to hear what Mr Swift said, following the exchange between Lord Castleford and his two guests, were you not?'

'I was, sir. Mr Jolyon followed the master across the hall, and said something like "It's *got* to be tonight . . ." – or it might have been "You *must* see me tonight." I couldn't exactly make it out.'

'The gentlemen were too far away, perhaps?'

'No, sir. It was only that Mr Jolyon's speech was a bit thick. From the drink, like,' said Cavanagh unhappily.

'I see. And what did your master – Lord Castleford – say in response to his brother's plea?'

Sir Anthony rose once more. 'My lord, as my learned friend well knows, Jolyon Swift was Lord Castleford's *half*-brother.'

'Thank you, Sir Anthony. Mr Riordan, we must endeavour to be precise.'

'Of course, my lord.' To the witness: 'What did Lord Castleford say to his half-brother?'

'He said, "All right. You'd better come into my study."'

'Which is where the two men went?'

'Yes, sir. I heard the study door close.'

'The rest of the party having gone into the drawing room?' This, too, was confirmed. 'What did you do then, Mr Cavanagh – once the gentlemen had left the dining room?'

'Well, sir, having loaded up the tray with the cheese plates and knives, and glasses – for the port, you see – I carried it through into the hall towards the scullery, for the maids to wash up.'

'I assume this took several journeys?'

'Two, sir. I had only to clear the crockery and glassware. The maids would see to the rest.'

'And did these two journeys take you past the door of the study where Lord Castleford and Mr Swift were closeted?'

'They did, sir.'

'Can you tell the court what you heard?'

'The first time or the second time, sir?'

'Begin with the first.' Riordan's tone was quiet, as it had been throughout this series of exchanges. There was no need to amplify the drama of what the footman was saying.

'I didn't hear too much, the first time,' said Cavanagh. 'I was in a hurry to clear, and the door was shut. I don't listen at doors,' he added sternly. 'All I could hear was the sound of voices. Angry, they were. That was the way of it. Once, I heard His Lordship shout something like "You scoundrel!" or maybe it was "You infernal scoundrel!" – but like I said, I didn't stop to listen to more.'

The courtroom sat as if spellbound. You could have heard a pin drop. 'And the second time?' Riordan barely had to raise his voice.

The servant drew an audible breath and let it out. 'The second time was a few minutes after – say ten minutes. I'd taken my tray to the scullery and . . . and passed a few remarks with one of the other servants.' It was pretty clear from Cavanagh's sheepish tone that the other servant had been female. 'Mr Monckton says to me to get on with my work, because they'd be wanting their drinks in the drawing room soon, the ladies and gentlemen. So I returned to the dining room, and loaded up the tray as before. Just as I came out into the hall, I saw the blind gentleman, Mr Rowlands, coming downstairs. Then the door of the study was flung open and Mr Jolyon came rushing out. "I'll not stay," he cries, "to be insulted." And then the master follows him out, looking very angry. "Get out o' my sight," he says. "Or by heaven I'll kill ye . . .""

Chapter Twelve

Worse was to come on the second day of the trial. It had begun undramatically enough, with the evidence of the Castleford servants following on from that of John Cavanagh. Much of this merely confirmed the chief points in the footman's evidence. The fact that Mr Jolyon had been drinking heavily, and that this was not an unusual occurrence. The fact that the master and Mr Jolyon had quarrelled (Mary, the parlourmaid, who had been passing through the hall on her way to tidy the dining room after John had cleared away, said that she had also heard the fateful words spoken by her master to his relative). Having established in the minds of the jury that matters between Ned Swift and his half-brother had reached boiling point, the counsel for the prosecution proceeded to confirm the notion of the former as having been the aggressor in the quarrel, by calling Sebastian Gogarty. According to Lady Celia (in a whispered aside to Rowlands), he had disappeared from Castleford a few days after her husband's arrest, and had not been heard of since.

Now he aired his grievance against his former employer in the witness box. 'Mr Gogarty, you were employed by Lord Castleford from the beginning of May this year to the end of August, were you not?'

'I was.' The young man's voice was so subdued that Riordan had to ask him to speak up.

'What was it you were employed to do?'

'I was c-cataloguing his – that is, Lord C-Castleford's – library.'

'I see. And during this time – four months – you must have formed an opinion of your employer.'

'My lord,' protested the counsel for the defence.

'Quite so, Sir Anthony. Mr Riordan, does this have a bearing on the case?'

'I hope to show that it does, my lord. But I will rephrase the question. Mr Gogarty, what was your opinion of Lord Castleford?'

'I thought he was a b-blackguard.' The shocked murmur that went around the courtroom at this blunt judgement was instantly quashed by the usher.

'How did you come to this conclusion?' Riordan's tone was as emotionless as ever. 'You must have had reasons for disliking the defendant.'

'I did. I . . . I thought him arrogant and h-high-handed.'

'I see. And was this high-handedness, as you call it, displayed only towards you yourself, or was it apparent in Lord Castleford's behaviour towards other members of the household?'

'It was.'

'Can you be more specific?'

Gogarty hesitated as if reluctant to commit himself. Then he burst out: 'Jolyon Swift was one. It s-seemed to me that he h-hated him.'

'By "he" you mean the defendant?'

'Yes.'

'Mr Gogarty, I should like to turn to the events of the night of 19th August. You were amongst the guests in the drawing room when the quarrel between Lord Castleford and Mr Swift we have heard described took place, I understand?' Gogarty confirmed that this was so. 'You heard the words that were said by Lord Castleford – words constituting a threat, one might reasonably suppose?'

'I d-did – and it *was* a threat,' said the librarian, provoking another murmur in the courtroom.

'Very well. I think the jury will have understood that. I would now like you to describe your movements in the hours that followed this incident. You left the drawing room, did you not?'

'I . . . I w-went outside for a b-breath of air.'

'Outside on the terrace, you mean?'

'Yes.' The young man's voice had lost its vehemence. Now it was hesitant, as if he regretted having exposed himself to such public scrutiny. Perhaps, thought Rowlands, he was remembering the embarrassing scene that had taken place on the terrace.

'But you did not remain there, did you?' Riordan was saying. 'You went for a walk.'

'I w-wanted to clear my head,' said Gogarty. 'I w-walked up the lane for a few minutes – a quarter of an hour . . . or p-perhaps longer. I lost track of time.'

'So it was between fifteen minutes and half an hour later, at the outside, that you met Lord Castleford, coming along the lane in the opposite direction?'

'Yes. He m-must have been coming from the home farm.'

'And did you have any conversation with him?'

'I did. I . . . I t-told him what I thought of him.'

'As a result of which, he struck you, did he not?'

'He d-did. But I h-hit him first,' said Gogarty proudly.

This was perhaps not quite the impression Riordan had intended to leave with the jury. He went on smoothly: 'During this scuffle, did you form an impression of the defendant's state of mind?'

'My lord . . .'

'Yes, Sir Anthony. You will have your chance to question the witness in due course. Go on, Mr, ah, Gogarty.'

'I . . . I w-wasn't thinking of anything much,' admitted Gogarty sheepishly. 'Except trying to p-pick myself up.'

'He knocked you down, then?'

'Yes . . . He . . . he s-seemed furious about s-something. As if . . . as if he'd have liked to k-kill me. Or s-somebody else,' said Gogarty.

'Thank you, Mr Gogarty, you may remain there,' said Riordan. 'My learned friend has some questions for you.'

'Mr Gogarty . . .' The counsel for the defence could not have sounded more affable. 'You have told the court that you were employed by Lord Castleford for a period of around four months – you came straight from your studies at Trinity College, I believe?' Gogarty agreed that this was so. 'During those four months – between May and August this year – you became very much a member of the household, I gather? Taking your meals with the family, passing your evenings with them, and spending your working hours in the library – is that correct?'

'Well, I was c-cataloguing the books,' said Gogarty, perhaps a bit too glibly, for Sir Anthony allowed a pause to ensue before replying, 'Quite so.'

Another pause, during which there was no sound but that of Sir Anthony rustling his papers.

'My lord,' he said at last. 'With your permission, I should like to show this document – a handwritten note – to the witness.'

'Proceed, Sir Anthony.'

The piece of paper was duly passed to Gogarty while the rest of those in the courtroom speculated as to what it said. 'Mr Gogarty,' said the counsel for the defence, in his sonorous accents. 'Do you recognise the handwriting on this, ah, note?'

'Y-yes.' Gogarty's cocksure manner had deserted him. 'It's m-mine.'

'Excellent. Will you read what it says to the court?'

'I . . . It's p-private,' blustered the youth. 'I don't s-see why I have to . . .'

'Read it, Mr Gogarty.'

'I . . . Oh, very w-well.' Gogarty dropped his voice so that it was barely audible. '"*I m-must see you,*"' he read.

'Louder, Mr Gogarty. I don't think the jury can hear you.'

'"*I . . . must . . . see . . . you,*"' read the witness again, between gritted teeth. '"*I can't b-bear it any longer . . .*"'

'Thank you, Mr Gogarty. And to whom was that note addressed?'

'I . . . I d-don't remember.'

'Then let me help you. It was addressed to your employer's wife, Lady Celia, was it not?'

A murmur of surprise went around the packed courtroom. Beside him, Rowlands heard his companion gasp. 'How on earth . . . ?' she whispered. 'I thought I'd thrown it away.'

'I . . .' Gogarty seemed momentarily to have lost his voice.

'Answer the question, Mr Gogarty. Was it, or was

it not, addressed to Lady Celia?'

'You can't p-prove anything of the kind,' said the young man defiantly.

'Oh, but I can,' said the counsel for the defence. 'This note was retrieved from the wastepaper basket in Lady Celia's office by another member of the household, who passed it to me.'

'I can't believe it of Mary or Biddy,' murmured Lady Celia to Rowlands. 'They'd never have done such a thing.'

'You'll admit that the note suggests a certain intimacy . . .' began Sir Anthony, when there was an angry intervention from the defendant: 'This is outrageous! I won't have it, do you hear?'

'Lord Castleford.' It was the judge who spoke. 'You are not permitted to speak.'

'Poppycock! I won't sit here and listen to my wife being slandered.'

'Lord Castleford, if you say anything more, I will have you taken down. Sir Anthony, is this really necessary?'

'My lord, the last thing I intended was to give offence,' said the counsel for the defence blandly. 'I merely wished to make a point.'

'Well, get on and do it,' said Mr Justice Walsh, with some acerbity.

'Very well, my lord. Mr Gogarty,' the barrister went on, in a less emollient tone. 'I should now like you to turn your mind to the night of 19th August. You were among the guests gathered in the drawing room after dinner in order to play cards, were you not? But you were not yourself playing cards.'

'I dislike c-card games,' said the young man coldly. 'They s-seem to me to be a w-waste of time.'

'Indeed. And so you occupied yourself with some other distraction, I take it?'

'I was reading,' said Gogarty. 'Byron's *Verses*, if you m-must know.'

'But you were not reading the *whole* evening, I gather?' said Sir Anthony, in a silkily insinuating voice. 'At just before midnight, you went out onto the terrace, did you not?'

'I've already s-said so. I n-needed a breath of air.'

'Quite so. But you did not find yourself *alone* on the terrace, did you?' pursued the other. 'You had, in fact, followed another member of the party – your employer's wife, Lady Celia – in order to speak to her, am I not correct?'

'I . . . I d-don't recall,' said Gogarty.

'Oh *come* now, Mr Gogarty! You can't expect the court to believe that! You followed her onto the terrace with the express purpose of making a declaration of love to her, is that not also correct?'

'No! That is, I d-don't remember what I s-said.'

'You were overheard, Mr Gogarty. I need not give your words verbatim, need I? But the person who heard them is willing to swear to what you said.'

'I . . . I m-might have said s-something of the kind,

I suppose,' said the unfortunate youth. 'I was a bit lit up that night.'

'So it would seem,' said Sir Anthony. Having successfully undermined the witness's credibility – for who would take seriously Gogarty's disparaging remarks about his employer, now that his juvenile crush on his employer's wife had been exposed? The counsel for the defence said he had no further questions, and the witness was told he might step down.

'It wasn't I who gave him away,' murmured Rowlands to Lady Celia.

'I know. The silly boy was making an exhibition of himself,' she replied. 'He might have been overheard by any one of the people in that room.' Although it struck Rowlands that only those seated near to the open French windows would have been in a position to hear exactly what was said. 'Ned will be furious about this,' went on Lady Celia as the courtroom settled down. 'He hates having his dirty linen washed in public.'

'It's hardly that,' said Rowlands. 'Neither he, nor you, can be blamed if a foolish young man lets himself be carried away by his feelings.'

'I suppose not,' she said. 'But there's always the thought that I might be to blame, for having encouraged Sebastian's attentions.'

'Well, you didn't,' he replied. 'I can vouch for that.'

'Ah, but . . .' she began to say when the court was called to order. *But what?* he wondered. Had she been about to say that his reliability as a witness was compromised by his own feelings for her? That the fact that he had been in love with her for years meant he could be trusted no more than that silly youth could be trusted where she was concerned? He was still brooding over this when the next witness was called.

This turned out to be another 'expert': a forensic scientist, it transpired. He (Rowlands failed to catch his name) gave as his opinion that the blood found on an item of clothing – a single leather glove – was identical with that of the dead man. The glove was produced, and the witness identified it as the one he had been asked to examine. The production in court of this object – as had happened with the gun – caused a frisson of horrified interest to go around the room.

'Silence!' said the usher.

The next witness was called. It was Monckton, the Castleford butler, sounding more wooden and on-his-dignity than ever as he took the oath, and confirmed his name – Joseph Henry Monckton – his occupation and the number of years he had been in the defendant's employ. 'You were presiding in your capacity as butler over the dinner which took place on 19th August, were you not?'

'I was, sir.'

'So you were present in the dining room all the time that this was going on, I take it?'

'Well, yes, sir,' said Monckton. 'Except for the times when I returned to the kitchen quarters to see what was happening about the next course.'

'Duly noted, Mr Monckton. But you had an opportunity to hear what was going on for much of the time – for example, any words spoken between your master, Lord Castleford, and his half-brother, Mr Swift – did you not?'

'I . . . I suppose so.'

'A little louder, Mr Monckton. The jury needs to be able to hear your replies clearly.'

'Yes. I mean, I did.'

'Thank you. And will your tell the court exactly what was said by Lord Castleford to Mr Swift?'

Monckton hesitated. 'He . . . His Lordship . . . said something to the effect that he thought Mr Jolyon was drinking too much, and that—'

'Can you give us his exact words?'

'I . . . I think he said, "You're putting it away rather fast, aren't you, Jo?"'

'And what did Mr Swift say to that?'

'He . . . he said that was his business, and that His Lordship should mind his.'

'Exact words again, if you please.'

'"Don't come the big brother with me! I'll drink as much as I please . . ."' Monckton was sounding increasingly miserable, Rowlands thought. Riordan, however, sounded more and more pleased with himself. 'Thank you, Mr Monckton. And what was the outcome of this conversation?'

'I . . . I don't follow, sir.'

'Did Lord Castleford say or do anything after this which might have had a bearing on Mr Swift's heavy drinking?'

'I see what you mean, sir. Yes, he called me over, and told me not to serve Mr Jolyon any more wine.'

'With what result?'

'Sir?'

'I mean,' said Riordan. 'Did this injunction have any effect on Mr Swift's consumption of wine?'

'I see, sir. No, it did not. He – Mr Jolyon – was sitting close to the sideboard, on which the decanters were set out, and so he could help himself to drink. He . . . well, it was obvious that by the end of the evening that he was the worse for it.'

'Thank you, Mr Monckton. I think we can get the picture. I now want you to turn your thoughts towards the morning of 20th August. A Sunday, was it not?' Monckton agreed that this was so. 'You were on hand to answer the door when William Baines, chauffeur to Mr Langton, arrived at the house at around 4.30 p.m., I understand?'

'I was, sir. I . . . I happened to hear the car arrive as I was passing though the hall, and so thought it would save time to open the front door in order to see what Mr Baines wanted.'

'I see.' Riordan allowed the import of what Monckton had said to sink in. 'Was there a particular reason why you expected to see Mr Baines that afternoon, then?'

'I . . .' Again, the butler hesitated. 'I thought perhaps he might have brought a message from Mr Langton I would have to attend to.' It was a valiant attempt to cover up the real reason why Monckton had been hanging about in the hall, thought Rowlands – but it didn't wash with the counsel for the prosecution.

'I put it to you, Mr Monckton, that you were in fact *waiting* for Mr Langton's car to arrive, because your mistress had received a telephone call from *Mrs* Langton to say that the car was on its way – and that as soon as you heard it pull up outside, you rushed out of the front door in order to intercept Mr Baines before anybody else could. Isn't that the truth of the matter?'

'If you want to put it like that, sir.'

'I *do* put it like that, Mr Monckton. You had a particular reason for wanting to catch Mr Baines, did you not? You were lying in wait for the Langtons' chauffeur because he had something to give you. Something you were very anxious that none of the other servants should see.' Riordan now addressed one of the court officials. 'Please hand Mr Monckton Exhibit B.' This was done, and he turned again to the witness: 'Mr Monckton, do you recognise this glove?'

'I . . . I believe so, sir.'

'This is the glove you were waiting for Mr Baines to bring you – the glove that, as we shall hear, he found on the steps of the house when he returned to Castleford late the night before in search of Mrs

Langton's diamond earring. That was why you were waiting for him, wasn't it?'

'I . . .'

'Answer the question, Mr Monckton,' said the judge.

'I thought perhaps the glove was one I had been looking for,' said poor Monckton, cornered.

'And was it?' said Riordan coldly.

'Yes,' was the reply – almost inaudible to those sitting in the public gallery.

'Thank you, Mr Monckton. You had been looking for the glove, you say? Presumably you had its fellow in your possession?'

'Yes. I . . .'

'The pair belonged to Lord Castleford, did it not?'

Monckton must have nodded, without speaking, for the judge said, not unkindly, 'You must speak up so that the jury can hear you, Mr Monckton.'

'Yes, Your Honour . . . I mean, my lord.' Nothing revealed the butler's state of mind more cruelly than the fact that he, generally a stickler for correct forms of address, had got the judge's title wrong. 'The gloves belong to His Lordship,' he added unhappily.

'Lord Castleford, you mean?' This was confirmed. 'And the gloves – just to make it clear for the benefit of the jury – were the ones the defendant had missed that very morning as he prepared to go out for his ride, is that not correct?'

'Yes, sir.'

'The very same gloves,' repeated Riordan slowly. 'One of which lies before you – stained with the blood of the deceased, Mr Swift. That concludes my questions for the witness, my lord.' Sir Anthony had no further questions.

'In which case,' said Mr Justice Walsh, 'we will leave calling the next witness' – this would be Baines, Rowlands surmised – 'until after lunch. Let us reconvene at two.'

'That was pretty bloody,' said Celia Swift as she and Rowlands emerged into the chill October wind that blew along the quayside. 'Poor Monckton did his best, but he only made things look worse for Ned, with his prevarications. That business with the glove put the lid on it.'

'They can't prove it was Lord Castleford who was wearing the glove – or that it was he who fired the gun,' said Rowlands. 'The evidence is all circumstantial.'

'Maybe so. But it still looks pretty bleak.' They began to walk along the riverside, with no clear idea of where they were headed. 'If only,' she said, 'there was definite proof that Ned *couldn't* have done it. Or proof that somebody else *did*.' But that, as they both knew, was going to be hard to find, two months after the event.

The question of the blood-stained glove – who had found it, and what was done with it – formed the substance of the examination of the next two witnesses, the first of whom was the chauffeur, William Baines, as Rowlands had anticipated. His account added little to what had already been said by Monckton. Yes, Madam had sent him back to Castleford from Slaney Park (that was the Langtons' place) sometime after two a.m. in order to look for the earring she had lost. No, he had not found the earring, although he had searched the steps going up to the terrace where Madam thought she might have dropped it. It was there he had found the glove. He had seen at once that it was a man's glove – the kind the master and His Lordship wore when they went riding. He had taken it home with him since it was by then too late to rouse up Mr Monckton. It was only when he had got it home that he had seen the stains upon it. Yes, he had thought that the stains might be blood. It sometimes happened that blood from a kill transferred itself to a man's gloves after a day's hunting.

'But you did not think this was the blood of a fox, did you?' asked Riordan sharply. Baines mumbled that he had not known what to think. He had taken the glove to Madam the next day and she had told him he had better return it. He had accordingly driven over to Castleford and given the glove to Mr Monckton. 'As we have already heard,' said Riordan, sounding thoroughly pleased with himself. Once more, Sir Anthony declined to question the witness, and the next witness was called. This turned out to be Mrs Langton.

'Venetia was very apologetic about having to give evidence against Ned,' whispered Lady Celia to

Rowlands as the court settled down once more. 'She tried to get out of it – but it was no go.'

Certainly, Mrs Langton was not the compliant witness that all the others had been. Questioned as to the reason for her presence at Castleford on the night of 19th August, she replied: 'Why, I was having dinner with me husband and me oldest friends – as anyone might've told you, young man.'

'You and your husband were among the party playing cards in the drawing room after dinner, were you not?' said Riordan, sounding a little nonplussed at being thus addressed.

'And what if we were?' Venetia Langton replied magnificently. 'Sure, and there's nothing wrong with a pleasant rubber of bridge to while away an hour or two with friends.'

'No, indeed,' said Riordan hastily, then, making an effort to recover his dignity: 'You were present in the drawing room, as I have said, and therefore overheard the defendant threaten the life of Mr Swift.'

'I heard nothing of the kind,' was the robust reply.

'Madam . . . Mrs Langton . . . let me remind you that you are under oath,' blustered Riordan. 'You were in the drawing room and must have overheard the words that were said.'

'Oh, I heard 'em all right,' replied this exasperating woman. 'What I *didn't* hear was a threat. It was nothing but a silly squabble between brothers. No sooner said than forgotten.'

'Except that it *wasn't* forgotten, was it, Mrs Langton?' There was a quiet satisfaction in Riordan's voice as he scored this point. 'The man whose life was threatened was found dead a few hours later.' Venetia Langton's only answer to this was a disdainful sniff. 'We now come to what happened *after* the dinner and the game of bridge attended by you and your husband. You missed one of your diamond earrings, I understand, and sent the chauffeur, William Baines, over to Castleford later that night to look for it – isn't that so?'

'Yes. The clip was loose. I'd been meaning to get it fixed.'

'Quite so. What time was this?'

'I suppose about half past one, or a quarter to two. I didn't notice the earring was gone until I was undressing. Baines hadn't yet put the car away, and so I asked him to return to Castleford to see if he could find it.'

'But your chauffeur didn't find the earring, did he? Instead, he found something else. Can you tell the jury what it was?'

'A glove.'

'A little louder, please.'

'A glove!' she snapped.

'Precisely.' Riordan's tone was smug. 'And it was this glove – a vital piece of evidence – that you told Baines to return to Castleford, and about which you telephoned the defendant's wife, Lady Celia Swift, not once but twice on the Sunday, first telling her that you had instructed your chauffeur to return it, and later warning her that the police, having questioned Mr Baines, knew of its existence.'

'What if I did?' she demanded. 'The Swifts are my friends. It may come as a surprise to you, young man, but in this country we don't believe in throwing our friends to the wolves. Yes, I telephoned Celia Swift as soon as that silly feller' – she meant Baines – 'confessed he'd told the Gardai about finding the glove. I told her to burn the wretched thing. Unfortunately, she didn't take me at my word.'

After this heroic stand by a defiantly hostile witness – Sir Anthony, of course, had 'no further questions' for Mrs Langton – the court adjourned for luncheon. At Lady Celia's insistence, their party, joined by a jubilant Venetia Langton, returned to Merrion Square. Over Dover sole, duchess potatoes and a crisp Chablis, they toasted Mrs Langton's spirited performance: 'Did you see his face, the red-headed eejit, when I said that about burning the glove?' But this euphoria was short-lived. On returning to the public gallery, the Swift contingent was confronted with a far more testing prospect. For Riordan was again on his feet. He had only one further witness to call before concluding the case for the prosecution, he informed the judge: to wit, Mrs Jolyon Swift.

As that lady took her seat in the witness box, there was an excited stirring from the watching crowd.

'She's certainly dressed the part of the grieving widow,' murmured Lady Celia to Rowlands. 'Black satin, dyed black furs and a *very* smart hat.'

Asked by the counsel for the prosecution to confirm that she was 'Mrs Jolyon Swift, widow of the late Jolyon Swift Esquire,' she replied in a trembling voice that this was so. She also confirmed her present address in Dublin as 'my late husband's flat, in St Stephen's Green.' Then Riordan got to the heart of the matter. 'Mrs Swift, I now want to turn to the events of August when you and your late husband were living at the home of his half-brother, Lord Castleford. You had been there for some weeks, I understand?'

'Yes. We . . . we always spent the summer months at Castleford. Jolyon . . .' Her voice broke. 'My . . . my husband thought of it as his home. And it was a healthier spot for our boy, being in the country.'

'Indeed.' Riordan's manner was at its most emollient. 'Mr Swift's mother was in residence at Castleford too, was she not?'

'She was. Jolyon . . . my husband . . . was very close to his mother.'

'To be sure. Mrs Swift, I am now going to ask you a few questions. I want you to cast your mind back to that summer when you and your husband and child were living at Castleford demesne. Would you say that the atmosphere was a happy one?'

'*We* were happy, Jolyon and I,' was the faltering reply. 'Blissfully happy.' Recalling the frequent quarrels he had witnessed between husband and wife during his stay that August, Rowlands wondered whether this was a deliberate falsehood, or merely the rosier view of the past often adopted by the recently bereaved.

Riordan's next question put paid to that idea, however. 'You say that you and your husband were happy – but that was not the case with Mr Swift and his half-brother, Lord Castleford, was it?'

'No. Ned – that is Lord Castleford – hated my husband, and never lost a chance of showing it.'

'So there was an atmosphere of tension between the two men, you would say?' She agreed that there was. It occurred to Rowlands that her answers were rather too pat, as if she had been coached. 'We now come to the night in question – the night of Saturday 19th August. You were present when Lord Castleford made his threat against your husband's life.'

'I was.'

'Objection, my lord. I understand that the witness was not actually present in the room where the exchange took place, but in another room.'

'Thank you, Sir Anthony. Mr Riordan, we must endeavour to be precise.'

'Yes, my lord. I'll rephrase the question. Mrs Swift, although you were not, as my learned friend has pointed out, in the room where the words were spoken, you were able to overhear Lord Castleford's threat towards your husband, were you not?'

'Yes. We all heard it.'

'By "we", you mean the people who were with you in the drawing room for the purposes of playing bridge, I take it?'

'That's right.'

'So – just to make it absolutely clear for the benefit of the jury,' said Riordan. 'You and all those present in the drawing room overheard Lord Castleford's words: "By God, if you come near me again tonight, I swear I'll kill you." Is that right?'

'Yes.'

'And – just to be clear – did it seem to you that Lord Castleford was in earnest when he made that threat, or was it said in a joking tone?'

'It wasn't a joke,' said Henrietta Swift. 'He meant every word. As I've said, Ned hated my husband.'

'Thank you, Mrs Swift. I'm now going to ask you some questions that you may find distressing. If so, please forgive me. I want you to cast your mind back to the moment you first heard the news that your husband had been killed, on the day after the quarrel between Lord Castleford and Mr Swift we have just heard described. Can you tell me what you felt when you learnt what had happened?'

'I was very upset,' replied the young woman, without hesitation. 'In fact, I fainted.'

'So you did,' said Riordan sympathetically. 'It must have been dreadful for you. But what I want to know, Mrs Swift, is what you thought, on coming round from your faint? Was the news – terrible as it was – a shock to you?'

'Not at all,' was the prompt reply. 'I thought, "He's done it at last."'

'By "he", you mean Lord Castleford?'

'Yes.' There was an air of satisfaction about her next words. 'I told him so as soon as I heard his voice on the stairs. I called him a murderer – which he is,' she added defiantly. Her voice wavered, and the tears she'd been holding back now fell. 'He killed my Jolyon,' she sobbed. 'My darling Reggie's Papa. I'll never forgive him – never!' A murmur of sympathy went around the court at the sight of the weeping woman.

'Bring a glass of water for Mrs Swift,' Riordan instructed one of the court ushers. He sounded well pleased with the effect he had created.

Now it was the turn of Sir Anthony. He waited a courteous few minutes until Mrs Swift had regained her composure, then he began: 'Mrs Swift, you have told us your feelings on overhearing the words that were allegedly said by Lord Castleford to Mr Swift on the night before Mr Swift was found dead. I think we are all clear on that. And I am sorry to ask you to revisit once more scenes you must find distressing. But I should like to know – what happened after that?'

'I . . .' For the first time, Henrietta Swift sounded unsure of her ground. 'I don't understand.'

'I'm sorry, I should have been more precise. I meant, what did you do immediately after you had heard the exchange between Lord Castleford and your husband?'

She hesitated a moment. 'Well, I was about to play bridge, as I said before. Our table was waiting for someone – Celia's friend – to join us, so we weren't actually playing at that moment.'

'But you began playing thereafter?'

'That's right.'

'And what of your husband? Was he one of the bridge players, too?'

'No . . . that is . . .' Again, she hesitated. 'He . . . he doesn't . . . he *didn't* . . . care for cards.'

'But he joined the party in the drawing room, I take it?'

'No. That is . . . I think he went upstairs.'

'You didn't actually *see* him do so?' Sir Anthony's tone was one of polite interest.

It seemed to unsettle the witness, however, for once more she paused before replying: 'Well, no. But he *must* have gone up to his room at some point in order to pack . . .' She broke off, perhaps realising that she'd said more than she meant to.

Sir Anthony allowed a further pause to ensue, then continued, 'Mrs Swift, at what time did you finish your game of bridge?'

'I . . . I don't know exactly. Some time after eleven, I think. Say half past.'

'What did you do then?'

'I went upstairs to bed.'

'So you joined your husband at around half past eleven?'

'Well, not exactly. My husband and I have . . . or rather, *had* . . . separate rooms.'

'Separate rooms,' echoed Sir Anthony. 'And did you, by any chance, enter your husband's room at that time?'

'No. That is, I . . .'

'Really, my lord,' protested Riordan. 'I fail to see the point of these questions. Mr and Mrs Swift's sleeping arrangements can have no bearing on the case.'

'I am sure Sir Anthony has his reasons for pursuing the matter, Mr Riordan. We will allow him to proceed.'

'Thank you, my lord. I will endeavour to be brief.' Sir Anthony turned again to the witness: 'Did you perhaps call out to your husband, Mrs Swift, as you passed his door? To wish him good night, perhaps?'

'I . . . I don't remember. I might have done.'

'But you didn't see him again that night?'

'No. I was tired. I went straight to sleep.'

'So – to conclude – you neither saw nor spoke to your husband after you and he parted at around nine o'clock that evening, he to speak to Lord Castleford in his study, and you to play cards, am I right?'

'I told you, I *heard* him.'

'Yes, yes. We already know all about that. But you didn't see him again, did you – nor make any effort to do so? The next thing you knew was he was dead.'

'Really, my lord,' protested Riordan. 'I think my

learned friend might have more consideration for the witness's feelings.'

'Indeed he might. Sir Anthony, is there much more of this?'

'My apologies, my lord. My intention was merely to show that a considerable period of time elapsed between Mrs Swift's last encounter with her late husband on the night of 19th August and the, ah, lamentable discovery of his body the next day. It was not my wish to distress the lady. I have no further questions.'

For all his apologetic words, Sir Anthony did not sound displeased with the outcome of his cross-questioning. Once more, he had managed to introduce a note of doubt into a witness's account of events. In this instance, Henrietta Swift's earlier assertion that her marriage had been happy had been subtly undermined by the revelation that not only did the couple not share a bed (admittedly a common enough state of affairs amongst the upper classes) but that, more significantly, they had not even exchanged a parting good night.

Chapter Thirteen

The case for the defence opened on the following day. Court 1 was utterly silent as the defendant took his seat in the witness box. Rowlands, seated next to Lady Celia in the public gallery, thought that there must have been the same kind of breathless anticipation at public hangings in the not too distant past. The respectful pause before the condemned man's last words upon the scaffold. The shouts and cheers as a popular villain made his adieux. Swift, Rowlands knew, had only agreed at the eleventh hour that he would subject himself to examination and cross-examination. 'It's all a charade, in any case,' he said, with the bitter resignation he had displayed throughout the trial. 'The evidence is against me. I've heard nothing to indicate that the verdict will be anything but the worst.'

'Now then, my lord!' cried the ever-jovial Sir

Anthony. 'You really mustn't take such a pessimistic line. We've a great deal in our favour, and I'm confident that once the jury have had a chance to consider matters fully and to take facts in their proper order,' – he meant after his closing speech – 'they will come to the right view.'

'Yes, yes,' said Swift impatiently. 'I'm sure you'll spin them a good yarn.' He turned to his wife, who had been standing silently by. 'What have you said to George about this business?'

'I've told him you've had to go away for a while.'

Swift laughed: a hollow sound. 'Well, it might be a longer while still,' he said, adding fiercely, 'I don't want him lied to, do you understand?'

'Ned . . .'

'Just tell him, if the worst comes to the worst, that I wasn't a coward.' It seemed to Rowlands, who was also present, that Swift's brusque manner towards his wife concealed a deeper hurt. Could it be, as she had feared, that he knew about her affair with his half-brother? Either that, or he was putting on a show of indifference towards his likely fate, and his apparent hard-heartedness towards her was a sign of its opposite. As their little party was about to leave the prison cell so that Swift could prepare himself for his ordeal, Rowlands felt a touch on his shoulder. 'I want to thank you again for standing by me, old man,' said Swift, with more emotion in his voice than he had previously shown. 'And for looking after *her*,' he added, in a low tone so that only the other could hear. 'It's made all the difference to me.'

Sir Anthony Griffin now rose to his feet. His manner when addressing his client, was grave – with none of the theatrical flourishes that had distinguished his performance so far. 'Lord Castleford,' he began once the peer's bona fides had been established. 'I have only two questions for you. The first is this: did you kill your half-brother, Jolyon Swift?'

There was an infinitesimal pause, during which the courtroom held its collective breath. Then: 'I did not.'

'Secondly, do you have any idea who might have done so?'

'I do not.'

'Thank you.' Sir Anthony turned to the judge. 'No further questions, my lord.'

It was a daring ploy, but Griffin was gambling on the fact that the jury would by now be thoroughly familiar with the evidence, as it had been relayed to them by successive witnesses over the past week. They had been led by the hand – first by the prosecution counsel, then by the defence – and had their attention drawn to this aspect of the case or that, depending on which arguments each side was trying to make. And there *was* something impressive about the quiet dignity with which Swift had answered the questions put to him. After days of listening to one lengthy examination and cross-examination after another, the taciturn responses of the accused would come as a welcome change to those twelve men, thought Rowlands.

Now it was the turn of Riordan, the fox, as Rowlands privately thought of him. 'I've a few questions for you, too, Lord Castleford,' he began. 'Would you say you were a patient man?'

Swift thought about it. 'That depends what you mean.'

'I mean, my lord, do you have difficulty controlling your temper?'

'I wouldn't have said so,' replied the other coldly. 'But of course it's a matter of opinion.'

'Indeed,' said Riordan softly. 'And we have heard, have we not, the testimonies of a number of witnesses as to what took place on the night of 19th August. I refer, of course, to your quarrel with Mr Swift.'

'What of it?' said the other.

If Riordan was taken aback by Swift's coolness, he did not show it. 'If I might remind you, you said—'

'I know what I said.'

'"By God, if you come near me again tonight, I swear I'll kill you . . ." Those were your words, were they not?'

'As far as I can remember.'

'Do these seem to you, my lord, to be the words of a patient man? Or are they not, rather, those of a man prone to losing his temper – a man who might easily be driven to violence?'

Sir Anthony was on his feet. 'My lord, must we

listen to any more of this? My learned friend is *leading* the jury.'

'Quite right. Less of this, Mr Riordan. I'm surprised at you.'

'My lord.' The counsel for the prosecution accepted the rebuke with characteristic mildness. Once more, he addressed the defendant: 'Can you tell us, Lord Castleford, what it was that made you so incensed that night in your study – so incensed, in fact, that you were moved to threaten Mr Swift's life?'

A pause ensued, during which Rowlands was aware of people around him in the public gallery shifting in their seats and craning forward. An expectant hush hung over the whole courtroom as those present waited to hear what Swift had to say. 'You're asking me what my half-brother said to me that night, which caused me to use those words to him?' he replied in due course. 'Very well. He told me that he had committed a fraud against me, by falsifying my signature on a document authorising the sale of a piece of land – without my permission, needless to say. Does that strike you as sufficient reason for a man to lose his temper, Mr Riordan?'

The murmur of surprise prompted by this information – which most of those in the courtroom were hearing for the first time – was instantly quashed by the usher: 'Silence!'

Riordan did not reply to the defendant's question, which was of course rhetorical, but asked another of his own. 'Your property, the demesne of Castleford, has belonged to your family for a long time, I believe?'

'Two hundred years,' was the reply.

'That is indeed a long time,' said Riordan. Was there a note of irony in his voice? Two hundred years was nothing, in the annals of history, he seemed to be implying. Ireland was an ancient land, which had seen off foreign occupation in the past, and would do so again. 'So you would be strongly opposed,' he went on, 'to any attempt – such as the one you have described – to sell off all, or a part of, the property?'

'Naturally,' said Swift. He sounded faintly bored with the discussion. Rowlands hoped that his friend's disdain for the process he was currently undergoing wouldn't be obvious to the jury.

'So strongly opposed,' went on the counsel for the prosecution, in his quiet, relentless voice, 'that you would have done anything—'

'My lord, this is mere speculation on the part of my learned friend.'

'Thank you, Sir Anthony. We will allow Mr Riordan to finish his question.'

'I repeat,' said Riordan, with deliberation, 'that you were so strongly opposed to this attempt that you would have done anything to prevent it – including murder. Is that not so, Lord Castleford?'

'If you're asking me if I felt like murdering my half-brother when he told me what he had done, the answer is yes,' said Swift calmly. A murmur went around the courtroom. 'If you're asking me if I murdered my half-brother, you have already heard my answer to that. I did not.' More murmuring.

'Silence in court!'

Oliver Langton appeared next as a character witness. He had known the defendant all his life, he said; their fathers, too, had been friends. Ned Swift had never done a mean or cowardly thing in his life, he opined. As for the idea that he'd shoot a defenceless man in cold blood – it was preposterous. Questioned about his attendance at the dinner party on that fateful Saturday night, Langton said that it had been no different from many such occasions in the past. The atmosphere had been relaxed and convivial. 'You could say Castleford was home-from-home, as far as my wife and I were concerned.' There'd been talk of the war, of course, but that was only to be expected, at this time. Asked whether he'd noticed any particular animosity between Lord Castleford and his sibling, Langton brushed aside the question. If there *had* been, it wasn't Ned's doing. Young Swift had been drunk – and not for the first time, either. *Nil nisi bonum* and all that, but the feller was a public nuisance. Why Ned had allowed him to go on living there at his expense – to say nothing of having to put up with his foolery – he (Langton) hadn't the least idea. But murder? No. Impossible. If he'd wanted to get rid of Jolyon Swift, he (Ned) would only have had to ask him to leave, said the landowner, adding: 'My wife and I could never understand why Ned put up with him.'

Cross-questioned by Riordan as to whether he had heard the threat made by Lord Castleford to his half-brother, Langton admitted that he had. 'But what's the harm of a few harsh words?' he said. 'In my opinion, it was no more than the feller deserved. He'd been up to his old tricks, no doubt – losing money hand over fist through betting on the horses, and expecting Ned to bail him out. What he (Ned) said was mild, considering the provocation.'

Next to be called to the witness box was Canon Wetherby. He, too, gave a glowing testimonial to the defendant's good character – his mild and unemphatic tones in contrast to Langton's hearty manner. He then gave an account of his movements on that Saturday night that matched Langton's in most details as regarded the earlier part of the evening, up until the guests departed and the household went up to bed. The canon's brief conversation with Jolyon Swift in the corridor later that night was the part of his testimony that interested the counsel for the defence. 'Now then, sir. You have told us that you spoke to Mr Swift for a few moments outside your room. What was your impression of his demeanour? That is to say, did he seem cheerful – or was he anxious or apprehensive?'

'Well, not exactly *cheerful*, you know,' said the old gentleman. 'Rather agitated, if anything. Young people, I find, are in rather too much of a *hurry*, these days. I feel like saying to them, "What's your rush? Life passes soon enough, without hastening it along."'

He gave a nervous cough. 'I wish now that I had detained him a bit longer. I might have persuaded him to change his mind, poor soul . . .'

'Change his mind?' echoed Sir Anthony. 'What about, exactly?'

'Well . . .' Again Canon Wetherby paused. When he spoke again, it was in graver tones than before. 'Self-murder is a serious crime,' he said. 'Not only a crime against the state, but against God. He must have been utterly desperate, poor fellow.'

'So you believe that Mr Swift killed himself?'

'What other explanation is there?' replied the other. 'I have already told you that it was not in Ned's – in Lord Castleford's – nature to destroy his own flesh and blood. The only alternative is that he – poor Jolyon – was driven to despair when he was called to account for his unprincipled behaviour, and took his own life. There was a very similar case when I was an army chaplain, during the last show. Poor fellow in my battalion hanged himself after being found out cheating at cards. Terrible waste of life.' Riordan waived his right to question the witness, whose gentle demeanour had left a powerful impression on those assembled in the courtroom.

The telephone rang, just as they were sitting down to dinner that night, interrupting a rambling account by the canon of a day's hunting he'd enjoyed at Castleford years before. Ned Swift had been just a boy, he said:

'Plucky little feller he was, even then.' He chuckled. 'Saw him jump a wall higher than he was on that pony of his. Starlight, I think it was – unless it was Mercury? Chestnut with four white feet. Pretty little beast. Flew over that wall like a bird, with Neddie clinging on for dear life. Never the least hint of funk.'

'Who can that be, I wonder?' said Lady Celia as the shrill sound of the instrument cut across these reminiscences.

A moment later, O'Driscoll put his head around the door. 'Mr Butler on the telephone for you, milady. He says it's urgent.'

'Thank you, O'Driscoll.' Their hostess excused herself, and they heard her voice in the hall: 'Yes, Mr Butler?' followed by a silence.

'I hope there's nothing the matter with young George,' said Canon Wetherby. 'Children do get ailments, from time to time, but generally they throw them off quite quickly.'

Rowlands murmured something in reply, but really his attention was entirely focused on the telephone conversation that was taking place outside the room. He wondered what was so urgent that it couldn't have waited until the morning. It wasn't long before he found out. 'Don't get up,' said Lady Celia as she joined her guests once more, then, as she resumed her seat: 'Rather beastly news, I'm afraid – but I don't think there's anything to be done from this end – at least, not at this time of night. There's been a shooting. *Another* shooting, I should say. A local quarrel, from the sound of it . . . although the body was found on Castleford land.'

'Whose body?' said Rowlands sharply.

'It's one of the men from the village – he used to work for Ned, as a matter of fact, but Ned had to sack him. Bit of a bad lot, I gather, from what Ned said. I suppose Mr Butler thought I should be told of his death, although to be perfectly honest, I don't see that it has much to do with us, since the man's no longer an employee.'

'What was his name?' persisted Rowlands, already half-expecting the answer.

'Christie Doherty. He was one of the stable hands until Ned sacked him. Oh yes, you met him, didn't you?'

'I did,' said Rowlands grimly. 'Did Mr Butler say how it happened?'

'Well, he didn't go into too much detail,' she replied, then, to the butler, who was hovering nearby: 'Yes, O'Driscoll, you can tell Mrs Keane to send up the next course.' When he had left them, she went on, 'It sounds as if it was a quarrel about money.'

'Ah,' said Rowlands, but made no other comment.

It was left to the canon to add a pious reflection: '"For the love of money is the root of all evil . . ." One Timothy, Verse Six,' he said. 'And it is so often the case, alas.'

'Indeed.' Again, Rowlands – his thoughts

preoccupied with what he had just heard – did not expand on this.

Further discussion was interrupted by O'Driscoll's bringing in the fish course, which was dressed crab: 'Caught this morning in Dublin Bay,' said Lady Celia. 'We've some restrictions here, of course, but we can still get plenty of fish.' For the next few minutes they addressed themselves to the enjoyment of this delicacy – one of Mrs Keane's specialities, said their hostess – and to other general topics of conversation. Only towards the end of the meal was the matter of the shooting at Castleford raised once more: 'I wonder, Frederick, if you would do something for me?' said Celia Swift. 'I can't leave Dublin while the trial's going on – I have to be there for Ned, whether he wants me or not.'

'Dear girl, I feel sure that—' protested the canon, but she waved the interruption away.

'Let me finish, Cousin Aloysius. I think somebody ought to go to Castleford, to see about this business with Christie Doherty. However much I might dislike it, it *is* our responsibility to get to the bottom of what happened.'

'The police will do that,' said Rowlands, seeing which way this was going.

'Yes, but I feel somebody from the family – or *representing* the family – ought to be there, to show that we take the matter seriously. I'm sure Ned would expect nothing less. Doherty might have been a rogue, but he *was* employed by the estate, at one time. So I wondered if you,

Frederick . . . in fact, if *both* of you . . . would agree to look into things for me? There'll be an inquest, of course, and I think the family should put in an appearance.'

Castleford in autumn had a very different feel to the place in high summer when Rowlands had first set foot there: the smell of damp leaves and smouldering bonfires now prevailed over that of flowers and new-mown grass. As the car pulled up in front of the house, Rowlands was conscious of an absence, which he soon identified as a silence, in place of the joyful barking of dogs that had greeted him on his arrival two months before. 'The poor beasts were making such a commotion with their howling that they couldn't be kept in the house any longer, but had to be sent up to the home farm,' said Canon Wetherby when Rowlands remarked upon this. 'They miss their master, of course.'

Nor was the atmosphere in the house itself any lighter where the servants were concerned – Mary, as she helped him off with his coat, saying tearfully to Rowlands, 'Oh, sir, what a change since you were last here!' while John, the footman, sounded no less morose as he carried the bags upstairs, apologising for the state of the rooms: 'We're short-staffed, you see, sir. Three of the maids have left this past month alone, not wanting to remain in an unfortunate house. I'll see to it that you have a fire lit, directly,' he added. ''Tis a cold house in winter.'

On descending from their respective rooms, the two

men had been met in the hall by Robert Butler, the land agent, who had seemed at first somewhat put out at their arrival. 'I told Her Ladyship that I'd be more than happy to attend the inquest,' he said. 'There was no need for you both to trouble yourselves.'

'Lady Celia felt that a member of the family should be there,' replied Canon Wetherby, his usual sweetness of manner softening the implied reproof.

'Well, yes, but I—' began Butler when his wife, who had noiselessly appeared at his side, intervened.

'I'm sure Robert would far rather *not* be involved. He has quite enough on his hands, dealing with the estate, now that Lord Castleford is . . . er . . . *detained* . . . wouldn't you say so, my dear?' To which Butler could only mutter an agreement.

Lunch was an awkward occasion, with the four of them squashed uncomfortably at one end of the long dining-room table – in order, said Mrs Butler, to save John the extra walk. 'With such a reduced staff, we're having to make economies,' she said. 'It won't be easy to get servants to replace the ones who've left, especially with a war on.' It seemed unnecessary to point out that the war had not yet affected Ireland directly.

Instead, Rowlands, doing his best with the rather dry rissoles that were evidently another of Mrs Butler's economies, addressed the land agent: 'I wonder if you could give me some more details about the circumstances of Christie Doherty's death, Mr Butler?

Lady Celia only gave us the bare facts.'

'Yes, indeed,' replied the other. 'But perhaps we should wait until a more . . . ah . . . *suitable* moment? My wife is sensitive about such matters.'

'Of course,' said Rowlands. 'I wouldn't want to upset Mrs Butler.'

'We'll leave you then, my dear,' said Butler to his spouse. He touched a bell, and when the servant appeared, said: 'We'll have our coffee in the smoking room, John. Mrs Butler will have hers in here.' The three men accordingly decamped to the other room where, once coffee had been brought and cigarettes lit, Butler said, 'So what exactly do you want to know?'

'First of all, where and when was he found, and who found him?' said Rowlands.

Butler laughed. 'Ah, Mr Rowlands – living up to your reputation as a detective, I see! Well, to answer your questions in the order in which you asked them: the body was found in the stable-yard at around nine p.m. last night, by one of the stable-lads. Michael Cullen. Mickey to his friends. The foolish boy hadn't the wit to make himself scarce, of course.'

'What do you mean?' said Rowlands sharply.

'I mean that it was he who shot Doherty,' was the reply.

Canon Wetherby gasped. 'No!' he cried. 'I don't believe it.'

'I assure you, it's true. The Gardai have him in custody this very minute.'

'But . . . but what *evidence* is there against him?' The old gentleman seemed shocked to the core by what he had just learnt. 'He's such a quiet lad.'

'Ah, appearances can be deceptive,' said Butler. 'He admits he quarrelled with Doherty over money. He claims that the man had borrowed a largish sum, and then refused to repay it, thus placing young Mickey in difficulties. He went to remonstrate with Doherty and a fight must have broken out. He – the Cullen boy – was found kneeling beside Doherty, who was dying from a gunshot wound. Cullen's fingerprints were on the gun, and there was blood on his clothes. Like I said, Mr Rowlands, the lad was foolish not to make his escape when he could . . . and to get rid of the weapon while he was about it.'

'Where did he get the gun?' said Rowlands.

Again, Butler laughed. 'When you have been in Ireland as long as I have, Mr Rowlands, you will know that a gun can always be obtained from someone. In this case, I imagine that the boy got it from his uncle – or one of his uncle's connections in the IRA. Seamus Cullen did time in Kilmainham Gaol for shooting a Gardai officer during the Easter Rising. Fortunately, the man survived, or Cullen would have swung for it. So I'd say that's your answer, Mr Rowlands. Any further questions about this unfortunate affair will doubtless be taken up at the inquest tomorrow. I'm afraid my knowledge of the business is partial, to say the least.'

'I must go and see the boy's mother at once,' said Canon Wetherby. 'And Mary Doherty, of course. This must have been a terrible blow for her.'

'She can't have been too surprised to have something like this befall her reprobate of a son,' said Butler. 'It's not the first time Mrs Doherty will have had the Gardai at her door on Christie's account.'

'Perhaps not,' said the clergyman. 'But she's still lost a son. I'll visit her this afternoon as soon as I've spoken to Mickey's family and to the lad himself. I still can't believe the boy could have done anything so heinous. He's a good lad, is Mickey Cullen.'

'Oh, they're all "good lads" – until they're not,' said Butler, stubbing out his cigarette. 'And now, gentlemen, if you've finished asking questions, I've some work to get on with. An estate doesn't run itself, you know.'

'Was there a witness to the shooting?' said Rowlands. Butler, who had risen to his feet, seemed momentarily disconcerted. 'I told you, the lad admits to quarrelling with Doherty.'

'That doesn't necessarily mean it was he who shot him.'

'But the evidence of the fingerprints is pretty conclusive, don't you agree? I'll see you at dinner, gentlemen, if not before.' Then he was gone, letting the door fall to behind him.

'I don't believe it,' the canon said stubbornly. 'It's completely out of character for Mickey to have killed that lad.'

'I hope you're right,' said Rowlands. 'But the question remains: if *he* didn't kill Doherty, who *did*?' To this question, the canon had no reply. Murmuring that he would see whether Patsy Connolly would run him into the village in the motorcar before he returned to Dublin, he went off to pay his visits to Mrs Doherty and the Cullen family, leaving Rowlands to his own devices. The house was very quiet – an echoing shell of the way it had been in the summer when, full of company, it had seemed a convivial spot. Now it had an abandoned air.

Rowlands decided to take a stroll in the grounds: from memory, the grounds below the terrace were the most level and easy to navigate, and so he made his way there, first collecting cap and stick from the boot room. It was from here, he recalled, that he'd set out on that first walk around the demesne with its owner. At the thought of Swift, and how he must be hating his present incarceration, Rowlands felt a stab of pity. He wondered how the trial was going – he'd ask if he might telephone Dublin that evening, to find out. He wished there was something he could do, to make things better for his friend – and for *her* – some scrap of evidence, previously overlooked, that would turn the case around . . . While he was musing on this, he heard a shout from the terrace: 'Wait for us! We want to come with you!' It was young George, who now ran up with his little cousin in tow. 'Hello! You were with Daddy when we got Rusty.' That was the name of his dog, Rowlands guessed. 'You showed me your knife.'

'I did,' said Rowlands, holding out his hand for the child to shake. 'How are you, George?'

'I'm very well, thank you,' was the grave reply. 'I thought you might have brought Mummy with you.'

'Your mother's in Dublin,' said Rowlands. 'But she said to tell you that she'll be coming to see you very soon.'

'Good,' said George. 'It's dull here, with only Reggie to talk to.'

The younger Mrs Swift had left Castleford some time before, Lady Celia had told Rowlands when, over coffee the night before, he'd asked what had become of the lady. 'She said she couldn't stay in a "murderer's house",' adding drily, 'She didn't mind availing herself of the murderer's nanny, however,' since Philomena had been looking after both children for the past month. 'I thought it best for Georgie to stay at Castleford while all this was going on,' she had concluded. 'He's happier there, with his dog and his rabbits. It's a healthier atmosphere for a child.'

At that moment, the young woman Rowlands remembered being introduced to as George's nurse hurried up, sounding a little out of breath. 'Master George! Master Reggie! Come away now! You're not to pester the poor gentleman. They *would* come out,' she said to Rowlands apologetically. 'Although I've told them and told them it's time for their nap.'

'I don't mind,' said Rowlands as the boys danced

around him. 'Let them come along if they want to.'

The nurse accordingly went to fetch her cloak, and coats for the boys – Master Reggie was prone to chills, she said, buttoning the younger child into his. 'And put your cap on straight, Master George,' she added as, with delighted shrieks, the little boys dashed ahead, leaving the two adults to follow at a more sedate pace.

'You'll have to be my guide, Miss McGurk,' said Rowlands. 'I'm familiar with several of the walks on the estate, but I'm sure you know a good many more.' Which turned out to be the case since Philomena McGurk's father was head gardener at Castleford, and she'd grown up in one of the tied cottages. 'Then your father must have been the man who grew those wonderful roses I so admired last summer,' said her companion as they strolled across the lawn towards the shrubbery where the boys were already playing a noisy game of hide-and-seek.

'Sure, the da loves his roses,' was the reply. '*He* wouldn't leave Castleford for the world.'

This prompted Rowlands to say, 'But *you* would?'

'Oh!' The nurse seemed taken aback by the question. 'It's a grand place – or used to be. Now . . .' She broke off. 'Master George, you're to stay out of them puddles!'

'You were saying?' said Rowlands.

For a moment, the girl was silent. 'Things have changed,' she said at last. 'Castleford isn't what it used to be. Oh, it's not just the terrible business with

His Lordship being accused of murder, which, by the way, I've never believed. It happened before that. Now this shocking business with Christie Doherty . . .' She lowered her voice although the boys were out of earshot, as far as Rowlands could tell. 'There's a few that knows more about *that* affair than they let on,' she said darkly. 'Master George! What have I said about climbing trees? You'll tear your nice coat. Come down this instant!' Before Rowlands could ask her what she'd meant by her previous remark, she left his side and hurried after her rebellious charges. As Rowlands caught up with her, she was remonstrating with the older child for having led his cousin astray. 'Will you look at Master Reggie's knees! They're all over mud. And where's your cap, Master George?'

'Stupid cap,' said the boy. 'Shan't wear it – and you can't make me, so there!' Then he ran off, followed by Reggie, both shouting 'Stupid cap! Stupid cap!' at the tops of their voices.

'He isn't always such a caution,' said the nurse to Rowlands. 'He's missing his da, is what it is.' Again she dropped her voice. 'It's a mercy little Master Reggie is too young to realise what's happened to *his*. Such a terrible thing.' She sounded really upset. 'I wouldn't have stayed, but for the children.'

'I'm sure it makes all the difference, having a steady person like yourself to look after them,' said Rowlands. 'Children need to feel safe. You said just now that things had changed a good deal at

Castleford. What was it you meant exactly?'

'Oh . . . It's just a feeling,' she replied. 'Nothing I can put my finger on. We used to be such a happy crowd – me, and Biddy, and Mary, and all the rest. We'd grown up together, you might say. Castleford was our home and His Lordship's family . . . well, we felt a sense of *belonging* to the family, if that makes sense.'

'It does,' said Rowlands. 'And now you feel that's no longer the case?'

'That's so. Since . . . since what happened with the poor little boys' fathers, it's as if nobody at Castleford *trusts* anybody else. We're all looking at each other and wondering "Did *she* know something?" or "Was *he* involved?" It's horrible.'

'I can see that it must be,' he said. They fell silent once more as the two boys ran up.

'Come and see our camp!' cried George, seizing Rowlands' hand. 'It's a good camp, isn't it, Reggie?' Reggie agreed that it was.

'Now then, Master George, Mr Rowlands doesn't want to drag himself through the mud to see your old camp,' said the nurse. But Rowlands said he didn't mind. Eagerly accompanied by the little boys, he and Miss McGurk made their way through the trees to where the children had made their camp – a rickety construction of branches and dead leaves, piled up at the base of large beech tree.

'See?' demanded George. 'It's a good camp. But

we're building a better one,' he confided to Rowlands while the nurse was occupied with brushing mud off Reggie's knees, much to the latter's displeasure. 'It's down by the river. You won't tell anyone, will you? It's a secret.'

Chapter Fourteen

Dinner that evening was no less uncongenial than luncheon had been. Once again, Rowlands and the canon found themselves at table with the Butlers. Lady Castleford, Butler explained, was dining alone in her room. Stunned by the double blow that had befallen her, in the loss of her son and the arrest on suspicion of his murder of her stepson, she kept to her room much of the time, he said, taking her meals on a tray, and only emerging, on the arm of Biddy the chambermaid, to shuffle a few paces up and down the corridor by way of daily exercise. 'Between you and me,' the land agent concluded, 'I think the unfortunate lady's not quite right in the head.'

'Robert – *really!*' said his wife reproachfully.

'Only making an observation, me dear.'

The meal itself – roast pheasant – was an improvement

on the midday fare, but conversation was stilted, with Butler throwing out jovial observations from time to time on the poor prospects for the season's hunting, and Mrs Butler complaining that the pheasants were not cooked to her liking. Canon Wetherby was preoccupied with the visits he had made during the afternoon: 'That poor woman,' he remarked as the men sat over their port. It was Doherty's mother to whom he referred. 'With the boy gone, she's got no one to look after her.'

'There's that brother of hers,' Butler reminded him. 'And the priest. Father O'Shaughnessy is a great man for keeping an eye on his parishioners. She won't starve.'

'I wasn't thinking only of her bodily comforts,' said the old clergyman. He sighed. 'But you're right, Butler. I'll have a word with Father O'Shaughnessy and see if we can't arrange for some of the local ladies to pop in.'

Coffee was served in the smaller of the two drawing rooms – 'We only keep a fire in *this* room, in the evenings,' said Mrs Butler. 'Coals are ruinously expensive, these days.'

'But you don't have rationing in Ireland, surely?' said Rowlands, to which Butler replied that with all these German U-boats sighted off the coast it wouldn't be long before they'd start to feel the pinch with regard to imported goods.

'Besides which,' added his wife, clicking her knitting needles as she worked at a garment she was producing for some good cause or other, 'it never pays to be extravagant.'

Soon after this irrefutable remark, Butler and his wife said they would turn in: 'I've another busy day ahead of me,' said the land agent, repeating his favourite adage that the estate didn't run itself.

When they were alone, Rowlands asked the canon what had been said during his meeting at the goal with Mickey Cullen, which had followed his visit to the boy's family. 'Well, it was most peculiar,' replied the old gentleman. 'Mickey swears he had nothing to do with the shooting. He admits he quarrelled with Doherty, but says he'd already left the stable-yard and had turned into the lane that leads to his mother's cottage when he heard the shot. He ran back, to find Doherty dying – he thought at first that the man must have shot himself. It was then that he picked up the gun, which was lying on the ground.'

'That was a foolish mistake,' said Rowlands.

'It was,' agreed the other. 'He panicked, poor lad.'

'What about the blood on his clothes?' persisted Rowlands.

'Mickey says it got there when he knelt to check if Doherty was still breathing. But I agree it looks bad for him. I've told him to keep his spirits up and to tell the truth at the inquest.'

'It's the best policy,' agreed Rowlands. But he was troubled by this account. Had he perhaps got it wrong about Christie Doherty? What if he *hadn't* been the one responsible for cutting the stirrup leather after all? Might it have been another of the stable hands – Mickey Cullen –

who'd been bribed to carry out this act of sabotage? Then the quarrel over money, and Doherty's shooting by Cullen made sense – as the silencing of a blackmailer . . . Only *none* of it made sense, thought Rowlands despairingly. The characters of both men told against such an interpretation. Doherty was too obviously untrustworthy and Cullen too obviously decent for such a story to be credible. And yet, and yet . . . 'Appearances can be deceptive,' Butler had said. Rowlands had had ample confirmation of this, in the past.

He decided he'd sleep on it, and accordingly left Canon Wetherby to his pipe, and his reflections: 'I seldom sleep well these days. I think I'll read for a while. The fathers of the church are good companions in the watches of the night, I find.' They said good night and Rowlands went to his room. It was bitterly cold – the fire had gone out. He decided to keep on his dressing gown to alleviate the chill, but still found it hard to fall asleep. Who had killed Doherty? That was the question on which all else hinged, he was sure. It had been Doherty, he was increasingly convinced, who had been responsible for cutting the stirrup leather. It wasn't inconceivable that whoever had put him up to it might have a reason for putting him away.

Thinking about the attempt on Swift's life brought him back to the trial that was going on in Dublin. His brief conversation with Lady Celia on the telephone earlier that evening had offered little more in the way of significant developments in the Castleford trial. She'd sounded so dispirited that he'd offered to come back to Dublin after the inquest on Doherty. 'That's good of you,' she said. 'And I could certainly do with the moral support. But I don't think it's going to change things, at this stage. Oh, Frederick, I'm so frightened.' He'd done his best to calm her, saying that if she'd send the car back for them, he and the canon could join her for the final day of the trial. 'All right.' But there'd been no perceptible lightening of her tone. It was as if she'd already resigned herself to the worst.

As he lay there, restlessly turning things over in his mind, he became aware that he was not the only one in the house who remained awake at that late hour. From outside in the corridor came the sound of sobbing. He got up and went to the door. His tread had been so noiseless that when he opened it, whoever it was who stood there was evidently taken by surprise. 'Oh! I . . . I wasn't expecting . . .'

'I'm sorry if I gave you a fright,' said Rowlands. 'No, don't run away. It's Bridget, isn't it?'

'Yes, sir. I thought that room was empty, so I did.'

'It was, until this morning. Now. Why don't you tell me what's upset you so much?'

'Oh . . .' A fresh outburst of tears ensued. 'Sure, I *couldn't* . . .'

'Then let me guess. It's to do with Christie Doherty, isn't it? You and he had an *understanding*, didn't you?'

'Who told you?'

'Let's just say I worked it out. *How* I did so doesn't

matter. What matters is what passed between you. You knew he was involved in something he shouldn't have been. You tried to stop him.'

'He wouldn't listen to me, the silly feller. And now . . . now he's *dead* . . .'

'What exactly was he up to?' asked Rowlands, cutting across what threatened to turn into another fit of sobbing. 'Whatever you tell me won't make any difference now, you know. He's past hurting.'

She acknowledged this. 'If only he'd listened to me!' she wept. 'He said he was doing it for *us* – to get money so that we could be married.'

'So what was it he was going to do in order to get this money?' said Rowlands, hoping that here, at last, would be the piece of evidence he had been looking for.

But her reply was disappointing. 'I don't know, sir. He wouldn't tell me. Only that he'd be "getting his own back" on His Lordship.' A thought seemed to strike her. 'Oh, sir, you won't say anything about this to Mrs Doyle, will you? I'll lose my position.'

'You needn't worry about that,' said Rowlands, although in truth he could make no such guarantee. 'So the thing he was going to do was in order to pay Lord Castleford back for some perceived injury, is that right?'

'I . . . I couldn't say, sir. Christie could get awful mad when he was roused. But he wasn't a bad feller, sir.'

'Now then,' said Rowlands, feeling he'd lost control of the situation somewhat. 'No need to upset yourself.'

He fumbled for the clean handkerchief that was in his dressing gown pocket. 'Here you are. Dry your eyes.'

'What's going on?' said a voice from a short distance away. It was Elspeth Butler. How long she had been standing there, Rowlands had no way of telling. 'Biddy, what are you doing out of bed? It's past midnight.'

'I . . . I'm awful sorry, Mrs Butler,' stammered the girl. 'I couldn't sleep, and . . .'

'You'd no call to go waking up the rest of the house,' was the retort. 'Go back to your room at once.' With which Biddy, with another stifled sob, fled, leaving the land agent's wife and Rowlands alone.

'I'm sorry you were disturbed, Mr Rowlands,' said the former coolly. 'These girls can be rather hysterical.'

'I thought she seemed thoroughly sensible,' replied Rowlands. 'Just a little upset. But that's hardly surprising, in the circumstances.'

'Indeed. Well, good night then,' she said. 'I hope you manage to get some sleep at last.' He thanked her, and wished her good night. But what he'd just learnt made him disinclined for sleep.

By contrast with the trial of his erstwhile employer, Lord Castleford, the inquest on the death of Christie Doherty was thinly attended. Here were no jostling crowds of onlookers outside the court; no packed benches of pressmen eager for a juicy quote to enliven a slow news day; no crowded public gallery, with spectators hanging on every word of the proceedings, as if they were at a play. Here, in the back parlour of the Crown public house, an altogether less theatrical affair was enacted. Only the main actors in the sorry little drama were called. First of these was Sergeant Flanagan, who gave his account in the dry, unemotional voice Rowlands recalled from his own interrogation by the Gardai officer. He had been summoned to Castleford at 21.35, he said, reading aloud from his notes. He had proceeded to the stable-yard where he found the body of a man identified as Christie Doherty lying on the ground with a bullet wound in his chest. The doctor had arrived at 21.42, and had confirmed that life was extinct. He (Flanagan) had taken statements from several witnesses, including Michael Cullen, and had then taken Cullen into custody for his own protection.

'What's that you say?' interrupted the coroner, whose name was Brady. 'Had somebody threatened the witness?'

'No, sir. But Doherty's uncle's an associate of O'Donovan's.'

'I see.' Brady sounded as if he *did* see. Presumably, thought Rowlands, the fact that the dead man's uncle was a friend of the IRA man was reason enough for Doherty's alleged killer to fear for his life. And indeed, Mickey Cullen, the next witness to be called, *did* sound fearful. In a trembling voice, he admitted to finding the body. He'd had a falling-out with Doherty that same evening, he went on, but he hadn't killed him. Another of the stable hands, Paddy Monaghan, was then questioned. He had overheard Cullen and Doherty 'having words' on the night of the murder, he said, adding that he thought the quarrel was over some money that Doherty owed Cullen. He'd gone home at around half past eight, he said, having given the horses their last feed, so he wasn't there when the shooting took place. The final witness to be called was Daniel Pheelan, the head groom. He testified to Cullen's previous good character, and hinted that the same account could not be given for the character of the deceased: 'I'm not a man to speak ill of the dead,' he said. 'But Christie Doherty could be a quarrelsome feller. Then there was that business with the money that went missing.'

'That was never proved!' shouted a voice from the body of the courtroom where Rowlands was sitting. He recognised it as that of Pat Doolan, the gamekeeper, and Doherty's uncle. After silence had been enjoined, and the last witness dismissed, the coroner retired to consider his verdict.

A short interval elapsed, during which a general muttering arose. Of this, Rowlands could make out only a few phrases: 'If the boy isn't taken up at once, the big feller'll have something to say.'

'Ah, he'll not let that pass, right enough.'

The import of this only became clear when – a verdict of 'unlawful killing by person or persons unknown' having duly been pronounced by the coroner – Rowlands and the canon made their way out of the pub, to find that a sizeable crowd had assembled. 'Oh dear!' murmured the old man. 'I was afraid that something like this might happen.'

They were just behind Sergeant Flanagan, who was escorting Cullen to the waiting police car. As these two emerged from the doorway of the Crown, a shrill voice rang out: 'That's him! That's the one who killed my Christie!' Rowlands supposed that this must be Doherty's mother. Then came a cry from Mickey Cullen as a missile – perhaps a stone – hit him. The next moment, pandemonium broke out.

'Get him, boys!' cried another voice from the crowd, which surged forward. Burly men jostled Rowlands and his companion aside. 'Teach the murdering swine a lesson!' Things looked ugly.

'Stand back!' shouted the Gardai officer. 'Stand back, I say! This is police business, Donnie O'Donovan. I'll not have ye interfering.'

'And just how are ye going to stop me?' sneered the IRA man. 'Ye're outnumbered.' His eye must have fallen on Rowlands at that moment, for he went on, 'Although I see ye've brought your *English* friends with ye, to back ye up.' At this gibe, there was a burst of rude laughter from the crowd.

'I have *not!*' cried the exasperated Flanagan – who, Rowlands guessed, had as little liking for the English as O'Donovan himself. 'They're nothing to do with me.'

'The sergeant's right,' said Rowlands, addressing his remarks in the direction of the IRA man. 'I'm here on my own account – to see justice done. I was told it's something that matters a good deal to your countrymen – but perhaps I was wrong?'

There came an angry growl from the crowd, but then, suddenly, O'Donovan laughed. 'The man's right,' he said. 'Even if he *is* an Englishman. We Irish *do* care about justice. Let the boy go,' he added to one of his lieutenants. 'He's better off in gaol until they hang him.'

'I didn't do it!' shouted Cullen, his voice breaking with fear. 'I swear, Donnie O'Donovan . . .'

'Save that for the trial,' was the reply. 'Come on, you men. Mary. . .' This was to Mrs Doherty. 'You'd better go home.'

And with that word from their stern leader, the crowd melted away – all except for O'Donovan himself. 'I liked what you said, Englishman,' he said to Rowlands. 'Were it not for the fact that I hate your kind, I'd be glad of a talk with you, one of these days.'

'I'm not your enemy,' replied Rowlands. 'But I know that probably cuts no ice with a man like you.'

'And what sort of a man is that?' said the other, with a hint of steel in his voice.

'A man who doesn't believe that the past can ever be forgiven or forgotten,' said Rowlands.

The other man considered this for a moment. 'There's a lot to forgive, as you put it. I had an uncle hanged in Kilmainham Gaol, during the War of Independence. He left a wife and child – my cousin Tommy. My father was a volunteer. He was in the crowd when the police fired on unarmed men at a football match.'

'That was after the killings on Bloody Sunday, wasn't it?' said Rowlands quietly.

'And what if it was? Those men were British spies and informers.'

'You mean they *deserved* to die – but your uncle and those men in the football crowd didn't?'

'It was war,' said O'Donovan harshly. 'And we got our independence in the end, didn't we? Now your country's got itself into another war.' He laughed. 'You won't find *this* one easy to win, either.'

'We'll see about that,' said Rowlands. 'Mickey Cullen's uncle was in Kilmainham Gaol, too, wasn't he?'

O'Donovan emitted a contemptuous snort. 'Indeed he was – and they let him out without a scratch on him,' he said. 'You can't trust a Cullen, is what I say.'

'I don't believe that boy killed Christie Doherty,' said Rowlands. 'But I'm quite sure Doherty tried to bring about Lord Castleford's death. It was he who cut the stirrup leather, wasn't it?'

'I don't know anything about that,' said the IRA man. 'And if I did, I wouldn't say. It seems to me that one dead English lord, more or less, is hardly a matter to grieve over.'

'Shame on you for those words, Donal O'Donovan,' said Canon Wetherby, who had been standing silently by during this exchange of views. 'To think that a man who calls himself a good Catholic should make light of any man's death.'

'I don't see that it's any concern of yours,' replied the Irishman, but he had the grace to sound abashed. 'You're not even of the true faith, Father.'

'It's all one whether you're Catholic or Protestant,' said the old man. 'You've heard of the Ten Commandments, I suppose? "Thou shalt not kill." We adhere to *that* precept in our church, just as you do in yours.'

'Ah, to hell with your Sunday school lectures!' snapped O'Donovan. 'I've no time to be standing here blethering like an old woman.' With which he took himself off.

'Well,' said Rowlands when the two of them were alone once more. 'I call that a very respectable draw.'

But the canon seemed unamused by the quip. 'I'm afraid that what you said just now was all too true,' he said sadly. 'For as long as men like O'Donovan refuse to forgive and forget, there'll be war in Ireland.' He was going to call at the gaol, he said, to check on Mickey Cullen. 'I don't imagine the boy has a solicitor who'll speak for him. I want to make sure that he isn't bullied into confessing to something he didn't do.'

Rowlands said he would go with him to the police station at Enniskerry where the boy was being held. He was curious to hear more of Cullen's story, and to make his own assessment of the lad's character. His previous encounter with Cullen had been when the youth's quick thinking had alerted the rest of the household to Swift's accident; it was hard to believe that the same young man could have planned and carried out a cold-blooded murder.

The Gardai station at Enniskerry was a modest building – 'one of the old-fashioned sort,' said Canon Wetherby as they got out of the taxi that had brought them to its door. The taxi itself – a Ford, at least twenty years old, whose suspension left something to be desired – could also have been described as old-fashioned, thought Rowlands as the canon, refusing the other's offer of sharing the cost, paid off the driver. 'That's for you, Mick Malone,' he said. 'And don't go spending it on drink.' The man assured him that he would not. 'Teresa Malone's boy,' said the old clergyman to Rowlands – by which the latter guessed he meant the Castleford cook. Once inside the police station, the canon fell into conversation with the officer behind the desk: 'How's yourself, Martin O'Connor? The missus up and about yet, is she?' – to which the policeman replied that indeed, she and the baby were doing fine. Rowlands wondered to himself if everybody in this part of Ireland knew everybody else's business, but he had little time to reflect on this, because Garda O'Connor was already leading the way towards the cells where Mickey Cullen awaited them.

'He's very low,' said the police officer. 'But he'll be glad to see you, Father.'

They found Cullen lying on his bunk in the tiny cell where, two months before, Ned Swift had also been held, the night before his transfer to the Dublin gaol. The boy's mood was indeed subdued: 'Will they hang me, Father?' he said, sounding close to tears.

'Now then, no need to fear the worst,' said the old man. 'You'll be entitled to a trial first, won't he, Mr Rowlands?' – a piece of information that didn't seem to reassure the boy much. Since there was no room for both visitors to sit down (the canon, as was proper, having taken the only chair), Rowlands remained standing at the door. Sergeant Flanagan, whom they'd encountered in the corridor on their way to the cells, had said that they might have ten minutes with the lad. It struck Rowlands that the Gardai officer had seemed less stand-offish than before. Perhaps it was the fact of Rowlands having bested the IRA man in argument that had tipped the scales in the Englishman's favour, perhaps not.

Whatever the reason, Flanagan had been almost cordial, remarking that it was good of them to take an interest in the Cullen lad. 'Not that he's been formally charged, as yet,' he added. 'But I judged it best to keep him here, for the time being. We wouldn't want anyone taking the law into their own hands. There are an awful lot of hotheads about.'

Now, as Canon Wetherby did his best to calm the

boy, Rowlands went back over the events of the night before last, as he had heard them described, in case there was anything he'd missed. 'I'd like to ask you a few questions, Mickey, if that's all right?' he said as, his business concluded, the canon got up to leave, having promised to carry a message to Cullen's mother. 'I don't mind,' said Cullen.

'All right,' Rowlands went on. 'I want you to cast your mind back to that night – Tuesday night – and think very hard about what happened.'

'I've already *told* the poliss what happened!'

'I'm not the police. And I'm not out to trip you up. I just want to know if there was anything you saw . . . or heard . . . that might cast some light on what went on.'

'What kind of thing?'

'That's for you to say.' Rowlands was anxious not to put words in the other's mouth. He smiled. 'It's my belief that people often notice a lot more than they realise. But let's start at the beginning. Was it you who asked Doherty to come to the stable-yard, or did he ask to see you?'

'Well, that's the funny thing,' said Cullen. 'He *said* he'd come because he got my note. But I never sent him a note.'

'I see. But when you saw him, you naturally asked him about the money he owed you?'

'I did. I thought that was why he'd come – to pay me back the ten pounds. He'd been saying for weeks he'd give it back as soon as he had the money.'

'So it wasn't you who asked him for it?'

'I've already told you. I never expected him that night.'

'All right, that's clear enough. So while you and Doherty were talking over this matter of the money he owed you, were you aware of anything – or anyone – else?'

'I don't understand.'

'I'll put it more plainly. Were you and Doherty the only ones there, at that time, in the stable-yard?'

'We were. All the other lads had gone home. I was just going off for my tea, too, when Christie Doherty arrived.'

'But you were overheard quarrelling with Doherty by another of the stable hands, were you not?'

'Ah, to be sure. That was Paddy Monaghan. He'd come back to collect his jacket. But he didn't stay more than a minute.'

'Was there anyone else there you were aware of?'

'I don't know what you mean, sir.'

'I mean,' said Rowlands carefully, 'did you see or hear anyone else in the stable-yard after Monaghan left?'

The boy thought for a moment. 'As to seeing or hearing anybody, I can't say as I did,' he replied. Rowlands' heart sank. 'But now you mention it, sir, I think there might have been somebody about . . .'

'Oh? What makes you think that?'

'Why, the dogs, sir. They was kicking up a fearful row. Since . . . since the master left, they've been shut up at nights in the shed where we keep the tack.'

'And you think they wouldn't have barked unless somebody was about?'

'Well, not to say as they *never* would,' admitted the boy. 'But they know me, and Paddy. Even Christie wouldn't have set them off, not the way they was going on.'

'So you think somebody – a stranger – might have been in the stable-yard, at the time you were having your set-to with Doherty?' persisted Rowlands.

'It's possible, sir.' With which Rowlands had to be content. Soon after this, Garda O'Connor put his head around the door to say that time was up.

'So . . . if I've got this right . . . you're suggesting that a vagrant or some other intruder might have been responsible for killing Doherty?' said Canon Wetherby as the two men left the Gardai station.

'It's one theory,' replied the other.

'I'm sure Mickey's family will be grateful to you for trying,' said the old man. 'But I'm not sure I quite follow what you're hoping to achieve.'

'I'm not entirely sure myself,' said Rowlands. 'It's only that if one could create a doubt in the minds of the jury, it might help Cullen's case.' When Malone's taxi had dropped them off at the house, Rowlands decided to follow up what he'd learnt by taking a walk to the stables. There was still over an hour to go before dinner, and he wanted to familiarise himself with the lie of the land once more. Leaving the canon writing letters in the small sitting room, he made his way, via the boot room, to the cobbled yard behind the house, and through the ornamental arch beyond that led to the stable-yard. He hadn't expected to find many others about – it being past six o'clock – but was surprised to find the place deserted. Then he remembered that a number of the Castleford employees had been at the inquest that afternoon and might now be refreshing themselves over a pint or two of the local brew in the Crown. Rowlands couldn't help envying them.

It was certainly quiet in the yard. Only the soft whinnying and stamping of the horses in their stalls disturbed the silence. 'Anybody there?' he called, but there was no reply. It struck him that the dogs mustn't yet have been shut up for the night, since there was no sound from them either. If Cullen's account was to be believed, they would otherwise have been 'kicking up a row'. Cautiously, Rowlands made his way towards the door that led into the main building. He remembered from his earlier visit with Swift that this was a lofty, barn-like structure, with a central aisle running between two rows of stalls. Four of the six facing onto the yard were occupied with the animals he had previously encountered: Lady Molly, Duke Humphrey, Delilah and the formidable Lucifer. The six facing these were empty. It was to these that he first directed his attention. Because where better, he thought, to conceal oneself in a stable-yard than in one of the empty stalls? He didn't really expect to find concrete evidence that anyone had been there on Tuesday night, but he saw how it might have been done.

He made his way along the row of empty stalls, all swept clean, but still smelling of the straw that had once covered the floor. 'My father kept a dozen hunters' . . . He remembered Swift's proud boast on that day, two months before and, for an instant, allowed his imagination to fill each stall with a fine thoroughbred, all glossy coat and haughtily arched neck. Those must have been the glory days of the Irish Ascendancy, he thought. Now, they were reduced in number as in circumstances, clinging to the vestiges of their power and wealth. He couldn't say he pitied them as a class: they had had things their own way too long. Others (he thought of O'Donovan and his crew) would take back what they claimed was rightfully theirs. It was happening everywhere, not least in England. The old order was dying – and good riddance.

And yet he couldn't help regretting the passing of that golden pre-war era (golden only for some, he reminded himself) with its devotion to the pleasures of the chase and the table; its wasp-waisted women in their white dresses and preposterous cartwheel hats; its hard-drinking men in their hunting clothes, with their cigars and their chaff, their unshakeable conviction that they were born to rule. Even though Rowlands himself had never belonged to such a world, it had been part of the national myth to which he and everybody else

280

had subscribed. The myth of Britain's greatness and invincibility, its civilised values and cultural superiority. All that had been blown away by the war, of course – the one that had also destroyed Rowlands' sight, and with it, his youth. Now there would be other young men who would pay the price, in this new war.

Finding nothing to interest him in the empty stalls on the left-hand side, Rowlands turned his attention to those on the right, at the end of the row furthest from the door. There were two of these – both fairly recently occupied, to judge from the straw that still covered the ground, and the faint smell of dried horse droppings. He recalled Swift telling him that his neighbour – Langton, presumably – stabled two of his horses at Castleford. No doubt with the falling-off in the numbers of staff since Swift's arrest, it had become necessary to move the animals elsewhere. After a brief word with Lady Molly, whose stall was next door – 'Hello, old girl. Remember me?' – he went inside the first of these, familiar now with the layout: a half-door (now bolted) that opened onto the stable-yard; an iron basket – or hay rack – fixed to the wall, and still half-full. For no reason that he could afterwards recall, he thrust his hand down into the hay, and felt around. Nothing. He was wasting his time in idle speculation. Yes, it was perfectly possible that somebody had stood where he was standing, eavesdropping on the row between Cullen and Doherty, and no, there wasn't the slightest bit of proof.

His hand encountered a hard object, which had been pushed down to the bottom of the hay rack. He knew at once what it was. A clasp knife. If he wasn't mistaken, it was the very one with which Doherty – or another – had scored the stirrup leathers on Swift's horse. Rowlands weighed the knife in his hand, with a feeling of mounting excitement. It was evidence at last. As he stepped away from the wall to which the hay rack was attached, he became aware, for the first time, that he wasn't alone. Someone had entered the stall behind him. 'Who's there?' he went to say, but before the words were out, he felt a shattering blow on the back of his head, and all was silence.

Chapter Fifteen

From all around came the screaming of horses, terrified by the constant shelling. Some – poor beasts – had been wounded in the attack, and now lay on the ground, thrashing about in their agony as the bombardment went on, their riders dying or dead, and thus unable to put them out of their misery. 'My God,' he said to Perkins, who crouched beside him, behind the big gun. 'I can't stand to listen to this.' But if the other man heard him, he gave no sign of it, perhaps deafened by the roar of the shells, so that for him the grey landscape of mud and stumps of trees was as silent as the smoke that drifted across it.

Smoke. The acrid smell of it was in Rowlands' nostrils. He gasped, drew a breath and choked. But the act of trying to catch his breath brought him back to consciousness. Painfully, he sat up, realising in the same moment that what had seemed the stuff of nightmares was in fact all too real: the stable building was on fire, and the terrified neighing that had seemed a part of his dream came from the stalls next to the one where he'd been attacked, where the Castleford horses were stabled. He staggered to his feet, his head throbbing from the blow that had rendered him temporarily unconscious. As he pulled himself upright, using the iron frame of the hay rack for support (the knife he'd found there was gone from his pocket, of course) he discovered that there was a full bucket of – now brackish – water standing beneath it. Quickly, he soaked his handkerchief and tied it around his nose and mouth – a rudimentary mask. He pushed open the door that led to the central corridor, but was immediately driven back by the heat of the flames. No wonder the horses were panicking.

Fighting his way through the choking cloud of smoke, he ran to the main door, only to find it locked and barred on the outside. Shouting and hammering on the unresponsive surface brought no answering shout from outside. Whoever had imprisoned him here had chosen his moment well. Returning to the stall he had just left, he tried the half-door that opened onto the yard, but it, too, was bolted on the outside. He didn't doubt that it would be the same in the other stalls, with the additional hazard, for a blind man, of trying to get past a frightened horse in order to reach the door. Well, he had little choice in the matter if he were to get out alive. He wondered how far the fire had established itself. Might there be a chance of putting it out before it took hold irrevocably? He seized the bucket and, glad of the protection of his mask, carried what remained of the water towards where he judged the fire was at its fiercest, and flung it over the flames. There was a hiss of steam, but it seemed to make little difference. Unless help came soon, he and the equine inhabitants of the stable building would suffocate in the smoke – or burn to death. He forced himself not to think of this.

Lady Molly was as restless as he had ever known her to be, tossing her mane and trembling as Rowlands edged his way into the stall, murmuring soothing words. 'It's all right, old girl. Don't be afraid. I'm going to get us out of here.' As he had suspected, the half-door was locked on the outside. Once more, he banged on the wooden shutter, shouting for help. Meanwhile, the mare was becoming increasingly agitated; Rowlands was afraid that she might kick out at him in her panic. 'It's all right,' he said. 'It's all right, Molly.' To his delight, he found that there was also a bucket of water, almost full, beneath the hay rack. He picked it up and, taking his time so as not to alarm the horse more than he had to, made for the door. Again, he flung the water, and again, there was a hiss and a spitting, but no appreciable diminution of the fire. Even if he managed to retrieve further buckets of water from the stalls of the other three horses, he was afraid it wouldn't be enough to extinguish the blaze.

Then it struck him: there was another, arguably more

effective way, of putting out a fire. He edged his way back into Lady Molly's stall, talking to her all the time. 'It's all right, it's all right. You're going to help me, Molly, my dear. Just let me get a bit closer, won't you?' Because as he'd edged past her the first time, careful to stay close to the wall, he'd brushed against the mare's solid flanks, and realised that she was wearing a blanket. This, with many apologies and endearments, he removed from around her shoulders, releasing the strap that held it in place and dragging the heavy cloth towards the door. Might it serve, with those of the other horses added to it, to smother the flames? Well, he would soon find out.

Duke Humphrey's was the next stall into which he must venture. This was an older horse and, like Lady Molly, renowned for his quiet behaviour. 'You remember me, don't you, old fellow?' Gently patting and stroking the trembling animal, Rowlands managed to detach the blanket from his back, and to lug it towards the fire, as before. Was it having an effect? It was hard to tell. No sooner did he succeed in smothering one part of the fire, it seemed to him, than another burst of flames sprang up elsewhere. Now for Delilah. This proved to be a more spirited creature than the other two, and for a few moments, Rowlands wondered if he would manage to get into the stall and remove the blanket without injury to himself. But as he flattened himself against the wall, waiting for the nervous animal to stop dancing around, it struck him that a greater challenge was ahead of him. Lucifer. Already he could hear the

286

furious neighing and stamping of hooves from the next stall. The sound of his voice, murmuring soothing words, appeared to calm Delilah – would it have the same effect on the stallion?

Having thrown the third horse blanket over the fire, adding the contents of two more buckets of water for good measure, it struck Rowlands that his strategy was having an effect. Certainly the heat seemed less extreme – unless it was just that he was getting used to it? Sweat poured down his face and back, but this was as much from his exertions as from the fire. Well, that made it all the more imperative to tackle Lucifer. Come on, my lad, he said to himself. He's just a horse – not the devil incarnate. But as he entered the stall, he wondered if, after all, he had taken a risk too far. Because in his panic, the terrified animal was crashing around, as if he wanted to kick his way out of the place. 'Steady on,' said Rowlands firmly. 'You'll do us both no good, carrying on like this.' But his words had no effect. As he stretched out his hand, Lucifer reared up, making it impossible for Rowlands to remove the blanket. Smoke filled the stall, threatening to choke both man and beast.

Then, just as he was giving up all hope of ever getting out of there alive – because if he wasn't suffocated or burnt to death, he'd be kicked to pieces by a rogue horse, he thought wildly – he heard the sound he'd been subconsciously listening out for all the time: the wonderful, exhilarating sound of barking dogs.

* * *

'Sure, it's a good thing we came along when we did,' said Daniel Pheelan when the fire – already waning, thanks to Rowlands' efforts – had been extinguished, and the frightened horses given temporary shelter in a neighbouring barn. 'Who knows what might have happened?' It was a thought that had occurred to Rowlands. If he'd remained unconscious for a few minutes longer, allowing the fire to take hold . . . If Pheelan and the Monaghan lad, alerted by the barking dogs, hadn't heard his shouts for help . . .

'I'm grateful to you both, but especially to the dogs,' he said.

'Ah, to be sure,' said the head groom. 'We'd taken the dogs with us to the hearing at the Crown this afternoon – you was there yourself, sir, I believe? Had to tie 'em up outside while the business was going on. Couldn't leave them shut up all day, and Tom O'Brien has his hands full at the home farm just now. Paddy was just after bringing them back to their quarters for the night when they started up their noise. O' course, it was the smell of the smoke that set them off.'

They were sitting in the room Pheelan had fitted up for the purpose in one of the buildings adjacent to the stables, with a couple of chairs and an oil stove presently giving off a good heat (although Rowlands had had more than enough of *that* for the time being). Pheelan had brewed up a mug of tea on the aforesaid stove, to which he'd added several spoonfuls of sugar – 'Good for the shock' – insisting that Rowlands should drink it down.

Now he said: 'What was you doing in the stables, sir, if I might ask? Was it myself you were wanting to see?'

'Not exactly.' Rowlands was wary of saying more. 'I had an idea I wanted to follow up, that's all.'

Pheelan was silent a moment as if turning something over in his mind. Then he said, 'The lad, young Paddy there, found these that you'd dropped in the yard.' He handed Rowlands what turned out to be a packet of his preferred brand of smokes – Churchman's. One cigarette was missing. 'But . . .' Rowlands thrust a hand into the pocket of his tweed jacket, and found it empty. 'I suppose these *are* mine,' he said. 'Only I hope you don't think that I'd do such a thing as to light up inside the stables? I know enough to realise how dangerous that could be.'

'Indeed, sir, indeed,' said the other, sounding uncomfortable. 'It'd be the most likely cause of a fire, with all the straw lying about.'

'You can't think it was *I* who set the place on fire?' said Rowlands indignantly.

'I'm sure I don't know what to think, sir,' replied the other. 'All I know is what I saw.'

'Then how do you account for the fact that I was locked in?' demanded Rowlands. 'The stable door – and the doors to each of the stalls – were bolted shut on the outside.'

'We always make sure that the horses are shut in for the night,' replied Pheelan, perhaps not grasping the implications of Rowlands' question. 'Wouldn't do for them to get out. It'd cause no end of trouble.'

'I realise that, but—'

'It may be, o' course, that a tramp or some gypsy feller was after stealing the horses, like,' Pheelan went on, in a more conciliatory tone. 'It'll have been *he* who dropped that cigarette, no doubt. Then when he heard you coming, he ran away, and bolted the door behind him. Yes, that'll have been the way of it.' Rowlands made no attempt to dignify this piece of fiction with a reply. In the mind of the head groom, he was evidently an irresponsible outsider who had blundered into the stables, carelessly dropping a lighted cigarette, and then found himself trapped. Everything else the man had said was mere face-saving.

Wearily, he made his way back to the house, looking forward to nothing else but his bed and a hot bath before that to wash away the smoke and grime of the past hour. At the kitchen door, he was met by an anxious Mrs Malone (evidently the tale of his misfortunes had already got around). Was he hurt? she wanted to know. Rowlands brushed aside her concern. He'd no more than a few cuts and bruises, he said. Nothing a good night's sleep wouldn't put right. 'Speaking of which, I think I'll go straight to my room,' he said. 'Perhaps you'd convey my apologies to Canon Wetherby and Mr and Mrs Butler, and say that I won't be joining them for dinner.'

'I'll have a tray sent up to you, sir,' replied the cook. Rowlands thanked her, although he didn't think he'd manage to eat much tonight. He realised, now that his ordeal was over, that he was bone-tired. The exertions of trying to fight a fire while grappling with a string of terrified horses, had made him ache in every limb. All he craved was the oblivion of sleep. But, having bathed and readied himself for bed, he found that his mind was still whirling. How was it that Pheelan and his lad had happened to be so conveniently absent from the stable-yard that evening? And – even if this could be put down to coincidence – who was it who'd locked him in, having first rendered him unconscious? Who, above all, had set the fire that might have killed him, destroying the Castleford stables and their valuable livestock in the process? He began to see that the mind behind all this – and all the horrors that had preceded it – was one of utter ruthlessness. A mind for which pity, remorse and reason were alien concepts.

In spite of his restless night, Rowlands awoke before six, mindful that today was the last day of Ned Swift's trial, and that he and the canon were due to attend the proceedings. Connolly was driving up from Dublin to collect them, directly after breakfast. Having washed and dressed, he descended the stairs to the breakfast room where he found, to his surprise, that he was not the first down that morning. Canon Wetherby was there, as expected, placidly eating his kipper, but he had been joined not only by the Butlers, but by the Dowager Lady Castleford. Since his arrival the day before yesterday, Rowlands had glimpsed the old lady only once, in the corridor on the way to his room that first night. He understood from everything he'd been told that she'd become a virtual invalid. Now, her shrill voice rose above that of the others as she chattered of this and that: '. . . *much* better for the nerves, I find. I always *insist* on a spoonful of honey in my tea. I even add it to my skin food. The results are quite noticeable after only a few weeks. You ought to try it, my dear,' she added, evidently addressing the land agent's wife. 'It might do something for you.'

Mrs Butler replied in an offended tone that soap and water was quite enough for *her*, while the canon, ever the peacemaker, murmured that *he* liked a spot of honey on his porridge, he didn't mind who knew it. 'Ah, Rowlands, *there* you are,' he said as the latter came in. 'No ill effects from your alarming experience yesterday, I hope? Shocking business, shocking. I gather from Daniel Pheelan that some vagrant got into the stable-yard last night. Dropped a match, too, from the sound of it. Dangerous thing. Whole place might've gone up in smoke.' Helping himself to eggs and bacon, Rowlands agreed that it had been a close call.

'Yes, most disturbing,' said Butler. 'I'll have to address the damage to the stables later.' He sighed. 'It'll be another charge upon the estate, at a time when it can be ill-afforded. However, no use crying over spilt milk, I always say.'

'Pheelan tells me that if it hadn't been for your quick-wittedness, the damage to the building would have been much greater,' said the canon. 'To say nothing of what might have happened to the horses. Merciful heavens! When I think that that fine thoroughbred of his might have perished in the flames, it sends a shiver up my spine.'

'To be sure,' said the land agent, pouring himself a fresh cup of coffee. ''Twould have been a calamity, and no mistake. Were you hurt yourself, Mr Rowlands?'

'Not to speak of,' replied the other. 'As you say, it could have been much worse.'

Mrs Butler opined that it was a pity that the police didn't spend more time catching vagrants and arsonists and the like, instead of meddling in things they didn't understand. 'Playing detective!' she said scornfully, in case anyone had missed her meaning.

'Now then, my dear,' remonstrated her husband. 'I'm sure our local constabulary are doing their best. Although it's true that they don't seem to have made much progress with our own unfortunate affair.'

'Ah, there's Patsy Connolly now,' said the canon as a car was heard drawing up outside. 'He's nice and early. I'll ask John to bring our bags down, shall I, Rowlands? As soon as you're ready, we can be off.'

'Where are you going? Anywhere exciting?' said Lady Castleford eagerly. She might have been a child, anticipating a treat.

'Only to Dublin, Eveline my dear,' replied Aloysius Wetherby.

'Not London, then?' She sounded disappointed. 'You're the man from London, aren't you?' she said to Rowlands, touching his sleeve. 'The friend of Celia's. You see, I *hadn't* forgotten! People tell me my memory's wonderful for my age.' She giggled naughtily. 'It's true!

I remember all sorts of things – sometimes things I *shouldn't*.'

'You always were a sharp one, Eveline, even as a girl,' said the canon.

'That's right!' She gave another delighted giggle. 'You have to get up *very* early in the morning to get past me. Or go to bed *very* late at night,' she added cryptically.

Butler rose from the table at that moment, saying in his usual self-satisfied way that if they'd all excuse him, he had a *mountain* of work to get on with. 'I take it you'll be attending this morning's hearing, with Her Ladyship?' he said, adding in a concerned tone, 'This morning's papers take a rather dismal view of the prospective outcome. But we must live in hope. That's what I always say.'

Chapter Sixteen

It was the closing day of the defence case. All the witnesses – for and against – had been heard. There was only the closing statement by the prosecution and defence counsels, and the judge's summing-up to go before the jury would be asked to retire to consider their verdict. Mr Justice Walsh accordingly addressed the jury: 'Members of the Jury, you have now heard all the evidence in this case. There remains only counsels' speeches and my own summing-up for you to hear. These will take place on Monday morning. However, there remain some Points of Law which I wish to discuss with counsel, which you are not required to hear. I will therefore discharge you a little earlier than usual for the weekend. I should like to remind you that you are not to discuss this case with anyone outside this courtroom, nor to read accounts of it in the press.' With a general shuffling of feet, and clearing of throats, the court rose, and the members of the jury began to file out. A general atmosphere of relaxation prevailed. Into this momentary calm, there came, from the back of the public gallery, an intervention: 'Everything you've been told is a pack of lies! All that nonsense about forged signatures and land sales . . . My husband was killed for quite another reason.'

Beside him, Rowlands felt Lady Celia give a start. 'Henrietta!' she gasped, her cry lost in the general uproar that greeted this bombshell.

'Madam,' the judge was saying. 'I cannot allow this kind of thing in my courtroom. If you say another word, I will have you removed.'

But Henrietta Swift was now on her feet. 'Ask Lord Castleford,' she said, 'about the letters his wife wrote to my husband. *There's* his reason for murder . . .'

'Enough! Clear the courtroom,' thundered Mr Justice Walsh. 'Members of the jury, you are to disregard what you have just heard. It is not evidence.' But the interloper had already gone, letting the door to the public gallery swing shut behind her, and leaving consternation in her wake.

Unsurprisingly, after Henrietta Swift's dramatic intervention, the press reaction was sensational: *Peer Accused of Murder in Court by Wife of Deceased* being the most restrained of the headlines in that evening's papers. All Dublin was agog to hear the outcome of what had been, for some, the event of the year. Even the reports, published the following day, of a speech Herr Hitler had delivered to the Reichstag, claiming to have countered alleged aggression by Polish forces through 'peaceful' means, and sending an ultimatum to Churchill that this supposedly conciliatory message would be his last attempt to broker a settlement, did not take precedence – in the Irish newspapers at least – over the Castleford murder trial.

Faced with the knowledge that he might now have to rethink his strategy entirely, Sir Anthony was unusually sombre. 'It's a facer,' he said when the five of them – the counsel for the defence, his junior, Mr Harker, Lady Celia, Rowlands and Canon Wetherby – were assembled in Griffin's chambers. 'I won't deny that it puts a very different complexion on this case.' He was silent a moment before addressing Lady Celia: 'I assume that the letters Mrs Swift referred to actually exist?'

'Yes.'

'I see. And was your husband aware of this?'

'You'll have to ask him.'

'Hmph.' Again, Sir Anthony hesitated, as if trying to find a way of phrasing what he had to say as delicately as possible. 'I take it, then, that the *contents* of the letters might be prejudicial to your . . . to Lord Castleford's . . . interests?'

'Almost certainly,' was the reply.

Sir Anthony considered this. 'It might mean a retrial,' he said gravely. 'It depends what my learned friend

Riordan wants to make of this. And whether Dicky Walsh will allow fresh evidence to be introduced at this stage. I do *wish*, m'dear, that you had been a little more *forthcoming* with me at the start of all this.' He gave a short, unhappy laugh. 'But never mind. What's done is done. We shall just have to make the best of it.' He and Mr Harker would go immediately to the Mountjoy, he went on, in order to consult his client as to how best to proceed.

'I'll come with you,' said Lady Celia. 'Frederick, I'd like you to come too. Cousin Aloysius' – this to the canon – 'perhaps you could return to Merrion Square? I'll need somebody to steady the ship, and to keep the servants from talking to the press. The next few days aren't going to be very pleasant for any of us.'

On their arrival at the prison, Lady Celia said that she wanted a private word with her husband, and so the three men waited outside in the corridor until she had finished. None of them spoke. Sir Anthony shuffled the documents he was carrying as if the clue to what had turned into a far less straightforward case than he'd anticipated might lie there; his junior, Mr Harker, whistled softly under his breath until told by his superior to desist. 'Whistling in a gaol – have you no care for people's feelings?' he said, with uncharacteristic sharpness.

The young man apologised. 'I wasn't thinking.'

'That's the trouble nowadays. People don't think.'

At last the door of the cell opened and Lady Celia

emerged. 'All right,' she said, touching Rowlands on the arm. 'Let's go.' There was an artificial brightness in her tone that told him all he needed to know. The interview with Swift had not gone well; Rowlands supposed there had been harsh words, or worse, cold indifference. Before he could consider the implications of this, she set off along the corridor at such a pace that he almost had to break into a run to catch up with her.

Sir Anthony, too, must have been taken aback by the suddenness of her departure. 'Lady Celia,' he cried as he came panting along behind. 'Lady Celia, where can I find you . . . if I should need to?'

'I'll be at Castleford.' She gave a grim little laugh. 'No sense in sticking it out in Merrion Square. The jackals will have surrounded the place by now.'

'Quite so. Then if I were to telephone you this evening . . .'

'What for?'

'Well . . .' He was still getting his breath back. Sir Anthony was not accustomed to running. 'If there should be any developments, you know.'

'You mean if my husband should decide to divorce me?' Again, the mirthless little laugh. 'I can save you the trouble of asking. He won't. He has far too much family pride for that.'

'So I may telephone, then?'

'If you like.' A thought appeared to strike her. 'I'll be taking the car.' (It had been the Bentley that had brought them all to the Mountjoy.) 'Do you want me to send it back for you?'

'No need, no need, dear lady. Harker will call us a taxi when we've finished with His Lordship.'

'Or perhaps,' she said, with the barest shade of irony, 'when he's finished with *you*.'

She took Rowlands' arm as they crossed the courtyard towards the prison gates. 'My husband said he didn't believe a word of it,' she said. 'He said Henrietta's accusations against me were the ravings of a madwoman.'

'He's right,' said Rowlands, but she wasn't prepared to let it go at that.

'I tried to tell him that there was more to it than he knew, but he said he didn't want to hear it. I was afraid it would come to this,' she added bitterly. 'He'll believe the worst, without ever giving me the chance to explain.'

'There'll be a time for that,' said Rowlands gently, but she didn't sound convinced.

'Will there?' They had reached the gate where a warder let them out, with a jangling of keys. 'Don't you think this has tipped the scales? If there was any doubt in the minds of the jury as to my husband's guilt, this will have removed it. It's what I feared would happen if the affair ever got out. It's given Ned a cast-iron motive for murdering Jolyon.'

'What Mrs Swift said won't be counted as evidence,' said Rowlands. 'If Riordan wants to pursue it, there'll have to be a retrial.'

'That would just about finish Ned,' said Lady Celia as the Bentley drew up alongside them. 'He's already had as much of this as he can stand. Oh, I almost forgot,' she added as the chauffeur got out to open the door for her. 'Ned said I was to thank you for saving his precious Lucifer, and for preventing the Castleford stables from burning down. I'm grateful, too. Castleford wouldn't have been the same without the horses.'

Nothing more was said on the drive back until the Bentley turned in to Merrion Square. Here, Lady Celia's remark that the 'jackals' of the press would be lying in wait proved all too prescient. As the car pulled up in front of the house, a crowd of reporters surged forward. Cameras clicked. 'Lady Celia! Is it true that you were romantically involved with your brother-in-law?'

'Would you like to comment on the allegations, Lady Celia?'

Doing his best to shield her from these audacious attacks, Rowlands had the satisfaction of stepping hard on the foot of one particular importunate pressman, who yelped in pain. 'Get out of the way!' said Rowlands angrily. 'You ought to be ashamed of yourself. Terrorising a woman.'

'Quite the Sir Galahad,' jeered the other, but he stepped back hastily when Rowlands turned to confront him, having first made sure that his charge was safely in the house.

'Who's he?' shouted another wag. 'The new boyfriend?' Rowlands didn't dignify this with a reply, but followed Lady Celia inside, leaving the chauffeur, Connolly, to fend off any further attempts on the part of the journalists to approach the house.

They were met in the hall by an anxious Canon Wetherby. 'There you are, my dear! It's been like this ever since I got back. People knocking on the door, and calling through the letterbox. The telephone ringing every few minutes. There it goes again!'

The butler made haste to silence the incessant ringing. 'No, you may *not* speak to Her Ladyship. Her Ladyship is not at home.'

'Take the receiver off the hook,' said his mistress. 'Tell Mrs K we'll have luncheon at one. And ask Bridget to pack me a bag. We'll be leaving for Castleford directly.'

Chapter Seventeen

The grey drizzle that had been falling all day, and which seemed to Rowlands a perfect expression of his present mood, lifted as they approached Enniskerry. A fitful sunshine grew stronger from then on, so that by the time they reached Castleford it felt almost like an Indian summer. 'It's one thing I've come to love about this part of Ireland,' remarked Lady Celia, breaking what had been a long silence. 'The weather can be absolutely foul, and then the clouds roll away, and you can see clear across to the mountains.'

Rowlands and Canon Wetherby murmured their appreciation of this fact – the weather being a safe topic when so much else could not be spoken of. 'I always think Castleford looks its best in the autumn,' said the old man as the Bentley passed through the gates and continued up the drive. 'You can see the bare bones of the place without all the greenery. Some people might find it too austere, but I like it.'

Again, there was a murmur of agreement. It was the last moment of concord there was to be that day. For as the car drove up to the front of the house, Celia Swift exclaimed, 'Oh no! What's *he* doing here?'

Before Rowlands had time to wonder who it was she meant, there came a shout from the terrace: 'I say, Celia!' It was Sebastian Gogarty. A moment later, the young man came hurrying down the steps towards the car. 'I h-had to come,' he stammered as Connolly, having got out of the car, went round to open the door for his mistress. 'I w-wanted to apologise.'

'You might have done that by letter, or telephone, Mr Gogarty,' she said, sweeping past him and up the steps to the front door.

'B-but Celia . . .'

As the youth went to follow her, Rowlands, getting out of the car at the same moment, put out a hand to detain him. 'Can't you take a hint?' he said. 'Lady Celia doesn't want to talk to you now.'

'W-what business is it of yours?' snapped the other. 'I've c-come to s-say I'm s-sorry for what I said.'

'Well, you've said it,' replied Rowlands. 'So there's no need for you to stick around.' His words were ignored, however. With an exclamation of impatience, Gogarty pulled away from him, and ran back to the house.

'Rather a hot-headed young feller,' observed the

canon. 'I'm sure he means well, but it might have been more considerate of Celia's feelings to stay away.' There was no arguing with this, and so Rowlands – whose feelings towards the 'young feller' were rather less forgiving – merely grunted.

Inside the house, they found other members of the household assembled. Monckton the butler was there, giving instructions to John the footman to carry the luggage upstairs. The land agent, too, had emerged from his office to boom words of greeting. 'Good to see Your Ladyship looking so well after your, ah, *ordeal*. I hope you left His Lordship in good health?'

'Thank you, Mr Butler. My husband was quite . . .' she began to reply, but at that moment there came a delighted shriek from the landing above.

'Mummy! You're here!' There followed a clattering of footsteps as young George Swift came running down the stairs, and hurled himself at his mother.

'Steady on!' She laughed. 'You almost knocked me over, Georgie.'

'Sorry for that, milady,' said the nurse, Miss McGurk, hurrying downstairs, with little Reginald tagging behind. 'He was that excited when he heard the car. I couldn't hold him.'

'Oh, *he's* the reason I've come,' said George's mother. 'We've heaps to talk about, haven't we, Georgie?' George agreed, and began jumping up and down in his enthusiasm, soon joined by Reggie, so that it was as if a couple of noisy puppies had taken over the hall – an illusion perfected by the arrival of George's pet spaniel, Rusty, whose frantic barking added to the commotion.

'Gracious! What's all the fuss?' demanded a querulous voice from the floor above. It was Lady Castleford, who had come out of her room to see what was going on.

'*Now* look what you've done, boys,' said Lady Celia, sounding anything but severe. 'You've woken poor Granny from her nap.'

'I wasn't asleep,' replied the elder lady with dignity. 'I'd only just closed my eyes. Doctor O'Leary said I was to rest for an hour every afternoon. I don't suppose I *shall*, now,' she said resentfully.

'I'm sorry, Eveline. Nurse, you'd better give the boys their tea. I'll come up and see you after you've had it,' she added to George, who was showing signs of mutiny. 'And we'll have tea in the library, Monckton.'

'Yes, m'lady.'

With which the party dispersed, to reassemble a few minutes later in front of the fire in the library where the tea trolley had just been brought in by Mary. As Rowlands entered the room – in his opinion one of the nicest in the house, with its distinctive smell of books, and its comfortably shabby furniture – he could hear Lady Castleford's shrill tones rising above the general murmur of voices. Her pug was being bullied by George's spaniel, she complained to Canon Wetherby. 'The wretched animal barks and barks. He quite frightens my poor Mitzie. She's very sensitive, you know.'

'I think he just wants to play,' said the canon, but Eveline remained unconvinced.

'Nasty, rough creature,' she said. 'He oughtn't to be allowed in the house.'

Across the room, Sebastian Gogarty was talking in low, urgent tones to Lady Celia. 'B-but you m-must see . . . It's the only s-sensible thing to do.'

Rowlands decided that the young man needed reining in. Celia had had quite enough to put up with today, without having to fend off this love-sick puppy. But as he started to make his way across the room, he found his path blocked by Elspeth Butler. 'Well, well,' she said. 'The resourceful Mr Rowlands. I hope you were not too shaken by your unpleasant experience in the stables, the other day?'

'I was lucky,' said Rowlands. 'Mr Pheelan came along at just the right time.'

'So he did,' was the reply. 'Oh, get *away* from me, you horrid little beast!' she cried suddenly, stepping back so hastily that she half-collided with Rowlands. It was the pug, Mitzie, she meant – a fact that became apparent when the dog's mistress rushed to defend her.

'You ought to look where you're putting your feet! You almost stepped on her! Poor little Mitzie.'

'You shouldn't let it run around like that. Sniffing

at people's ankles,' was the indignant retort. Leaving the two women to fight it out, Rowlands continued his progress across the room.

'Ah, Frederick, there you are!' Lady Celia did not conceal her relief at having her tête-à-tête interrupted. 'Mr Gogarty was just telling me that he intends to join up as soon as possible. I call that admirable, don't you?'

'Very,' said Rowlands. 'Which of the services are you hoping to join?' he asked the young man, who replied sulkily, 'The RAF, if they'll take me. Otherwise, the Irish Guards. I think *somebody* has to do *something*,' he added.

'I agree,' said Rowlands.

There was a moment's awkward silence before Lady Celia said, 'If you *really* want to do something for me, Mr Gogarty, you can fetch me another cup of tea.' She held out her empty cup for him to take, which he did, with what seemed to Rowlands an ill grace.

'What's got into him?' said Rowlands when Gogarty had taken himself off, although he had a fair idea.

Celia Swift laughed. 'He's angry because he asked me to go away with him, and I refused. So he says he'll join up instead. I suspect,' she added wryly, 'that he was trying to make me feel guilty about turning him down.'

'I don't doubt it. Silly young ass! Was that why he came back to Castleford?'

'So it would seem.' She sighed. 'Do me a favour, would you? Don't leave me alone with him. I don't think I could stand another declaration of love.'

'I'll do my best,' he said, wincing a little as it struck him that the remark might have been directed at him. Not that he'd ever made such a declaration, but after all these years, she couldn't be unaware of how he felt about her.

As if she realised that she'd made a faux pas, she reached out and touched his hand. 'Thank you,' she said softly. 'I don't know what I'd do without you.'

'I've done nothing.' Her words touched him, nonetheless.

'Oh, but you have,' she said, then, in a changed tone, 'Ah, here's my tea. Thank you, Mr Gogarty.'

'I *said* you could call me Sebastian,' replied the youth, in a resentful tone. He had doubtless noticed that Rowlands was 'Frederick' to her.

'And *I* said that I hadn't known you long enough,' she replied. 'I'd like to walk over to the stables after tea,' she said to Rowlands. 'I want to get an idea of how much damage there is, and what it would cost to repair.'

'I'll come with you,' said Gogarty at once.

'No. I'd prefer it if you'd stay here, Mr Gogarty. It's Mr Rowlands' advice I need. If it hadn't been for him, there'd be no stables left to inspect.'

'B-but . . .'

'If you really want to do something to help me,' she said, 'you can carry on with the job you started a few months ago – cataloguing the library. It'll need to be done, whatever happens.'

Gogarty mumbled a reply – really, he was a sullen

youth, thought Rowlands, resisting the urge to kick him. But he said no more about accompanying them, and when the party in the library began to drift away to bathe and change for dinner, Rowlands and his companion made their way to the stables. When they reached the fire-damaged buildings, Celia Swift stood for a while in silence. 'I hadn't realised quite how bad the damage was,' she said at last.

'It can be repaired,' said Rowlands, guessing that it was a deeper damage to which she referred.

'Perhaps. But if things go badly for Ned . . .' Her voice faltered. 'The truth is, I don't know if I'll be able to carry on at Castleford without him.'

'He'd want you to carry on,' said Rowlands quietly. 'For George's sake, as much as for his own.'

She said nothing for a moment, scuffing the ashes in which they were standing with the toe of her boot. 'How they must have hated us,' she said. 'The people who did this.'

'I'm not sure—' he began, but she cut across him.

'Maybe they're right, whoever they are, and it's time our sort were gone.' It wasn't too far from what he'd been thinking himself that day when he'd been poking around the stables, and had been knocked on the head for his inquisitiveness. Their sort – the Swifts and the rest of the landed class – had had their day, it was true. But he could take no pleasure in the thought.

* * *

Back at the house, they found the Langtons had just arrived; Monckton had shown them into the drawing room, he said. 'Shall I bring the drinks tray in, milady?'

'Yes, do,' she replied, then, sotto voce to Rowlands, 'I wonder what brings them here? Venetia! How nice of you to call!' she exclaimed – all at once the perfect hostess – as they entered the room where her guests waited. To hear her, no one would have guessed that only a few hours before she had been sitting in a grimy cell in Mountjoy Gaol, with a man on trial for a capital crime.

Mrs Langton, it seemed, wasn't taken in by this brave show. 'Ah, me dear,' she said. 'We heard you were back. Couldn't leave you all on your lonesome, could we?'

'Indeed we could not,' said her spouse, who was even then helping himself to a drink from the tray just brought in by Monckton.

'Although it looks as if ye've got plenty of company already,' went on the good lady. 'How are ye, Mr Rowlands?'

Rowlands said that he was fine.

'But we had to come and make sure that you were all right,' said Mrs Langton. 'If there's anything we can do – anything at all – we want you to say, don't we, Ollie?'

'To be sure,' said Oliver Langton.

'And how's himself?' said his wife. 'Bearing up, is he, the poor soul?'

'You know Ned,' was the reply. 'He doesn't let things get him down.'

'No, indeed. Although it's a terrible cruel thing for a man to be locked up for weeks on end through no fault of his own,' said Venetia Langton feelingly. 'I can tell you, when I was sitting in that witness box, it was as much as I could do not to jump down and bang those lawyers' heads together.'

'It might have been a good thing if you had.' Celia Swift laughed, giving a passable imitation of someone without a care in the world.

Oliver Langton seemed convinced, at any rate, for he said: 'Next time you see him, be sure and tell Ned that the horses are settling in. The black stallion gave us a bit of trouble at first – nearly kicked the stall down – but he's calmed down now, praise God.'

'Ollie, shut up about the horses,' said his wife.

'Yes, m'dear. Whatever you say.'

A silence followed.

'Well, if you're sure there's nothing we can do, we'd best be on our way,' said Mrs Langton. 'We only just looked in for a moment, ye know.'

'You'll stay to dinner, won't you?' said their hostess, still in the same bright tone.

'Thank you, me dear, but we're not dressed.'

'Oh, none of us are dressing,' was the reply. 'What with the war, and . . . and everything else . . . it doesn't seem right, somehow.'

Whether informal as to dress or not, dinner was an

uncomfortable affair. The presence of the Langtons, affable as they were, only served to point up the awkwardness of the situation. The absence of two family members – one dead, and the other in prison – was the spectre at the feast, thought Rowlands. No amount of inconsequential chit-chat about whether next Saturday's meet was likely to go ahead, or which horse was most fancied for next year's Dublin Races, could lift the prevailing gloom. Lady Celia said little, listlessly toying with her food, and leaving it to her mother-in-law and the canon to keep these interesting topics going. No less silent and preoccupied was Gogarty, whose only contribution to the proceedings was when he knocked over his water glass, exclaiming repeatedly that he was sorry, he was a clumsy oaf – until his hostess told him sharply not to make such a fuss. The Butlers, as was their wont, spoke mainly to one another, Mrs Butler seeming especially concerned about the acid effect that accepting a second glass of wine might have on her husband's stomach.

And so it was with relief that Rowlands got up from the table and, together with the rest of the company (it having been decided that the ladies would not precede the gentlemen on this occasion), made his way towards the drawing room where coffee was being served. Having no desire to be kept awake, he thought he'd forgo this beverage in favour of a small whisky and soda. He guessed that he wasn't alone in wanting to bring the evening to a close. It had been a long and exhausting day. But as he crossed the hall, with Lady Celia at his side, he heard the car. Indeed, they all heard it. Whoever was behind the wheel must have been driving at some speed, for there was a screech of brakes and a crunching of gravel as the vehicle pulled up abruptly. 'Who can *that* be so late?' said Lady Celia. A moment later, there came an impatient jangling of the bell. 'See to it, Monckton, will you? I'm not at home.'

'Yes, milady.'

As the party entered the drawing room, the sound of voices could be heard from the hall: the butler's low and conciliatory as he made his mistress's excuses, then that of the visitor, shrill with indignation. 'Don't give me that!' It was Henrietta Swift. 'I *know* she's here. And she'd better see me, or it'll be the worse for her.'

'Oh dear,' sighed Lady Celia, then, to the assembled company, 'Do help yourselves to coffee and drinks. I'd better see what my sister-in-law wants.' She left the room, closing the door behind her so that whatever she said to Mrs Swift could not be overheard.

Only the latter's angry reply came loud and clear: 'I've come to take him away, I said! And you can't stop me.'

'It'll be the kiddy she's after,' said Mrs Langton to her husband.

'So it would seem,' he replied. 'A pity she didn't think to remember him before. What'll you have, Rowlands? Whisky?'

'Oh . . . yes . . . thanks,' said Rowlands distractedly. All his attention was focused on what was happening behind the closed door. Langton poured him out a measure, adding a splash of soda at his request, and handed it to him. Rowlands raised the glass in a silent toast.

A moment later, the door was flung open, and the younger Mrs Swift came rushing in. 'I won't leave my boy another moment in this house, I tell you! I . . .' She stopped short when she saw that the room was occupied. 'So you're all here, are you?' she said in a sneering tone. 'Come to back her up, I suppose. But it won't work. They'll still hang him. And I for one will be cheering.'

'Come now, me dear!' said Mrs Langton. 'That's a terrible thing to say. I'm sure you don't mean it.'

'I *do* mean it.' Suddenly, Henrietta Swift burst into tears. 'I do, I do,' she sobbed.

'Pull yourself together, Henry,' said Celia. She poured a glass of something – brandy, from the smell of it – and handed it to the weeping woman. 'Here. Drink this.'

'I don't want it.' But she drank it, nonetheless. 'I've come to take Reggie away,' she said again. 'He can't stay here. Not now.'

'Why? What's different from the way it was before?' said her sister-in-law coolly. It struck Rowlands that she was enjoying the moment. It was doubtless a relief after all the tiptoeing around the subject, to have it out in the open at last.

'What's *different*,' said Henrietta, 'is that a murderer's about to receive justice for his crime.'

'I wouldn't be too sure about *that*,' said another voice. It was Eveline Swift's. 'Sometimes they hang the wrong man, you know, and the real villain gets off scot-free.' She laughed – an eerie sound, which sent a shiver up Rowlands' spine. Perhaps the shock of losing her son had turned the old woman's wits, he thought. 'Oh yes.' She chuckled. 'It's easy enough to mistake one man for another, in the dark.'

'Eveline . . .'

'I saw him, you know, that night,' persisted the dowager. 'Creeping across to the garage, he was. Oh yes, I saw him quite plain. You can't mistake a Swift.'

There was an uncomfortable silence. So Eveline Swift had seen her stepson on his way to intercept his half-brother in the garage, thought Rowlands. He wondered if she'd mentioned this to the police. It was certainly a damning piece of evidence – albeit from a somewhat questionable source. Because what she'd said didn't make sense . . . if it was Ned Swift she'd seen, then what had she meant about the real villain getting off scot-free?

'You're tired, Eveline,' said Lady Celia. 'I'll get Biddy to bring you up a hot drink, to help you sleep.' She pressed a bell.

'I'm not tired,' protested the other, but when the servant arrived Eveline allowed herself to be led out of the room, with Bridget fussing over her as if she were a child.

When she had gone, Mrs Langton said it was time she and her husband made a move. 'You'll promise to let us know if there's anything you need?' she said, for the umpteenth time. 'Ollie can drive round at any time, can't you, me dear?' He agreed that he could. 'And keep your chin up, won't you?' she added, enfolding Celia Swift in her embrace. 'It's always darkest before the dawn.'

Chapter Eighteen

A dog was howling – on and on it went, a mournful and unsettling dirge. Rowlands was instantly awake, and reaching for his Braille watch on the beside table. His fingertips sought the raised dots on the watch's face, which told him it was five a.m. He sat up and slid his feet out of bed and onto the floor. Still the dog howled. Something was very wrong; Rowlands could feel it in his bones. With a mounting feeling of unease, he put on his dressing gown and stepped out into the corridor. Here he met Canon Wetherby, always a light sleeper, by his own account. 'What can be the matter with that poor creature?' he said. 'It's Eveline's dog, isn't it? She must have inadvertently shut the animal out . . .'

'I think the barking's coming from *within* the room,' replied Rowlands grimly, fearing what this might portend. 'Does anyone have a key?' Because it was obvious that the alternative was to break the door down since the chances of its being unlocked from the other side looked increasingly unlikely.

They were joined at that moment by Lady Celia. 'Is something the matter with Eveline?' she demanded. 'Why doesn't she answer?' Rowlands repeated his question about the key and she said at once: 'Of course. I'll go and find Mrs Doyle myself. She has all the house keys.' But the appearance just then of Biddy, the chambermaid, made this unnecessary. 'Tell Mrs Doyle we need the key to Lady Eveline's room – at once, do you hear?'

'Yes'm. Oh, milady, is Her Ladyship all right?' cried the girl.

'I hope so,' was the terse reply. Now hurry – do!'

As they waited – joined by Mrs Butler, who enquired sweetly if there was anything she could do, as she was very unlikely to be able to get back to sleep in the circumstances – the anguished howling on the other side of the door turned to a whimpering as the little dog, hearing their voices, sensed that her vigil was coming to an end. At last, Mrs Doyle arrived, with Biddy panting after her. 'Here's the key, milady.'

The door was opened. At once Mitzie, imprisoned for so long, dashed out, eager to be petted. But her mistress, it was immediately apparent, would never perform this service again. A dreadful stillness prevailed in the room, into which Lady Celia, Rowlands and the canon were the first to step – the others remaining outside. That there was nothing to be done for the poor lady was soon established. 'Her heart, no doubt, poor soul,' murmured Canon Wetherby.

'Yes,' said Lady Celia. 'I'm afraid you may be right. Send for Doctor O'Leary, will you, Mrs Doyle?'

At which Biddy burst into tears. 'She was right as rain yesterday night which I brought her her cocoa,' she sobbed. 'Who'd have thought she'd end up cold and stiff the morning after?'

'That will do, Biddy,' said the housekeeper, then, to her mistress: 'Will I make the room tidy, milady, before the doctor gets here?'

'I suppose you'd better,' was the reply, but Rowlands, stepping forward, barred the housekeeper's way.

'I think, if you don't mind, it would be better to leave things untouched, for now,' he said. 'It may be that this is a matter for the police.'

'An overdose of heart medicine,' said Doctor O'Leary when he had finished his examination of the body. 'I'll have to wait until after the post-mortem to be absolutely sure, but all the signs point to it . . . Dilated pupils, extreme lividity, and . . . well, no need to go into all that,' he added hastily as Rowlands, conscious that Lady Celia was listening to this, held up a warning hand. 'We see it all the time,' the doctor went on, putting away the instruments in his bag. 'An elderly lady gets confused about whether or not she's taken her pills and swallows another lot "just to be on the safe side", which turns out not to be very safe at all,' he added with a grim little laugh.

'Perhaps,' said Rowlands, 'it might be a good idea to find out when Lady Castleford was accustomed to take her medicine? That might help to clarify what happened.'

But when Biddy was questioned, she could shed no light on the matter. 'Sure, and she'd take 'em before or after she had her hot drink at bedtime,' she said. 'I never watched her take 'em, but sometimes she'd say, "Open the bottle for me, Bridget. You've young, strong fingers", and Mr Heaney – he's the pharmacist – always seals it up too tight. Oh, the poor lady!' cried the chambermaid. 'She was always so good to me, she was . . .'

Beyond this touching encomium, there was not much more that Bridget could add. She had escorted Lady Eveline to her room the previous night at around ten p.m. She had helped her make ready for the night, brushing her hair and putting on her nightgown and cap before settling her into bed. She had fetched her her cocoa, as always, and let the little dog, Mitzie, into the room to sleep at the end of milady's bed. 'She has her basket, o' course,' said the kind-hearted maid. 'But milady liked her little doggie next to her, she said.' Another storm of tears threatened to overcome her at this reminiscence, only averted by Mrs Doyle, standing nearby, who told her to pull herself together.

'So you didn't actually see Lady Castleford take her pills?' persisted Rowlands.

The girl said that she had not. 'The bottle was open, with the cap off, like I said,' she added. 'She'd take out as many tablets as she needed and then leave it like that for me to screw the lid back on, in the morning.'

'Was the lid off when she was found?' This time, Rowlands addressed the doctor. They had all by this time adjourned to the corridor outside Eveline Swift's room – Rowlands having suggested that the room should be left undisturbed as far as possible.

'I didn't notice,' O'Leary replied. 'Let me check.' He returned, briefly, to the room. 'No, the lid's on,' he said. 'I remember now that it was when I looked to see how many pills were left in the bottle.'

'Then I think the police should be called,' said Rowlands. 'And it might be an idea to seal the room,' he went on, addressing Lady Celia.

'So you think . . .' she began, then made a decision: 'Mrs Doyle, I want this room left alone for the present. You can get John to stand outside, to prevent anyone going in . . . accidentally.'

'Yes, milady.'

'Doctor O'Leary, perhaps I can offer you some breakfast, as you've had such an early start?' He replied that he'd appreciate that. 'And I'd better ring the Gardai,' she said. 'They'll be getting rather used to coming to Castleford.'

The body had been taken away, and the cup that had contained the deceased's last drink of cocoa sent for analysis, at Rowlands' insistence. He'd met with some resistance from Sergeant Flanagan when this had been proposed. The officer had made it clear that he considered his summons to the house to be a waste of time. An old woman had taken too many pills and died. It wasn't a matter for the police, as far as he could see. He'd completed his cursory examination of the room, and taken his leave – grudgingly admitting that there'd probably have to be an inquest – by the time the younger Mrs Swift came down. When she learnt what had happened, and that she'd missed 'all the fuss', as she put it, she was suitably outraged. 'Why wasn't I called? I was Eveline's daughter-in-law. Jolyon . . .' Her voice cracked 'was very fond of his mother.' Then, when Celia made as if to console her: 'Don't give me that soft-soap! You hated her – as you hate all our family.'

'You know that's not true, Henry. You're being ridiculous.'

But she wouldn't be hushed. 'If you think I'm leaving before the inquest, you've got another thing coming. I'm going to tell everyone how you belittled and undermined my mother-in-law – and my husband.'

'My dear,' put in Canon Wetherby. 'You don't mean any of that. You're upset. Now, why don't you sit down and have some breakfast?' His words had no more effect than Lady Celia's had done. Saying that she was too distressed to eat a thing, and that she'd not the smallest intention of sitting down to breakfast with any of them, she stormed off.

'You'd better take a tray up to Mrs Swift's room,' said Lady Celia, summoning Mary. 'And bring us some fresh coffee.' She herself, Rowlands guessed, had consumed nothing apart from this. When only she and Rowlands and the canon remained in the breakfast room – the Butlers having rather ostentatiously departed, to see to their various tasks – she said, in a low voice, 'You think she was murdered, don't you?'

'I think it's a possibility,' Rowlands replied guardedly. 'We'll have to wait until after the post-mortem to be sure.'

'Is it because of the top being put back on the bottle of pills?'

'Not only that.' It was hard for him to explain that it was a feeling he had – one he'd had for some time – that something wasn't right. It was this atmosphere of fear and suspicion more than any actual evidence of wrongdoing that had convinced him that Eveline Swift had been murdered – the accumulation of apparently random facts rather than a single, conclusive fact, that pointed to foul play. An overheard conversation between a servant girl and a would-be assassin. Dogs that barked when no one was around. A knife concealed in a hay rack. An old woman's incautious words on the night before she herself was found dead . . . It all added up, and what it added up to was extremely disturbing. Not an impulsive killing after a quarrel between brothers, but deliberate, cold-blooded murder. Not a brawl over an unpaid debt but the elimination of a blackmailer. Not an old lady forgetting she'd taken her pills, but the cruel silencing of a witness . . .

The door opened. 'Oh . . . Ah,' said Sebastian Gogarty. 'H-have I missed breakfast? I didn't r-realise it was so late . . .'

'Of course not, Mr Gogarty,' said his hostess. 'And it's not late. Help yourself to whatever you want. There should be some fresh coffee . . . Thank you, Mary,' she added as the servant entered.

But the young man continued to apologise. 'I m-must have overslept,' he muttered as he served himself from the hotplate. 'N-not like me to sleep in.'

'It doesn't matter in the least,' said Lady Celia, taking a sip of coffee. 'As a matter of fact, you might have to remain at Castleford for another day or two. I don't know if you've heard, but there's been another death. The police may have to look into it.'

'*What?*' He sounded genuinely shocked. 'Who . . . who was it?'

Lady Celia explained.

'B-but that's terrible!' cried Gogarty. If he was bluffing, then he must be a very good actor, thought Rowlands. 'W-was it her heart?'

'We don't know yet,' said Rowlands. 'There'll probably have to be an inquest, so it's likely that some of us will have to give evidence.'

'B-but surely . . .'

'I shouldn't worry, Mr Gogarty,' said Lady Celia. 'You were asleep when all this happened, so I don't imagine the police will be very interested in you.' She got to her feet. 'If you'll excuse me, I've things to see to.

Cousin Aloysius, perhaps you'll join me in the study? Ned's asked me to look out some papers, and I wondered if you'd mind helping me?'

'Of course, my dear,' said the old man. The two of them left the room, leaving Rowlands and Gogarty to finish their breakfasts.

This the former did within a minute or two, and was on the point of getting up when the younger man said, 'It's too bad. I only c-came to Castleford b-because of her – Celia – and now *this* . . .'

'As we've said, you're most unlikely to be asked to give evidence,' said Rowlands.

'But I want to help her!' cried the wretched youth. 'I c-can't let her deal w-with this on her own! D-don't you *see*?'

Rowlands could see all too well, but he made no response to this outburst. 'Your bacon and eggs'll be getting cold,' he said, pushing back his chair. Really, young men in love were a nuisance, he thought irritably.

He decided to take a walk up to the home farm, to clear his head of the troubling thoughts that had been swirling around his mind ever since the discovery, earlier that morning, of what he was increasingly sure was another murder. As with those that had preceded it since his arrival at Castleford nearly three months before, it had been designed to look like an accident, or an act of self-harm. As he shrugged on a borrowed overcoat and cap, and took a stick from the rack in the boot room, he considered each of these crimes in turn, reflecting on what they said about the mind that had conceived them. First there had been the shooting of the dog – not, as it had appeared, an act directed at the master of Castleford by local malcontents in order to warn him of further reprisals by nationalists, but part of a carefully orchestrated campaign whose end was the destruction of the Swift family.

Then there was the murder of Jolyon Swift. Far from its being a case of mistaken identity, as Rowlands had first assumed, with one red-haired sibling being mistaken for another, this, too, had been meticulously planned. The only fortuitous element was the quarrel between Swift and his half-brother, which had prompted not only the timing of the killing but also provided a plausible motive. That had been a lucky break for the killer, thought Rowlands. As, stick in hand, he strode off along the lane towards the farm, he went over once more the list of those who had been in the house that night, and what each had said about his or her movements between the crucial hours. Canon Wetherby, Gogarty, Henrietta Swift, Lady Castleford, the Langtons, the Butlers – even Celia Swift herself. One of them was lying: the question was, which? He was beginning to have an idea, but he wasn't certain yet.

The killing of Christie Doherty, Rowlands was sure, had been carried out by whoever had commissioned the attempted murder of Ned Swift. Doherty had undoubtedly been responsible for cutting the stirrup leathers, and thereby precipitating the 'accident'. When he had threatened to reveal this, doubtless demanding money for his silence, he'd had to be eliminated. Now there was this. Rowlands didn't imagine for a moment that Eveline Swift had resorted to blackmail – at least not for money. But that she knew something that the killer had wanted to be kept quiet, he was not in doubt. What was it she had said about the ease with which one person could be mistaken for another? It must have been that remark that had brought about her death. But who had killed her, Rowlands couldn't yet be sure.

He lit a cigarette as he went over the various possibilities. Because they had all been there last night: the very same people who'd been present on that first occasion, the night of Jolyon Swift's murder. Even the Langtons, who'd left at the end of the evening on both occasions, had been present during the quarrel, just as they'd been present when Eveline Swift made her fatal remark. Hadn't Oliver Langton wanted to buy the land – the very piece of land about which Ned Swift and his half-brother had quarrelled? Yes, even the jovial Langton had a motive for murder. Then there was Gogarty. *His* motive was that of thwarted love and jealousy rather than greed and acquisitiveness – but its effects could be no less lethal, Rowlands knew. The canon? He couldn't believe that the gentle old man would be capable of such violent acts. But even he had served as a chaplain during the last war, and might be inured to such horrors. Nor had Lady Eveline specified that the 'person' in question was a man. Henrietta Swift had certainly displayed plenty of resentment towards her in-laws, but there seemed no earthly reason why she should want to kill her husband, reprobate as he was.

Then there were the servants and 'upper servants' – who were as much a part of Castleford's world as all the others: Monckton the butler, John the footman, Mary the parlourmaid, Robert Butler and his wife. What possible motive could any of them have for murdering one brother and ensuring that the other was hanged for the crime? He couldn't see it. It would mean an end to what had been, for most of them, a comfortable and not-too-onerous livelihood. No, it didn't make sense, he thought.

He reached the farm, taking care to extinguish his cigarette before entering the yard where straw and other debris lay about. A dog ran up, barking; he held out his hand for it to sniff, but it continued its racket. 'Down, Folly, down!' cried a voice, which turned out to belong to O'Brien, the cowman. 'She's only a pup,' he added apologetically. 'Hasn't learnt her manners yet.'

'She was only doing her job.' Rowlands smiled. 'How are you, Mr O'Brien?'

'Well enough, sir,' was the reply. 'Was it something particular you wanted?'

'No, I just felt like a breath of air. I didn't mean to disturb your working day.'

'Ah, you'll not do that, sir. Things go on pretty much the same as they ever did.' He hesitated, then went on, 'When you see His Lordship, tell him I'm doing my best. He'd not see a difference if he were to walk in this minute.'

'I'll tell him,' said Rowlands. 'I'm sure he'll be glad to hear that.' Both men were silent for a moment, the dog now sitting quietly at their feet. 'Well,' said Rowlands, 'I'd best be getting back. It was good to see you.' The familiar phrase had long ago ceased to sound incongruous to him.

Again, the other man hesitated. 'If you've nothing better to do, you might walk over to the Long Acre with me,' he said. 'I want to take a look at one of the Kerries that's about to calve.' Rowlands said he'd like nothing better, and the two men set off across the fields, with Folly bounding at their heels. As they walked, Rowlands breathed in the sweet, loam-scented air of the fields, now bare of their summer growth. 'Tell His Lordship we got the hay in before the rains started,' said O'Brien. 'We was short-handed this year, but the men worked double-time, and we got the ricks covered.'

'He'll be pleased,' replied Rowlands, although he'd no idea whether this was true or not. It seemed important to say so, however. Another silence followed.

'Is it as bad as they say?' said O'Brien at last. 'I mean, about how things might end for His Lordship?'

'It's pretty bad,' admitted Rowlands.

The other man sighed. 'It's a terrible thing, what's happened,' he said. 'I've known His Lordship since he was a lad, and a finer, straighter man you'd never meet.'

'I agree.'

'The pity of it was that he ever let that other one . . . the brother . . . into the house. There's a bad strain in that family, although I say it as one that knows His Lordship and knew his father before him. Not that he . . . the old master . . . was entirely without his faults, but . . .' He broke off, covering whatever he'd been going to say with a cough. They'd reached the pasture where the cattle were, and so the next few minutes were taken up with visiting this animal and that, and with checking the progress of the gravid cow. 'Another day or two before she delivers, I reckon,' said O'Brien. 'She'll need to be kept in the barn when the others go out – eh, lass?' He patted the sturdy little beast on her flank.

'How do you tell them apart?' said Rowlands, apropos of nothing. 'I mean, they're all the same colour, aren't they? No white patches or distinctive markings.'

'Oh, I could tell one from t'other in the dark.' The cowman laughed. 'They've all got their own characters – haven't you, my beauty?' he said, addressing the Kerry once more. 'This one – Buttercup – is a tough little lass, aren't you, me dear? This is her third calf in as many years, and she never makes a fuss, do you, darlin'? Oh no, I'd never mistake one for another.'

They parted soon after this – O'Brien to continue his perambulations around the farm, and Rowlands to return to the house, following the route suggested by the former. 'You just keep on downhill, with the wood on your left,' he said. 'The path's quite clear once you set your feet on it.' Armed with these directions, and with his stick to help him on his way, Rowlands found himself, after a few minutes' brisk walking, in the vicinity of the Castleford stables. The acrid smell he'd noticed the night before, on visiting the ruined building with Lady Celia, struck him anew. And there was something else: the sound of voices. As he drew nearer, these became identifiable as that of the head groom, Pheelan, and Robert Butler's.

'Yes, it'll all have to be pulled down,' the latter was saying. 'There's simply no money to rebuild – not with the difficulties we're having with getting supplies of metal and wood, in the current emergency.'

'What's to be done about the horses?'

'They'll have to be sold. The estate's in as bad a way as it's ever been. I'm sorry, Mr Pheelan, but there it is.'

'His Lordship'll have something to say about that,' said Pheelan. 'He loves them horses.'

'Unfortunately, Lord Castleford's feelings in the matter are of little account just now,' was the reply. 'Since I have the unenviable task of keeping things running in his absence, I'm afraid I have no choice . . . Ah, Mr Rowlands, been out for a walk, have you?' said the land agent, catching sight of him. Rowlands said that he'd been up to the home farm. 'That'll have to be sold, too,' said Butler. 'It's been making a loss for years. That's the trouble with these great houses – they simply *eat* money.'

'Have you discussed all this with Lady Celia?' said Rowlands, thinking that the man was taking rather too much upon himself. 'Surely she – and Lord Castleford

– should be the arbiters of any decision relating to the property?'

'Under normal circumstances of course,' said the other. 'But Her Ladyship is somewhat *preoccupied* at present, and His Lordship is, shall we say, *incommoded*.'

He really is a pompous fool, thought Rowlands. But he kept his tone civil. 'I still think Lady Celia ought to be consulted before any decision is taken regarding the stables.'

'Just what I've been tellin' Mr Butler!' put in Pheelan. 'And the damage isn't so very bad – thanks to yerself, Mr Rowlands. All it needs is a bit o' patching up and it'll be as good as new.' The tone of this appeal was a good deal more friendly than Rowlands remembered from the last time he and Pheelan had spoken, when he'd got the distinct impression that the man blamed him for the disaster.

'Yes, it does seem a rather drastic solution to the problem, Mr Butler,' he said. 'Perhaps you need to get a surveyor in first, to assess the damage before making any decision?'

'As I said, there isn't the money for renovations,' said Butler. 'But I'll keep your suggestion in mind. Well, must be getting back. My wife will scold me if I'm late for luncheon. The ladies, eh?' A thought appeared to strike him. 'Would you care to take my arm, Mr Rowlands?' He chuckled. 'It wouldn't do for you to take a tumble on these uneven cobblestones.'

'Thank you, but I can manage quite well with my

stick,' said Rowlands, who hated being reminded of his disability. 'I'll walk back with you, though. As you say, we'll be expected for lunch.'

He took his leave of Pheelan, who wrung his hands, saying again, 'It only needs patching up, Mr Rowlands, sir. You tell Her Ladyship I said so.'

'The poor fellow's obsessed with his precious horses,' said Butler as the two of them crossed the stable-yard towards the back of the house. 'He doesn't have the faintest idea what it costs to keep four or five of the beasts in fodder – let alone pay for the upkeep of the buildings. You might think me hard, Mr Rowlands, but even though Ireland isn't at war – yet – we're already feeling the effects of the blockade.'

'Yes, I see that,' said Rowlands evenly. 'But I still think the question of what to do with the stables – and anything concerning the Castleford demesne – should be a matter for its owners.'

There was a silence as the land agent digested this. Then he laughed. 'You're absolutely right,' he said. 'Ah, here's my wife now!' Because they had entered the kitchen door, and now stood in the corridor, which led, in one direction, to the main body of the house, in the other to the Butlers' private quarters. 'Won't be a moment, my dear,' he sang out. 'Mr Rowlands and I have been having such an interesting talk.'

Mrs Butler barely acknowledged this. 'Do hurry up,' she said to her husband. 'As soon as luncheon is over, I want you to drive me into Enniskerry.'

'Why, my dear, it isn't market day, is it?'

'You know it isn't. The fact is,' said Mrs Butler. 'I need a black costume. It might have escaped your notice, Robert, but there'll be another funeral to attend.'

Chapter Nineteen

The rest of that day passed in a kind of blur. A settled gloom had descended upon Castleford, which only the antics of little George and his cousin relieved to some degree. Saturday afternoon, which turned out to be too wet for a walk, was devoted instead to a lengthy game of Happy Families in the library, where tea was being served in front of the fire. Only Henrietta Swift had absented herself from this ceremony – saying that the children's row had given her a frightful headache, and asking for tea to be sent up to her room. As the demands for Miss Bun the Baker's Daughter from the holder of the rest of the Bun family grew louder, with the keeper of the missing card seemingly reluctant to part with it, Monckton came in, saying that the doctor was on the telephone. This, guessed Rowlands, would be the news they had been waiting for.

'You were right,' said Celia Swift bluntly when the

two of them were together in the study after she had taken the call. 'There were traces of the heart medicine in the cup of cocoa, doubling the dose that Eveline would already have taken. It might have been forgetfulness on her part, but . . .'

'So it was murder,' said Rowlands, who had not expected anything else.

'It would appear so. What I *can't* understand,' said Lady Celia angrily, 'is who could have wanted to hurt Eveline? She was a harmless creature.'

'Whoever killed her obviously didn't think so,' said Rowlands. 'She must have known something that was dangerous to that person. I think she recognised him – or her – as the same person she'd seen on the night of your brother-in-law's murder. Unfortunately, she couldn't resist letting out that she knew more than she was saying.'

'Poor, silly Eveline,' said Lady Celia. 'I was fond of her, you know, although she could be maddening, at times. But she didn't deserve this.'

'I think,' said Rowlands, 'that as the police are now bound to investigate Lady Castleford's death as an instance of foul play, it would make sense to inform Sir Anthony of this development. *Two* suspicious deaths – if we count Doherty's as one – can't be so easily brushed off. It might give him the ammunition he needs to ask for a retrial.'

But the counsel for the defence seemed less than enthusiastic when this was suggested. 'My difficulty, dear lady,' he said during the telephone call that followed, 'is that this is an entirely *different* case. Even if the police *do* decide to follow it up – and they haven't yet agreed to – it seems unlikely that I can persuade the judge that what happened to Lady Eveline has a bearing on your husband's case . . . which, as you know, is about to reach its conclusion.' This speech, relayed verbatim to Rowlands afterwards (displaying a gift for mimicry on Lady Celia's part he hadn't previously suspected) was dispiriting. More so was the indifference shown by the local Gardai towards the circumstances of Eveline Swift's death.

'It's what it seems – an accident,' said Sergeant Flanagan, recalled to the house. 'If the police investigated every death of this kind, we'd have no time to look into *real* crimes.'

'Stupid, pig-headed man!' cried Lady Celia when the Gardai officer had taken his leave. 'I believe he's actually *glad* that things are going so badly for the family. As far as he and his Republican cronies are concerned, the sooner the Swifts are gone from Castleford the better.'

'Yes, it's frustrating, but don't despair,' said Rowlands. 'Look at it this way: Lady Castleford's death shows that our murderer's becoming increasingly desperate. It's then that he'll make mistakes . . .'

'Or she.'

'Or she,' he echoed, knowing from past experience that murder was not exclusively the preserve of the male sex.

* * *

Court 1 was packed to the rafters on that Monday morning. An atmosphere of barely suppressed excitement prevailed as those in the body of the courtroom – the briefs, their juniors and the court officials – rustled their papers and exchanged remarks in low voices as they waited for the judge to take his seat. There came, too, a subdued murmur from the public gallery as those who had observed the trial from the beginning exchanged views on how it would end. There was not much dispute about this. 'Looks bad for him, doesn't it?' said one self-styled expert – a comment Rowlands, turning round to frown at the speaker, hoped that Lady Celia hadn't heard. There was no time for a word of reassurance because at that moment the judge entered, the court rose and the prisoner was brought up from the cells for the last act of the drama in which he had played so central a part.

Mr Riordan was already on his feet for his closing speech, in which he would summarise the case for the benefit of the jury one last time.

'Ladies and gentlemen,' he accordingly said, his tones as dry and unemotional as they had been throughout. 'Over the past week, you have listened patiently to the story my learned friend the counsel for the defence has constructed. You have been told of possible conspiracies by members of local Republican groups, intended to oust the accused from his property. You have heard, too, of simmering resentments in the accused's family circle and of alleged fraud on the part of the deceased,

Mr Jolyon Swift. I could go on – but what is clear from these, and other attempts by my learned friend to throw sand in your eyes, is that there is only one possible interpretation of the facts of what took place that night, the night of 19th August. That is, that a violent quarrel took place between the accused, Edward Swift, and his half-brother, Jolyon Swift, in the course of which the former threatened to kill his younger sibling. You have heard evidence that the relationship between these two men was one of animosity – for what reason, various explanations have been suggested. That is not your concern. What you have to decide is whether the man who was heard by several witnesses to utter the following: "By God, if you come near me again tonight, I swear I'll kill you", did in fact carry out his threat, a matter of hours later – shooting dead Jolyon Swift in cold blood as the latter was about to make his escape by car from the house where he had been so unfairly and, one might say, *cruelly* used.'

'My lord . . .'

'All right, Sir Anthony, you will have your turn in a few moments. Mr Riordan, stick to the essentials, if you please.'

'Yes, my lord. I repeat, the facts are not in doubt. A threat was made, and Jolyon Swift was killed. There are no other suspects – no others with the motive, opportunity and means to have carried out this act. I must remind the jury that the weapon used to kill Mr Swift belonged to the accused, as did the glove that was stained with Mr Swift's blood. There you have it, ladies and gentlemen, and there is only one verdict you can bring in: a verdict of guilty.'

The awful word hung in the air so that – try as he might – Sir Anthony could not dispel it. All his attempts to dismiss the prosecution's case as having been based on the flimsiest of evidence, his rousing encomiums of his client's standing in the community, his demonstrable worth as a landowner, churchgoer and family man, fell on deaf ears – or so Rowlands feared. The more Sir Anthony harped on these virtues, the more he reminded the men and women of the jury that the defendant, like himself, was an Englishman – and that his tenure as lord of Castleford had only ever been provisional. Now that tenure, by his own rash action, had come to an end.

'You cannot – you *must* not – convict on such insubstantial evidence,' said Sir Anthony, towards the end of his speech. 'I say to you, ladies and gentlemen of the jury, that if the *smallest* doubt that this man did what he is accused of doing persists in your minds, you *must* acquit.' Even though Rowlands was unable to see them, he could picture to himself the stony expressions on the faces of the jury as the counsel for the defence made his plea.

At last it was over. The judge's summing-up, which followed, summarised the evidence once more, emphasising that in order to reach a guilty verdict, the jury's conviction that a crime had been committed had to be 'beyond reasonable doubt'. If that was so, said Mr Justice Walsh, echoing Sir Anthony's words, 'then you must acquit. I repeat: you must acquit.' With this injunction ringing in their ears, the jury then retired to consider its verdict, the prisoner at the bar was taken down and the courtroom rapidly emptied of its respective legal teams, leaving only the spectators to make their own way out. At Rowlands' suggestion, he and Lady Celia and the canon waited until the crowd had dispersed somewhat before descending from the public gallery. But if he'd hoped to avoid the attentions of the press – gathered in a predatory huddle at the foot of the stairs – he was mistaken.

'Lady Celia, do you think your husband will be found guilty?' cried one of these jackals.

'Lady Celia! Lady Celia! This way, please!' yelled another as a flash went off.

'Stand back, all of you!' shouted Rowlands, doing his best to shield her from the worst of this. 'Isn't there another way out of here?' he said to Sir Anthony, whom they found waiting in the foyer with his junior.

'Indeed there is. Mr Harker'll show you. Is your driver outside? Perhaps you could tell him to go round to the side entrance, Mr Rowlands?' Rowlands said that he would. 'Good, good. All we have to do now is wait. Chin up, dear lady,' he added to Lady Celia. 'One must never lose hope, you know . . .'

She said nothing to this. Only when she and her companions were seated in the Bentley, on their way back to Merrion Square, did she mutter as if to herself, 'Hope is the worst thing. It's better not to hope.'

When they arrived at the house, she went straight to her room to rest, saying she didn't want any lunch. Rowlands and the canon made a poor meal of it, too, with neither much inclined to talk – the strain of the morning's events hanging over them both. After lunch, the canon dozed in an armchair in the library while Rowlands, with nothing to distract him, went over the facts of the case once more. It was plain to him that the murderer of Jolyon Swift was still at large, and that he or she had killed twice more. The list of suspects was small: he considered each one in turn. It seemed to him that one name stood out. The question was: how to prove it? If the Gardai had only agreed to investigate Eveline Swift's death as suspicious, it would have bought them some time. Now time was running out. At four o'clock, tea was brought in, and Canon Wetherby started from his sleep. 'Goodness me! Is that the time? I must have slept longer than I realised,' he said. 'I suppose there's been no word?'

'No.'

Then, out in the hall, the telephone began to ring.

If the atmosphere in Court 1 had been one of foreboding before, now it was electric: as the jury returned to its box, a ripple of anticipation went around the assembled crowd. From his bench below the judge's seat, the clerk of the court waited until the hubbub had subsided and absolute silence reigned before putting the all-important question: 'Foreman of the jury, have you reached a verdict?'

'We have.'

'Is your verdict guilty or not guilty?'

'Guilty.'

Another moment passed before the silence was broken: a murmur that might have been satisfaction at justice done – or horror – rose like a wave. 'Silence in court!' And beside him, Rowlands heard Celia Swift gasp, then felt her slip sideways as unconsciousness overcame her.

'Let's get her out of here,' he hissed to Canon Wetherby, who was seated on her other side. He accordingly lifted her, and carried her towards the doors at the back of the gallery, which the canon held open for him. It was a small mercy, he thought, that she was therefore not in court to hear sentence of death pronounced. Rowlands, who had heard the dreadful words on more than one occasion at the end of a murder trial, had no wish to hear them again, least of all when addressed to a man he liked – a man, moreover, of whose innocence he was convinced.

Once out of the stifling air of the courtroom, Lady Celia revived, murmuring that she was fine, she could bear it; she owed it to Ned to return.

'No, my dear,' said the canon, with unexpected firmness. 'You'll do no good to him by going back in there, or by making yourself ill. Here, drink this.' He handed her the glass of water an usher had brought. 'Then I'll take you home. The car's outside.' She said she wouldn't hear of it. She must go at once to Ned.

Rowlands, guessing that the condemned man would now be taken back to prison, suggested that they might all go together before the crowds started to make their exit from the courtroom. Lady Celia might therefore be spared the vulgar curiosity of strangers as well as the grosser attentions of the press. 'Come on,' he said. 'I told Connolly to wait for us at the side entrance, as before. If we leave now, we can get ahead of the traffic.'

As the Bentley pulled out onto the quayside, it fell in behind the prison van. 'There's Ned, up ahead of us,' whispered Lady Celia. 'Faster, Connolly! We mustn't lose him.' As if gaining a few more precious minutes might make up for the greater loss that lay ahead. After this, she fell silent for a moment, perhaps thinking about what she would say to her husband when they met. 'How could they do it?' she murmured at last. 'Those good men of the jury. How could they condemn an innocent man to death?'

At the Mountjoy, they found Sir Anthony, seemingly not at all perturbed by the verdict's going against them. '*Nil desperandum*, dear lady,' he said, coming forward to greet them with his customary good humour. 'In a case like this where the evidence is largely circumstantial, we've strong grounds for an appeal.'

A guard arrived just then with a message from the prison governor: if Lady Celia and her friends would care to join him in his office for a few minutes, he would personally conduct them to Lord Castleford's new quarters. 'We like to make sure our guests are as comfortable as possible,' said the governor – whose name was Halloran. After a quarter of an hour's delay in his pleasant sitting room, during which tea and biscuits was offered and refused, he led the way to the section of the prison where Swift was to be housed for the next three weeks until the sentence was carried out. Rowlands knew that this – the condemned cell – would be located next to the execution shed, separated only by the width of a wall from the apparatus that would end the life of the cell's present incumbent. He hoped this grim fact would not be evident to the prisoner's wife even if Swift himself must be aware of it.

Governor Halloran himself seemed anxious to gloss over this unpleasantness, murmuring only that he hoped Lord Castleford had everything he needed. 'Books, pen and paper – just name it, and I'll have it brought,' he said.

'Thank you,' was the reply. 'I can't think of anything just now.'

'Then I'll leave you,' said the governor. 'Do ring if Her Ladyship changes her mind about the tea, won't you?' Swift said that he would. The two men shook hands.

'Decent cove,' said the former when Halloran had gone. 'He plays a good game of chess, too.' He gave a bark of laughter. 'I really can't complain about the standard of accommodation here! It's quite civilised – wouldn't you say, Celia? Armchairs for my guests, a desk, a rug on the floor . . . I'll warrant even the mattress is comfortable. I'll sleep well tonight.'

'*Don't*, Ned . . .'

'Now, now, my dear – no tears, if you please. There's nothing to cry about. We did our best – or rather, Sir Anthony here did *his* best – but we lost the game, that's all.'

'We'll be appealing, of course,' said Sir Anthony. 'I've high hopes we'll be successful. No, my lord, hear me out,' he went on as Swift gave a sceptical laugh. 'Lady Eveline's death has changed everything. If the coroner finds that she was unlawfully killed, then the Gardai will have no choice but to investigate.'

'I thought you said there was no chance of that.'

'There is now,' said Sir Anthony complacently. 'I happen to know that the coroner they've appointed to try the case is a Dublin man. Jack Sullivan. He and I play golf together,' he added slyly. 'With the evidence Mr Rowlands here discovered – about the pill-bottle lid being found to be on – pointing to the fact of its being a suspicious death, I feel sure we'll have grounds to ask for the verdict to be overturned. If Lady Eveline was murdered, then the flimsiness of the case against you becomes all too clear.'

'You're saying that whoever killed Eveline is the same person who killed my half-brother?' said Swift.

'Just so,' said Sir Anthony happily. 'It's one and the same case.'

'You might find it difficult to convince the judge of that,' said Swift, but his tone was noticeably less gloomy than before.

'Oh, I think I can persuade him to grant a . . .' *Stay of execution*, he'd obviously been going to say, but thought better of it. 'A delay.'

'Hmm,' said Swift. 'It sounds a bit of a thin story to me. I mean, it's not hard to believe that Jolyon had enemies given the kind of circles he moved in . . . but who would have wanted to kill a harmless old thing like Eveline?'

Hearing the guilty verdict pronounced seemed to have knocked Celia Swift for six, thought Rowlands as, having left the Mountjoy, they drove back to Merrion Square. It was a subdued and listless woman who sat next to him in the Bentley, replying to any conversational overtures in monosyllables, if at all. Nor did her mood lift for the rest of that evening as the three of them sat over dinner. It was a relief to turn in at last, although it soon became apparent to Rowlands that sleep would prove elusive once more as the day's events went round and round in his head, with all their unanswered questions. In the absence of Lady Celia, who naturally wanted to remain in Dublin while her husband's life hung in the balance, Rowlands and Canon Wetherby would once more represent the family at the inquest on Lady Eveline. He needed to get his facts straight, he thought, so that if he was called to give evidence, it would strengthen the case for reopening the investigation into Jolyon Swift's murder.

He thought again of what Eveline Swift had said the night before she was found dead. 'It's easy enough to mistake one man for another, in the dark . . .' Had she seen the murderer on the night of 19th August, and mistaken him for someone else? Or not realised that was who she'd seen until afterwards? In which case, she would have presented a definite threat to the killer, who must have been one of those present when the words were spoken. After tossing and turning for half an hour or so, Rowlands found he was now wide awake. A quarter past two, by his Braille watch. *The dead waste and middle of the night.* He got up and lit a cigarette, opening the window a little wider than before to allow the smoke to escape. Ah. That was better. Nothing like a decent smoke to quiet the restless brain. But if he'd hoped to conceal the fact of his being awake and smoking at this hour, he wasn't successful, for a few moments later, he heard a soft tap on his bedroom door. 'It's me.'

'Lady Celia. I'm sorry if I disturbed you.'

'You didn't. I was awake. May I have one of those?' she added.

'Of course.' He lit the cigarette for her.

'Thanks.' She took a deep drag and exhaled. 'Yes, sleep's out of the question for me tonight, I'm afraid.' Her tone was artificially bright. 'I keep thinking about it,' she went on. 'What it must be like, to die in that way. "To be hanged by the neck until you are dead",' she intoned, quoting the terrible words of the death sentence – words Rowlands had hoped she'd been spared. 'Choking . . . strangling . . . fighting for air . . .'

'Celia, *don't* . . .'

'I can't help it. It's such a dreadful way to die. So ugly and undignified.' Which was true, Rowlands thought, but only for those who had to watch the procedure. For the condemned man, it was all over very quickly . . . that is, if the hangman knew his business, which most of them did. He said nothing of this, however. 'It's the *dread* of it . . . the waiting, that's so cruel,' she said. 'I can't bear the thought of him having to go through that . . . *knowing* what the end will be.' She was on the edge of hysteria, he thought. At any moment, she would break down.

'It's probably worse for you than it is for him,' he said. 'Your husband was a soldier. One gets used to such things. Waiting to go over the top was a rather similar experience, you know. More enervating than frightening. One just wanted it to be over.'

She was silent a moment, smoking her gasper. 'You always say the right thing,' she said at last.

'Oh, I don't know—' he began, but she cut across him.

'Can I ask a favour?'

'Anything.'

'Would you . . . *hold* me for a moment?' Then

she was in his arms. He felt her soft weight against him, smelt the sweet, musky scent of her hair as he gathered her to him. She was trembling; her face, when he touched it, was wet with tears. For a long moment they stood there, on the brink.

Chapter Twenty

The inquest was to start at ten, and so the car was ready to leave soon after breakfast. Lady Celia was not yet down when Rowlands and his companion left the house. After what had passed between them the night before, he wondered if she was deliberately keeping out of his way. He wouldn't have blamed her if that was the case; he didn't feel too good himself about what had happened. Over the years, he'd nursed a hopeless passion for a woman he knew was out of reach, not least because they were both married. He loved his wife too much not to feel bad about betraying her, even in thought. And yet, when Celia Swift had reached for him, in the depths of her misery, he hadn't hesitated for a second before responding. Even though he could tell himself that he was only comforting her, he knew it wasn't true. He was still as much in love with her as ever. What she felt for him, if anything, he didn't dare to ask.

His silence throughout much of the journey didn't seem to trouble Canon Wetherby, who was evidently preoccupied with his own thoughts. 'I knew her as a girl,' he said after a long silence. 'Eveline Swift, I mean. Eveline Dooley, she was then. Pretty as a picture. Hardly surprising she caught George Swift's eye . . .'

'Lord Castleford's father, you mean?'

'I do. He was back from Africa, then – this would have been the year 1902 – and looking for a wife. Caroline – the first wife – had died three years before, leaving him with the two boys, John and Neddie, to bring up. John died in France, in '16,' he added. 'Terrible thing. I don't think George ever got over it. Eveline was young enough to be his daughter, of course, but then he'd always had a penchant for a pretty face. There was that unfortunate affair when he was a young feller. Hushed up at the time, of course. It was after *that* blew over that he and Caroline were married and John was born. Neddie came along soon after. Such a dear little lad, he was. Yes, yes. Who could have imagined how things would turn out? Shocking business. Very.' The old man seemed to lose the thread of what he was saying, and lapsed into silence. Nor was Rowlands keen to pursue the topic. He felt he'd heard more than enough of the Swift family history, with all its ancient scandals and heartbreak.

As it was already a quarter to ten, Rowlands told Connolly to take them straight to the Crown where the inquest was being held, as it had been on Doherty's death. The chauffeur was to remain outside while the court was in session, because there was every chance, Rowlands said, that they'd have to return to Dublin straight away. If Sir Anthony was right, and the coroner decided that the circumstances of Eveline Swift's death merited a police investigation, then the sooner the barrister was told of the news the better. Rowlands hoped that it wouldn't take too long to get through the evidence, and that the significant fact he'd elicited from Doctor O'Leary – that the cap had been on the bottle of pills when he'd examined it, although according to Bridget the maid it had been left off the night before – would be enough to convince the coroner that the death had been suspicious.

Already seated in the courtroom were the Langtons, who had come to see justice done. Venetia Langton whispered to Rowlands as she drew him down to sit beside her. 'Eveline could be a bit flighty, but she wasn't a complete fool,' she opined. 'I don't believe for a moment she'd have taken a double dose of her medicine without realising it. Ridiculous that the police have been dragging their heels about this.' Rowlands suspected that her carrying tones must have reached the ears of Sergeant Flanagan, the first witness to be called. His dour recital of the facts conveyed his opinion that the affair had been blown out of all proportion. Yes, he'd been called to Castleford on the Saturday morning – the 7th, it was. He'd arrived just as the doctor was leaving – Doctor O'Leary, that was. He'd made a thorough examination of the room, and had observed the bottle of pills on the small table beside the deceased's bed. He understood that the lady had been in the habit of taking those pills for a heart condition. No, he had observed no signs of violence or disorder in the room. It had not occurred to him to confiscate the cup in which the deceased had taken her cocoa. It had not seemed necessary to him to investigate further.

Doctor O'Leary was next to the witness's chair, and it was as he was giving his evidence (necessarily of a technical nature) that a commotion was heard outside.

'Let me in! I tell you, I *demand* to speak to the police!' It was Henrietta Swift.

'Sergeant, see to that woman at once, do you hear?' said the coroner irritably. 'I will not have my courtroom disrupted in this way.'

'Sir.'

But before Sergeant Flanagan could stop her, Mrs Swift burst into the room. 'I *insist* you come with me at *once*, officer!' she cried. 'It's my boy, Reggie. He's gone missing – and his cousin George with him. I don't trust that child not to lead my boy into mischief. As for that nurse, I want her locked up, for dereliction of duty.' She stamped her foot. 'Well, don't just *stand* there! *Do* something!'

'Madam,' said the coroner. 'I must remind you that this is a court of law. I really cannot allow—'

She ignored him. 'Come on!' she shouted at the astonished police officer. 'I want you to organise a search party. We're wasting time!'

But it was Rowlands who made the decision to act. This was what he had feared – and she was right, of course. There was no time to lose. 'I'm going with her,' he said in an undertone to the canon. 'Connolly can run you back to Dublin when the inquest's over. You've got your car here, I assume?' he said to Mrs Swift. 'Then let's get back to Castleford. You can fill in the details on the way.'

His air of quiet authority must have convinced her, for she abandoned her attempt to persuade Flanagan to accompany her, and led the way to where she had left the roadster. Before he got in, he stopped and spoke to Connolly. 'You're to take Canon Wetherby back to Dublin,' he said. 'He'll have a message for Lady Celia, concerning the outcome of the inquest. And there's something else . . .' He hesitated. 'I don't want her alarmed, do you understand? But it appears her son – little Master George – and his cousin are missing. You'll need to collect Lady Celia from the Mountjoy, and bring her back here at once.' Connolly said he understood, and would return at all speed with Her Ladyship. 'Now then,' said Rowlands to Henrietta Swift. 'Tell me exactly what's happened.'

'It's all the fault of that stupid nurse,' she said as the car (surely not the same one in which her husband had been killed?) set off at a pace along the High Street. 'She didn't wake up until about an hour ago – although what she was doing sleeping so late when she was supposed to be getting the boys up and giving them their breakfasts, God only knows.' She crunched the gears as they plunged into the network of narrow lanes that led towards the Castleford demesne. 'When she went to wake them at last, she found the nursery empty. Their beds had been slept in, but their outdoor clothes were gone. Reggie's tweed coat and cap weren't on their hook. His gumboots were missing, too.' She gulped as if holding back tears.

'What makes you think that they haven't just gone off for an adventure?' said Rowlands. 'You know what boys are like.'

'It's what I thought at first,' she agreed, swinging the car so wildly around a bend that they scraped the hedge. 'But we searched the grounds thoroughly – the girl and I – and the rest of the servants, too,' she added. 'Not a sign of them. I'm afraid something terrible's happened. They could have fallen in the river and been swept downstream. Or wandered off into the woods . . .'

'Let's not jump to conclusions,' he said, although he, too, feared the worst. The timing of this could not be a coincidence.

Reaching the house, they found a distraught Philomena McGurk waiting for them. 'I'll never forgive myself if anything's happened to those children,' she sobbed. 'I can't think what possessed me, to sleep so late.'

Rowlands had a fair idea what it was that had induced

this – a sleeping draught of some kind, no doubt – but he wasted no time in such speculations. 'When was it you last saw the boys?' he demanded.

'Last night, at around seven,' was the reply. 'I always check on them an hour after I put them to bed. They was sleeping soundly, the dear little fellows.'

'And this morning when you found they were missing from their room . . . Did you notice anything untoward? Any sign of a struggle?'

'No, sir. Nothing like that.'

'Mrs Swift told me their outdoor clothes were missing.'

'Yes, sir. Georgie's waterproofs and boots, and the little feller's tweed coat. They're wrapped up warm, at least,' said the girl plaintively. 'You don't suppose, sir, that they simply took off somewhere for one of their games?'

'It's possible,' said Rowlands, who didn't suppose anything of the sort. 'But I think we have to act as if this isn't just a game.'

In the morning room, Henrietta Swift was complaining to Mrs Butler about the uncooperative behaviour of the local police: '. . . flatly *refused* to help,' she was saying. 'I mean, what are the police *for* if not to investigate something like this? Two children vanishing into thin air. *Anything* might have happened to them.'

'Typical of the Gardai, I'd say,' remarked Mrs Butler. 'A lazy lot. What we pay our taxes for, I can't imagine . . . Oh, it's you again, Mr Rowlands! You're getting to be quite a fixture at Castleford.'

'Mr Rowlands is helping to look for the boys,' said Henrietta Swift. 'Which is more than can be said for the police.'

'Yes, it comes to something when—' Mrs Butler broke off, with a laugh. Rowlands guessed she'd been going to make some reference to his blindness, and the fact that it must render him more or less ineffective when it came to 'looking' for anything. If she'd hoped to embarrass him, she'd be disappointed, he thought, concealing a smile. He was used to people underestimating him.

'Speaking of which, shall we carry on with our search?' he said to Philomena, who was hovering in the doorway. She was all too eager to get away from that unfriendly company. The phrase 'dereliction of duty' floated after them.

In the hall, they found an anxious Mrs Doyle. 'Oh, sir, is there any news?' she asked. 'I've had the house searched from the attics to the cellars – thinking the young gentlemen might have been playing hide-and-seek, you know – but there's no sign of them.' Rowlands replied that there was, as yet, no news, and left the housekeeper and her team of maidservants to continue their search while he and Philomena went outside, to where the latter's father, who was head gardener, was organising a search of the grounds.

'Sure, we've looked in all the places the nippers – I mean Master George and t'other little feller – liked to go,' he said. 'The potting sheds, and the glasshouses. My lad' – he meant the one assistant gardener left to him – 'is after checking the orchard now. No sign of 'em in the walled garden – I've just come from there . . . Now then, no need to take on, me dear,' he said to his daughter, who showed signs of breaking down.

'It's all my fault, Da. If I hadn't overslept . . .'

'You mustn't blame yourself,' said Rowlands. 'You're doing your best to find them – as we all are.' They left McGurk to continue his search of the shrubbery, and crossed the lawn towards the wood that bordered the property. It was here, at the foot of one of the great beech trees that lay at the heart of it, that little George Swift had proudly shown off the camp he had made. He'd boasted that he was making another, even better one, somewhere else. Now if Rowlands could only remember what it was he'd said. 'Miss McGurk, did George ever mention that he was building another camp?' he asked as they wandered between the trees, the nurse calling the boys' names from time to time.

'He was always building his old camps,' she replied. 'But I can't think of any special one. Master George! Master Reggie! You can come out now. Nobody's cross with you.'

'Try and remember,' said Rowlands. 'It might be the clue we need.'

'Well, he was always wanting to go to the stables,' she said. 'Especially after his da – I mean His Lordship – said he'd get him a pony of his own.'

'Then that's where we'll go next.'

But their search turned out to be fruitless. Pheelan, whom they found gloomily surveying the wreckage of the stables, said that the boys hadn't been near the place since the fire. 'I'd have given them what-for if they'd tried to go in there,' he said. 'Too dangerous. And there are no horses left for them to feed sugar lumps to,' he added sadly. 'Nor will be again, if Mr Butler has his way.'

So that was that. A visit to the home farm proved no more successful. Tom O'Brien said he hadn't seen Master George and his cousin since the previous afternoon. 'I had to tell them off about playing in the hayricks,' he said. 'They don't realise how easy it is to get trapped inside.' His men were searching down by the river, he said. 'I'll be joining 'em myself once the milking's done.'

'It's hopeless,' said Philomena, but something the farmer had said had suggested another possibility to Rowlands.

'Isn't there a boathouse down by the river? I seem to remember Lord Castleford mentioning that there was a skiff he used for fishing.'

'That's right,' said the nurse. 'But it hasn't been used for months and months. And the boathouse is all shut up now.'

'Let's go there,' said Rowlands. It struck him that there couldn't be a more perfect site for a secret camp: a deserted building that hadn't been used for months.

The fact that it was near water would make it doubly attractive to an adventurous child. A few minutes' walk brought them to the place.

'It's all locked up,' said Miss McGurk dubiously. 'I don't think there's anybody there.'

'Even so, I'd like to take a look around,' said Rowlands. He tried the door, which did indeed turn out to be locked. 'Could you go and fetch the key? I'll wait here.'

'All right.'

When she had gone off on her errand, Rowlands took his knife from his pocket and, opening one of the blades, slid it into the lock. A few moments' jiggling had the desired result: the lock clicked, and the door opened. He pushed it, and stepped inside the rotting and seemingly abandoned structure. It would consist (he knew from his rowing days) of a large hut, surrounding a central basin in which the skiffs would be moored when in use, with boardwalks running along three of its sides, and a water gate – no doubt closed and locked now – on the fourth side, opening onto the river. Along the walls would be stowed the oars or 'blades' as well as tarpaulins and other necessary equipment. An ideal hiding-place for two small boys. 'George,' he called softly. 'It's your father's friend, Frederick Rowlands – the one who showed you his pocket-knife. You and Reggie can come out now. It's perfectly safe. I've come to take you home.'

For a moment, the silence that had greeted him prolonged itself so that he wondered, after all, if he'd been mistaken in thinking that somebody else was there. Then came a soft scuffling from the far corner of the boathouse. It might have been a rat . . . but then a small voice said, 'Is Daddy with you?' Relief flooded over him: the child was alive.

'No, George,' he said. 'But you'll see him very soon.'

'*He* said Daddy would be here,' the boy went on. '*He* said we mustn't tell anyone about our camp. If we did, then Daddy wouldn't come after all.' So that was how it was done, thought Rowlands: the boys had been lured away with false promises, and then kept in this temporary prison until the man who had brought them here did what he intended to do . . .

'Your father'll be coming soon,' he said again. 'Only there's no need for you to wait for him here. Why don't you go back to the house, with Reggie – he's here, too, isn't he?'

'But he *said*—' began the child, then broke off with a shrill cry of fear as the door of the boathouse opened and someone else came in. In the same moment, Rowlands felt a sharp prod in the middle of his back from what he guessed was the barrel of a gun.

'I won't hesitate to use this,' said a voice he knew. Robert Butler. 'A pity you couldn't let well alone, Mr Rowlands. Now you're going to put me to the extra trouble of disposing of *another* body.' He laughed. 'Or rather, *three* bodies.'

'Let the boys go,' said Rowlands. 'You've got me, now. You don't need them.'

'That's where you're wrong,' said Butler. 'I do indeed need them, as you put it. They're the end of the line, as it were. I couldn't think of stopping until I've made sure that these little scions of the Swift family won't trouble me any more. Only *then* will I come into my own.'

'You're George Swift's eldest son,' said Rowlands.

'So I am. Clever of you to guess since you can hardly have seen the family likeness with your own eyes, so to speak.' Butler laughed. A chilling sound. 'Although as a matter of fact the likeness between me and my half-brothers isn't that obvious. I haven't inherited the family red hair, for one thing – for which I'm grateful . . . Get back, you!' he snarled at the little boy who had crept closer to Rowlands during this exchange. 'Or it'll be the worse for you . . . Yes,' he went on, 'I take after my mother's side as to looks – she was a mere servant girl, of course. Of no importance, except to have given me life, and to die in the process. The resemblance between me and the late Lord Castleford – may he rot in Hell – is one of build and posture, so I'm told.'

'It was that that struck Lady Castleford's attention, the night of Jolyon Swift's murder. She saw you from her window, going towards the garage – but it was dark, and at first she mistook you for one of your siblings. It was only later that she put two and two together.'

'Unfortunately for her, she couldn't resist boasting about what she knew,' said Butler. 'Which meant she had to be removed . . . just as you will have to be 'removed,' he added softly, jabbing the gun viciously into Rowlands' back.

'There'll be a witness before long,' said Rowlands. 'Miss McGurk has gone to fetch the key.'

'She'll search a long time for it. My wife will see to that,' was the reply. 'By which time it will be too late for you.' Another jab.

'If you shoot me,' said Rowlands, 'it'll be obvious that it's murder.' It seemed important to keep Butler talking. 'On previous occasions, you were careful to create the impression that it was accident, or suicide or – in the case of the Doherty shooting – that someone else was responsible.'

'Yes, I made sure *that* one was laid at the door of young Cullen.' The other laughed.

'Doherty was blackmailing you, I take it?' said Rowlands.

'He was. Venal fool. Thinking he could threaten *me* and get away with it!'

'And Jolyon Swift. I imagine you mistook him for Lord Castleford in the dark?'

'I did no such thing!' Butler sounded outraged to have been accused of such a blunder. 'I knew quite well who it was when I fired that shot. It was always my intention that the so-called Lord Castleford should take the blame for the killing, especially after he so obligingly provided himself with a motive for the same.' He chuckled. 'Yes, it certainly helped, having the two of them fall out so publicly over that land business . . . A golden opportunity, you might say. Oh, he'll hang for that, I've no doubt.'

'Not if there are any further killings,' said Rowlands. All the time they'd been talking, he'd been wondering if there was a way he could grab the weapon, whilst preventing injury to the children. '*Then* it'll be all too apparent that the wrong man has been arrested.'

Again Butler laughed: an inhuman sound. 'You don't think for a moment that I'll let that happen? After I've worked for this for so long – the restoration of my birthright as heir of Castleford . . . Oh yes, that day will come. Once all the usurpers have been cleared away, I'll be the last *true* Swift left. My father's last remaining son. Oh, I've waited a long time for this.' At which moment, Rowlands took a step back, treading hard on the other man's foot. Simultaneously, he reached behind to wrench the gun from Butler's grasp, taking a chance that the latter would refrain from firing it if he hoped to avoid alerting others to their presence there. 'Why, you—' expostulated the land agent. For a few tense moments, the two men grappled together. Initially, it seemed to Rowlands that he had the advantage as to agility and skill, although Butler was the heavier man.

'Run, boys!' he cried, hoping to keep his opponent occupied long enough to allow them to make their escape.

But then a crafty move – a leg hooked around his – knocked Rowlands off balance, and he fell to the floor. As he was trying to get up again, a stunning blow from the barrel of the gun laid him low. He lost consciousness for a moment. When he came to, it was to the icy shock of water as his adversary forced his head down below the level of the boathouse deck and into the basin of river water that lay beneath. Gasping, he struggled to break free of the other's stranglehold, but to no avail; the weight of Butler's body kept him from rising. '*Now* do you understand?' hissed Butler in Rowlands' ear. '*This* is how you're going to die. A foolish accident. Unable to see the danger, you tripped and fell into the river where you unfortunately drowned. By the time your body is found, I and my little charges will be gone. Although *their* fate – similar to yours, I fancy – will not be delayed long.' Once more, Rowlands' head was forced down into the freezing water, which filled his mouth and nostrils with its muddy, vegetable tang. His lungs felt as if they were bursting. A blackness greater than any he had ever known threatened to overwhelm him.

Suddenly, the weight that had been crushing the life out of him was released, and he reared up, vomiting water and gulping in great lungfuls of air. From somewhere nearby came a dull groaning, like that of a wounded bull. A smell of cordite hung in the air. 'Rowlands! My dear fellow,' said a voice. 'Good to see you're still alive.' It was Canon Wetherby.

'What . . . what happened?' said Rowlands when he was able to speak.

'That sound you can hear is Mr Butler,' was the

reply. 'I'm afraid I had to shoot him. Regrettable, but if I hadn't, he'd have drowned you.'

Butler let loose a mouthful of foul invective.

'Be quiet,' said the old man sternly. 'Or I might regret not finishing you off the first time. As it is, you'll live long enough to meet the hangman.'

Chapter Twenty-One

'Of course my father knew about him,' said Ned Swift. 'There was even a codicil in his will, referring to "any son of my body" having the same rights as any other – by which he meant myself and Jolyon, I suppose.' Swift's laugh had no mirth in it. 'That was like my father – to set one son against another, in effect, and to hug the knowledge of what he'd done to himself. It was his way of paying back the family for forcing him into a marriage he didn't want. My mother was made to pay for it, too,' he added bitterly. 'Robert Butler knew about the will. As my land agent, he was privy to all that kind of information.'

'Presumably, he knew of his relationship to your late father when he applied for the post?'

'I've no doubt he did. Butler was obsessed. He'd got it into his head that he was the *true* heir of Castleford, and that John, my elder brother, and I – and then later,

Jolyon – had denied him his birthright.'

'"Popped in between th'election and my hopes",' murmured Rowlands.

'What's that – Shakespeare?'

Rowlands said that it was.

'Well, it pretty well sums up the blighter's attitude,' said Swift. 'He thought that by wiping out his rivals, he'd be able to sweep in and claim his inheritance.'

'Surely that would have made it obvious that he was the one responsible for the killings?' said Celia Swift. She shuddered. 'If he'd succeeded, he'd have got rid of you as well as Jolyon, and then the children.'

'To say nothing of poor Eveline,' her husband reminded her.

'I wasn't forgetting Eveline,' she said. 'But she had no claim to the estate, beyond a life interest. So killing her was merely an act of spite.'

'She presented a threat to Butler's plan,' said Rowlands. 'She'd seen him from her window, going towards the garage, the night your brother-in-law was murdered, and hinted as much the night before she died. Having already killed twice, Butler had no compunction about eliminating her.'

'It's all so horrible,' said Lady Celia. 'The fact that we were harbouring that man . . . and his awful wife . . . under our roof.'

'It's over now,' said Swift. 'Thanks to Frederick here, we can all sleep in peace.'

'Oh, I can't possibly take all the credit,' said

Rowlands. 'If it hadn't been for Canon Wetherby, I'd be lying at the bottom of the river. It was his quick thinking that saved the day.'

'I've been to see him, you know,' said the old gentleman, having shrugged off this testimonial with characteristic modesty. 'Robert Butler, I mean. Went to see if there was anything he wanted . . . or if he felt in need of any spiritual consolation.'

'And did he?'

'No. I suggested he might ask for forgiveness from a higher power for what he had done, and his answer was that I myself was probably more in need of forgiveness than he was . . . given that I am a man of God,' he explained, 'and therefore theoretically opposed to killing of any sort. "Instead of which," he said to me, "you have delivered me to my death as surely as if you had fired a fatal shot, instead of just disabling me." He had a point, you know,' Wetherby added. 'I don't feel very proud of myself for the part I played in bringing him to justice.'

'Nonsense, Cousin Aloysius!' said Lady Celia. 'You did the right thing. If you hadn't fired that gun, Frederick would have died horribly, as would George and Reggie.'

'And you brought about justice for Jolyon and Eveline,' put in Swift. 'Even Doherty – scoundrel that he was – didn't deserve to die for what he did.'

'Oh, I know,' said the old man, and his tone was subdued. 'It's only that justice can be a hard taskmistress.'

Three days had passed. Robert Butler was now in prison, awaiting trial, the conclusion of which was not in doubt. Ned Swift had been released. He and his wife were having coffee in the morning room, with Rowlands and Canon Wetherby – as on that earlier occasion, three months before, when murder had yet to leave its bloody mark on Castleford. It was a mild October day – the storms of the past week having receded, to be replaced by a watery sunshine. This warmed the back of Rowlands' neck as he sat, absent-mindedly stirring the spoon round and round in his cup, and reflecting on all that had passed. He'd quoted *Hamlet*, and certainly the events he'd witnessed had resembled the sanguinary last act of that play, with bodies strewn about the stage – the would-be usurper's among them.

He thought of how Butler's resentment must have grown, over the years – the shame of his illegitimacy compounded by his inferior social status as the adopted child of a farm manager, trained up for a job as an upper servant while his younger siblings, blithely unaware of his existence, enjoyed all the benefits that money and a good education could confer. How that unfairness must have rankled until it became his raison d'être. Getting the job as Castleford's factotum must have been part of a calculated strategy, to exact revenge for all the slights he had suffered, and to restore him to what he saw as his rightful place in the scheme of things, even if it meant the ruthless elimination of an elderly woman and two defenceless children.

Rowlands shivered, recalling what had so nearly been his own last moments, fighting for breath as that relentless hand pressed his head down into the water, and that cruel voice whispered its taunts into his ear. 'I hope you're not coming down with a cold after being half-drowned in that freezing river,' said Lady Celia, who was sitting next to him on the sofa.

Rowlands smiled. 'I'm fine. How are the boys bearing up?'

Before she could reply, the door burst open and George rushed in, the puppy barking at his heels. A few steps behind, his younger cousin followed. Bringing up the rear was an apologetic Miss McGurk: 'Master George! Master Reggie! I've told and *told* you not to run in the house. They're that excited to have His Lordship home,' she added to the assembled adults, as if this was not already apparent.

'Daddy! Daddy! Guess what Rusty's done? He's chewed up Reggie's bedroom slippers!' cried the son and heir of Castleford delightedly. 'It's ever so funny.'

It seemed as if the boys had suffered no ill effects from the horrors they had witnessed two days before, in the boathouse – or so Rowlands hoped. The only person who found it all too much to bear was young Reggie's mother, who had taken to her bed as soon as she'd heard about the fate that had so nearly befallen her child. Even though she'd had to concede that she'd been mistaken in blaming her brother-in-law for her husband's death, she still seemed to hold him responsible for all that had happened. It had been Ned, after all, who had hired Robert Butler as his land agent, thus exposing her husband and child to the man's murderous intentions. As far as Mrs Swift was concerned, the finger of blame still pointed firmly in Ned Swift's direction.

'Henrietta's very bitter,' said Celia Swift. 'She thinks that if Ned hadn't invited her and Jolyon to Castleford, he – Jolyon – would still be alive. And so, in a sense, it's all Ned's fault.'

'Hmm,' said Rowlands. 'I had the impression it was Mr Swift's idea to come to Castleford, in the first instance.'

'Oh, it was. He was after money, of course. But Henry doesn't see it that way. I'm rather afraid,' she said, 'that we won't be seeing too much of her after this. She's already talking about going back to London. She finds Dublin provincial, she says.'

'I don't think London's a very pleasant place to be just now,' he said. 'Mrs Swift might be better staying here. Safer for her little boy, too.'

'Oh, Reggie'll be staying on at Castleford,' said Lady Celia. 'He's company for George, and Henrietta won't want the encumbrance of a child if she's planning to launch herself back into London society.'

It was late in the afternoon of the following day. Rowlands and Lady Celia stood on the quayside, awaiting the Liverpool ferry, which was to take him back to his own home and family. Apart from a brief telephone call to say when he was intending to return, he'd had little communication with his wife during these few weeks. There hadn't been much opportunity for writing letters, and those he had written were circumspect as to detail. There'd be time enough when he was back beside his own fireside to tell Edith all that had happened since his arrival in Ireland a fortnight before – and the part he had played in bringing matters to a satisfactory conclusion.

Now he stood, feeling a little awkward as the conversation lapsed into silence. He wondered if his companion felt it too – the fact that there was too much to say, and not enough time in which to say it. She'd been the only one of the Castleford party to have accompanied him to Dublin, Ned Swift having remained behind in County Wicklow. After so many months idling in gaol, as he put it, he was eager to get on with the business of restoring the demesne to full productivity – or as much as could be achieved with a reduced staff and diminished funds. He'd begin by restoring the stables, he said: 'I can't thank you enough for saving Lucifer, and the other horses,' he said to Rowlands as the latter took his leave. 'And for rescuing the nipper, of course,' he added. The saving of his own neck he appeared to regard as of little account.

Whether his decision not to see his guest off was also

out of consideration for his wife's feelings towards her elected champion, Rowlands preferred not to speculate. The company had dined together at Castleford for the last time the previous night. Only the Langtons, both repeatedly declaring their relief and delight at the happy outcome of it all, remained to swell the sadly depleted numbers. Even young Gogarty had gone – to fulfil his promise to join up. 'Somebody has to stand up for Ireland,' he'd said, taking his leave. Rowlands had wished him well.

That morning, he and Lady Celia had driven to Dublin together, lunching at the house in Merrion Square, from where, three months ago, Rowlands had set out on his uncertain quest. Now it was over, and he had a sense that everything was ending at once: not only the case he had been trying to resolve, but also his relationship with the woman he had loved for so long, without expecting or indeed desiring any return. A few nights before, when things were at their lowest ebb, he had held her in his arms. That had been a moment out of time – a moment to be cherished, but which could never be repeated.

She must have felt something of the same melancholy, for as the ferry's whistle blew to summon those passengers who still lingered on the quayside to come aboard, she touched his hand. 'Write to me,' she said. He felt her reach up, and brush his lips with hers. He could feel the lingering sensation of that kiss as he walked away, knowing her gaze was upon him.

He climbed the gangplank. As he took his place at the rail, he turned his face towards the spot where he knew she would still be standing, as the boat began to move away from the quayside, watching him out of sight.

Acknowledgements

With thanks to Jill Evans, for her expert advice on legal matters, Sophie Geake for her invaluable equestrian advice, and Mitch, of course.

CHRISTINA KONING has worked as a journalist, reviewing fiction for *The Times*, and has taught Creative Writing at the University of Oxford and Birkbeck, University of London. From 2013 to 2015, she was Royal Literary Fund Fellow at Newnham College, Cambridge. She won the Encore Prize in 1999 and was long-listed for the Orange Prize in the same year.

christinakoning.com

MURDER AT BLETCHLEY PARK

THE BLIND DETECTIVE INVESTIGATES

MURDER AT BLETCHLEY PARK

CHRISTINA KONING

Spring, 1941. The Second World War has entered a dangerous phase, with British ships being torpedoed in the Atlantic and nightly bombing raids on major ports. At Bletchley Park, top secret home of the nation's code-breakers, the race is on to crack the German Enigma code and thus prevent further naval and military losses. This endeavour is suddenly very close to home for Frederick Rowlands, blind veteran of the Great War, when his daughter, Margaret, who works at 'the Park' as a cryptographer, is arrested on suspicion of betraying secrets to the enemy.

Then a young woman is found murdered, and Rowlands is drawn into a deadly battle of wits where he must decode a series of clues that will lead him to the killer and enable him to discover the real traitor at Bletchley Park.